LIFETIME

LIFETIME

A Novel

LIZA MARKLUND

EMILY BESTLER BOOKS

—

ATRIA

NEW YORK LONDON TORONTO SYDNEY NEW DELHI

ATRIA BOOKS
A Division of Simon & Schuster, Inc.
1230 Avenue of the Americas
New York, NY 10020

Copyright © 2007 by Liza Marklund
English language translation © 2013 by Neil Smith

Originally published in Swedish as *Livstid.*

Published by agreement with Salomonsson Agency.

First Emily Bestler Books/Atria Books hardcover edition April 2013

EMILY BESTLER BOOKS / ATRIA BOOKS and colophons are trademarks of Simon & Schuster, Inc.

For information about special discounts for bulk purchases, please contact Simon & Schuster Special Sales at 1-866-506-1949 or business@simonandschuster.com.

The Simon & Schuster Speakers Bureau can bring authors to your live event. For more information or to book an event, contact the Simon & Schuster Speakers Bureau at 1-866-248-3049 or visit our website at www.simonspeakers.com.

Manufactured in the United States of America

10   9   8   7   6   5   4   3   2   1

The Library of Congress Cataloging-in-Publication Data has been applied for.

ISBN 978-1-4516-0697-3
ISBN 978-1-4516-0706-2 (ebook)

LIFETIME

PART 1

June

THURSDAY, JUNE 3

The call went out at 0321. It was sent from the regional communication center to all patrol cars in the center of Stockholm and was short and lacking in detail:

"Control to all units, report of shots fired on Bondegatan."

Nothing more. No house number, no information about casualties or who made the call.

Even so, Nina felt her stomach clench in a way she didn't quite understand.

Bondegatan's a long street, there must be a thousand people living there.

She saw Andersson in the passenger seat reach for the radio, and she quickly grabbed the mouthpiece of the S80 system and pressed the transmit button on its left-hand side while at the same time turning up onto Renstiernas gata.

"Patrol 1617 here," she answered. "We're one block away. Have you got a house number?"

Andersson let out a theatrical sigh and looked demonstratively out of the side window of the police car. Nina glanced at him as the car rolled toward Bondegatan. *Okay, sulk if you want to.*

"Control to 1617," the operator said over the radio. "You're the closest unit. Is that you, Hoffman? Over."

The number of the patrol car was linked to the number on her police badge. One of the routines before each shift started was to feed the car's registration number and your badge number into the Central Operations Planning System, handily abbreviated to COPS. This meant that the operator in the communication center could always see who was in which vehicle.

"Affirmative," she said. "Turning in to Bondegatan now . . ."

"How does it look? Over."

She stopped the car and looked up at the heavy stone buildings on either side of the street. The dawn light hadn't reached between the buildings yet, and she squinted as she tried to make out shapes in the gloom. There were lights on in one top-floor flat on the right-hand side, but otherwise everything was dark. It was evidently a street-cleaning night, no parking allowed, which made the street look particularly empty and abandoned. One rusty Peugeot stood alone, a parking ticket on its windscreen, halfway down toward Nytorgsgatan.

"No visible activity, as far as I can tell. What number was it, over?"

The operator gave her the address and she went completely cold. *That's Julia's number, that's where Julia and David live.*

"And he's got a flat on Söder, Nina! God, it'll be nice to get away from this corridor!"

"Don't just take him because of his flat, Julia . . ."

"Take a look, 1617, approach with caution . . ."

She wound down all the car's windows to make it easier to hear any sounds from the street, put the car in gear, turned off the headlights, and drove slowly down the familiar street. Andersson had perked up and was leaning forward intently.

"Do you reckon it's anything, then?" he asked.

I hope to God it isn't anything!

She stopped outside the door and switched off the engine, then leaned forward to peer up at the gray cement façade. There was a light on in a window on the second floor.

"We'll have to assume the situation is dangerous," she said tersely and grabbed the radio again. "Patrol 1617 here. We're in position, and it looks like there are people awake in the building. Should we wait for 9070, over?"

"Patrol 9070 is still in Djursholm," the operator said, referring to the operational command vehicle.

"The Nobel murderer?" Andersson wondered, and Nina gestured to him to be quiet.

"Are there any other cars in the area? Or the armed response unit? Over," she asked over the radio.

"We're switching frequency," the operator said. "All concerned, switching to zero-six."

"That whole Nobel business was quite a story," Andersson said. "Did you hear they've caught the bastard?"

Silence spread through the car, and Nina could feel her bulletproof vest rubbing at the base of her spine. Andersson squirmed restlessly in his seat and peered up at the building.

"This could very easily be a false alarm," he said.

Oh, dear God, let it be a false alarm!

The radio crackled, now on the designated frequency.

"Okay, has everyone switched? Come in, 1617."

She pressed the transmit button again, feeling her tongue stick to the roof of her dry mouth as she clung desperately, anxiously, to the procedures and routines.

"Zero-six, we're here. Over."

The others responded as well, two patrols from the city center and one from the county force.

"The armed response unit isn't available," the operator said. "Patrol 9070 is on its way. Hoffman, you have operational command until the command unit gets there. We need a considered response, hold some units back. We'll form a ring around the location, get cars in place. All units to approach in silence."

At that moment a patrol car swung into Bondegatan from the other direction. It stopped one block away, the headlights going out as the engine was switched off.

Nina opened the car door and stepped out, her heavy boots echoing in the street. She pressed her earpiece tightly into her left ear as she opened the boot of the car.

"Shield and baton," she said to Andersson, as she tuned in to frequency zero-six on the handheld radio.

She saw two policemen get out of the patrol car over at the next block.

"Is that you over there, 1980?" she said quietly into the speaker microphone on her right shoulder.

"Affirmative," one of the officers replied, raising his hand.

"You're coming in with us," she said.

She ordered the other patrols to take up positions at opposite corners of a square to ensure they had all lines of sight covered, one at the corner of Skånegatan and Södermannagatan, the other over on Östgötagatan.

Andersson was rummaging around among the bandages, fire extinguishers, shovels, flares, lamp, antiseptic gel, cordon tape, warning triangles, files full of forms, and all the other clutter that was stuffed into the boot of the car.

"Patrol 1617 to Control," she said over the radio. "Do you have a name for the person who called in? Over."

A short silence.

"Erlandsson, Gunnar, second floor."

She looked up at the façade of the 1960s block, with its square picture windows, and noted a light on in a kitchen on the second floor, behind a red-and-white-checkered curtain.

"He's still up. We're going in."

The other officers came over and introduced themselves as Sundström and Landén. She nodded curtly and tapped in the entry code on the keypad beside the door. None of the others reacted to the fact that she knew what it was. She stepped through the door, turning the volume on the radio down to barely audible. Her colleagues filed in silently behind her. Andersson, who was bringing up the rear, wedged the door open wide so that they could retreat to the street quickly if need be.

The stairwell was dark, deserted. The only source of light came from the lift, seeping through the oblong glass window in the metal door.

"Is there a courtyard?" Landén asked quietly.

"Behind the lift," Nina whispered. "The door on the right leads to the cellar."

Landén and Sundström each checked a door. Both were locked.

"Open the lift door," she said to Andersson.

The officer wedged the door open so no one would be able to use the lift, then stopped by the stairs and awaited her order.

She could feel panic thudding at the back of her head and took refuge in the rulebook to conquer it.

Make an initial evaluation of the position. Secure the stairwell. Speak to the man who made the call and find out where the suspected shooting occurred.

"Okay, let's take a look!" she said, heading quickly and carefully up the stairs, floor by floor. Andersson followed her, keeping one flight of stairs below her the whole time.

The stairwell was gloomy. Her movements were making her clothes rustle in the silence. There was a smell of cleaning fluid. Behind the closed doors she could sense the presence of other people without actually hearing them, a bed creaking, a tap running.

There's nothing here, no danger, everything's fine.

Finally, slightly out of breath, she reached the flats on the top floor. It was different from the others, with a marble floor and specially designed security doors. She knew that the housing association had renovated the attic space as luxury apartments in the late 1980s, just in time for the crash in property prices. The flats had stood empty for several years, almost bankrupting the housing association. Today, of course, they were hysterically expensive, but David was still angry at the poor judgment shown by the previous committee.

Andersson came up behind her, panting heavily. Nina could sense her colleague's irritated disappointment as he wiped his forehead.

"Looks like a false alarm," he declared.

"Let's see what the man who called in has to say," Nina replied, going back downstairs.

Sundström and Landén were waiting on the second floor, beside a door marked *ERLANDSSON, G & A.*

Nina stepped up to the door and knocked quietly.

No response.

Andersson shifted his feet impatiently behind her.

She knocked again, considerably louder.

A man in a blue-and-white-striped toweling dressing gown appeared through the crack behind a heavy safety chain.

"Gunnar Erlandsson? Police," Nina said, holding up her badge. "You called about some suspicious noises? Can we come in?"

The man closed the door, fumbled with the chain for a couple of seconds. Then the door swung open.

"Come in," he whispered. "Would you like some coffee? And there's some of my wife's swiss roll, with homemade rhubarb marmalade. She's dozing at the moment, she has trouble getting to sleep and took a pill . . ."

Nina stepped into the hall. The layout of the flat was exactly like David and Julia's, but this one was considerably tidier.

"Please, don't go to any trouble for us," Nina said.

She noted that Gunnar Erlandsson had been addressing Landén, the largest of the men. Now he was looking anxiously from one to the other, uncertain of where to look.

"Gunnar," Nina said, gently taking hold of his upper arm, "can we sit down and go through what you heard?"

The man stiffened.

"Of course," he said. "Yes, of course."

He led them into a pedantically neat living room with brown leather sofas and a thick rug on the floor. Out of habit he settled into an armchair facing the television, and Nina sat down on the coffee table in front of him.

"Tell me what happened, Gunnar."

The man swallowed and his eyes were still flitting between the officers.

"I woke up," he said. "A noise woke me up, a bang. It sounded like a shot."

"What made you think it was a shot?" Nina asked.

"I was lying in bed, and at first I wasn't sure if I was dreaming, but then I heard it again."

The man pulled out a pair of glasses and started polishing them nervously.

"Do you hunt?" Nina asked.

Gunnar Erlandsson stared at her in horror.

"Good grief, no," he said. "Murdering innocent animals, no, that seems utterly medieval to me."

"If you're not familiar with firearms," Nina said, "what made you think that you heard a shot, precisely? Could it have been a car backfiring, or some other sudden noise out in the street?"

He blinked several times and looked beseechingly up at Landén.

"It didn't come from outside," he said, pointing at the ceiling. "It came from the Lindholms'. I'd swear that's where it came from."

Nina felt the room lurch and stood up quickly, clenching her teeth to stop herself screaming.

"Thank you," she said. "We'll be back later to take a formal statement."

The man said something else about coffee, but she went out into the stairwell and up the stairs to the floor above, taking the steps two at a time, to David and Julia's door.

David and Julia Lindholm.

I don't know if I can go on, Nina.

You haven't gone and done anything silly, have you, Julia?

She turned and gestured to Sundström and Landén that they should cover the stairs in both directions and that Andersson should approach the door with her. They took up position on either side of the door, leaving any line of fire clear.

Nina felt the door gently. Locked. She knew it closed automatically if it wasn't held open. She fumbled for the ASP baton in her belt, then opened it with a light flick of the wrist. She pushed it gently through the letterbox and peered in cautiously.

There was a light on in the hall. The air smelled of newsprint and cooking. She could see the morning paper on the mat. She quickly moved her baton, laying it horizontally so that it held the letterbox open. Then she pulled out her pistol and made sure there was a bullet in the chamber, gesturing to the others to be on the alert. She nodded toward the doorbell so that Andersson realized she was about to make their presence known.

Pointing her weapon at the floor, she pressed the doorbell and heard it ring inside the flat.

"Police!" she called. "Open up!"

She listened intently to any sound from the letterbox.

No response.

"Julia!" she called in a slightly quieter voice. "Julia, it's me, Nina. Open up. David?"

Her vest was tight across her chest, making it hard to breathe. She could feel the sweat breaking out on her forehead.

"Is that . . . Lindholm?" Andersson said. "David Lindholm? You know his wife?"

Nina holstered her gun and pulled out her personal mobile from the inside pocket of her jacket, and dialed the familiar number to the flat.

Andersson took a step closer to her.

"Listen," he said, standing far too close to her. She resisted the impulse to back away. "If you have a personal connection to anyone in there, then you shouldn't . . ."

Nina stared blankly at Andersson as the phone started to ring on the other side of the door, long, lonely rings that seeped out through the letterbox.

Andersson took a step back. The ringing stopped abruptly and the answer machine clicked in. Nina ended the call and dialed another number. A cheerful tune started to play on the floor just inside the door. Julia's mobile must be on the hall floor, probably in her handbag.

She's home, Nina thought. She never goes out without her bag.

"Julia," she said once more as the mobile's voicemail clicked in. "Julia, are you there?"

The silence was echoing. Nina took several steps back, pressed the transmitter on her radio, and spoke quietly into it.

"This is 1617. We've spoken to the informant, and according to him he heard what he thought were shots, probably from the flat above. We've made our presence known but there's been no response from inside the flat. What do you advise? Over."

There was a short pause before the answer reached her earpiece.

"The armed response unit it still unavailable. Your call. Over and out."

She let go of the radio.

"Okay," she said quietly, looking at Andersson and the other two officers on the stairs. "We'll force the door. Have we got a crowbar in 1617?"

"We've got one in our car," Landén said. Nina nodded toward the stairs and the officer hurried off.

"Do you think it's appropriate for you to be leading the operation if . . ." Andersson began.

"What's the alternative?" Nina cut him off, more harshly than she intended. "Handing over command to you?"

Andersson gulped.

"Wasn't there something funny about Julia Lindholm?" he said. "Wasn't she involved in some sort of scandal?"

Nina took out her mobile and called Julia's number once more, still no response.

Landén returned to the landing with the necessary equipment in his arms, a length of metal almost a meter long that was basically an outsized and reinforced crowbar.

"Can we really do this?" Landén said breathlessly as he passed her the tool.

"Any delay could just make things worse," Nina said.

Paragraph 21 of police legislation. *The police have the right to gain entry to a property, room, or other location if there is reason to believe that someone inside may be dead, unconscious, or otherwise incapable of summoning assistance . . .*

She passed the crowbar to Andersson and clicked off the safety catch of her pistol, nodding to the others to take up their positions.

As Andersson inserted the end of the crowbar beside the doorframe, she put her foot down close to the door so that it wouldn't fly open and injure her colleague, in the event that there was actually someone inside who might try to force their way out.

After three carefully judged attempts, the door gave way, and the lock broke. The air that streamed out into the stairwell carried with it the last smells of cooking.

Nina listened intently for any sound within the flat. She shut her eyes and concentrated. Then she jerked her head quickly to her left, taking a first glance at the hall, empty. Another glance, this time toward the kitchen, empty. A third, toward the bedroom.

Empty.

"I'm going in," she said, pressing her back against the frame of the door, turning toward Andersson. "Cover me. Police!" she called again.

No response.

With her thighs tensed she slid round the doorframe, kicking the newspaper aside and stepping silently into the hall. The lamp hanging from the ceiling was swaying slightly, presumably from the draft. Julia's bag was indeed lying on the floor to the left of the front door. Alexander's jacket was next to it. David and Julia's coats were hanging from hooks on the rack to the right.

She stared straight ahead, toward the kitchen, hearing Andersson's breathing behind her.

"Check the nursery," she said, gesturing with her gun toward the first open door on the left, without taking her eyes from the entrance to the kitchen.

Her colleague slid in; Nina could hear the fabric of his trousers rustling.

"Nursery clear," he said a few seconds later.

"Check the wardrobes," Nina said. "Close the door behind you when you're done."

She took a few steps forward and took a quick look inside the kitchen. The table was bare, but there were plates with the remains of spaghetti bolognese on the worktop.

Julia, Julia, can't you be a bit tidier? I'm so damn tired of clearing up after you.

Sorry, I didn't think.

The draft was coming from the bedroom; one of the windows had to be open. The curtains were drawn, making the room completely dark. She stared into the shadows for a few moments, detecting no movement. But there was a smell, something sharp and unfamiliar.

She reached out a hand and switched on the light.

David was lying on his back across the bed, naked. Where his genitals should have been was a bloody mass of entrails and skin.

"Police," she said, forcing herself to act as if he were still alive. "You have a weapon aimed at you. Show your hands."

Thundering silence in response, and she noticed that she had tunnel vision. She looked round the room, the curtains were moving slightly, there was a half-full glass of water on the bedside table on Julia's side of the bed. The duvet was in a heap on the floor at the end of the bed. On top of it lay a weapon identical to hers, a Sig Sauer 225.

Nina felt mechanically for her radio.

"This is 1617 to Control. We have one casualty at the scene, unclear if he's still alive. Looks like gunshot wounds to the head and groin. Over."

As she waited for a reply she went over to the bed, looked down at the body and realized the man was dead. His right eye was closed, as if he were still asleep. In place of the left eye was a gaping entry hole into his skull. The flow of blood had stopped, his heart had stopped beating. His bowels had opened, leaving a brown sludge of acrid-smelling excrement on the mattress.

"Where's the ambulance?" she asked over the radio. "Didn't they get the same alarm as us? Over."

"I'm sending an ambulance and forensics," Control said in her ear. "Is there anyone else in the flat? Over."

Andersson appeared in the doorway, glancing at the body.

"You're needed out here," he said, pointing toward the bathroom door.

Nina put her gun in its holster and hurried out into the hall, opened the bathroom door and held her breath.

Julia was lying on the floor next to the bath. Her hair was like a pale halo around her head, partially smeared in a mess of vomited spaghetti and sauce. She was wearing pants and a large T-shirt; her knees were pulled up to her chin in a fetal position. She was lying on one hand and the other was cramped in a fist.

"Julia," Nina said gently, leaning over the woman. She brushed her hair away from her face and saw that her eyes were wide open. Her face was covered with pale-red splatters of blood. A string of saliva was hanging from the corner of her mouth down to the floor.

Oh God, she's dead, she's dead and I didn't save her. I'm sorry!

A rattling breath made the woman jerk, as she gasped before her stomach retched once more.

"Julia," Nina said, loudly and clearly now. "Julia, are you hurt?"

The woman retched in vain several times before subsiding back on the floor.

"Julia," Nina said, putting her hand on her friend's shoulder. "Julia, it's me. What happened? Are you hurt?"

She pulled the woman up into a sitting position, leaning her against the bath.

"Patrol 1617," Control repeated in her ear. "I say again, Are there other casualties in the flat? Over."

Julia closed her eyes and let her head fall back against the enamel. Nina caught it with her left hand as she checked the woman's pulse in her neck. It was racing.

"Affirmative, two casualties, one presumed dead. Over."

She let go of the radio.

"Andersson!" she called over her shoulder. "Search the flat, every inch. There should be a four-year-old here somewhere."

Julia moved her lips, and Nina wiped the vomit from her chin.

"What did you say?" she whispered. "Julia, are you trying to say something?"

Nina looked around and made sure that there was no sign of a weapon in the bathroom.

"How much do we want to cordon off?" Andersson asked from the hall.

"The stairwell," Nina said. "Forensics are on their way, and people from the crime unit. Start questioning the neighbors. Take Erlandsson first, then the others on this floor. And check to see if whoever delivers the papers saw anything, he must have only just been. Have you searched all the rooms?"

"Yes. Even checked the oven."

"No sign of the boy anywhere?"

Andersson hesitated in the doorway.

"Is there something you don't understand?" Nina asked.

Her colleague shifted his weight from one foot to the other.

"I think it's bloody inappropriate, you being part of this investigation," he said, "considering that . . ."

"Well, I'm here and I've got it," she said curtly in a sharp tone of voice. "Get the cordon sorted."

"Okay, okay," Andersson said, and lumbered off.

Julia's lips were moving nonstop, but she wasn't making any sound. Nina was still supporting her head with her left hand.

"The ambulance is on its way," Nina said, as she examined the woman with her free hand, following the outline of her body under the T-shirt, tracing her skin.

No wounds, not even a scratch. No weapon.

In the distance she could hear the sound of sirens and was gripped by panic.

"Julia," she said loudly, slapping the woman on the cheek with the palm of her hand. "Julia, what happened? Tell me!"

The woman's eyes flickered and cleared for a moment.

"Alexander," she whispered.

Nina leaned down close to Julia's face.

"What about Alexander?" she asked.

"She took him," Julia gasped. "The other woman, she took Alexander." Then she fainted.

As Julia Lindholm was being carried out on a stretcher from the flat she shared with her husband on Södermalm, Annika Bengtzon was sitting in a taxi on her way into the center of Stockholm. The sun was rising over the horizon as the car passed the city limits at Roslagstull, coloring the rooftops a blazing red. The contrast with the black, empty streets hurt Annika's eyes.

The taxi driver kept glancing at her in the rearview mirror, but she pretended not to notice.

"Do you know how the fire started?" he asked.

"I told you, I don't want to talk," she said, staring at the buildings flashing past.

Her house had just burned down. Someone had thrown three incendiary grenades through the windows, first one at the foot of the stairs, then one into each of the children's rooms. She'd managed to get her son and daughter out through the window of her own bedroom at the back of the house, and now she was clutching them tight as they sat on either side of her in the backseat of the car. Both she and the children smelled of smoke, and her cornflower-blue top had soot stains on it.

I bring death and misery with me. Everyone I love dies.

Stop it, she thought sternly, biting the inside of her cheek. I made it, after all. It's all a matter of focusing and then acting.

"I never usually drive anyone on credit," the taxi driver said sullenly, pulling up at a red light.

Annika closed her eyes.

Six months ago she had discovered that Thomas, her husband, had been having an affair with a female colleague, an icy little blonde called Sophia Grenborg. Annika had put a stop to the relationship, but she had never confronted Thomas and told him that she knew.

Yesterday he had found out that she had known all along.

You've been lying and pretending and fooling me for months, he had yelled, *and it's the same with everything you do. You decide what the world looks like, and anyone who doesn't agree with you is an idiot.*

"That's not true," she whispered, aware that she was about to burst into tears in the backseat of the taxi.

She wanted us to meet again. I'm on my way there now.

Her eyes were stinging and she opened them wide to stop the tears from overflowing. The stone façades of the buildings flickered and shone.

If you go now, you can never come back.

He had stared at her with his new, strange, narrow gaze; his red, terrible, dead eyes.

Okay.

And she had watched him cross the parquet floor and pick up his briefcase and open the front door and go out into the gray mist. He walked out the door and closed it behind him, and he didn't look back once.

He had left her, and someone had thrown three firebombs into the house. Someone had tried to kill her and the children, and he hadn't been there to save her, she'd had to cope alone, and she knew perfectly well who'd thrown the bombs. The neighbor on the other side of the rear hedge, the one who'd ruined her lawn by driving across it, dug up her garden, and destroyed her flowerbeds, the one who'd done all he could to get rid of her: William Hopkins, chairman of the villa owners' association.

She held the children more tightly.

I'm going to get you back for this, you bastard.

She'd tried calling Thomas, but his mobile was switched off.

He didn't want to be reached, he didn't want to be disturbed, because she knew what he was doing.

So she hadn't left a message, she'd just breathed into his new, free life and then clicked to end the call. It served him right.

The betrayer. The deceiver.

"What number did you say it was?"

The taxi driver turned into Artillerigatan.

Annika stroked the children's hair to wake them up.

"We're here," she whispered as the taxi pulled up. "We're at Anne's. Come on, darlings . . ."

She opened the door, and the night chill swept into the car and made Ellen curl up into a little ball. Kalle whimpered in his sleep.

"I want your mobile as security," the taxi driver said.

Annika shepherded the children out of the car, turned round, and dropped her phone on the backseat.

"I've turned it off, so you can forget about making any calls," she said, slamming the door.

Anne Snapphane turned her head to take a cautious look at the man lying on the pillow beside her, at the dark, gelled hair sticking out over his forehead, his quivering nostrils. He was falling asleep.

It was a long time since she'd slept next to anyone, actually not since Mehmet got engaged to Little Miss Monogamous and abandoned their open, functional relationship.

How pretty he is, and how young. Scarcely more than a boy.

I wonder if he thinks I'm too fat, she thought, checking to see if her mascara had run. It had, but not much.

Too fat, she thought. Or too old.

What had been most exciting for her had been the taste of strong lager in his mouth.

She felt rather ashamed at the realization.

It was six months since she last drank any alcohol.

How come it wasn't longer than that? It felt like an eternity.

She rolled onto her side and studied the profile of the young man beside her.

This could be the start of something new, something fresh and fun and good.

It would look great in the little boxes of basic information when the papers interviewed her:

Family: daughter, 5, and boyfriend, 23.

She reached out a hand to touch his hair, the hard clumps almost like dreadlocks.

"Robin," she whispered in a soundless exhalation, moving her fingers just above his face. "Tell me you care about me."

The angry buzz of the doorbell out in the hall woke him with a start, and he looked around in confusion. Anne pulled her hand back as if she'd burned herself.

"What the fuck?" he said, staring at Anne as if he'd never seen her before.

She pulled the sheet under her chin and tried to smile.

"It's just the doorbell," she said. "I won't bother to answer it."

He sat up in bed, and she noticed that all his hair-care products had left a big stain on the pillowcase.

"Is it your old man?" he said, looking at her skeptically, anxiously. "You said you didn't have a bloke."

"It's not a bloke," Anne said, and got up, still holding the sheet, trying in vain to wrap it around herself as she stumbled out toward the hall.

The doorbell rang again.

"All right, for fuck's sake," Anne said, feeling disappointment rising. She'd wanted this for so long, had tried to appear experienced, sensual, but now he was just embarrassed. Shit.

She fumbled with the lock and swallowed something which may have been a sob.

Annika was standing outside with Kalle and Ellen.

"What do you want?" Anne said, and she could hear that her voice sounded broken.

Annika looked tired and cross, sighing like she didn't have the energy to explain what they were doing there.

"Do you know what time it is?" Anne said.

"Can we sleep here?" Annika asked. "Our house burned down."

Anne looked skeptically at the children. Burned down? Behind her she could hear Robin flush the toilet.

"This isn't a good time," she said, hoisting the sheet further up her chest.

Kalle started to cry, which started Ellen off as well. Anne felt the chill from the stairwell around her feet and tucked the sheet around her legs.

"Can you just be a bit quieter," she said. "It's the middle of the night, after all."

Annika was staring at her with her big, moist eyes.

Christ! Don't tell me she's going to start as well?

"We haven't got anywhere to go."

Robin coughed from the bedroom. *Please, don't let him go now!*

"But, Annika," Anne said, glancing over her shoulder. "That's hardly my fault, is it?"

Annika took a step back, drawing breath as if to speak, but nothing came out.

Anne tried to smile.

"I hope you understand."

"You can't be serious," Annika said.

Anne could hear Robin moving in the bedroom.

"I'm not on my own right now, and you've no idea how much this means to me."

Annika's eyes narrowed.

"How selfish can you get?"

Anne blinked. What? Who?

"I didn't manage to take any money out of the house," Annika said, "so I can't even pay the taxi. Perhaps you think I should sleep in the street with the kids?"

Anne heard herself gasp as she felt herself getting angry. *Who the hell is she to accuse me?*

"Time for me to pay you back," she said, "is that it? Because you paid for this flat? Is that what you're thinking?"

Annika Bengtzon's voice rose to a falsetto.

"Is it really too much to ask for a bit of help, just this once?"

He's getting dressed, he's going to leave.

She knew it, he was going to leave her now, and to get him to stay a bit longer she went out into the stairwell and closed the door behind her.

"After all the times I've had to listen to you!" Anne said, trying to restrain herself. "Year in, year out, I've had to put up with your constant whining, everything going wrong, your boring husband and your awful job. I'll tell you one thing, *I'm* not the one letting anyone down!"

She could feel her legs beginning to tremble.

"You can't be serious?" Annika said.

Anne could hardly keep her voice under control when she replied.

"All the energy I've wasted on you," she said unsteadily, "I could have spent it on myself instead. Then I'd have been the one who made it, I'd have been offered a presenter's job and found a sack full of money."

"Presenter's job?" Annika said, looking confused now.

"Don't think I've forgotten," Anne said. "I remember how bloody arrogant you were. After Michelle died, when Highlander rang you and offered you her job, but *I* was the one who should have got that job! Who's the one who put in all those years of toil at that shitty company?"

"What on earth are you talking about?" Annika said, her eyes welling up once more.

"You see, it didn't mean anything to you! Nothing I've achieved is good enough."

Annika started to cry, her tears spilling over and running down her cheeks. She'd always been such a crybaby.

"I realize that it's completely irrelevant to you, but now I've *finally* got a chance that could lead somewhere. Do you begrudge me that chance? Do you?"

Annika lowered her eyes and head in defeat.

"I won't bother you again, ever," she said.

She took hold of the children's hands and turned back toward the staircase.

"Good," Anne said. "Thanks!"

She went back into her hall, but was so full of rage that she leaned out again.

"Book yourself into a hotel!" she shouted at Annika's back. "You're rich as Croesus, after all!"

Robin was standing behind her as she closed the door. He had pulled on his jeans and top and was doing up one of his trainers.

"Where are you off to?" she said, trying to smile through her anger.

"Got to get home," he said. "I've got an early start in the morning."

Anne fought an impulse to pull the sheet tighter around her. Instead she tried to relax and let it fall to the floor, reaching out her arms to him, to show him that she was opening herself to him.

He leaned down, embarrassed, looking for his other shoe.

"But," Anne said, her gesture stiffening, "I thought you were unemployed?"

He glanced up at her breasts.

"I've got a band rehearsal," he said, and the lie was so heavy it never left the ground.

Anne picked up the sheet again and wrapped it around her.

"I like you," she said.

He paused just one awkward second too long.

"And I like you too," he said.

Just don't say: It isn't you, it's me.

"Call me?" she asked.

He swallowed and looked down, then kissed her quickly on the ear.

"Course," he said, then went out, shutting the door behind him.

The doctor stepped into Accident and Emergency with his white coat flapping behind him. Nina was surprised at how young he was, younger than her. He gave her a quick glance as he walked over to the gurney where Julia was lying.

"Do we know what happened?" he asked, shining a little pocket torch in one of Julia's eyes.

The door closed behind him.

"She was found in her flat," Nina said. "There'd been a murder, her husband was found shot on the bed."

"Have you made any contact with her?" the doctor said, moving the torch to the other eye.

Nina suppressed an urge to unbutton her bulletproof vest.

"Negative. At first I thought she was dead."

"Her pupils are reacting normally," he declared, switching the torch off. "Do we have an ID for the patient?"

He reached for a computer tablet.

"Julia," Nina said. "Julia Maria Lindholm, thirty-one years old. Maiden name Hansen."

The young man glanced up at her, made some notes, and put the tablet down. He hung a stethoscope round his neck and put a blood-pressure monitor around Julia's upper arm. Nina waited quietly while he took Julia's blood pressure.

"Slightly high, but stable," he said.

Then he picked up a pair of scissors and cut off Julia's T-shirt.

"Where there any traces of blood where the patient was found?"

"Apart from the splatters of blood on her face I didn't see any," Nina said. "I don't think she's physically wounded."

"No entry or exit wounds? No cuts?"

Nina shook her head.

"She could have been hit by a blunt instrument that hasn't left any visible traces," the doctor said as he moved his hands over her body, squeezing her abdomen and chest firmly.

Julia didn't react.

He felt her neck.

"No stiffness, pupils normal, she hasn't got concussion," he stated.

He raised her legs and muttered, "No fractures to the hips."

Then he took her hand and stroked it.

"Julia," he said, "I'm going to check your level of consciousness. I want to see if you react to pain. It isn't dangerous."

He reached over her and squeezed her rib cage. Julia's face contorted and she screamed.

"There, there," the doctor said, and noted something on his tablet. "Okay, I need to do an ECG, then I'll leave you in peace . . ."

He fastened some electrodes to Julia's chest, then wrapped her in a thick blanket.

"Do you want to sit with her?" he asked Nina.

Nina nodded.

"Hold her hand, stroke it, and talk to her."

Nina sat on the edge of the gurney and took Julia's hand; it was damp and cold.

"What's wrong with her?"

Just don't let her die! Tell me she's not going to die!

"She's in a state of psychological shock," the doctor said. "They sometimes get like this, mute and paralyzed. They stop eating and drinking. You can look them in the eye but they don't notice you're there, the lights are on but no one's home."

He glanced up at Nina, then quickly looked down again.

"It's not dangerous," he said. "It'll pass."

It'll pass? Will everything get back to normal?

Nina stared at the woman's white face, her pale eyelashes, her hair. The blood on her face had dried up and got darker. Fragments of their last meeting were rolling through Nina's head like short film sequences.

I can't bear it any longer, Nina. I've got to do something about this.

Just tell me, what's happened?

Julia had looked desperate, chapped red marks on her cheeks. They were still visible under the blood. How long ago was that, three weeks?

Four?

"Julia," she said quietly. "It's me, Nina. You're in hospital. Everything's going to be all right."

Really? Do you believe that?

Nina looked up at the doctor, who was sitting by the end of the gurney, focusing on filling in a form.

"What happens now?" she asked.

"I'm sending her for a CAT scan," he said, "just to rule out any other sort of injury to the brain. We'll give her a sedative and she can go up to the psychiatric ward. With a bit of luck, she'll get a course of therapy."

He stood up, his wooden sandals clattering on the floor.

"You know her personally?"

Nina nodded.

"She's going to need a great deal of support over the coming months," the doctor said, then went out into the corridor.

The door closed slowly with a sucking sound. In the silence after the young man's crackling efficiency every sound seemed much louder: the rumbling fan, Julia's gentle breathing, the bleep of the ECG machine. Steps hurrying past in the corridor, a phone ringing, a child crying.

Nina looked round the sterile room. It was cramped and cool, windowless, harsh light coming from flickering tubes in the ceiling.

Nina freed her hand from Julia's and stood up. Julia's eyelashes fluttered.

"Julia," Nina said quietly, leaning over her friend. "Hello, it's me. Look at me . . ."

The woman reacted with a little sigh.

"Listen," Nina said. "Look up, look at me, I want to talk to you . . ."

No response at all.

Anger rose through Nina like acrid vomit.

"You're just giving up," she said in a loud voice. "That's so typical of you, you just lie back and leave everyone else to clear up your mess."

Julia didn't move.

"What do you imagine I can do?" Nina said, taking a step closer to the gurney. "I can't help you now! Why didn't you tell me? Then at least I'd have had a chance . . ."

Her radio crackled, making her take a couple of steps back in alarm.

"Car 1617 from 9070. Over."

Her superiors trying to locate her.

She turned away from Julia and stared into a cupboard full of bandages as she pulled out the microphone and pressed the transmit button on the side.

"This is 1617. I've gone with Julia Lindholm to Södermalm Hospital. She's just been examined in A&E. Over."

"You can't just sit there waiting," her superior declared. "We need your report as soon as possible. I'm sending Andersson with the car, and he can stay until I've found someone else who can guard her. Over and out."

Nina let go of the radio, fear clutching at her throat.

Someone who can guard her.

Of course, Julia was a suspect.

The prime suspect in a police murder.

She left the room without looking at Julia again.

www.eveningpost.se

BREAKING NEWS
DAVID LINDHOLM MURDERED

Updated June 3, 0524

Police Superintendent David Lindholm, 42, is reported to have been found murdered in his home on Södermalm.

Lindholm is Sweden's most well-known and respected detective, not least for his role as an expert commentator on the television program *Criminal.*

He was also personally responsible for several of the most remarkable police operations of recent decades, helping to solve the most brutal and complex cases in Swedish criminal history.

David Lindholm grew up in a well-to-do home in Djursholm on the outskirts of Stockholm. In spite of his background he opted for a career as a regular police officer. After several years in the tough environment of the rapid-response unit of Norrmalm Police, he was promoted to detective and chief negotiator.

He became familiar to the Swedish public as the straight-talking and fair-minded police superintendent in the television program *Criminal,* but it was his handling of the hostage crisis at the Cowslip Nursery School in Malmö five years ago that made him a legendary figure in the police force.

A desperate armed man had barricaded himself in the toddlers' room and was threatening to kill the children one by one.

David Lindholm established contact with the man, and after two hours of negotiation he was able to walk out to a waiting patrol car, arm in arm with the disarmed criminal.

Evening Post photographer Bertil Strand won Picture of the Year in the category Best News Image in Classic Photography.

While questioning an American who had been sentenced to life imprisonment two years ago, David Lindholm successfully extracted information that led to the robbery of a security van in Botkyrka being solved. Five men were arrested and the majority of the takings, thirteen million kronor, was recovered.

(updates ongoing)

Andersson came roaring up to the entrance to A&E, skidding to a stop and leaving black lines on the tarmac. Nina opened the driver's door before he had come to a halt.

"Julia Lindholm has just been examined," she said. "Stay here and keep an eye on her until you're relieved; it shouldn't take too long."

Andersson swung his heavy legs to the ground.

"So what's wrong with our killer, then?" he said lazily. "Period pains?"

Nina clenched her fists to stop herself from hitting him.

"I'm heading back to write my report," she said, getting into the patrol car.

"Have you heard the preliminary evaluation of the cause of death?" he said to her back. "First she put a bullet in his brain stem, then she blew his cock off . . ."

Nina shut the door and let the car roll down toward Ringvägen. It was daylight now, and the traffic was already building up. She glanced at her watch—twenty-five minutes to six. Her shift ended at six, but it would probably be seven, eight o'clock before she had finished her report and filled in the P21 form . . .

A form? How can I be thinking about what forms need filling in? What sort of person am I?

She took a deep breath that ended up as a sob. Her hands were shaking on the wheel, and she had to make a real effort to calm them.

Right onto Hornsgatan. Change gear. Pull away gently.

Then the thought that had been lurking at the back of her mind since she walked through the door into the flat: *Must ring Holger and Viola.*

She would have to talk to Julia's parents as soon as possible. The only question was what justification, what excuse she could find for telling them what had happened. None at all, really; she obviously couldn't spread any information about what she'd seen at the crime scene to anyone not involved in the case, but this was about something else. *Decency, possibly just basic morality.*

She'd practically grown up with Julia and her parents. They had probably saved her from the life that her two siblings ended up with. She had spent many long weeks each summer out on the farm while her mother worked shifts in the chicken factory in Valla. During term time, she would often go home with Julia and have tea at the big gate-legged table in the farmhouse kitchen. She could still remember the taste of the oxtail soup and sandwiches, the faint smell of farmyard that always hung around Holger. Then, when her mother's shift ended, she would leave the warm surroundings and take the bus home to Ekeby . . .

Nina shook herself to stop herself from getting too sentimental.

I didn't have it hard at all. I was lucky, having Julia.

Some drunk teenagers wearing school-graduation caps were staggering about on the pavement to her left. She sharpened her gaze and looked at them carefully. They were walking along, arm in arm, three boys and a girl. The girl could hardly stand, and the boys were more or less dragging her along.

Watch out, little one, take care they don't take advantage of you . . .

One of the boys caught sight of her and started making obscene gestures at the police car, first one finger, followed by rutting movements. She switched on the blue lights and siren for three seconds, and the effect on the youngsters was instantaneous. They ran off like antelopes in the other direction, the girl as well.

So much for being drunk.

She pulled up and parked outside the station, switching off the engine. The silence that followed was so great that it echoed. She sat there for several minutes, listening to it.

Then she sighed, undid the seat belt, and picked up Andersson's

hamburger wrapper and her own Diet Coke can to throw into the rubbish bin in the car park, the can as well. There had to be some limit to her
responsibility for humanity on a morning like this.

Pettersson, the station head, was on the phone when she went in, and
waved at her to sit down opposite him.

"At five?" he said into the phone. "Isn't that a bit late? A lot of our
officers . . . yeah, that's true enough. Yes, you're right. Okay, 1700 it is,
then . . ."

He put the receiver down and shook his head.

"What a terrible business," he said, rubbing his bald head. "What's
happening to this society?"

He sounds like Inspector Wallander, Nina thought.

"We're going to have a minute's silence for David Lindholm," Pettersson went on. "At five o'clock, the evening shift will have turned up, but
the day shift won't have left yet, which means that most people will be
able to take part. Every police district in the country is joining in. After
all, Lindholm was known and respected everywhere, and after all those
years lecturing at the Police Academy he's got friends throughout the
force, new recruits and older officers alike . . ."

"Just don't tell the media," Nina said.

Pettersson lost his train of thought with a look of surprise, then irritation.

"Of course we're going to inform the media. Apparently radio news
want to do a live broadcast."

"If you were planning on robbing a local shop, when would you
choose to do it if you found out that all police activity throughout Sweden was going to be idle between 1700 and 1701? Anyway, how do you
do a live broadcast of a minute's silence? Won't it be a bit . . . bleak?"

Her boss stared blankly at her for a few seconds, then leaned back,
making the Ikea chair creak.

"Okay, let's get down to business," he said.

Nina took out her notebook. She ran through all the facts in a mo-
notonous voice, the call at 0321, suspected shots heard on Bondegatan.
Because the command unit and rapid-response squad were both out in

Djursholm, Hoffman in 1617 was put in charge of the operation. The informant, a Gunnar Erlandsson, a resident of the building in question, reported that he had been woken by what he thought were shots in the flat above. When there was no response from the apartment in question, patrol 1617, together with patrol 1980, gained entry under paragraph 21 of police regulations, suspecting that any delay could exacerbate the situation. In the flat they found two people, David Lindholm and Julia Lindholm. David Lindholm was lying on the bed, shot twice, in the head and torso. Julia Lindholm was found in the bathroom in a state of severe shock. She had been taken to Södermalm Hospital for treatment.

Nina closed her notebook and looked up at Pettersson.

He was shaking his head again.

"What a terrible business," he said. "Who would have thought it would end like this . . ."

"There's one more thing," Nina said, looking down at her closed notebook. "Julia said something odd before she fainted."

"What?"

"She mentioned her son, Alexander. She said: 'She took him. The other woman, she took Alexander.'"

Pettersson looked up, eyebrows raised.

"'The other woman?' What the hell did she mean by that? Was there anyone else in the flat?"

Nina felt stupid.

"No," she said.

"Were there any signs of a break-in or struggle?"

Nina thought for a moment.

"Off the top of my head, I don't think so, but forensics will . . ."

"And the door was locked?"

"It closes automatically if you don't wedge it open."

The station head let out a deep sigh.

"Bloody hell, poor David. Looks like she was more crazy that anyone imagined."

"Alexander is missing, though," Nina said.

"Who?"

"Julia and David's son. He wasn't in the flat. His room was empty."

Her boss inserted a dose of chewing tobacco.

"And?" he said. "Where is he, then?"

"Don't know."

"Has he been reported missing?"

Nina shook her head.

"Do we know if anything's happened to him?"

"No," Nina said. "It's just that . . . we searched the flat and couldn't find him anywhere."

Her boss leaned back.

"Well, then," he said. "Obviously the information about the other woman and the missing boy will have to go in your report. Just choose your words carefully."

She could feel her cheeks starting to burn.

"What do you mean by that?" she asked.

Pettersson looked at her intently for a few seconds, then he stood up and stretched his back.

"You weren't supposed to be on patrol last night, were you?" he said. "Weren't you meant to be off?"

"I was doing an extra shift," Nina said. "I go back on my normal rota at 1600 hours."

Her boss sighed.

"The papers have already started calling," he said. "Don't talk to them. All comments go through the press officer, no leaks to that woman on the *Evening Post* . . ."

Nina got up and walked away down the corridor, past the staff room, and into a small office containing a desk and computer.

She sat down, switched on the computer, and went into the database for reporting incidents. She systematically set about clicking and filling in the relevant information in the correct boxes, time of call, personnel involved, address of crime scene, injured party, deceased, suspect . . .

Suspect?

She would be listed as the author of this report. It would be attached to the case of David Lindholm's murder forever, would probably be examined and investigated at the Police Academy in fifty years time, and she would be named as the person behind it. She was the one who had to record all these first, preliminary details, she had to formulate the case.

Suspect: Julia Lindholm.

She pushed the keyboard away and went out into the corridor, taking a few aimless steps to the right, then turning and going left instead.

I need something, she thought. Coffee? Then she wouldn't sleep. A sandwich from the machine? The very idea made her feel queasy. She went over to the confectionary vending machine instead. All that was left were bags of sour sweets. She found a ten-kronor coin in her pocket and bought the last-but-one packet. Then she went back to the station head's office and knocked on the doorframe.

Pettersson looked up from his computer screen and glanced at her.

"Sorry," she said, "but who should I put as the injured party? The murder victim, or his family?"

"The murder victim," Pettersson said, and went back to his screen.

"Even though he's dead?"

"Even though he's dead."

Nina lingered in the doorway.

"There's one more thing," she said. "Alexander . . ."

Pettersson sighed.

"He ought to have been in the flat," Nina said quickly. "I think we should . . ."

Her boss let out a small sigh of irritation and leaned toward his screen again.

"If mummy did shoot daddy, then it's probably a good thing the kid wasn't around to see it," he said, and Nina realized the conversation was over.

She turned to leave.

"Listen, Hoffman," the station head called after her.

She stopped and looked back over her shoulder.

"Do you need a debriefing?" he asked, and his tone revealed that he thought a debriefing would be the most ridiculous thing she could ask for in a *tragic case* like this.

"No, thanks," she said breezily and went back to the little room, opened the bag of sweets, and gasped as she put the first one in her mouth. They really were sour.

Instead of clicking in the box for *suspect*, she picked up a form for recording instances where paragraph 21 of police legislation had been applied. It was easier to fill in than Julia's name.

In the end she had filled in all the forms she could find to fill in, including the spontaneous interview with Erlandsson on the second floor.

She stared at the screen.

Clicked on *suspect*.

Quickly typed *Julia Lindholm*.

She logged out and closed the program, then hurried out of the room before her thoughts caught up with her.

"Mummy, I'm hungry. Do they have peanut butter here?"

Annika opened her eyes and found herself staring at a white curtain. She had no idea where she was. Her head was like a big lump of rock, and there was a big black hole in her chest.

"And milk chocolate and jam, have they got chocolate?"

The hotel. Reception. The room. Reality.

She rolled over in bed to look at her children. They were sitting next to each other in their pajamas, bright eyed, hair a mess.

"Did our peanut butter burn up in the fire?" Kalle asked.

"And Poppy," Ellen said, her lip starting to quiver. "Poppy and Leo and Russ burned up in the fire too . . ."

Oh God, what can I say? How can I answer that?

Groggily, she fumbled her way out of the damp sheets and pulled the children toward her without a word and held them, held them in her arms and rocked them gently while the hole in her chest grew.

"They've probably got some chocolate," she said in a thick voice. "And jam. I'm not so sure about peanut butter."

"My new bike," Kalle said. "Did that burn up as well?"

The computer. All the emails stored in it. My phone book and diary. Our wedding presents. The pram. Kalle's first shoes.

She stroked the boy's hair.

"We've got insurance, so we can get them back again."

"Poppy too?" Ellen asked.

"And we can rebuild the house," Annika said.

"I don't want to live in that house," Kalle said. "I want to go back home and go to my proper preschool."

She shut her eyes and felt the world lurch.

The family had only been living in the villa on Vinterviksvägen in Djursholm for a month when it went up in flames. Their old flat on Kungsholmen had been sold to a gay couple who had already moved in and ripped out the kitchen.

"Let's go and have breakfast," she said, forcing her legs over the side of the bed. "Okay, let's put some clothes on."

Ellen wiped her tears and looked at her reproachfully.

"But Mummy," she said, "they burned up in the fire too."

By the time Annika got back down to the street after Anne had refused to let them in, the taxi had driven off. She couldn't call for another one and they didn't have anything else left to barter with, so she had no choice but to pick the children up and start walking. She had a vague idea that there was a hotel in the neighborhood, but she spent three quarters of an hour walking round in circles before she found it. She was on the point of collapse when she stumbled into reception. The receptionist got a scared look in her eyes when Annika explained how they came to be there. They were given a room on the second floor.

Now she let the door of the hotel room swing shut behind them, took the children's hands in hers, cold and sweaty, and got into the lift.

The restaurant was a minimalist, ambitious affair with a glass wall onto the street, walls covered by bookcases and steel and cherrywood furniture. The clock behind the counter said quarter past nine, she had slept for about four hours.

The breakfast buffet had been stripped bare, a real mess, and the room was half empty. The businessmen had all gone off to their important meetings, leaving just one middle-aged couple and three Japanese tourists to stare at her and the children, at her torn jeans and soot-stained designer top, at Kalle in his silky Batman pajamas and Ellen in her flannel pajamas with butterflies on.

Sorry if we're disturbing your lovely breakfast with our unbrushed teeth and bare feet.

She clenched her jaw and filled a teacup with coffee, then helped herself to a yogurt and three slices of gravlax. The yogurt was the only thing she managed to get down, but she took the salmon because it was included in the price, 2,125 kronor for a "twin standard room" that was more like a lift shaft than a room.

I can't do this on my own. I need some help.

"That's impossible," Berit Hamrin said. "You sound completely normal."

"The alternative is just lying down and dying, and if I was going to do that I might as well have stayed in the house," Annika said, checking that the bathroom door was closed.

She had found the Cartoon Network on the hotel television perched up near the ceiling, and had put the children back to bed, each with a little box of frosted cereal in place of sweets. Then she had shut herself inside the bathroom, where there was another phone, and called her colleague in the newsroom.

"And you didn't manage to take anything with you? I read about the fire on the agency feed, but I had no idea it was your house. Bloody hell!"

Annika slumped onto the toilet seat and leaned her head on her hand.

"According to the news agency, the house was completely burned out," Berit said. "Hasn't anyone from the paper called to ask what happened?"

"Don't know," Annika said. "I left my mobile as a deposit with Stockholm Taxis. But I don't think anyone's been in touch. No one died, after all."

Berit fell silent. Annika could feel the chill of the porcelain creep up toward her neck.

"So what do you need help with first?" her colleague asked.

"The children have only got their pajamas and I didn't take any money with me . . ."

"What size are they?" Berit asked, clicking a ballpoint pen.

"They're 110 and 128."

"And shoes?"

Her throat tightened and Annika was finding it hard to breathe.

Don't start crying, not now.

"Ellen takes size 26, Kalle 31."

"Stay where you are. I'll be there in an hour or so."

She remained seated on the toilet, staring at the towel rail, feeling the hole in her chest throb and ache. All around she saw drifting veils of self-pity and hopelessness, bitter tears at how everything had been taken from her, but she didn't want to give in to them, because in amid the fog there was no visibility, and she was bound to get lost.

Your life is gone, the fog whispered, but she knew that wasn't true, because she was sitting here and Scooby-Doo was howling that he was scared of ghosts out in the hotel room.

You've got nothing left!

"Of course I bloody have," she said out loud.

Home was important, the place you belonged, but it didn't necessarily have to consist of four walls. It could just as easily be people, or projects, or ambitions.

You've got nothing that means anything.

Was that true?

She didn't actually have much less today than she had yesterday.

The children had no clothes, and her computer had gone up in flames, but pretty much everything else was still there.

Apart from Thomas.

And Anne.

She got up and looked in the mirror.

Only the children left.

Me and the children, everything else has been stripped away.

She had lost.

Shouldn't it feel worse than this?

The editor in chief of the *Evening Post*, Anders Schyman, had surrendered his privileged corner office in the name of cutbacks and installed himself in a cubbyhole behind the comments desk, something he regretted more with each passing day. The only advantage of the reorganization was that he was in direct contact with the newsroom, and could sit in his office and watch the work in progress out there.

Even though it was only eleven o'clock in the morning, the level of activity going on out there would have been unthinkable just a few years before. Nowadays the website was updated round the clock, apart from a few hours of downtime around four in the morning, and not just text had to be updated, but video content, radio, adverts too. The ever-earlier print deadlines for the paper meant that the whole production process had been brought forward, and these days everything was done during the day, which was new. Tradition dictated that the evening papers were put together at night, preferably by a gang of hard-drinking, weather-bitten editors with red eyes and nicotine-stained typewriter fingers. Today there were hardly any such relics left on the paper. They had either adapted to the new age, kicked the booze, and polished their shoes, or been cleared out during one of the rationalization programs and sent off with a redundancy package and early pension.

Anders let out a deep sigh.

Over the years the feeling that something was slipping from his grasp had been getting stronger and stronger. Recently he had begun to get an idea of what it was: the very point of what they were doing, the fundamentals of journalism.

Nowadays it was so important to keep the website updated above all else that occasionally everyone forgot that you actually had to have something to say as well.

He remembered the old mantra that their rivals used to throw at the *Evening Post* in the old days when the paper sold more copies in Sweden than any other: biggest, but never first. Most, but never best.

Now everything was done much faster, at the cost of truth and good reporting.

But it isn't all crap, he forced himself to think.

Today's paper was another bloody good edition, with Annika Bengtzon's inside story of the Nobel Killer, Berit Hamrin's incisive articles about terrorism, and Patrik Nilsson's interview with a docu-soap star speaking out about her eating disorder.

The problem was that all this was old news. Even though the paper had scarcely reached the newsstands, the articles were already boring and uninteresting, because now David Lindholm had been found murdered in his bed, and his wife was suspected of murder.

There was an endless torrent of praise for the dead police officer on the net.

His talent lay in his insight into human nature, and in his astonishing ability to communicate. As a interviewer he was unbeatable, he was the most loyal friend ever, his intuition was staggering.

How do I handle this? Anders wondered, realizing that his thoughts were going slowly in a brain that was no longer particularly used to wrestling with ethical dilemmas. His marrow, which should have been dominated by basic journalistic principles like news evaluation, checking sources, and reflecting upon whether or not to identify people by name, had little space for anything but financial analysis and sales figures.

He looked out over the newsroom.

The first thing I need to do is get an awareness of the situation, he thought, standing up decisively and striding out into the newsroom.

"What are we doing with the murdered supercop?" he asked Spike, the head of news, who was sitting with his feet up on his desk, eating an orange.

"Front page, newsbill, seven, eight, and the centerfold," Spike replied without looking up.

"And the fact that his wife is a suspect?" Schyman asked, sitting down on the desk, demonstratively close to the head of news's feet. Spike picked up the hint and dropped them to the floor.

"You mean what point size we're making the headline?" he asked, tossing the orange peel in the recycling bin.

"If we name David Lindholm as the murder victim, and then say that his wife is a suspect, we're identifying her as the murderer," the editor in chief said.

"And?" Spike said, looking up at his boss in surprise.

"She hasn't even been taken in for questioning," Schyman said.

"Just a matter of time," Spike said, staring at his computer screen once more. "Besides, it's everywhere already. Our rivals and the oh-so-refined morning rag have already got character assassinations online."

Okay, Spike thought, so much for taking the ethical initiative.

"Can you really get oranges at this time of year?" he asked.

"They're a bit chewy, but then so am I," Spike said.

Berit Hamrin came over to the desk with her handbag swinging from her shoulder and her coat over her arm.

"Bloody good articles in today's paper," Schyman said, trying to look encouraging. "Has there been any response?"

Berit stopped in front of him and nodded toward Spike's screen.

"Julia Lindholm," she said. "Have we taken a conscious decision to identify her as the murderer on the Internet?"

"'We' meaning the collected journalists in Sweden," Spike said.

"As far as I understand it, only the other evening paper and one of the morning papers are running with the story that his wife is a suspect," Schyman said.

"We don't have to give the name of his wife," Spike said.

The reporter took a step closer to Schyman.

"The very fact that we're publishing David Lindholm's name, describing how he was shot on his bed, and then writing that his wife is a suspect, means that we don't have to give her name. Anyone who knows Julia will know that she's the person we're referring to."

"We have to be able to cover sensational murder cases," Spike said indignantly.

"I wouldn't exactly describe what we've got on our website right now as 'coverage,'" Berit Hamrin said. "It's called 'gossip.' So far the police haven't confirmed anything, so all we're publishing is rumors."

Anders Schyman could see how the journalists at desks around the main news desk were raising their heads to listen. Was this good or bad? Were ethical discussions at the news desk a sign of rude health, or did they made him look weak?

He decided it was probably the latter.

"We'll continue this discussion in my office," he said firmly, ushering them toward his cubbyhole with his hand.

Berit Hamrin responded by pulling on her coat.

"I'm heading out to meet a source," she said.

The reporter turned and disappeared toward the stairs leading down to the garage.

Schyman realized that he was still holding out his hand toward his office beyond the comment section.

"So we've already put what we've got about his wife being under suspicion on the website?" he said to Spike, letting his hand fall heavily to his thigh. "Who made that decision?"

Spike looked up with an expression of wounded innocence.

"How should I know?"

No, that was true enough, the printed paper and the online edition had different editors.

Anders Schyman turned on his heel and went back inside his office.

A thought took root and chafed against his ego: *What am I actually doing here?*

Berit was carrying eight big bags.

"I tried not to get too caught up in gender stereotypes," she said as she squeezed her way into the crowded room and dropped the bags on the floor. "Hello Kalle, hi Ellen . . ."

The children looked up at Berit for a moment, then went back to the television. Annika switched it off.

"Look, Kalle," she said. "Aren't these great jeans!"

"Those are for Ellen," Berit said, sitting down on the bedside table and unbuttoning her coat. "Underwear's in that bag, and that one's got some bits and pieces, soap, toothbrushes, and so on . . ."

The children got dressed of their own accord, silent and serious. Annika helped Ellen brush her teeth and caught sight of her own eyes in the mirror. Her pupils were enlarged, almost covering her irises, as if the hole in her chest were visible in her eyes.

"How much do I owe you?" she asked Berit.

Her colleague stood up and pulled an envelope out of her handbag, and handed it to Annika.

"I went past a Cashpoint and got some money out. You can pay me back later."

The envelope contained ten thousand kronor in five-hundred-kronor notes.

"Thanks," Annika said quietly.

Berit looked around the cramped room.

"Shall we go out for a bit?"

The children put on their new outdoor clothes. They walked silently through reception and out into the street, crossing the road toward Humlegården.

The clouds were hanging thick and gray in the sky; the wind was gusty and cold. Annika pulled her new cardigan more tightly around her.

"How can I possibly thank you?"

"If my house burns down, I'll be in touch," Berit said, turning up her collar against the wind. "You have to make a start by phoning the insurance company. They'll cover any costs you have to pay for staying somewhere until your house is rebuilt."

They reached the park. The children were a bit hesitant in their new trainers, Kalle's green, Ellen's blue.

Annika forced herself to smile at them.

"You run ahead," she said. "Berit and I will wait here."

Carefully, looking back over their shoulders, they headed off toward the playground.

"Where's Thomas?" Berit asked quietly.

Annika gulped.

"I don't know. We . . . we had a fight. He wasn't home when it happened. I don't know where he is. His mobile's been switched off."

"So he doesn't know what's happened?"

Annika shook her head.

"You have to try to get hold of him."

"I know."

Berit looked at her thoughtfully.

"Is there anything you want to talk about?"

Annika sat down on a bench, pulling the cardigan around her.

"Not right now," she said.

Berit sat down beside her and looked over at the children, who had slowly started to take possession of the playground.

"They'll get over it," she said. "But you have to hold yourself together."

"I know."

They sat for a while without talking, watching the children play on the slide. Ellen was laughing her little head off.

"By the way, have you heard who got shot this morning?" Berit said. "David Lindholm, that police superintendent."

"What, the one on the television?" Annika said, waving to Ellen. "Married to Julia Lindholm?"

"Do you know them?" Berit said, sounding surprised.

"I spent one night in a patrol car with Julia. Do you remember that series of articles, about women exposed to danger in the course of the their work?"

Berit shook her head and pulled a bag of foam sweets from her pocket.

"They're allowed sweets, aren't they?" she asked Annika. "Kalle, Ellen!"

She waved the bag and the children came running.

"How many can we have?" Ellen asked.

"You can't even count," Kalle said scornfully.

They each took a handful, she picking out the pink ones, and he the green.

"I was actually doing a profile of Julia's colleague," Annika said, as she watched the children walk away. "Nina Hoffman, that was her name. It was the night we stumbled across that triple murder on Södermalm, if you remember."

Berit took a handful of sweets and offered the bag to Annika, who declined.

"The ax murders? Hands chopped off and all that?"

Annika gulped.

"Bloody hell, yes," Berit said. "Sjölander and I covered the court case."

Annika shivered and crossed her legs.

She had been heavily pregnant with Ellen that spring, and at the *Evening Post* pregnant reporters were treated as if they were suffering from severe senile dementia: in a friendly, firm, and utterly undemanding way. Eventually she had nagged her way into a fairly relaxed job, a series of workplace reports about women doing what were usually dangerous jobs for men. On the night of March 9 five years ago she had gone on patrol with two female police officers on Södermalm. It was a cold night, quiet, and she had plenty of time to talk to the two officers. They had been close friends since they were children, had attended Police Academy together, and now worked at the same police station. One of them, Julia, revealed that she was pregnant as well. No one at work knew about it yet, she was only in the fourteenth week, and she felt violently sick all the time.

Just before midnight they got a call about a disturbance in a flat on Sankt Paulsgatan, at the Götgatan end. It was a routine call; a neighbor had phoned in to complain about fighting and shouting from the flat downstairs. Annika asked if she could come along, and they let her, as long as she agreed to stay in the background.

They went up the stairs to the second floor, and that's where they found the mutilated woman. She had crawled out into the stairwell and was still alive when the police patrol turned up. Her right hand was missing and blood was pumping out of the severed veins, running over the stone floor and down the stairs and splashing the walls whenever she moved her arm. Julia had thrown up in a window alcove, and Nina had forced Annika back down to the street with astonishing force and efficiency.

"I didn't see much, but I can still remember the smell in the stairwell," Annika said. "Sweet, and sort of . . . heavy."

"There were two men in the flat," Berit said. "They'd both been mutilated as well."

Annika changed her mind and reached for a sweet.

"They solved the case pretty quickly."

"Filip Andersson," Berit said. "A financial expert. He denied it but was still found guilty. He's in Kumla Prison. Life."

Berit tipped the last of the sweets into her hand and dropped the empty bag into a rubbish bin.

"If you're going to fall out with your friends, it's probably a good idea not to be a drug dealer," Annika said.

"Yes, but we're not talking about little bits of drug money," Berit said. "These were serious financial transactions, between Spain, Gibraltar, and the Cayman Islands."

"Crazy," Annika said, "leaving your fingerprints all over the place if you've just chopped up three people."

"Well, the criminal element of the population doesn't usually register as being particularly smart," Berit said, standing up to help Ellen, who had fallen over and scraped her hand.

Annika didn't move. Her body felt heavy as cement, and she could no longer feel the cold. The wind was pulling at her hair, but she couldn't be bothered to brush it from her face.

"The last I heard before I left the newsroom was that they think Julia killed her husband," Berit said as she sat back down again.

"Really? She seemed so timid . . ."

"Looks like their son's missing as well."

"Oh, so she had a boy, then . . ."

They sat in silence again, watching the children, who had evidently found something interesting beneath a large oak on the other side of the playground.

"Listen," Berit said, "have you got anywhere to go?"

Annika didn't answer.

"Your mum?" Berit suggested. "Thomas's parents?"

Annika shrugged.

"Do you want to come out to Roslagen with me? Thord is in Dalsland this weekend, fly-fishing with his brother. You can stay in the guest cottage, if you like."

"Are you serious?"

A couple of years ago Berit and her husband, Thord, had sold their house in Täby and moved out to some stables between Rimbo and Edsbro. Annika had been out there a couple of times. In the summer it was absolutely idyllic, with the lake, and horses in the paddock.

"Of course. It's only standing there empty."

"That would be so great," Annika said.

"I have to go back to the newsroom and finish my follow-up piece on the terrorist articles, but I should be finished by eight at the latest. I'll pick up your mobile, then collect you from the hotel, if that sounds okay."

Annika nodded.

Nina stopped in the doorway, feeling uncertain.

There were an unusual number of uniforms in the small staff room. They were standing in small groups with their backs to her, their heads close together. The hum of their voices sounded like air-conditioning, low and constant.

This is what grief sounds like, she thought, without quite understanding where the idea came from.

It was quarter to two, and her shift didn't start until 1600, but she hadn't been able to sleep, hadn't *wanted* to sleep. When she eventually drifted off, her dreams had been so confused and unsettling that she chose to get up instead.

She pushed her way in behind Pettersson, who was blocking the door, and made her way over to the coffee machine. In places she had to squeeze sideways between people, muttering apologies and stepping over helmets and boots and jackets.

The further she got, the quieter it seemed.

By the time she reached the coffee machine there was complete silence around her. She raised her head and looked round.

Everyone in the room was staring at her. They looked skeptical, their faces closed. She got the feeling that they were all leaning back, away from her.

"Is there anything you'd like to know?" she asked.

No one spoke.

She turned away from the coffee, stood with her legs fairly wide apart, put her hands behind her back, and looked her colleagues in the eye.

"Is there anything you want to know that isn't obvious from the report?"

They started to look uncomfortable, and some of the officers standing closest to her looked away.

"How come you were first on the scene?" someone shouted from the back of the room.

All of a sudden there was total silence again.

Nina craned her neck to see who had shouted.

"Why I was first on the scene?" she called out, loud and clear. "And why would anyone wonder about that?"

Christer Bure, one of David's former colleagues from his days in uniform with the Norrmalm force, stepped forward. His face was dark from lack of sleep and grief, his shoulders were up by his ears, his heavy body moving only with difficulty.

"I just think it's bloody odd," he said, stopping half a meter away from her. "I think it's bloody odd, that you're the one who storms into the flat where David was shot, and I think it's bloody odd that you're the one who whisked away his crazy fucking wife and hid her in hospital. How the fuck did that happen? How do you explain that?"

Nina looked at the man and suppressed an impulse to back away from him. She wouldn't get far anyway; the coffee machine was in the way. He was glaring at her with such undisguised derision and ill will that she had to take a deep breath before she spoke.

"The answer is perfectly simple," she said. "Andersson and I were sitting in 1617, and we were closest. Anything else you'd like to know?"

Christer Bure took another step closer to her and clenched his fists. There was a ripple around him, as if several other men were following his example.

"His crazy wife," he said. "Why did she do it?"

Am I really supposed to put up with this?

"Julia Lindholm is the prime suspect for David's murder," Nina said, hearing that her voice was trembling. "I presume that the investigation will uncover the murderer's motivation, whether it was Julia or someone else who . . ."

"Of course it was her, for fuck's sake!" Christer Bure shouted, his forehead deep red. "Why the fuck are you still pretending?"

A few drops of saliva hit Nina's face. She turned and forced her way toward the door. She could feel tears burning in her throat and had no intention of standing there and giving him the satisfaction of seeing her break down in front of the entire station.

"The press conference is starting!" someone yelled above the noise that had suddenly erupted. The introduction to Swedish Television news flickered across the screen in front of Nina. Everyone fell silent and the uniforms turned in unison to face the screen. Nina stopped and looked at the television, where someone in a Hawaiian shirt settled behind a desk up on the rostrum of the large conference room of Police Headquarters over on Kungsholmen. Two men and a woman sat down beside him; Nina recognized the police press officer and the head of the National Crime Unit. She had never seen the woman before. A storm of flashbulbs broke over their clenched features, and the press officer said something into the microphone.

"Turn the volume up!" someone shouted.

"... by the murder of Detective Inspector David Lindholm," the press officer was saying as the volume was increased. "I will hand you over to the head of the preliminary investigation, Prosecutor Angela Nilsson."

The woman leaned toward the microphone. She had a blond page cut and was wearing a bright-red suit.

"I have today remanded one individual in custody," she said, "on serious suspicion of having murdered David Lindholm."

Her voice was cool and had a faintly upper-class accent.

On serious suspicion, the higher level of suspicion.

"An application for the formal arrest of this individual will be presented to the magistrate's court by Sunday at the latest," she went on, without changing her tone of voice. "I would like to point out that as head of the preliminary investigation, I am keeping an open mind as far as this case is concerned, and that we are not focusing on just one scenario, even though we have made a breakthrough in our work at such an early stage."

She leaned back to indicate that she had finished.

"Well," the press officer said, clearing his throat. "In that case I will now hand you to the detective superintendent leading the case for the National Crime Unit."

A large police officer with his cap still on moved to stand right in front of Nina, and she had to step to one side to see.

"David Lindholm was found shot in his home early this morning," the man in the brightly colored shirt said. "One person who was found alive at the crime scene was taken to hospital, and has today been re-manded on grounds of reasonable suspicion. We have secured some fo-rensic evidence, but there is still one large question mark hanging over the work of our investigation."

A blown-up picture of a small child appeared behind the people on the rostrum.

"This is Alexander Lindholm," the detective in the shirt said. "He's David Lindholm's four-year-old son. Alexander Lindholm was reported missing this morning. The boy lives in the apartment that is also our crime scene, but he wasn't there when officers first arrived on the scene this morning. We are extremely interested in any information about Al-exander Lindholm and where he might be now."

There was feverish activity in the press conference as the photogra-phers started taking pictures of the image on the wall.

The press officer adjusted his microphone and spoke quickly to calm the press corps down.

"The boy's picture will be distributed to all media," he said, "both digitally and as hard copy . . ."

The detective scratched his head, and the head of National Crime looked uncomfortable.

Pictures and disks containing the image and other press material were distributed among the journalists and the hubbub subsided.

"Murders of police officers are extremely rare in Sweden," the head of the National Crime Unit said slowly, and a heavy silence fell, both in the press conference in Police Headquarters and in the staff room of Söder-malm police station. "David Lindholm is the first such victim since the murders in Malexander in the late 1990s, and we should be very grateful that we are spared such occurrences more often."

He took off his glasses and rubbed his eyes. When he spoke again it was with greater focus and solemnity.

"But when one of our fellow officers is killed," he said, "we don't just lose a person, but also a friend. Part of our social structure has been at-tacked, part of our democratic foundations."

He nodded thoughtfully at his own words, and Nina saw several of her colleagues nod along with him.

"David was also . . . special," he said, lowering his voice. "He was a role model for people far beyond the police force, an inspiration for people from every class in society, from every background."

Now the head of National Crime's voice was almost trembling.

"I myself had the honour of watching David at work, and could appreciate the impact of his dealings with serious criminals, those with drug addictions and lifetime sentences, how he made people like that feel hope again, and believe in the future . . ."

Nina suddenly felt that she didn't want to hear any more. She turned away, pushed her way past two fellow officers, and hurried out toward the changing room.

Thomas steered his heavy jeep through the streets of the suburban idyll and could feel the early summer rush in through his window, swirling through his hair and tugging at his clothes. Sophia's smooth thighs were still burning on his skin, her scent was still in his stubble.

He felt alive. *Bloody hell, he felt so alive!*

He had spent the past twenty-four hours in Sophia's big double bed. She had called in sick: For Sophia, some things were more important than her career. They had eaten breakfast and lunch beneath the sheets.

Was it really only a day since he had been out here? Only one day, one night since he had lived here, among these birch trees?

He saw lawns flash past, unfamiliar, as if they belonged to another world.

All those years with Annika already felt like a long, dusty trek through a desert, a drawn-out ceasefire with regular skirmishes and protracted negotiations.

How did I put up with it? Why didn't I leave her before?

The children, of course; he had done his duty.

He cruised through the cars parked outside the local supermarket, waving at a neighbor he thought he recognized.

Practically the first thing that had happened in his relationship with Annika was her getting pregnant, so he hadn't really had much choice. He could either try to live with the mother of his child, or be one of those absent fathers whose child ends up disadvantaged and ostracized.

But now that was over. He would never have to put up with her contrary outbursts again. He would just gather up a few clothes, pick up his computer and record collection, and on Monday he'd get hold of a hot-shit divorce lawyer. Sophia had good contacts in that world, among doctors and lawyers and academics; she didn't have to sit down with the Yellow Pages like Annika did whenever she needed a qualified professional.

No two women could be less alike, he realized. Sophia was everything that Annika despised, mainly because she could never be like that herself: educated, feminine, and well mannered.

And Sophia liked having sex, unlike the frigid goat that Annika had become.

Wow, that was mean. Was he allowed to be that mean?

He turned right, into the area they lived in, his eyes roaming over the pale-green trees and white fences. Houses loomed up on either side of the road, patrician villas and big brick palaces in the national romantic style, with ornate verandas, pools, and summerhouses.

She'll have to buy me out of the house, and it won't come cheap.

He was prepared to fight, he really was, because the house was just as much his. Annika may have stumbled over a load of money when she uncovered that terrorist cell up in the far north of the country, but they had no prenuptial agreement, so half of that was actually his.

Now that he came to think about it, he had no idea how much money she had actually found. She had handed the sack in to the police, which meant that she had only received ten percent as a reward. Which meant that they weren't exactly talking about buying property in the smartest part of the city, Östermalm. Sophia had been born into money; the building where she occupied the penthouse suite was owned by her family.

He saw the turning to Vinterviksvägen ahead of him and felt his pulse increase; this was likely to be very unpleasant.

Sophia had asked if he wanted her to come along, had said she would be happy to support him through this horrible situation. He had been firm and said that seeing as he had got himself into this mess, it was his job to sort it out.

She had thought him very responsible.

I'll sort this out. I can do this.

He turned into the road with a heavy sigh.

I don't want to fight, I've just come to get a few things . . .

At first he couldn't work out what was wrong with the scene that greeted him, what it was that didn't make sense. Reality took a few moments before it hit him, like a punch in the face, before his brain identified the smell of smoke and ash, before he worked out what he was looking at.

He stopped the car out in the road, leaning over the wheel and staring through the windscreen, mouth wide open.

His home was a smoking ruin. The whole building had collapsed. The remains were blackened and warped, charred roof tiles lay scattered over the grass. Annika's car stood on the drive, a blackened wreck.

He turned off the engine and listened to the sound of his own panicked breathing.

What the hell have you done, you fucking witch? What have you done with the children?

He opened the door and got out onto the road, as the car alarm shrieked to tell him he had left the key in the ignition. The noise followed him as he made his way unsteadily toward the police tape and stared helplessly at the shattered walls against the sky.

Oh God, where are the children?

His throat constricted and he heard himself whimper.

Oh no, oh no, oh no!

He sank to his knees, hardly noticing the damp creeping through his trousers. All his things, all his clothes, the soccer ball from that tournament he played in over in the States, his student graduation cap, the guitar from Sunset Boulevard, all his reference library and vinyl records . . .

"Terrible, isn't it?"

He looked up and saw Ebba Romanova, their closest neighbor, leaning over him. He didn't recognize her at first. She usually had a dog with her, and without it on the end of a leash she didn't seem herself. She held out a hand and he took it and stood up, brushing some wet ash from his trousers.

"Do you know what happened?" he asked, wiping his eyes.

Ebba Romanova shook her head.

"It was like this when I got home."

"Do you know where the children are?" he asked, and his voice broke.

"I'm sure they're fine," she said. "They haven't found any . . ."

She fell silent and gulped.

"And when it comes down to it, it's just possessions," she went on, staring out over the ruins. "The only thing that really matters is life itself."

Thomas felt his rage rising from his stomach.

"Easy for you to say."

She didn't answer, and he saw her eyes fill with tears.

"Sorry," she said, wiping her nose. "It's Francesco, he's dead."

Francesco?

"My dog," she said. "He was shot last night. He died in the living room."

The woman pointed toward her house, and before Thomas could think of anything to say she had turned and started to walk unsteadily back toward her gate, sobbing.

"Wait," he called after her. "What happened, exactly?"

She looked over her shoulder.

"They caught the Nobel Killer," she said, and carried on.

Thomas was left standing on the road, confused and lost.

What do I do? What am I supposed to do?

He fished his mobile from his pocket and checked the display. No messages, no missed calls.

That told you, eh? Well, it serves me right!

He may have had his phone switched off last night, but only so she wouldn't call him screaming and crying. She could have left a message. She could have told him his house had burned down.

Is that too much to ask?

He went to call her, but realized he didn't know her mobile number. He had to look it up, dialed, and was met by the automated voice message.

She didn't even have a personalized message.

He turned his back on the pile of ruins and went back to his car.

*   *   *

Work at the station had slowly got going again, but the 1600 handover had passed without any great enthusiasm. Nina was told to go out with Andersson again, and couldn't think of a reason not to. None of the other young bucks was much better.

Now they were sitting in the staff room talking, no one was going to head out before the minute's silence at 1700. Nina walked silently down the corridor, glanced quickly over her shoulder, then snuck into an empty interview room. She listened at the door and heard Andersson's deep voice rolling along the walls.

How am I supposed to handle this? How am I going to balance all this?

She went over to the telephone, picked up the receiver, and listened to the dial tone for a few seconds. Then she dialed the ten-digit number and waited quietly as the phone rang.

Eventually someone answered with a muffled cough.

"Hello. It's me, Nina."

She could hear someone breathing heavily and sniffing at the other end.

"Holger? Is that you?"

"Yes," Julia's father said.

Nina checked that the door was properly closed, then sat down at the empty desk.

"How are you both?" she asked quietly. "How's Viola?"

"Desperate," the man said. "Utterly desperate. We're . . ."

He fell silent.

"I know," Nina said when he didn't go on. "Have you heard anything about Alexander?"

"Not a thing."

Silence again.

"Holger," Nina said, "I want you to listen very carefully to what I say. I'm about to tell you something that I'm not supposed to, not to you or anyone else. You mustn't tell anyone what I tell you, apart from Viola. I was the one who took the call. I was the first into the flat. I found Julia on the bathroom floor, I looked after her and went with her up to the hospital. She wasn't hurt, Holger, do you hear what I'm saying? She wasn't physically wounded at all. She was in deep shock, not really there, but there's nothing wrong with her. Julia's going to be fine, she'll soon be back to normal. Holger, do you understand what I'm saying?"

"Did you . . . ? What were you doing in Julia's flat?"

"I was on duty, I was doing an extra shift. I was the closest patrol when the call came in, so I responded. I thought that was the best thing to do."

"And Alexander, he wasn't there?"

"No, Holger, Alexander definitely wasn't in the flat when I got there."

"But . . . where is he, then?"

She could feel the tears rising in her throat.

"I don't know," she whispered, then cleared her throat, there was nothing to be gained from her bursting into tears. "Are you getting any help? Have you got anyone to talk to?"

"Who would that be?"

No, that was true. Holger and Viola weren't regarded as relatives of a murder victim, but of a murderer. There was hardly likely to be any crisis team ready to help them with their grief.

"I'm working Saturday and Sunday," Nina said, "but I can come down to see you on Monday, if you like?"

"You're always welcome here," Holger said.

"I don't want to intrude," Nina said.

"You never intrude. We'd like it if you could come and see us."

There was another silence on the line.

"Nina," the man finally said, "did she shoot him? Was it Julia who shot him?"

She took a deep breath.

"I don't know," she said, "but it looks like it. The prosecutor has remanded her in custody."

Julia's father took several deep breaths.

"Do you know why?"

Nina hesitated, she didn't want to lie.

"Not exactly," she said. "But I think they'd been having problems recently. Julia hasn't really told me much lately. She hasn't mentioned anything to you?"

"Nothing," Holger said. "Nothing to indicate that things were seriously wrong. About a year ago she mentioned that she thought it was a shame that David didn't seem to like Björkbacken, but she never said anything else . . ."

She could hear noise out in the corridor, then Andersson's voice.

"I have to go," Nina said quickly. "Call me whenever you like on my mobile, you hear me, Holger? Whenever you like . . ."

The electronic bleeping was forcing its way inside Annika's head. She resisted the urge to put her fingers in her ears.

She had used some of Berit's money to buy the children a new Game Boy each. They were sitting curled up at the head of the bed, staring intently at the small screens. Ellen was playing Disney Princess, and Kalle was playing a Super Mario golf game, to the accompaniment of much bleeping and pinging and popping.

She didn't seem to be able to see any further ahead than a couple of minutes at a time. In some peculiar way this actually made her feel calmer.

Now I'm going to buy a new purse. Now we're going to eat hot dogs. Now I'm going to make a phone call . . .

At that moment the phone beside her rang and she jumped in surprise. She went into the bathroom and picked up the receiver in there.

It was Detective Inspector Q.

"How the hell did you know I was here?"

"I spoke to Berit. It's about the fire. Forensics have just got back, and they've got a preliminary cause. The level of destruction and the explosive way that the fire spread suggest that the fire broke out in several places simultaneously, and probably on more than one floor, and that in turn suggests that the fire was started deliberately."

"But that's exactly what I told you!" Annika said animatedly. "I saw him, I know who started it."

"Who?"

"Hopkins. The neighbor. He was standing in the bushes spying on us after we got out."

"I think you're wrong, and I think you should think very carefully before pointing the finger at anyone. Arson is a serious offense, one of the worst in the book. It can carry a life sentence."

"It would serve him right," Annika said.

"And insurance fraud is also serious," Q said. "We investigate that sort of case very thoroughly."

Annika snorted.

"Don't try that one," she said. "I know exactly what happened. Anyway, haven't you got anything else to worry about but the fire? The Nobel Murders, for instance? Or David Lindholm getting killed? By the way, have you found the boy yet?"

There was a noise on the other end of the line, someone entering the detective's office. Annika heard voices in the background. The receiver was put to one side, she could hear rustling and clattering.

"I'll be in touch," Q said, then hung up without waiting for an answer.

She was left sitting there with the phone in her hand, listening to the sounds of the computer games seep under the door.

Suddenly she was overwhelmed by a desperate longing for Thomas.

You never gave me a chance. Why didn't you say anything?

She wanted us to meet again. I'm on my way there now.

And he walked across the parquet floor, picked up his briefcase, opened the front door, and looked out at the gray gloom. He stepped outside and the door closed behind him and he didn't look back, not once.

"Mummy," Kalle said from the hotel room. "There's something wrong with Mario. He won't hit the ball."

She pressed the palms of her hands to her eyes for a few seconds, breathing through her mouth.

"Coming!" she said, standing up.

She ran some water in the basin and rubbed her face hard for a few seconds.

Kalle opened the bathroom door.

"I can't press *Hit,*" he said, holding out the computer game.

She dried herself on a flannel and sank onto the edge of the bath, looking at the game and pressing various buttons before realizing what had happened.

"You must have pressed *Pause*," she said, showing him the command to start the game again.

"No I didn't," the boy said, insulted.

"You probably didn't mean to," Annika said, "you must have done it by mistake."

"No I didn't!" her son cried, his eyes full of tears, and he snatched the game from her.

For a moment Annika's eyes flashed black, and she could feel herself lifting her arm to slap him across the face.

She stopped herself with a gasp, let her arm fall and looked at the boy standing in front of her, his lower lip trembling.

Oh God, I mustn't fall apart. What would I do if I fell apart?

"Well, at least Mario can hit the ball now," she said breathlessly.

The door of Detective Inspector Q's office was ajar. Nina hesitated, not sure if she should press the button beside the three little lights on the wall labeled *Busy, Wait,* or *Come In,* or if she should just knock.

Before she had made her mind up, the door opened abruptly and the detective was standing there in front of her, his hair all over the place and his loud shirt only half tucked into his jeans.

"What the hell?" he said. "What are you doing, eavesdropping?"

He held out his hand.

"Nina Hoffman, I presume?"

She looked him in the eye.

"Yes, that's right. And you're Q, I presume?"

"Come in, for God's sake. My leggy blonde secretary isn't here today, so I'll have to get the coffee myself. How do you take it?"

Nina stared at him. What was he going on about?

"Thanks, I'm okay," she said, stepping into the office.

The detective inspector's office, on the third floor of Police Headquarters on Kungsholmen, was so impersonal that it bordered on spartan. There weren't even any curtains. A dead potted plant stood abandoned in the window; she presumed it had been part of the furnishings when he moved in.

She stood there for a minute or so while the detective went off to the coffee machine farther down the corridor.

"Don't worry, the chair isn't booby-trapped," he said, pointing at it as he came back with a steaming plastic mug in his hand.

Nina sat down on the worn old chair that had been offered to her, feeling extremely uncomfortable.

She had heard about Detective Inspector Q, even if he wasn't anywhere near as well known as David Lindholm. And, unlike David, he wasn't universally liked either. There were a lot of officers who thought his weird clothes were a bit affected, and then there was his passion for cheesy pop music. There were stubborn rumors that he was gay.

Q settled down on the other side of the desk.

"That was a bit of a bloody coincidence, wasn't it?" he said, blowing on his coffee.

"What?" Nina wondered.

"That you just happened to be first on the scene of that particular crime."

"Is this an interrogation?" Nina asked, tilting her chin slightly.

The detective inspector threw out his arms.

"Absolutely not!" he said. "Call it a conversation between fellow officers, if you like. I'm just curious to hear what you think, about the things that don't have their own little box on the official report."

Nina tried to relax. He really was extremely odd, considering that he was such a senior officer.

"What do you want to know?" she asked.

"How did you react when you got the call?"

Bondegatan's a long street, there must be a thousand people living there.

She looked out of the window.

"I didn't," she said. "Why would I have thought anything in particular?"

The man on the other side of the desk toyed with his mug of coffee and looked at her in silence for a whole minute. Nina felt her tongue swell in her mouth and got an unbearable urge to lick her lips.

"Do you know what?" Q said eventually, his voice now tired and muted. "I think you're lying. I think you know much more than you've reported so far, because you want to protect your best friend. But believe me, you won't help her by keeping quiet. If I'm to stand any chance of sorting out this mess, I need to know what happened."

Nina made an effort to keep her back straight, and nodded, yes, she could see that.

"I knew David Lindholm," Q said. "Better than most people. Let's just say that I'm not an unqualified supporter of the current claims that he was a great hero."

She looked at the detective in surprise.

"What do you mean by that?"

"We trained together. Why David joined up is one of life's great mysteries. He wasn't remotely interested in police work, just wanted to carry on with his extreme sports and chase women."

He was looking at Nina, evidently to see how she reacted.

"That's just part of being young," she said.

"He could be violent as well, at times, went in far too hard. Is that anything you've noticed during your career?"

"I never worked with David. He'd left active fieldwork behind long before Julia and I got to know him."

Q sighed and leaned forward over the desk.

"Yes, well," he said, "right now there's something considerably more important than David Lindholm's character and the question of Julia's guilt, and that's their son. Have you got any idea where Alexander might be?"

Nina tucked a strand of hair behind one ear.

"Julia's parents live in Södermanland, on a farm just outside Katrineholm. They look after Alexander sometimes, but he's not there. I spoke to them yesterday . . ."

"Julia's parents were the ones who reported the boy missing," Q said.

Nina sat completely still.

"David's father died years ago, and his mother lives in an old people's home; I haven't spoken to her but he's unlikely to be there. Julia didn't have much to do with her neighbors or the other mums at nursery, but I suppose he could have been spending the night with one of them anyway . . ."

"The boy hasn't been to nursery for the past week. No one's seen him since last Friday, neither the staff nor the other parents."

This is worse than everything else. How did it get to this?

"So what . . . what do you think's happened?"

"Was the Lindholms' marriage in trouble?"

Nina looked down at her lap.

"I suppose you could say that," she said.

"Enough trouble for Julia to be on the point of leaving him? For her to have prepared her departure somehow?"

"I don't know," Nina said.

The detective leaned across his desk and fixed his eyes on hers.

"Could she have hidden the boy somewhere?" he asked. "Could he be alive, locked up somewhere?"

She gulped hard and looked out of the window. *Could Julia have done that? Could she have locked Alexander away somewhere and then gone home and shot David?*

"It's now thirty hours since the murder," Q said. "Time's running out. If the boy doesn't have access to water, we need to find him within twenty-four hours, forty-eight at most. I hope you appreciate just how serious a situation this is."

A draft from the door made her shiver.

"Julia's got a summer cottage," she said. "Out in the woods near Katrineholm; she rents it from her parents' neighbors. They don't spend much time there. David thinks it's too basic, but Julia's very fond of it . . ."

She fell silent when she realized she was using the present tense.

Detective Inspector Q was making notes.

"So she rents it? That'll be why we haven't found any trace of it in the property register. Where is it?"

"In the woods outside Floda, halfway toward Granhed," Nina said. "I can draw you a map . . ."

She took a sheet of paper and drew a shaky map showing the way to Julia's cottage.

"It's called Björkbacken," she said, "but there's no sign. You can't see the house from the road; the post gets delivered to a box in Floda itself. But there's an old milestone beside the track, an iron sign saying how far it is to Floda Church. You can't miss it."

She pushed the sheet over the desk and the detective picked it up.

"How often does she go out there?"

Nina thought.

"I don't know," she said. "We haven't seen much of each other over the past few years . . ."

"Why not?" Q asked quickly.

Nina hesitated.

"David," she said. "We . . . we didn't really get on."

"Because?"

She looked away at the dead plant, remembering the first time they met David.

He came to give a lecture at Police Academy, dressed in jeans and a white T-shirt, big cowboy boots on his feet. His hair was short and spiked, and he had several days' stubble.

She recalled their teacher's breathless enthusiasm.

We should really have been looking at crime prevention today, with a particular focus on racism, but now that we've got the opportunity to hear David Lindholm instead, obviously we're delighted . . .

Several of the other teachers had turned up in the lecture room, which was extremely unusual.

David had sat down on the table at the front of the room, one boot dangling, the other firmly on the floor. He leaned forward with one elbow on his thigh. The impression was at once nonchalant and authoritative.

Julia's whisper like a warm breeze in her ear.

Just look at him! He's even better-looking in real life than on television . . .

The lecture had been fascinating, one of the best of the whole course. David talked about the art of negotiating with criminals in extreme situations, when there were hostages involved, for instance. He described situations and events that made everyone gawp, shifting between deadly seriousness and genuine humor with ease. His smile was radiant and white, and he noticed Julia straight away. Nina saw him turn toward her when he made a number of his jokes, and once he even winked at her. Julia blushed.

Afterward several of the teachers and students flocked round the famous lecturer. He was laughing and joking, but when Nina and Julia were getting ready to leave he excused himself and came over to them.

There is a future for Sweden, he said. *With you two in the force, the yobs will be queuing up to get arrested . . .*

He was pretending to talk to both of them, but he was looking at Julia as he spoke.

Julia smiled her wonderful smile and her eyes sparkled.

Nina could still remember the prick of jealousy.

She looked up at Detective Inspector Q.

"I think David felt that I was too close to Julia. Some men find that sort of thing difficult."

Q looked at her intently for several seconds.

"You were the one who reported that Julia mentioned another woman in the flat."

Nina nodded.

"Yes, that's right. There was nothing to indicate that that was the case, but obviously I made a note of what she said."

"Do you think she was telling the truth?"

Nina said nothing for a few moments.

"I don't know. It's probably up to forensics to see if there's any evidence of an intruder . . ."

"There were a lot of different fingerprints in the flat," Q said. "It must have been a while since it was last cleaned properly. You didn't see any signs of a break-in, no indication that the door had been forced?"

"No."

"Forensics have found traces of blood on the floor of the hall. Did you notice anything there?"

"No. But I saw a gun on the bedroom floor, by the end of the bed."

"That was Julia's."

Nina fell silent and looked down at her lap.

"Could this other woman have got in any other way?" Q asked. "Through an open window?"

Nina looked over at the detective's filthy windows. *The breeze from the bedroom, a window open slightly. Curtains drawn, a room in complete darkness. Shadows but no movement. Only the smell, sharp and unfamiliar.*

"The bedroom window was probably open," she said. "I didn't check, but there was a draft from in there."

"Which way does the bedroom face?"

"Toward Bondegatan."

"Is it possible to get in or out that way?"

"The flat's on the third floor, and the façade of the building is plastered. In theory it would probably be possible, using a rope, but you'd have to attach it somehow, either up on the roof or somewhere inside the flat."

Q sighed.

"And you're quite sure about the information about the other woman?"

Nina stiffened.

"What do you mean?"

"There's no way you could have misunderstood it?"

What were they really thinking? And what was the real reason for this peculiar conversation?

"Do you think I fabricated it in order to help my friend?"

"I don't think anything. But I would appreciate your help in trying to work out what happened."

Q leaned forward in his chair and held her gaze.

"It's like this: Julia isn't talking to us. We're extremely keen to get her to communicate. I was wondering if you could pay her an informal visit, to hear what she's got to say."

Aha. So that's it. This is where we've been heading.

Nina folded her arms.

"You want me to spy on my best friend? Is that what you're suggesting?"

"Call it whatever you want," the detective said calmly. "I'm offering you the chance to see Julia and find out how she is. If you think it fitting, you could always ask about the other woman, and about what happened in the flat yesterday morning."

"So I'm supposed to conduct some sort of interrogation without there being any sort of defense lawyer present?" Nina said. "That's completely unethical!"

"Maybe," Q said, looking at his watch. "She's in Kronoberg Prison as of now, more or less. I could get you permission to get in—if you think it would help, I mean."

"So she's been discharged from hospital? Already?"

"I saw her last night," the detective said. "She was fit as a fiddle."

"But," Nina said, "she was completely out of it yesterday morning."

"She wasn't particularly talkative, but that's hardly unusual. She's behaving like people normally do in custody."

The detective inspector wrote something on a sheet of paper and stood up.

"There's nothing wrong with Julia," he said. "I think she'd appreciate a visit from you. These are my telephone numbers. Call me when you've made up your mind."

Nina took the piece of paper and stood up as well.

"Just one question," she said. "How come you're in charge of this case?"

"I work here, and I had nothing better to do," Q said.

"But police officers suspected of any crime are supposed to be investigated by the police authority," Nina said. "Why isn't that happening with Julia?"

The detective held the door open for her.

"Julia Lindholm resigned from the force on May 15," he said. "The senior prosecutor with the police authority has decided that she should be treated as an ordinary mortal. She can hardly be investigated by her former colleagues on Södermalm, which is why the case has come to us at National Crime rather than going to the local district."

Nina stared at him.

"That's not possible."

"I can assure you that I take the rivalry between the district police authorities and the National Crime squad very seriously, but in this case we had no option."

"She can't have resigned. She would have talked to me first."

"Because my secretary is off today, I'm the one who's got to sit and file my nails today. So, if you don't mind . . ."

He nudged her out of the bare room and left her standing in the corridor.

Annika was leaning against the doorframe with a mug of coffee in her hand, watching the children chasing Berit's dog around the large lawn in front of the house. Kalle was quicker, of course, but Ellen was keeping up fairly well on her little legs. The girl had a good stride; maybe she'd turn out to be a good sprinter.

I was good at sprinting once. Long distance too, come to that: I managed to run away from Sven . . .

She stopped midthought and thrust it aside.

The view from the porch of Berit's guest cottage was wonderful. Up to the right lay the main house, two stories, a terrace, ornate woodwork. To the left the meadow sloped down toward the lake and the beach, where the neighbor's horses usually went to shit in the summer. Straight ahead, on the far side of the paddocks, lay the forest.

Maybe this is the way to live, close to nature.

But she knew she'd get cabin fever within a week.

"Mum, I caught him!"

Kalle had managed to get his arm round the neck of Berit's good-natured old Labrador. The boy and dog were rolling around the grass together, and Annika could already see that his new clothes were going to have permanent grass stains.

"Don't be too rough!" she called. "And the dog's a she!"

Berit was coming over to the guest cottage, a mug in one hand and Annika's mobile in the other.

"Did you sleep well?"

Annika tried to smile.

"Sort of. Funny dreams."

Berit sat down on the steps.

"About the fire?"

"About . . ."

Annika stopped herself. She hadn't told Berit that Thomas had been unfaithful. She had been tormented by macabre nightmares about Sophia Grenborg for months now, making her wake up breathless and in a cold sweat.

"There's something wrong with Thord's old charger," Berit said, "so I'm not sure how full the battery is."

She put the phone down on the porch. Annika sat down next to her and looked out over the meadow with the mug of coffee between her hands.

"You've got a lovely place here," she said.

Berit screwed her eyes up against the reflection of the sun in the water of the lake.

"This was the last chance for me and Thord," she said, still looking off toward the beach. "We grabbed it, and it worked out."

Annika followed her colleague's gaze, down toward the water.

"How do you mean?"

Berit glanced at Annika with a little smile.

"I had an affair," she said, and Annika gasped.

Berit? An affair?

"I got very fond of another man," Berit went on, "but of course it was just an illusion. I fell in love with love itself, it was great feeling that sparkle again, being head over heels in love again."

She laughed, slightly embarrassed.

"But of course it didn't last. When I saw him in the full light of day, he was just another bloke. There was no reason to throw away everything I had with Thord just for a bit of decent sex for a while."

Annika was staring down into her mug, unable to think of a single thing to say.

Berit? An affair? Decent sex for a while? But she was fifty-two years old!

"I know what you're thinking," Berit said, "and I can assure you of one thing: It felt exactly the same as when I was eighteen. In some ways I'm glad it happened, but I'll never do it again."

Without being conscious of what she was doing, Annika put the mug down, wrapped her arms round Berit's neck, and started to cry. She wept silently, her body shaking, for several minutes, with her colleague's arms holding her tight.

"He's got someone else," she whispered, wiping her nose with the back of her hand. "I keep dreaming of killing her. He left me for her, and then the house burned down."

Berit sighed and stroked her back.

"And you still haven't spoken to him?"

Annika shook her head and wiped her cheeks with the sleeve of her cardigan.

"You have to get through this," Berit said. "There's no way around it."

Annika nodded.

"I know."

"There's a phone in the office. The children can stay here if you need to go out for a while."

Berit stood up, brushed the dirt from her behind, and headed off toward the house again, mug in hand.

Annika watched her go, trying to see her with different eyes, a man's eyes.

She was fairly tall and thin, with broad shoulders and cropped hair. She was wearing a loose top that swung out at her hips. She didn't dress like that for work. She usually wore a jacket and dark trousers, perhaps with a bit of expensive but discreet jewelry.

It had never even occurred to her that Berit might be capable of having an affair!

That her serious and well-educated colleague was a sexual being.

It was actually a bit uncomfortable, a bit like realizing that your mum and dad must have had sex once upon a time.

Then she was struck by the most obvious thought of all: *But who with?*

Whom had she had an affair with?

Someone at the paper?

It was almost bound to be.

Or one of her sources? Berit met a lot of different people to get information.

She said the farm was the last chance for her and Thord, and when had they bought it? A couple of years ago? She was already working at the paper herself by then! Maybe it had been when she was on maternity leave, so perhaps it wasn't so strange that she'd never noticed anything.

As long as it wasn't Spike!

Please, don't let it be Spike!

Somehow the idea of Berit having an affair was strangely heartening. Annika felt like calling her colleague back and asking her all about it to find out more.

It was possible to carry on; everything wasn't finished just because things had been a bit difficult.

Her eyes fell on the mobile phone; she must remember to buy a charger next time she was in the city.

Angst suddenly took a stranglehold of her and she took several shallow breaths to keep it at bay.

Got to get through this. There's no way round it.

So she went back into the house and picked up the phone and dialed the number of Thomas's mobile.

One ring, she could hear the children racing around outside.

Two rings, the sunlight on the water caught her eyes.

Three rings . . .

"Hello, this is Thomas . . ."

She gulped audibly.

"Hello," she managed to say, and it sounded like a squeak.

Her heart was thudding so hard that she could hardly hear what he replied.

"Where the hell have you been?"

She was shaking, and had to hold the receiver with both hands.

"I've . . . the house has burned down."

"Really, so you didn't think it was worth telling me before now?"

"It was yesterday morning . . ."

"Why haven't you called? Why didn't you tell me? How the hell do you think I felt, driving out there and seeing the house like that, in ruins? Have you any idea what sort of shock it was?"

"Yes, sorry . . ."

"And how the hell did the fire start? I mean, the whole house is a wreck! What on earth did you do?"

"I didn't do anything, I just . . ."

He cleared his throat loudly.

"How are the kids?"

"Fine. They're playing. Do you want to see them?"

He put the phone down and was gone for a long while.

"Now isn't a good time," he said when he came back. "What do the insurance company say?"

He doesn't want to see the children! He doesn't care about Ellen and Kalle!

Her tears overflowed and ran down her cheeks.

"I haven't sorted that out yet," she whispered. "I suppose I'll do it next week."

"Fuck," he said. "How long does it take to get the money?"

She wiped her tears away with her sleeve.

"Don't know . . ."

"I need to get this sorted as soon as possible," Thomas said, and it sounded like he really meant it.

"I'm so sorry," Annika said.

"Not half as much as I am," Thomas said, and ended the call.

She put the receiver down carefully and let a wave of self-pity course through her body. She snorted a couple of times and wiped her cheeks with her fingertips. She stood there, looking out through the window at the sunlight and the children playing.

Why isn't this enough for me? Why isn't life ever enough?

She went out onto the porch again and sat down, watching the children.

Where was she going to go with them?

Their nursery was out in Djursholm, but the thought of taking them back there made her feel ill.

No more suburbs, never again.

The countryside was fine, but she was happiest in the city.

Maybe they could go back to Kungsholmen. Things had been good there. If they were lucky, their places at nursery and preschool would still be available: They didn't usually take on new children until the start of term.

Maybe she should phone and find out?

She picked up her mobile and switched it on. Thord's old charger had managed to squeeze a bit of power into the battery. She dialed the manager's number and got a message telling her that the nursery was closed for a training day.

She huddled up and wrapped her arms round her shins.

Was she wrong about this? Would it be better to make a fresh start? Move to a new part of the city, maybe even a different town entirely? Home to Katrineholm?

Her mobile started to buzz. It had connected properly to the network and the messages were tumbling in.

Annika looked at the screen.

There weren't that many. Five voicemails and three ordinary texts.

The voicemails were, in order, from Spike, Schyman, Spike, Thomas, and Thomas. The texts were all from Thomas, and got progressively more angry in tone.

Spike wanted her to go in and write about David Lindholm, then Schyman wanted the same thing, then Spike wondered if she could write an eyewitness account of her house burning down, then finally her husband had called with the same fury as in the text messages.

This was actually fairly symptomatic of her life, she realized. This was what happened whenever she was hit by some catastrophe, these were the people who got in touch. Two of her bosses, wondering if she could do some work, and an angry bloke who didn't think she fucked him often enough.

She went back into the house and called Schyman.

"How are you?" the editor in chief asked. "You're still in one piece, then? Are you okay?"

She sat down.

"I'm okay. Berit came to get me last night; I'm out at her place in the country now."

"We've been trying to call you, but couldn't get through."

"I know, but now I've got my mobile going again. Was it anything in particular?"

"First of all it was this business with Julia Lindholm: You know her, don't you?"

"Well, sort of: I spent a night in a patrol car with her five years ago."

"They're keen to publish the story," Schyman said. "But I understand the situation you're in. Did you have time to rescue anything from the house?"

"The children."

He fell silent and coughed awkwardly.

"Bloody hell," he said. "It's hard to imagine. Do you need some time off?"

"Yes," she said, "I've got a lot of things to sort out."

"Do you think you could write up the story about Julia Lindholm? My night with the cop killer? You could do that from home."

"I don't have a computer."

She didn't have a home either, but she didn't mention that.

"You can pick up a new laptop here at the newsroom. I'll sign a requisition slip at once. When can you get in to pick it up?"

She looked at her watch.

"This afternoon," she said. "And if I'm going to write about Julia Lindholm, I ought to talk to the other officer who was with us. Nina Hoffman, that was her name. She was the one I was actually doing the profile of."

"Okay, I'm counting on you."

She left the children in Berit's care, playing on the lawn, and went off to the bus stop. She took out her mobile and checked the contact list. She tried Nina, then Hoffman, and finally found a mobile number under "Police Nina H."

She pressed *Dial,* and waited as the phone rang.

"Hoffman."

She swallowed.

"Nina Hoffman? My name's Annika Bengtzon, I'm a journalist on the *Evening Post.* We met five years ago, I spent a night with you and Julia . . ."

"Yes, I remember."

"Is this a bad time?"

"What's it about?"

She looked out over the fields and meadows around her, at the clouds slowly drifting north toward the horizon, at red-painted wooden houses, the old glass in their windows sparkling.

"You can probably guess," Annika said. "My editors want an update on what we did that evening, what Julia said and did, what I made of it all. I've said I'll do it, but I wanted to talk to you first."

"We have a press spokesman who looks after all communication with the media."

"Well, I know that," Annika said, and could hear that she was sounding irritated. "But I wanted to check with you before I write anything about Julia, because I got the impression that you were quite close."

Nina Hoffman said nothing for a few moments.

"What are you thinking of writing?"

"Julia said quite a lot about David. And now our idle chat that night has suddenly become very interesting. Have you got time to meet me?"

Annika could see the dust of the approaching bus at the brow of the hill.

"I'm not planning on dishing the dirt on anyone," she said. "That's not why I'm calling. In fact, it's rather the opposite."

"I believe you," Nina Hoffman said.

They agreed to meet at a pizza restaurant close to where Nina Hoffman lived on Södermalm an hour and half later.

The bus drove up and stopped. Annika clambered aboard and held out Berit's last five-hundred-kronor note as payment.

"Haven't you got anything smaller?" the driver said.

Annika shook her head.

"I can't change a note that big. You'll have to take the next bus."

"You'll have to throw me off," she said, picking up the note and walking toward the back of the bus.

The driver looked after her for a few moments, then put the bus in gear and pulled away.

She sat right at the back by the window, and watched the landscape flash past. Everything was different shades of green. The speed of the bus blurred the edges and turned the world into an abstract painting.

Annika shut her eyes and leaned her head back.

Thomas walked briskly into the government offices at Rosenbad with his back straight. Without looking left or right, he slid past a group of citizens queuing at the security desk in the white hallway, and prayed that his pass would still work.

Officially his secondment had come to an end on Monday, and he hadn't had his pass renewed, which had come as an unexpected and unpleasant surprise. So far in his career he had been recruited from one job to the next without ever having to produce lengthy CVs or tortured applications. It would feel like a blow if that were to change now, when he had finally managed to get a research post with the government.

Yesterday the head of his section in the Ministry of Justice, Per Cramne, had called and asked him to look in, and Thomas had been careful not to sound too keen. So he had made out that he had a meeting in the morning, which was actually true, even if it was with Sophia.

If he was in luck his entry code would still work, and he could avoid the humiliation of having to wait in the queue of visitors. He held his breath and pressed the number, there was a whirring sound from the door, and the green light came on.

With measured force, he pulled open the white steel door and stepped into the corridors of power. He could feel the eyes of the people in the queue on the back of his neck: *Who's that? What does he do? It must be someone important!*

Naturally, he went over to wait by the lift on the right, seeing as the one on the left was a goods lift that stopped at every single floor (waiting for the one on the left was an elementary mistake).

He got out on the fourth floor and walked straight to the head of section's office.

"Bloody good to see you," Cramne said, shaking his hand as if they hadn't met for several months. In fact that had eaten dinner together at the house out in Djursholm as recently as Monday.

"Awful business about the house," his boss went on, gesturing to a chair. "What's it like, are you going to rebuild it?"

Nice and calm, Thomas thought, just breathe gently and wait for what he's got to say.

"Yes, I suppose so," he said, sitting down and leaning back, letting his knees slip open slightly, it felt suitably relaxed.

"Well, the bugging proposal's going through like a knife through butter," Per Cramne said. "Everyone's very happy with the research you did for us, I want you to know that."

Thomas swallowed and held up his hands as if to stop the praise.

"It was really just a continuation of my work for the Association of County Councils . . ."

Cramne was leafing through some files in a cabinet to the right of the desk.

"Now we've got to take care of the follow-up work," he said. "The government will be appointing a parliamentary inquiry which will go through all the clauses and suggest changes."

"A proper inquiry?" Thomas wondered. "Or to bury the proposal?"

The problem with inquiries is that they were set up both to get something done, and if you *didn't* want something to be done. The method was exactly the same, whether you wanted to bury something or promote it.

The assistant undersecretary opened another drawer and carried on leafing through it.

"You haven't read the memo? I thought that went out while you were still here."

Thomas fought an impulse to cross his legs and arms in a sort of basic defense posture.

"No," he said, still sitting the same way. "What are the conditions?"

Cramne slammed one of the drawers shut and looked up.

"The directives are bloody simple," he said. "Any proposed reforms mustn't drive up the cost of criminal custody. We need an economist in the group to analyze the consequences of any proposals, and it's going to require a fair bit of political dexterity. One of our aims is to abolish lifetime sentences, and some of our critics are already screaming that this is going to be bloody expensive. I'm absolutely convinced that they're wrong."

He smiled and leaned back in his chair, and the backrest hit the wall.

"This is where you come into the picture," he said.

"As an economist?" Thomas said, his heart sinking.

He hadn't reckoned on this. He'd hoped for something else, some sort of position within the department. Being an economist for the Justice Ministry didn't sound anything much, scarcely better than caretaker.

"We need an expert on the committee," Cramne said with a nod.

"To provide economic analysis?"

"Exactly. We're extending your appointment until the inquiry is complete, and that could take a couple of years."

Thomas could feel the blood rushing to his head. A couple of years! His immediate reaction had been mistaken, this was brilliant! It meant that he'd be guaranteed employment protection and would have first chance at any permanent post, and he'd get to stay in the department. A government official! That's what he'd be, properly.

He had to show how sharp he was, right from the start.

"Abolishing lifetime sentencing," he said, "why should that be expensive? Shouldn't that make things cheaper?"

Cramne looked slightly irritated.

"Any change has cost implications. Today a lifetime prisoner serves on average thirteen, fourteen years. You know that they get out after serving two-thirds of their sentence? If you get rid of the lifetime sentence, the new maximum term would be something like twenty-five years."

"Really?" Thomas said.

"Which would obviously place a severe strain on the prison service. But we can deal with that later. We have to start by going through what the direct consequences would be today, then look at how they would change over time, and how the range of sentencing is being applied."

He leaned forward and lowered his voice.

"Up to now, the government hasn't increased any sentences, apart from some adjustment to the Sexual Offenses Act, so in my opinion it's high time that that was done."

He leaned back once more, his chair hitting the wall again. Thomas lifted one foot onto his knee and rubbed at a spot on his shoe to avoid having to look up and reveal that he was blushing.

"So the job would be to do cost analysis of possible legislative proposals?" he said. "And then carry on as usual?"

"You'll keep your office, and work the way you've been doing up to now. I've already discussed this with Halenius, the undersecretary of state, and he's given it the okay. Welcome to the team!"

Per Cramne held out his hand again and Thomas took it with a grin.

"Thanks, boss," he said.

"This business of statistics," Cramne said, lowering his voice as he leaned forward, "it's like herding cats."

The assistant undersecretary got to his feet and gestured toward the door with one hand. Thomas got up clumsily and realized that his legs felt a bit unsteady.

"When do I start?" he asked.

Cramne raised his eyebrows.

"Well, what the hell?" he said. "There's no point hanging about, is there? Get hold of someone at the National Council for Crime Prevention and get them to put together an analysis of current sentences so we've got something to get our teeth into."

Thomas headed off toward his old office, his feet not quite touching the floor. The room was only on the fourth floor, far below the real center of power up on six and seven, it was cramped and dark and looked out on Fredsgatan, but at least it was in Rosenbad.

He stopped in the doorway and gazed silently at the furnishings, took a deep breath and shut his eyes.

He'd had so much sex that his crotch ached, he was living in a huge apartment on Östermalm, and he worked for the government.

Fuck me, it doesn't get better than this, he thought, stepping into the room and hanging his jacket on the back of the chair.

The bus braked sharply, throwing Annika forward and banging her head on the seat in front. Confused, she rubbed the bridge of her nose and looked out of the window. The bus had stopped at a red light just in front of the Eastern Station.

She jumped out and caught the underground at Tekniska Högskolan and checked her watch.

If everything went according to plan, she would have time to go to the bank before she met Nina Hoffman.

She got off at Slussen and headed along Götgatan until she came to a branch of her bank.

She had to wait twenty minutes before she got to see a cashier.

"I've got a problem," Annika said, putting the form she had filled in on the counter. "My house has burned down. I haven't got an ID card, nor any bank cards, because I didn't manage to get anything out of the house. That's why I need to withdraw money this way. I hope that's okay."

The cashier looked at her with a completely neutral expression behind her thick glasses.

"Obviously I can't hand any money over to someone if the person in question can't identify themselves."

Annika nodded emphatically.

"Yes," she said, "I understand that. But I don't have any identification documents, seeing as they all went up in the fire, and I haven't got any money either, that's why I need to withdraw some now."

The woman behind the counter was starting to look as if Annika smelled.

"That's out of the question," she said.

Annika gulped.

"I know my account number off by heart," she said. "And I know exactly how much I've got in my current account. I've got a phone account as well, I know all the codes . . ."

She held up her mobile and smiled to show how friendly she was.

"Sorry," the cashier said. "I'll have to ask you to step aside."

White-hot fury flashed up instantly.

"Listen," Annika said, leaning toward the cashier. "Whose money is it, yours or mine?"

The cashier raised her eyebrows and pressed to call the next customer in the queue. A man stood up and walked over to Annika, stopping demonstratively close to her.

"I have almost three million kronor in various accounts in your damn bank," Annika said, far too loudly. "I want to withdraw every single öre and close every account."

The woman looks at her with unconcealed loathing.

"You have to be able to give proof of your identity before you can close an account," she said, turning to the man who was muscling past Annika in annoyance.

"But it's my money!" she shouted.

She turned round and walked quickly toward the door, and from the corners of her eyes she could see the other customers staring at her with a mixture of fear and distaste.

Close to tears, she tore the door open and started running down Folkungagatan toward Danvikstull.

I've got to calm down, otherwise everyone will think I've robbed the bank.

She slowed down and forced herself to go at normal walking speed.

Five minutes later she reached the pizzeria.

It took her a few moments to recognize Nina Hoffman. The police officer was sitting in a corner at the back of the restaurant, studying the menu intently. Without her uniform she looked like any other young Södermalm woman, jeans and jumper, her light-brown hair down loose.

"Hello," Annika said breathlessly, holding out her hand. "I'm sorry I'm a bit late, I was trying to get some money out of my bank account, but I haven't got any ID at the moment . . ."

She realized she was about to burst into frustrated tears again, and took a deep breath.

"Sorry. It's very good of you to see me at such short notice," Annika said, sitting down at the table. "My house has burned down and I didn't manage to get anything out with me."

There was a flicker in the police officer's eyes.

"In Djursholm? That was your house?"

Annika nodded.

Nina Hoffman looked at her carefully for a few seconds, then picked up the menu.

"Do you eat pizza?"

"Absolutely."

They each ordered mineral water and a sealed-crust calzone.

"It's a while since we last met," Annika said when the waitress had disappeared into the kitchen with their order.

Nina Hoffman nodded.

"Down at the station," she said, "just before your article was published. You brought me a printout to look through."

"It was the day that financial consultant was locked up," Annika said. "Filip Andersson. I remember everyone being relieved that those terrible ax murders could be sorted out so quickly."

"I've hardly ever felt such unanimous loathing within the force for one individual criminal," Nina said.

"Rich, cowardly, and sadistic," Annika said. "Not a combination of characteristics that's ever going to win any popularity contests. He's in Kumla Prison, isn't he?"

Nina Hoffman raised her chin.

"What exactly do you want to find out from me?"

Annika got serious.

"I don't know how much you remember, but Julia talked a fair bit about David that night. David didn't want her to work in the force while she was pregnant. David didn't like the fact that she'd had her hair cut. David didn't like the fact that her stomach was starting to show. David hoped it would be a boy. He called three times just to find out where we were. I got a hint of control-freakery."

Nina looked at her coldly.

"How come you remember it so well?"

"David was already a television celebrity, even then. Besides, I'm allergic to control-freakery, it brings me out in a rash. How was their marriage, really?"

Nina folded her arms.

"Don't you think that's a very personal question?"

"You don't kill your husband without a very good reason."

The calzones arrived and they started to eat in silence.

Annika paused halfway through, put her knife and fork down and leaned back.

"Eating a whole calzone's like putting a big rock in your stomach," she said

Nina carried on eating without looking up.

This isn't going well.

"How have things been for you since we last met?" Annika asked. "Do you still work at the Katarina station?"

Nina shook her head and wiped her mouth with the napkin.

"No," she said, glancing up quickly, then looking down again. "I got promoted, I've been an inspector for the past year or so."

Annika studied her. Nina Hoffman was a smart woman who played according to the rules.

I'll do this the overpedagogical way.

"It's always a sensitive matter, writing about tragedies within relationships like this," she said. "While there's a lot of public interest, everyone in the media has to consider all the people involved. David was one of the best-known police officers in Sweden. I don't know if you saw the press conference yesterday when they announced that Alexander was missing, but the head of National Crime said straight out that David's murder was an attack on the structure of society as a whole, an attack on democratic principles."

Now Nina looked up with a different expression on her face.

"He seemed personally affected in a way I haven't seen before," Annika went on. "The head of National Crime usually looks like a fairly wooden character. If I've understood it correctly, his reaction is shared by a lot of police officers. The entire Swedish police force seems to have taken David's murder personally. That makes our job in the media even more difficult."

The police officer put down her knife and fork and leaned forward.

"How do you mean?"

Annika chose her words carefully.

"We're always walking a tightrope when we write about ongoing criminal investigations," she said slowly. "We want to publish as much information as possible for our readers, but at the same time we have to take into account the work of the police. The police have the same conflict of interest, only reversed. You want to work undisturbed and as effectively as possible, but at the same time you wouldn't get anywhere if you didn't communicate with the public, which usually happens via the media. Do you know what I mean?"

Nina Hoffman was looking hard at her.

"To be honest, no, I don't," she said.

Annika pushed her plate aside.

"We need to know what happened with this murder, and we need an open dialogue about what we can and ought to publish. That requires trust and loyalty from both sides. If we can establish that, then maybe we have a chance of succeeding, you and us alike."

Nina blinked several times.

"We always know much more than we publish," Annika went on. "You know that. I mean, I was there when you and Julia walked right into the ax murders, but I didn't write a thing about it in the paper the next day. Whereas I let you approve the way I described your work in the profile I did of you. That's the way I work, and that's what I mean about us both taking our responsibility, on both sides . . ."

It was entirely true that Annika hadn't written anything about the ax murders the following day, because she had promised Nina that she wouldn't. Instead she had given all the details to Sjölander, who got a scoop and a front page for nothing.

"So what do you want to know about Julia?" Nina asked.

"Did she do it?"

"The investigation has only just got started," Nina replied.

"Are there any other suspects?"

Nina sat silent.

"This must put you in an extremely odd situation," Annika said. "Professionally as well, I mean. You can't be part of the investigation, I realize that, but at the same time . . ."

"I'm involved whether I like it or not," Nina Hoffman interrupted. "I was the one who responded to the call first; my colleague and I were the first officers inside the flat."

Annika jerked.

"That must be hard for you," she said, "trying to remain objective."

A couple near them burst into simultaneous laughter. Another couple stood up, chairs scraping. Annika moved her cutlery.

"Objective?"

Annika waited until the couple near them had gone out.

"Not having a preconceived idea of culpability."

"David was shot in his sleep," Nina said. "We found a gun right by the bed. We've already linked it to the culprit."

"With fingerprints? That was quick."

"It was even easier than that. It was Julia's service revolver."

Annika had to stop herself from letting out a gasp.

"How do they know? Don't they all look alike?"

"Most officers have a Sig Sauer 225. But each gun has a serial number that links it to a particular officer, a particular individual."

"Can I publish that?"

"Absolutely not."

A silence rose up between them. Groups of people around them were getting up and leaving.

"What do the police think about Alexander? Is he still alive?" Annika asked when the silence had become too oppressive. "Is there any point in asking the public to help look for him?"

Nina Hoffman looked at her sternly for several long seconds.

"We don't know if Alexander's alive," she said. "For the time being we're assuming that he is. It's extremely important that the public keep their eyes open."

"If he is dead, what might have happened to him?"

"He hasn't been at nursery all week. Julia rang to say he was ill. The last person to see him was the downstairs neighbor, Erlandsson. He looked out through the spyhole in his door and saw Julia going out with the boy on Tuesday morning. They had a flowery fabric bag with them."

"But I can't write about that either?"

They sat in silence for a while. The waitress took their plates away. Neither of them wanted coffee, just the bill.

"By the way," Annika said after she had paid with Berit's money and Nina was gathering her things. "Why aren't National Crime taking care of this? Aren't all crimes committed by police officers supposed to be investigated by them?"

"Julia resigned a couple of weeks ago," Nina Hoffman said, standing up.

She was tall, a head taller than Annika.

"She did?" Annika said. "Why?"

Nina looked at her.

"I can come with you to the bank if you like. They usually only need someone to confirm your identity."

Annika stopped midstep, her mouth open in surprise.

"Could you? That would be great."

They walked off toward the branch on Götgatan in silence.

The queue of lunchtime customers was gone. Annika filled in a new withdrawal form and walked straight up to the cashier with the thick glasses.

"Hello," Annika said. "It's me again. I want to withdraw my money now."

Nina Hoffman put her driving license and police badge alongside the form.

"I can vouch that the person in question is the person she claims to be," she said firmly.

The cashier's mouth pursed slightly and she nodded curtly.

She counted out twenty-five thousand kronor in thousand-kronor notes, and held them out to Annika with a little flick of the wrist.

"Can I have them in an envelope, please?" Annika said.

The cashier let out a little cough.

"As soon as I've opened a new account with another bank I'll come back and shut down everything I've got here," Annika said, then turned and walked out.

When they emerged onto the street Annika breathed out, a deep, drawn-out breath.

"Thank you," she said, holding out her hand. "Imagine, that it could suddenly be so easy . . ."

"The police badge usually helps," Nina Hoffman said, and smiled slightly for the first time.

"Have you still got my mobile number?" Annika asked.

They went in different directions, the police officer heading down toward Danvikstull, Annika off toward the underground station at Slussen.

Schyman was sitting at his desk staring helplessly at the report from the steering group of the management board, dated the previous day.

Sixty employees.

Sixty employees had to go.

He stood up and did the short circuit of his tiny cubbyhole, one step in each direction.

He sat down again and tugged at his hair.

If he protested, there would be only one outcome: He would have to take his things and leave. There was no other option, he had learned that during his years in the warm embrace of the Family. Anyone could run the paper; he was under no illusions that he was indispensable. The question was just what journalistic ambitions any new management might have. Would they turn the *Evening Post* into a gutter-press rag with naked girls on page three? Cut out anything political, investigative, or analytical and focus exclusively on gossip and celebrities?

Or would they simply close it down?

The *Evening Post* wasn't one of the Family's most warmly regarded publications, to put it mildly. If it weren't for the fact that the paper brought money into the business, it would have been dead and buried long ago.

Running at a profit had been one of the basic demands when he accepted the position of editor in chief and legally responsible publisher some years before, and Schyman had never let them down, but—*sixty employees*?

He would of course have to discuss the matter with the new managing director, a lad who had graduated from business school a few years ago and had got the job at the *Evening Post* because he was best friends with one of the Family's sons. So far the young pup hadn't made too many waves (much to everyone's relief and delight).

Schyman put the report down on his desk.

That wasn't such a bad idea, damn it.

Perhaps it was time for the Pup to take some responsibility and do something in return for his million-kronor salary.

On the other hand: The Pup couldn't judge which measures needed to be taken, nor which employees could be let go of, so it would obviously have to be him who identified the priorities and thus the entire project. If he sent the Pup into battle and the cutbacks worked, then the Pup would be the one who got all the credit. And he would be left looking weak and ignorant.

And that would never do.

So where would the points of conflict be, exactly?

The unions, of course: There'd be a terrible fuss.

The newspaper had approximately five hundred employees, half of them on the editorial side, which meant that they were members of the Swedish Journalists" Association. (Those who weren't already members would join up the moment the proposed cutbacks were announced. There was nothing better for promoting a bit of solidarity than a serious threat to people's own wallets.)

The other 250 were in the Salaried Employees' Union (advertising, marketing, administration), and then there were a couple of dozen poor sods still working in graphics.

What could be cut?

Not advertising, that was out of the question. They would have to accelerate out of the crisis, and advertising was the only way to rake in profits. And the analysts and distribution people couldn't be touched either. Technical support had already been pared to the bone.

Which left editorial staff and admin.

Anders Schyman sighed and wondered if he could be bothered to go and get a plastic mug of coffee from the machine. He closed his eyes and imagined the bitter taste on his tongue and decided against it.

The other way of raising profits was to increase the number of copies sold, which placed serious demands on the competence of the journalists. Which in turn meant that every cutback in editorial staff needed to be done with surgical precision.

And that brought him back to the union, and likely conflict.

He needed to keep and fire people according to their abilities and work, but the union was guaranteed to trot out the old maxim, "Last in, first out."

If they got their way, everyone who had been recruited recently would be thrown out, leaving just the old hacks, and that was simply impossible if the paper was going to survive.

The new website people were essential, otherwise the entire online investment would collapse. But he also needed to retain the experience and competence of the older employees, the ones who still knew who and what the chancellor of justice was, for instance.

He let out a loud groan.

The Salaried Employees' Union and the Journalists' Association were relatively weak and flexible unions. They seldom rode into battle for any-thing, and even less often for something sensible. Schyman could still remember his astonishment when the Journalists' Association had uni-laterally suggested that trainee reporters should be forced to accept other types of work (dishwashers, cleaners, the Volvo production line) as soon as they became unemployed, a suggestion so controversial that not even the government or business community had thought of it.

He scratched his beard.

The local branch of the union had its annual general meeting on Monday. They would be choosing a new chair, seeing as the previous one was going on study leave from August.

The post of chair of the union branch was much sought after, seeing as it meant that you spent all your time on union matters, and therefore played no part in the editorial work of the paper. And it meant power, be-cause you became part of the management group and took part in some sections of committee meetings as the representative of the staff.

Just let it be someone with a brain, Schyman thought, and made up his mind to go and get that cup of coffee after all.

Annika thought people were looking at her rather oddly as she walked through the newsroom with her newly purchased bag over her shoulder. Naturally, her colleagues loved gossip—it went with the job—and she realized that her burned-down house must have been at the top of yes-terday's list of gossip.

She hoisted the bag higher on her shoulder and quickened her pace.

First she had to get the requisition note to pick up the new laptop from technical support, then check if she could track down her old notes on the Internet, and then put together a piece about Julia Lindholm.

But before any of that she needed a cup of coffee.

She dropped her bag and her new jacket at the long desk shared by the day-shift reporters and went off to the machine.

She found Anders Schyman staring shortsightedly at all the buttons.

"Strong with sugar but no milk, how do you get that?" he asked. An-nika swiftly pressed + *Strength,* + *Sugar,* –*Milk* and pressed *Make.*

"The computer," she said. "Can I get it now?"

"The requisition's ready and waiting on my desk," the editor in chief said. "Is there anything else you need?"

She paused.

"A car," she said. "If I could borrow one of the paper's cars for the weekend . . ."

"That will probably be okay," Anders Schyman said, and started to walk toward his office. "By the way, do you know what the CJ is?"

"The chancellor of justice?" Annika said. "A dinosaur. Why?"

The editor in chief stopped.

"A dinosaur?"

"Or some other prehistoric relic," Annika said. "It's completely absurd that a post like that is still bestowed for life, just because that's what happened in the 1700s. Everyone in Sweden has the right to change their lawyer, apart from the government. It's completely ridiculous."

"Can't the CJ be dismissed?" Schyman said.

"Nope," Annika said.

"Follow me, and I'll give you the requisition note."

She trudged after the editor in chief to his office. The room wasn't actually that small, but Anders Schyman was so expansive that it shrank when he went in.

"Here you are," he said, handing her the sheet of paper. "Have they found whoever set fire to your house yet?"

She shook her head and swallowed.

Hopkins, the miserable old bastard. May he burn in hell!

Schyman hunted through a desk drawer and pulled out another requisition request which he signed with a quick scribble.

"You can have the car for a week," he said. "If Tore makes a fuss, refer him to me."

She put the piece of paper in her bag and headed off to see the caretaker. She could feel people's eyes on her as she crossed the newsroom, and looked down at the floor to avoid them.

She had to wait for five minutes as Tore, the caretaker, concluded an important telephone conversation about racing tips.

"You can have this one," Tore said, putting a battered laptop on the counter when she had explained why she was there.

"Does it work?" Annika said.

Tore looked up at her with an affronted expression.

"Of course it bloody works. I'm the one who checked it over."

"Hmm," Annika said, switching the machine on.

The programs loaded. Explorer logged in automatically to the paper's wireless network. MS Word turned out to be full of Sjölander's old articles.

She sighed quietly.

"Great," she said. "And a car as well, please . . ."

She handed over the requisition note with Schyman's signature.

Tore looked skeptically at the sheet of paper.

"And what do you need a Volvo V70 for?"

"I'm thinking of robbing a bank, and I need a discreet getaway car," Annika said.

"Sounds fun," Tore said, handing her the keys. "It's got a full tank. Make sure it's full when it comes back."

She went back to the newsroom and set up the laptop on the reporters' desk. She began by reading everything she could find about the police murder from the main news agency and in the *Evening Post*'s internal files.

"Annika," Spike said, putting his hand on her shoulder. "How do you feel about writing a true story? 'How I Escaped the Flames'?"

She looked up and saw a troop of people gathering around her.

"Is it true they know who started the fire?" wondered crime reporter Patrik Nilsson, currently the only reporter with that title on the paper apart from Berit.

"I need you to fill in a report about the loss of your old laptop as soon as possible," said Eva-Britt Qvist, the editorial secretary who had been promoted to paper shuffler in admin. She looked almost happy for the first time ever.

Even the girl with the piercings who ran the commercial radio station with all the adverts had left her nest in Annika's old office and come out to stare.

"I mean, like, what the fuck?" she said. "Like, poor you."

"Okay," Annika said, rolling her chair back to the edge of the table.

"I'm fine, everything's fine. Thanks for your concern, but I'm kind of busy . . ."

Nobody moved.

"Must be really fucking awful for you," said the girl with all the things on her face, taking a step closer.

"Go and get on with your work," Spike said, slightly too loudly, and people began to move again, muttering in disappointment.

"I want the loss report by Monday at the latest, otherwise you'll be liable for the loss," Eva-Britt Qvist said over her shoulder.

The head of news turned back toward Annika.

"We haven't put anything in the paper, but if you feel like writing an eyewitness account, we've got a gap on eleven."

Annika cleared her throat.

"Thanks, but no thanks," she said. "Schyman's asked me to write about Julia Lindholm."

"That's great," Spike said. " 'Exclusive: Cop Killer's Secret History.' "

"Mmh," Annika said. "She hasn't been found guilty yet, of course."

"That's just a technicality," Spike said, and went back to his desk.

She left the news pages and logged in to her annika-bengtzon@hot-mail.com address, and found the file marked archive. Slowly she began to click open notes and documents from several years before.

There were things there that were so old that she had almost forgotten them: excerpts from a conversation with Patricia who worked in the porn club, Studio Six; notes from her first meeting with Rebecka who ran the Paradise Foundation; copies of articles she'd written in the *Norrland News* offices when she was up there digging about in an old bomb attack on the F21 airbase and found herself in the middle of the murder of the journalist Benny Ekland.

All of a sudden it hit her: *This is all I've got left. Everything else went up in flames. What a relief that I thought to keep my archive on the Internet . . .*

She pushed her hair from her face and carried on clicking. She had a definite memory that it ought to be here somewhere.

Finally she found the document, and leaned over to glance through the single-page file.

Nina Hoffman and Julia Lindholm grew up in the Södermanland

countryside, had been in the same class since their third year at school, and were both good at athletics. They shared out the victories in the regional championships. They both joined the youth wing of the Social Democratic Party in Katrineholm when they were fifteen, but they didn't really like Göran Persson, and used to call him Nivea (slimy and unpleasant). They both studied social sciences at Duveholm School, just as she herself had done. If they had been just a year or two older, maybe she would have remembered them, but four years was a big difference at that age. After high school Nina went traveling in Asia for six months while Julia got a job as a teaching assistant in Stenhammar middle school in Flen. When Nina returned to Sweden they both applied to Police Academy, and were accepted at once. By the time Annika spent a night with them, they had served about five years as neighborhood police officers in the Katarina district of Stockholm.

Both girls agreed that they were fed up with the macho atmosphere in the police station. You could never show any sign of weakness, because then you were finished.

Pretty much like the Evening Post.

She logged out of her archive and began reading through the articles about David Lindholm, both in the *Evening Post* and the rest of the media.

All the obituaries were uncritical in their praise and admiration, precisely as the situation demanded. She made a note of a couple of the officers who had commented on the dead man: a Christer Bure of the Södermalm Police, and a Professor Lagerbäck at Police Academy. They both described David Lindholm in terms that suggested he was Christ reincarnated.

She looked through the great work the officer had done for society. Naturally, there was the famous hostage drama in Malmö. The pictures of David and the hostage taker emerging from the nursery, arm in arm, were classics.

Then there was the security van: He had single-handedly cleared up a big robbery where two guards were shot and wounded, and he managed to reclaim the stolen money. He had got the decisive information from an American who was serving a sentence for murder in Tidaholm

Prison. The arrests of the five young men from Botkyrka who had carried out the raid were well documented across the media.

This wasn't the whole picture of David Lindholm, she knew that much.

The hero who solved all these spectacular crimes had been murdered in his bed, shot by his wife.

There's another truth. She must have had a reason.

She closed her battered laptop and went over to Patrik Nilsson. The crime reporter had his nose almost pressed against the screen, and was reading intently.

"Have you ever thought about glasses?" Annika asked as she sat down on Berit's seat.

"National Crime have been searching a farm in Södermanland, trying to find the boy," Patrik Nilsson said, without looking up from the screen with his shortsighted eyes. "There are signs that he may have spent time at the location during the past week."

"I hope you're not thinking of writing that," Annika said.

The reporter looked up in surprise.

"Of course I am," he said.

"'May have spent time at the location' is police-speak," Annika said. "Anyone normal would say 'may have been there.' What makes them think that?"

Patrik read on intently.

"They've found evidence to support the idea," he said. "Doesn't say what. I'll have to check my source."

"Something that suggests a child has been there," Annika said slowly. "The floor covered with Disney comics? Half-eaten lollies in the bin? A plastic bath on the kitchen table full of lukewarm water, bubbles, and rubber ducks?"

Patrik was chewing on a Biro.

"Or clear signs from boots exactly the right size in the sandpit," he said.

"I'm guessing the bin," Annika said. "If anyone ever throws anything in a bin, you can tell pretty much exactly when they were there."

"How do you mean?" Patrik said.

"Date stamps," Annika said. "Every family with children buys and drinks milk. All milk cartons have a best-before date."

"But the bins are always being emptied," her colleague said.

"Not that often," Annika said. "Katrineholm council has fortnightly collections. Or you can request collections only during the summer, although the bin men are so nice they usually empty them anyway . . ."

Patrik looked at her skeptically.

"I used to be a local reporter for the *Katrineholm Courier*," Annika said. "I've written thousands of articles about rubbish collections from the farms between Floda and Granhed."

Her colleague leaned back in his chair and folded his arms.

"How do you know where the cop killer's summer place is?"

"Julia told me," Annika said, getting up. "I don't know exactly which house it is, but I have a rough idea. It's outside Floda, on a road called Stöttastenvägen. My grandma used to live in a cottage not far from there, just outside Granhed. Called Lyckebo."

"Julia's place is called Lyckebo?"

"No, Grandma's. I don't know what hers is called."

"There's nothing in the property register."

"Yes there is, just not under her name. I think she rented it. Have the police released anything about the murder weapon?"

Patrik shook his head without looking away from the screen.

"Anything about when Alexander was last seen alive?"

Her colleague looked up.

"What do you mean?"

"Has anything got out about David? Have you heard any gossip about him?"

"What are you after?" Patrik asked, looking at her suspiciously.

"Have we done all the usual checks on him: money, businesses, property, cars, TV license, tax . . . ?"

"No, but I mean . . ." Patrik said.

"You never know," Annika said. "It might give us an idea of what he was like without his halo, some kind of lead or explanation for what made his wife flip out like that . . ."

"You can't find that sort of thing in the archive," Patrik said, and returned to the screen.

Suddenly something clicked inside Annika's head.

"The Personnel Committee of the National Police Board," she said. "Has anyone checked there?"

Patrik pulled a face.

"To see if there were any complaints about him?"

"As if they'd be public," Patrik said.

"You can check everything they do," Annika said. "You just have to go in and ask the clerk, and they give you the information."

"They always hush up that sort of thing," Patrik said.

Annika went back and opened up her laptop again, then did a search for "Lindholm, David, Stockholm" on the National Registry. She made a note of his date of birth and ID number in her pad, then slung her bag over her shoulder and walked out.

The entrance to the National Police Board was via the main doors of Police Headquarters on Polhemsgatan, the part of the complex that was built in the 1970s, its façade covered in shit-brown paneling. The taxi dropped her off beside a cluttered motorcycle park and she zigzagged her way toward the doors and went into reception.

"I need to check some information with the personnel office," she said without introducing herself or showing any ID: She was there to look at public documents in her capacity as an interested citizen.

"Have you made an appointment?" the receptionist asked, a young man with a heavy fringe and thick-framed glasses.

Annika shifted her weight to the other foot.

"I don't need one," she said. "I'd like to check possible complaints."

The receptionist sighed and picked up the phone. He turned away and muttered something into the receiver.

"He's coming," he said, then went back to his Sudoku.

Annika looked out through the doors and up toward the park.

There, on the other side of the hill, was the cemetery where Josefin Liljeberg's body had been found that hot summer. It must be ten years ago now.

She went over to the door and peered down to the left.

Down there was where Studio Six had been, the porn club had closed down the autumn after its owner was jailed for a series of financial crimes.

He was never charged with Josefin's murder.

"How can I help you?"

An older, bearded man in a cardigan was blinking amiably at her. Annika was at a loss for words for a few seconds, then remembered why she was there.

"I'd like to know if a particular police officer has ever been prosecuted for any criminal activity," she said.

"Is there reason to believe that he might have been?"

"Isn't there always?" she said.

"This way," the man said.

He led her through a glass door and into a lift and pressed *11,* and the lift glided up through the building.

"You've got the ID number of the person in question?" the man asked, and Annika nodded.

The lift came to a halt with a little sigh, and Annika's stomach lurched. She followed him through the police complex, through winding corridors and low doors, until finally they reached a cramped little room with a wonderful view of the park. She craned her neck.

You still can't see the cemetery. It's on the other side, over toward Fridhemsplan.

She held out her notepad with David's date of birth and ID number and the man typed the details into the computer.

"Do you hold all the records of police officers who have been charged with offenses?" she asked as the hard disk chewed its way through its files.

"Not all of them," the clerk said. "Only from 1987 onwards. The older records are kept by the County Administrative Board."

He looked up at her.

"Which one of the reports did you want to look at?"

Which one . . . ?

Her heart skipped a beat.

"There's more than one?"

The man looked at the screen.

"Two."

She gulped.

"Both."

"I need to check that they're not confidential. Could you come back on Monday?"

Annika leaned across the man's desk to peer at his screen. It was angled in such a way that she couldn't see anything.

"Couldn't you check now?" Annika asked. "Please?"

The man looked more closely at the screen.

"Interesting cases," he said. "They were a long while ago, but the subject has of course become very interesting now, through no fault of his own."

He smiled and looked over his shoulder.

"Our lawyer is here today," he said. "The files are in the archive, I'll go and get them and see if we can't get them checked at once."

He disappeared out into the labyrinth of corridors.

Annika resisted the urge to go round his desk and sneak a look at the screen, and went and stood by the window instead, looking out over Kronoberg Park.

Their old flat was on Hantverkargatan, just two blocks from here. She had passed by down below every day with Kalle and Ellen, in rain and sun and snow. She had struggled up the slopes to take the children to the playground by the fire station. She always ended up on a hard park bench surrounded by café-latte mothers trying loudly to outdo each other with their tales of troublesome building work and trips to France.

She leaned against the window and let her thoughts wander.

If she was honest, she hadn't really been particularly happy in the city either, but at least the neighbors had never tried to burn her house down.

"That didn't take too long," the clerk said, unbuttoning his cardigan. "There's nothing confidential in these reports. Here you are."

He handed the copies to Annika.

She glanced through the main points and felt the adrenaline kicking in.

"Thank you, thanks very much indeed!" she said, and hurried off toward the lifts.

Pp. 6–7

EVENING POST STOCKHOLM EDITION
SATURDAY, JUNE 5

POLICE SEARCH FOR ALEXANDER
- **Search expanded**
- **Army called in**
- **Forest searched last night**

By Patrik Nilsson

Evening Post (Södermanland). Efforts to find the missing four-year-old, Alexander, are getting increasingly desperate.

"We're close to a breakthrough," a police source said.

It's now a matter of hours rather than days.

The missing little boy has to be found on Saturday, otherwise hope of finding him will start to fade.

In the middle of idyllic countryside, near a cottage called Björkbacken in the depths of the Södermanland forests, an intensive search is currently under way to try to find Alexander. The trees whisper quietly, and only the cries of the search teams disturb the peace.

The police have confirmed that the boy has been here, close to the summer cottage used by Julia Lindholm, currently in custody, within the past few days.

"This is probably based upon material gathered from bins," a well-placed source has told the *Evening Post*. "Milk cartons are always a valuable source of information in this sort of search, because all families with young children buy milk. Using the sell-by and best-before dates on the packaging, the police will have been able to confirm that the child was at this location. The bins are only emptied fortnightly in the forests around Katrineholm, which has made the work of the police easier."

The police are also believed to have found small footprints in the mud outside the house, which means that a small child has been at the cottage since the last downpour on Tuesday.

The police in Södermanland have expanded the search to the surrounding district. A helicopter equipped with a heat-seeking camera joined the search yesterday.

"That will only work if the boy is still alive," a source in the investigation said. "If he's dead, his body would be the same temperature as the surroundings."

Do you believe the boy is still alive?

"The fact that we're using an infrared camera indicates that we believe the boy is alive, and simply missing."

As of today, Saturday, the military will also be joining the search. Conscripts from the P4 Skaraborg Regiment in Skövde will be taking part.

There have been indications from the National Crime Unit that the evidence implicating Julia Lindholm is mounting up. It is believed that she will be formally charged shortly. Negotiations could take place this weekend, or on Monday at the latest.

Police analysis suggests that they are close to a breakthrough in the case.

"Naturally, we are still hoping to find the boy alive."

Any information regarding the disappearance of four-year-old Alexander Lindholm should be given to the National Crime Unit in Stockholm, or your nearest police station.

Nina was walking through the long glass corridor that constituted the official entrance to Police Headquarters on Kungsholmen. Even though she had been working for the Stockholm Police for almost a decade, she had hardly ever used this entrance. The glass walls and the sloping glass roof made her feel both enclosed and exposed at the same time, and oddly guilty.

She quickened her pace.

The man in reception made her wait almost a whole minute before deigning to notice her. Seeing as she was dressed in plainclothes, Nina understood that he took her for an ordinary, troublesome member of the public.

"I'm here to see Julia Lindholm," she said, holding out her police badge.

The man's eyes narrowed and his mouth set hard. There may have been 301 people in custody, but he knew exactly who Julia was.

"Lindholm's in isolation," he said. "There's no question of her receiving any visitors."

Nina raised her chin slightly and made sure her gaze was firm when she replied.

"Obviously this isn't an ordinary visit, it's an informal interview. I was assuming that had been agreed to and sanctioned."

He looked at her skeptically, took her police badge, and disappeared into an office.

She waited at the counter for ten long minutes.

I'm going. I can't be bothered with this. Julia, I can't help you . . .

"Nina Hoffman?"

She turned round and saw a female guard standing by the door that led further into the complex.

"I must ask you to put all personal items like outdoor clothing and your mobile phone in a locker before I can let you enter the prison. This way."

Nina put her shawl, jacket, and handbag in a locker to the left of reception. She was given a badge that had to be visible at all times while she was in the prison, then was let through the gates.

She followed the guard down a corridor. It ended in a lobby in front of some lifts, painted a gaudy blue color.

"Aren't we going to one of the visitors' rooms?"

"My orders are to take you to Julia Lindholm's cell in the women's section," the guard said, rattling a ring of keys at the end of a long chain.

Nina didn't reply. She had never been inside Kronoberg Prison itself before.

They got into the lift and the guard pressed a button. There was a short pause before the machinery began to work, and Nina glanced up at one of the cameras.

"The lifts are kept under surveillance," the guard said. "All movement through the building, up or down, is controlled remotely."

They stopped on the third floor. Nina made to leave the lift but the guard stopped her.

"This is where police jurisdiction ends," she said. "We need further authorization before we can go up into the actual prison."

A few seconds later the lift juddered into action again.

They got out on the sixth floor and went through three locked doors before reaching one of the secure units.

"If you just wait here for a moment, the food trolley can get past," the guard said.

Nina looked down a long corridor, a gray linoleum floor running the whole length of the building and ending at a barred window. The sunlight outside and the neon tubes on the ceiling cast reflections on the floor. Green metal doors lined the walls, each with a small sign giving information about the cell's occupant, box number, restrictions, case number. Each door had a hatch so that the staff could look in, and they had substantial locks. She heard someone cough behind the nearest door.

"So are you full?" Nina asked.

"Are you kidding?" the guard said.

Two men lumbered past them with a trolley full of trays and disappeared into the next corridor.

The guard walked to the end of the corridor and unlocked one of the green doors with her jangling keys.

"Julia Lindholm," she said. "You've got a visitor."

Nina took a deep, calming breath before walking into the cell, and noticed that her mouth felt dry. The walls closed in on her, and she realized just how cramped it was.

This isn't remotely humane! How can they treat you like this?

Julia was sitting curled up on the desk that was fixed to the wall, looking out of the small window of the cell, up at the sky. She was wearing regulation green and gray prison clothing, and was clutching her knees tight and rocking quickly back and forth. Her toes were moving frenetically inside her thick socks. Her hair was tied up in a blond knot on top of her head. She didn't seem to notice that someone had come into the cell.

"Julia," Nina said quietly so as not to startle her. "Julia, it's me."

The cell door closed behind Nina. There was no handle on the inside.

At first Julia didn't react, just carried on staring out of the window.

Nina stopped, her back to the door, for several long seconds as she looked around carefully. The pine desk was connected to a bed that was also fixed to the wall. The wood was yellow from old varnish and covered in cigarette burns. A chair, two small shelves, and a metal washbasin. It smelled of stale smoke.

"Julia," she repeated, taking two steps over to the desk and carefully putting a hand on the woman's shoulder. "Julia, how are you?"

Julia looked away from the sky, turned toward Nina and her face lit up in a happy smile.

"Nina," she said, wrapping her arms round her neck, hugging her as she rocked. "How sweet of you to come and visit me! What are you doing here?"

Nina disentangled herself from her friend's arms and looked at her intently. Her eyes were bloodshot and the rash on her cheeks had got worse, but her smile was open and friendly. She seemed alert and energetic.

"I wanted to see how you are," Nina said. "So, how are you feeling?"

Julia shrugged, pushing past Nina and jumping down onto the floor. She went over to the door and felt it with the palms of her hands.

"What are you doing?" Nina asked.

Julia went back to the desk again, sat down, then stood up again and went and sat on the bed.

"Julia," Nina said. "I heard that you resigned. Why?"

Julia looked up at her in surprise, then started biting one of her thumbnails and looking round the cell.

"I need to buy washing-up liquid," she said. "I've run out of powder. I've got those little cubes, but they never dissolve properly . . ."

Nina felt her throat tightening.

"How are you feeling? Is there anything I can help you with?"

Julia got up again and went over to the door, running her hands aimlessly over the green metal.

"Nina," she said, sounding suddenly scared and nervous. "Do you really think we ought to apply to Police Academy? Wouldn't it be better to go into social work instead?"

Something's seriously wrong here.

"What are you talking about?"

Julia got up from the bed and stamped her feet impatiently, her gaze meandering out of the window and flickering restlessly over the brown wall on the far side of the inner courtyard.

"David hasn't come home yet," she said anxiously. "He was supposed to pick up Alexander on the way, and the nursery's been closed several hours now."

She looked at Nina hopefully.

"Has he called you?"

Nina opened her mouth but couldn't reply, she could feel tears choking her and making her speechless. Julia saw her reaction and blinked at her in surprise.

"Come and sit down with me," Nina said, taking Julia's hand and pulling her friend to her. "Come on, we'll just have a little talk . . ."

She sat Julia down in front of her on the bunk and put her hands on Julia's cheeks, looking her in the eyes.

"Julia," she whispered, "where's Alexander?"

Julia opened her eyes wide, bright streaks of confusion flickering through them for several long moments.

"Don't you remember what happened to David?" Nina said quietly. "In your bedroom? Do you remember the shot?"

Something dark landed at the bottom of Julia's eyes, she seemed to be looking at something just above Nina's head. She gasped and her face contorted.

"Get her out of here," she whispered.

"Who?"

"The other one. She's evil."

Nina turned round and looked at the wall above her, and saw scratched marks left by a previous prisoner who had carved her initials in the wall.

"Do you mean the other woman? The one who took Alexander?"

Julia's body jerked and she struggled to get free, her lower arm hitting Nina across the nose. Without a word Julia staggered to the door and starting banging on it, first with her fists, and then with her head. A whimpering sound was coming from deep in her throat.

Oh no, what have I done?

With two long strides Nina was over at the door, taking a firm grip on Julia from behind to calm her down, but her embrace had the opposite effect. Julia started screaming, an angry howl that was only muffled when she tried to bite Nina.

"Julia, I'm going to lay you down on the bunk, on your side," Nina said, twisting her arms up behind her back.

She put the screaming woman down with her head in the pillow.

The hatch opened and the female guard looked inside the cell.

"She needs a tranquilizer," Nina said.

Julia was crying hysterically, her whole body shaking. Nina kept a firm grip of her, trying to calm with the weight and warmth of her body.

"The medics are on their way!" the guard called through the hatch.

Slowly the convulsions ebbed away and Julia's body stopped moving. The screaming turned into a wailing sob.

Eventually she fell silent, lying quite still and panting for breath.

"It was my fault," she whispered. "It was my fault."

Nina called Detective Inspector Q the moment she emerged into the glass corridor outside reception.

"You can't keep her locked up like that, not in a prison cell," she said abruptly when he answered. "She's verging on psychotic and needs proper psychiatric care."

"What makes you think that?"

"She's seeing things and obviously suffering from delusions."

Nina was walking quickly toward the exit, eager to escape the unpleasant glass tunnel.

"So our informal interviewer has been transformed into a psychiatric expert?" the detective said at the other end of the line. "Did you get anything out of her?"

Nina pushed the door open and stepped out into the gale on the street. *Quisling, quisling.*

"She spoke incoherently about irrelevant things, said she's forgotten to buy washing-up liquid, that she wasn't sure about applying to Police Academy. She seemed confused about time and space, and isn't aware of what's happened. She asked where David had gone with Alexander."

"Did she mention the other woman?"

"Yes, she said she was evil. She asked me to get rid of her. I think Julia should be sent for paragraph seven investigation, immediately."

"So she didn't say anything about whether or not she was guilty?"

Nina breathed in and out twice.

"Maybe I haven't made myself clear. Julia was so confused that she didn't know where she was. When I tried to ask about the murder she became extremely agitated. A medic had to come and give her a tranquilizer. She's sleeping now."

Detective Inspector Q sighed loudly.

"Well, I suppose it's progress," he said. "She hasn't spoken to us at all."

"Nothing at all?"

"Not a sound. And no washing-up liquid either."

Nina stopped and looked up at the façade of Police Headquarters, trying to imagine the caged walkways on the roof where the prisoners got their fresh air for an hour each day.

"So you were aware of how disturbed she was," she said. "You knew how bad she was, but you didn't tell me before you asked me to question her?"

"Hey, now," Q said, "she was just refusing to talk. That's hardly unusual."

"If you want to have anything like a sensible interview with Julia, she has to get some sort of treatment first," Nina said. "I don't know the details, but people experience traumatic events every day and get psychiatric treatment."

"In an ideal world," Q said. "That's going to be difficult in this case."

She started walking toward the underground.

"So why wouldn't the health service have the resources to deal with this case?"

"I'm not talking about the health service, but whether there's any desire to do it. Let me put it like this: There's a certain resistance in the force against treating David's murderer with kid gloves."

Nina stopped midstride.

"Kid gloves . . . ?"

"If everything goes according to plan, Julia will be formally charged on Monday. Naturally, that's just a formality, but I'd like you to be there. It's possible that there'll be questions about her arrest that the court will need to clear up."

Nina stopped, standing squarely on both legs. Two teenage boys went past giggling, but she didn't bother to lower her voice to stop them from overhearing.

"Let's get one thing absolutely clear," she said. "I did this for Julia's sake, not yours. I've got no intention of getting involved in this."

"Right now this is about finding the boy."

She rocked back and forth on the balls of her feet.

"You haven't got an easy job," she said. "Either you keep our colleagues happy, or you solve these crimes. Good luck."

She ended the call and went down into the underground station on shaky legs.

Only when she was standing on the escalator did she realize what she'd said.

Crimes, plural.

I'm assuming that Alexander has been killed as well.

She hurried toward the platform.

The children were parked in Berit's living room watching a Moomin cartoon on television. Annika put the breakfast things in the dishwasher, wiped the kitchen table and worktop, and then took out the copies of the misconduct reports against David Lindholm from her bag. She sat down beside the drop-leaf table and let her gaze wander out the window toward the lake.

People really did treat each other so atrociously badly. Was there any hope for humanity at all with so much evil everywhere?

She could hear Little My shouting something at Moominmamma on television and put her hands over her ears.

Berit had gone shopping for something for dinner, ages ago.

Why do I get so upset at being on my own? Why am I so restless?

She grabbed the photocopies from the Police Board's personnel committee and read through the reports once again.

The first case concerned a young man called Tony Berglund. The complaint had been made by a doctor in A&E at Södermalm Hospital. The file describing the man's injuries was three pages long and extremely detailed. In the doctor's opinion, the injuries had been inflicted during a prolonged and vicious attack, leaving him with four fractures and extensive internal bleeding as a result.

The victim had said in the ambulance that "a cop" had kicked him. In A&E he had described the policeman as well built, blond, with a prominent brow.

The description certainly fitted David Lindholm very well.

Every time he was questioned, Tony Berglund stuck to exactly the same version of events on Luntmakargatan.

He and two friends had been on their way to see a girl over on Frejgatan, up by St. Stefan's Church, when five blokes wearing caps had jumped them at the corner of Rehngatan. Mostly it was just shouting and pushing—there hadn't been any real physical violence—but it was more than a minute or so before the rapid-response team of the Norrmalm Police came tearing up on screeching tires from the direction of Norra Real School. Four cops had leapt out, and the big blond one had led the charge.

"Are you Tony?" he had asked, and when Tony said "What the fuck's it got to do with you?" the attack began.

Tony Berglund couldn't say how long the attack had gone on: He had lost consciousness when his cheekbone was fractured, and he hadn't woken up until he was in the ambulance. The description of the police officer had been made in writing, seeing as his jaw had been set. The crumpled note was among the documentation.

Then the lad had changed his story during the trial.

Extremely peculiar.

David himself claimed that by the time the police arrived a fight was already in progress, and that the police had probably saved Tony Berglund's life with their rapid intervention.

The two friends who had been with Tony had been chased off by a couple of other officers, and were unable to support any of his statement.

The other officers on the unit had all backed up David's version.

The background information revealed that Tony Berglund had a criminal background. Foster homes, remand school, probation for minor drugs charges.

Annika sighed. *Poor sod.*

She put Tony Berglund's case down and moved on to the second report.

A man named Timmo Koivisto (*Was his name really Timmo? Apparently so*) had been on his way to a minor amphetamine deal in Ropsten. He had gone to take a piss in the Central Station, but just as he was on his way into the gents the door had been yanked open and a large, blond man in a police uniform had come into the toilet. At first Timmo had thought it was some sort of joke, that it was someone dressed up as a policeman, then the man had grabbed him by the ears and asked "Are you

Timmo?," and Timmo had got scared and tried to twist free. Then the man had started banging his head against the tiles on the toilet wall, and he couldn't remember anything after that.

The ambulance had been called by David Lindholm, who said he had found a seriously wounded man lying unconscious in the toilet, and that he had probably saved his life thanks to his rapid intervention.

Timmo Koivisto stuck to his story right until the case went to court, when he had suddenly changed his mind.

Timmo Koivisto's background details also revealed him to be one of society's more unfortunate children, with a similar history to Tony Berglund. Three short prison sentences for drug dealing.

He's guilty. He did it. He beat these small-time crooks to within an inch of their lives, but for what reason? On whose orders?

Annika got up and went over to Berit's electric coffee machine. She could never work out how they worked. At home she had always had a French press, the sort where you poured in coffee and boiling water, then pressed down a filter and it was all done. Here you had to pour water into various containers and fit paper filters into other bits and measure out the coffee and then wait for ages.

She went in to see the children in the living room instead.

"Hello," she said. "Is Moomin good?"

Ellen leaned to one side.

"Mummy, you're in the way."

Annika went back out into the kitchen. She ran her fingers over the reports. Made a feeble attempt with the coffee machine but gave up.

She wondered about getting her computer out but didn't want to take over Berit's kitchen table with her stuff. Instead she called directory inquiries and asked for the number to a Tony Berglund.

"Do you have the address?"

No, she didn't, of course.

"I've got sixty-three results in Stockholm and the northern district."

"What about Timmo Koivisto?"

"In Norrtälje? The Vårtuna Home? He's the only one I've got in the whole country. It's a mobile number. Do you want me to connect you?"

Annika said yes and immediately ended up with voicemail, with a long personal recorded message. The man speaking had a strong Finnish accent, and explained in a rather long-winded way that this was Timmo, and that he'd call back as soon as he had time. He wished the peace of the Lord to everyone, and said that the love and forgiveness of Christ applied to everyone no matter where on earth they were.

Then came the bleep, and Annika hesitated.

"Er," she said, "yes, I'm calling from the newspaper, the *Evening Post*, my name's Annika Bengtzon. I was wondering if this was the Timmo Koivisto who had a rather unpleasant . . . encounter . . . with a police officer, his name is . . . or rather, was . . . David Lindholm, eighteen years ago . . . because if you *are* that Timmo, and *if* you feel like talking about what happened so long ago, please give me a call on . . ."

She gave her mobile number, then ended the call.

She got up and looked out toward the road, still no sign of Berit.

She went back to the kitchen table, picked up her mobile again, and called Nina Hoffman.

The police officer answered after four rings.

"Is this a bad time?" Annika asked,

The reply sounded tired and sad.

"What do you want?"

"I've had a few thoughts about David," Annika said. "I understand that he was accused of physical abuse, and I know it was a long time ago, and I know he was never found guilty, but I was wondering if you knew anything more about these cases . . ."

There was silence at the other end of the line, she could hear a faint sound of traffic, so the line hadn't gone dead.

"How did you find that out?" Nina said eventually.

So she knows.

"Why do you ask? Is it strange that I should know about the complaints?"

More silence.

"I don't want to discuss this over the phone."

Annika glanced toward the living room. She'd just have to take the children with her.

"I can come in to the pizza place," she said.

"No. Too many of my colleagues go there. Do you know where Nytorgsgatan is? The café on the corner of Bondegatan?"

They agreed on a time and hung up.

Berit came into the kitchen and put three large bags from the ICA supermarket on the draining board.

"It's going to rain this afternoon," she said. "The clouds are practically sitting on the tops of the trees."

"Did you know that David Lindholm was accused of physical abuse?" Annika said. "Not just once, but twice?"

Berit leaned against the worktop and thought for a moment.

"No, I've never heard about that. Was he found guilty?"

Annika stood to help her empty the bags.

"Of course not. The first incident was twenty years ago, when he was with the rapid-response unit in Norrmalm. He worked with a Christer Bure, who seems to have been one of his big buddies."

She opened the fridge and put in the milk and a pack of chicken drumsticks.

"According to the prosecution, David Lindholm kicked and broke the cheekbone of a young lad who was arrested during a street brawl on Luntmakargatan. The lad changed his mind in court and said he'd only made the complaint against David to cause trouble for the police, and that one of the gang they were fighting must have kicked him, he just didn't see which one."

"That could well be true," Berit said.

"Of course," Annika said. "In the other case, David was said to have attacked a drug dealer in a toilet at the Central Station, banging his head against the wall so hard that he ended up with serious concussion. The bloke was left with permanent injuries as a result, including double vision and impaired hearing in his left ear."

"Which could have been the result of serious drug use, maybe . . . ?"

"Sure. The weird thing is that the same thing happened as before: The lad changed his mind when the case got to court. Said another junkie beat him up, and that he tried to blame David to cause trouble for the police."

"What did David himself say?"

"Exactly the same thing the victims ended up saying in court: that they were attacked by other criminals and blamed the police to damage the force."

"So David was cleared?"

"The cases were dropped. And even if he'd been found guilty he'd have been allowed to keep his job, the personnel committee had already decided that."

Berit nodded thoughtfully.

"He was evidently a controversial but popular officer right from the start," she said. "How long ago was the most recent complaint?"

"Eighteen years ago."

"So he's kept his nose completely clean since then?"

Annika was folding up the bags.

"Well, he wasn't ever charged, at least. Where do you keep plastic bags?"

Berit pointed at the bottom kitchen drawer.

"Have you seen the papers? We're running your piece on Julia on page twelve. It's very good."

She handed both tabloids to Annika, who sat down at the kitchen table with the papers in front of her. Both the *Evening Post* and the competition had exactly the same picture and headline on the front page:

WHERE IS 4-YEAR-OLD ALEXANDER?

The photograph dominating the front covers showed a small boy, smiling uncertainly at the camera. The classic marbled background indicated that it was a picture taken at nursery, the sort that was taken in every preschool and classroom throughout Sweden every year.

So that was how he had turned out, the little boy who was born six months after Ellen.

He had untidy blond hair and small, finely chiseled features, almost girlishly pretty. A shirt collar could just be seen at the bottom of the picture, presumably a gesture in honor of the occasion.

The picture unsettled her. He looked so defenseless, so vulnerable, and the headline somehow seemed to imply that he was already dead.

What if it was my child? What if Ellen or Kalle were missing?!

She shuddered and opened the paper. Berit put on her reading glasses and sat down next to her.

"Did they put him on the fly sheets as well?" Annika asked.

"Both papers," Berit said, "same wording."

They read in silence for a while. Moomin had been replaced by Pingu, the little penguin, and the jaunty theme tune found its way into the kitchen. The wind was whistling through a gap under one window.

"I don't understand this," Berit said. "Where could the boy have got to? If the mother hasn't hidden him somewhere, then she must have killed him, but when could she have done that?"

Annika opened the other evening paper and made her way to pages six and seven, which always carried the heaviest news. Both pages were covered by a big picture, stretching across ten columns, of a forest clearing with a little red cottage in the middle, white eaves and a water pump out the front. It was an atmospheric picture, the light filtering through the treetops onto the white shutters beside the windows, and across the whole picture ran the blue and white tape of the police cordon.

POLICE SEARCH FOR ALEXANDER, 4, Annika read.

"They've got exactly the same angle as us," she said.

Berit shook her head with a sigh.

"I still don't see how it all fits together. If the mother took him out to their summer cottage and killed him there, did she go straight home afterward? Or did she wait a day or two? And didn't the father think it was odd that she came home without the boy?"

"Maybe she lied about where he was?" Annika suggested. "Said he was staying with a friend, or with Grandma and Grandpa?"

Berit read on for a while.

"But why go to such trouble hiding him? She wasn't remotely bothered about trying to hide the murder of her husband, after all."

"Maybe she's sent him away somewhere," Annika said. "Abroad, to distant relatives or something."

Berit shook her head.

"What sort of mother would do something like this?"

"Or maybe: What sort of person?" Annika said.

"Maybe something went wrong when she shot the father," Berit reasoned. "Maybe she'd planned to kill him and hide his body as well. Is that your phone ringing?"

Annika sat up straight and listened.

Yes, it was her mobile.

She ran over to the dresser by the door and looked warily at the screen. The phone carried on ringing.

"Aren't you going to answer it?" Berit asked, turning a page of the paper.

Annika put the phone down on the dresser, and it bounced and vibrated against the wood.

"It's Anne Snapphane. I have absolutely no desire to talk to her."

"Oh," Berit said. "I thought you were friends."

"So did I," Annika said.

The telephone fell silent, only to start jumping and ringing again a moment later. Annika groaned, picked it up again, and looked at the screen.

"Jesus," she said. "It's my mother. I have to take this."

She went out and stood on Berit's porch.

"Annika?" her mother said in an agitated voice. "Annika, is that you?"

She sank onto one of the steps, letting the wind tug at her clothes.

"Yes, Mum, it's me. How are you?"

"What's all this I hear?" her mum said. "Has your house *burned down*?"

Annika shut her eyes and put her hand over them.

"Yes, Mum, our house has burned down. There's nothing left."

"Buy why haven't you called and *said* something? Well? I found out in the shop, from someone I work with. What on earth were you thinking?"

Annika sighed quietly.

"Well . . ." she said.

"Do I really have to hear news like that as gossip? *About my own child?* Do you have any idea how that made me look?"

Annika couldn't stop a cruel laugh.

"So *I'm* supposed to feel sorry for *you*?"

"Don't be so mean," her mother said. "Can't you see how insulting it is, to have that sort of thing thrown in your face? As if I don't know what's happening to my own child?"

"Well, you don't, do you?"

"I still think . . ."

Annika stood up and looked out across the lake.

"Now that you've got me on the phone, you can ask me how we are," she said. "You can also ask what really happened. Maybe you'd even like to volunteer to help somehow, with a place to stay, or help look after the children, money maybe . . ."

Now it was her mother's turn to laugh.

"You want money from me, when I might have to take early retirement on grounds of illness? Social security are looking into it, I have to go to the Mälar Valley Hospital once a week nowadays, but I don't suppose that's important to someone living in Stockholm . . ."

"Goodbye, Mum."

She clicked to end the call, and in the silence that followed she could hear her own heart racing.

Berit came out onto the porch with a mug in each hand.

"Coffee?"

Annika took the mug gratefully.

"Can you trade in your parents?" she asked.

Berit smiled.

"Don't be so hard on her, she's doing the best she can."

Annika sat down on the step again.

"She only ever thinks of herself. It doesn't matter what happens to me, she's always the interesting one."

"She's a small person with a narrow frame of reference," Berit said. "She hasn't got the capacity to see you for who you are, and it's a lack she isn't even aware of."

Tears welled up in Annika's eyes.

"It just feels so fucking . . . miserable," she said. "Why can't I have a mum like everyone else's, someone who supports and helps me, someone who cares?"

Berit sat down beside her.

"Not everyone has a mum like that," she said. "A lot of people have no mum at all. I think you have to realize that you can't change her. She's never going to be the sort of mum you'd like. You just have to accept her the way she is, just like she's going to have to accept you."

They sat in silence for a while, looking out toward the forest. The wind had got up, and the firs were swaying in the breeze. Annika looked at the time.

"Is it okay if the children stay here with you while I head into the city for a bit? I'm meeting Nina Hoffman again."

Berit nodded.

"I can't stop thinking about this business of the missing boy," she said. "The whole story really is very peculiar."

"Anyone can go mad," Annika said. "If everything's going to hell, I think human beings are capable of absolutely anything."

Berit looked at her thoughtfully.

"I don't agree," she said. "Not everyone could kill their child. There has to be something missing for someone to do that, some sort of internal barrier that just isn't there."

Annika looked at the shimmering gray water of the lake.

"I'm not so sure about that," she said.

A moment later it started to rain.

Nina Hoffman was waiting for her at a messy table in the café on Nytorgsgatan. The police officer didn't notice that Annika had arrived; she was sitting with her back to the door, staring blankly out of the misted-up window. Her hair was tied up in a ponytail and she was wearing a gray padded jacket, and the light fell across her profile, giving nothing away. She was resting her chin on one hand and seemed to be a very long way away.

Annika went round the table.

"Hello," she said, holding out her hand.

Nina Hoffman stood up and they shook hands.

Annika went over to the counter before she sat down: "One coffee, black."

The café was starting to fill up with lunchtime diners. Wet outdoor clothes spread a smell of damp wool through the room. Nina looked out of the window.

"There was something you were wondering about?" she said. "Something about the allegations against David?"

No small talk, then.

Annika lifted her bag onto her lap and hunted through it, finding a bag of sweets and the folder of documents from the National Police Board's personnel committee.

"So you know what David was accused of?" she said, putting the sweets back in the bag.

Nina Hoffman's eyes flashed.

"How did you find out?"

Annika stopped and put her hands gently on the tabletop.

"I went and checked at the NPB," she said. "Why do you sound so surprised?"

Nina looked out of the window again.

"I didn't know . . ."

She fell silent and sat quietly for a long while. Annika waited. A woman with a stroller forced her way past them to get to the next table, but Nina didn't react. Eventually the police officer turned toward Annika, pulling in her chair and leaning over the table. She had dark circles under her eyes.

"I've never told anyone this," she said, "because I don't really know what it means. Can I trust you?"

Annika suppressed an urge to swallow.

"I won't write anything without your consent, you know that. You're my source, and your identity is protected under the Constitution."

"I got a bit confused when you called me, because I thought those old complaints had been buried and forgotten."

"So how did *you* find out about them?"

Nina adjusted her ponytail.

"Julia showed me. The last time we met before the murder. She'd come across them in David's archive down in the cellar."

Annika suppressed an instinct to reach for her pen and start taking notes. *I'll just have to try to remember.*

"Why did she show them to you?"

Nina hesitated again.

"I've always tried to support Julia, and it hasn't always been easy. But when it really mattered, she always knew she could come to me. I thought she was on the verge of leaving him. She never said as much, but I just got the feeling . . ."

She moved even closer to the table and lowered her voice still further.

"Did you see any police on your way in here?"

Annika looked carefully at the woman opposite her.

"Should I have done?"

"I chose this place because none of my colleagues usually come here. David often treated Julia very badly, and the rest of the force are no better. The way they're treating her now is appalling. Regardless of what she may have done, they've decided she's guilty, she's never going to get a fair trial."

The espresso machine behind the counter hissed and whined, and Nina waited until it had stopped.

"You were right about him being a control freak. Julia always had to watch herself when David was listening. She could never be really honest then."

"Did he hit her?" Annika asked.

Nina shook her head.

"Never, he wasn't that stupid. But he threatened her, even when I could hear. Said he'd make life hell if she didn't go home at once, things like that. He could be very sweet and loving one minute, hugging and kissing her even in front of other people. The next minute he could say such cruel, hateful things that she was practically in tears. He would frighten her, then regret it and ask for forgiveness. Julia isn't a strong person, she could never stand up to anything like that. And it got even worse when she found out that he was repeatedly unfaithful . . ."

The juice machine started up with a tremendous noise, and Annika shifted in irritation when the woman with the stroller wanted to take her baby to the toilet.

"Repeatedly?" she said.

Nina sighed quietly and waited until the mother had struggled past.

"I don't really know how to explain in a way you'll understand," she said eventually. "David was a notorious womanizer before he met Julia. They still talk about his escapades in the station—well, it's mainly Christer Bure and his crew who keep the stories alive. Mostly because it also shows how popular they themselves were, once upon a time. But when Julia came into the picture, all that stopped, at least the public boasting about his conquests did, and the lads weren't particularly pleased about that . . ."

"They lost their iconic shagger," Annika said.

"Outwardly, at any rate, but only for a while. He must have been having affairs the whole time, but Julia didn't realize until several years later. One of the women called Julia at home and told her that she was the one he really loved, and that she should realize that and set him free. That was just after Alexander was born."

"Jesus," Annika said.

"She found a letter to David containing an ultrasound picture of a fetus. 'I've killed our daughter, her name was Maja. Now it's your turn,' it said in the accompanying letter. I thought that was going to shake her out of it."

"What did she do?"

"I presume she tried to talk to David, but I don't know for sure. It wasn't so easy keeping in touch with her. David's career was always pretty unconventional. Sometimes he was posted abroad. Once they lived in a row house outside Malaga for six months."

"Malaga?"

"In the south of Spain. The house was in Estepona, just east of Gibraltar. I went down to visit them. Julia looked like a ghost. She said she was fine, but it looked like she was lying . . ."

A gang of teenage boys tumbled into the café, jostling and shouting and making the café-latte mothers frown with distaste.

"When Alexander arrived things got really bad," Nina went on without taking any notice of the teenagers. "He was born prematurely, and Julia got postnatal depression, and it was like she never quite shook it off. When she came back to work she couldn't handle anything happening to children, whether it be abuse, traffic accidents, anything that hurt them.

She was signed off sick with nervous exhaustion; that was over two years ago. She hasn't worked at all this past year . . ."

Annika looked at the policewoman and tried furiously to structure the information she'd been given.

He tormented Julia until she got ill.

He was a notorious womanizer.

And where do the allegations of misconduct come into the picture?

"If I could just rewind a bit," Annika said. "Can you tell me a bit more about Julia? What happened to her when she met David?"

The detective cleared her throat.

"There was a small gang of us girls who stuck together after we'd graduated from Police Academy, but Julia pulled away. She changed the way she dressed, stopped wearing jeans. We were active in the Social Democratic youth movement, but suddenly she started voting for the Moderates. We had a discussion about it that ended with her in tears. To begin with it was just little things like that . . ."

Annika waited in silence.

"So it all got worse after Alexander was born?" she asked eventually when Nina didn't go on.

"I knew something was wrong, but I didn't understand just how badly until the last few weeks before the murder. David was incredibly jealous; once I heard him call her a whore and a slut. He must have locked her in the flat at least seven times—it was like she stopped counting. Once she was shut up for something like a whole week. Another time he threw her out into the stairwell without any clothes on. She got so cold she had to go to hospital. At A&E she said she'd got lost out in the countryside."

"And you got to hear about all this quite late?"

"Julia's been terribly fragile the past couple of years; she was taken in for psychiatric treatment on one occasion. She hasn't been in touch with me much, but I made the effort to visit her when I knew that David was working or away traveling. It was on one of those visits that I went round to see her and found that she was locked in. It was only then that I realized just how bad things were for her."

"Why didn't she report him?"

Nina actually smiled slightly.

"You make it sound so simple. I wanted her to, of course; I offered to support her all the way. Maybe that was why she started going through his old files and found the old allegations: She was getting ready to leave."

"And what about the affairs? Did they ever stop?"

"No, quite the opposite. It got worse and worse. Even David evidently thought that it was becoming a nuisance toward the end. He'd asked Julia to forgive him, said he was sorry, but that was just the sort of thing he used to say . . ."

"And what do you think about the allegations of abuse? Did he do it?"

Nina snorted.

"Well, what do you think?"

Annika thought.

"I think it's strange that two insignificant small-time criminals had exactly the same thing happen to them, and with exactly the same result."

Nina studied her in silence, so Annika went on.

"They were very badly beaten, and every time they were questioned they said it was David who'd done it, and they stuck to their stories right up to the trial, when they suddenly went into reverse. Their stories are also identical on several points, for instance when David speaks to them and asks their names."

Nina looked at the misted-up window.

"That struck me as well," she said quietly. "The chances of them both inventing exactly the same lie strike me as being fairly slim."

Then she looked at Annika.

"You're not going to write about any of this, are you?"

Annika studied her weary face.

"Why did you tell me, if you didn't want it to get out?"

Nina looked away.

"As far as I'm concerned, you can put it all over the front page, but it has to be Julia's decision. I don't know if she'd want it to come out, everything she had to put up with . . ."

Nina got up and wrestled with her dark-green raincoat.

"You can use the information if you can get it corroborated elsewhere. But I'd still like you to tell me first."

"Of course," Annika said.

Nina Hoffman left the café without saying goodbye and without looking back.

Annika was left sitting there with her cold coffee.

Nina didn't like David Lindholm, that much was crystal clear. If what she said was true, then that was completely understandable. It must be awful to watch your best friend get drawn into a destructive relationship without being able to do anything about it.

It must be awful to have to sit on all that knowledge, and then have to read acres of coverage about what a hero he was.

Annika gathered her things and went out to the car that she had parked illegally on Bondegatan, but she hadn't got a ticket. Which was something, at least.

She'd just started the engine when her mobile rang. She sighed, hesitated, then fished it out of her bag. She checked the display; it wasn't a number she recognized. She took the call anyway.

"Annika Bengtzon? It's Timmo. You tried to call me."

Timmo? The man who was beaten up!

"Hello," she said, putting the car in neutral again. "Thanks for calling back. Would you like to meet up with me for a chat?"

"About David Lindholm? I'd be happy to. I owe that man everything."

Nina let the patrol car roll slowly across the Djurgård Bridge. Andersson was sitting beside her, staring sullenly through the passenger window, his gaze sweeping over the crowd of drenched civilians on their way to the open-air museum at Skansen to celebrate National Day.

"None of these people really give a shit about Sweden," he said. "They're only going to try to get on telly and stare at the royal family."

Nina clenched her teeth and thought to herself, *Patience, patience.*

The rain had been tipping down when she had gone to work, and had carried on all the way through her shift. Sometimes it had been raining so hard that she had had no visibility at all. The wind forced her to keep a firm grip of the steering wheel.

He won't survive weather like this. If he's been outside since Thursday, he must be dead now.

Nina braked at the junction with Långa gatan. An elderly woman on a bike had been hit by a car; she was sitting on the edge of the pavement holding her left ankle. The driver was sitting in his car, looking simultaneously embarrassed and annoyed.

She opened the car door but paused before she got out.

"I wasn't planning to get soaked on my own," she said. "You talk to the driver and I'll take the old dear."

"God, I could do without a fucking awful day like this," Andersson said, getting out into the torrential rain.

He had been in a dreadful mood ever since the handover meeting at 0630 that morning. There had only been six of them plus a superior officer, everyone else had been called in for Special Police Operations, as always on National Day celebrations, or the anniversary of the death of Charles XII, and other loaded dates.

"So how did this happen, then?" Nina asked as she squatted down beside the woman. The old woman was wearing a poncho with a hood made of some sort of waterproof material, but the rain had got through anyway and she was soaked to the skin. Nina noticed she was crying.

"My foot hurts," she said, pointing at her ankle.

Her ankle was at such an odd angle that Nina realized it must be broken.

"We need to get you to hospital at once," she said. "That foot needs to be plastered, and we can't have you sitting here like this. You'll catch a chill!"

She called Control over the radio and asked for an ambulance to the junction of Djurgårdsvägen and Långa gatan.

"He was driving like a maniac," the woman said, pointing to the man in the car. "I was cycling along, nice and safely, and he comes up and hits me from behind. I mean, it's not on, is it?"

Nina put her hand on the woman's arm and smiled at her.

"Don't worry," she said. "We'll get to the bottom of what happened. The main thing now is to get you to a doctor . . ."

Andersson came over to her, holding in his hand the Breathalyzer that the motorist had just blown into.

"Looks like someone started celebrating National Day at lunchtime," he said.

"We'll take him in for a proper test," Nina said, as she saw the ambulance emerging through the veils of rain.

Once the woman was being looked after by the paramedics, Andersson put the suspected drunk driver on the right side of the backseat of the car, then slid his seat back so as not to give him any room to maneuver.

"The old bag was weaving all over the road," the driver said. "It was impossible not to hit her."

I wonder how it's going. I wonder if they've found him.

During the handover meeting that morning, when they were told who was going out and in which cars, they had gone through new missing person reports as well as ongoing cases. *The search for David's lad was due to start again at six o'clock this morning, but they're holding off to see if the rain eases . . .*

"If I were you," Andersson said, "I'd keep seriously fucking quiet until I got hold of a good lawyer."

Nina glanced at her watch. Their shift ended in a hour, and they hadn't managed to get back to the station all day.

It took a long while to get all the way back to Torkel Knutssonsgatan on Södermalm. Nina drove straight into the garage, then took the drunk driver with her up to the duty officer, where he was made to blow twice more, with the same result.

Zero point eight parts per thousand.

"That's not too bad," the driver said, relieved.

"You could have killed someone," Nina said. "That woman's foot may never be right again. You might well have ruined her life."

The man glowered at her.

"I'll go and write the report," she told Pelle Sisulu, leaving the drunk to his fate.

Nina felt exhausted, even though it had been a relatively calm shift. She had felt herself close to tears most of the day.

It was going to be good to have a few days off now.

She quickly filed the report and logged out.

On her way to the changing room she stopped at the duty officer's room again, standing in the doorway. The drunk was gone.

Pelle Sisulu was a black man in his forties, and he'd worked at the station for as long as she could remember.

"Anything special to report?" he wondered.

Nina shuffled her feet slightly.

"No, nothing special, RTAs, a couple of slight injuries, and this drunk driver . . . Has anything happened in the search? For . . . Alexander, I mean?"

She had been on the point of saying "Julia's son."

The duty officer looked up at her.

He must have been the first black police officer in Sweden.

"They've called off the search for today," he said. "Visibility's too poor. The helicopter never got up."

He turned back toward his computer screen.

"But what about the ground search?" she said. "Surely they could have carried on with that?"

The man looked up again.

"Evidently some of the local officers from out in the bush are poking about in the mud," he said, "but we haven't got anyone there."

Nina nodded to herself.

"That's probably the village squad from Valla," she said.

The duty officer looked at her questioningly.

"Julia comes from around there. Her dad's chair of the local business association."

"I'd be surprised if they found anything."

He went back to his computer.

Nina went through to the rear part of the station, which was empty and deserted. Yellow brick walls and red doors absorbed most of the light from the strip lights in the ceiling, leaving the corridor to the changing room dark and gloomy. The ventilation system hummed quietly, stirring up dust from the gray linoleum tiling on the floor, and there was a smell of garbage from the recycling facility next door.

She unbuttoned her jacket and bulletproof vest, and let out a deep sigh.

She could still remember the very first time she was ever here, and how nervous and tense it had all been. During the fourth term of their course she and Julia had done their practical experience here, known as "integrated study orientation in the workplace." Julia had been over-joyed.

Just think, this is it for us, our careers, we're going to have such a chance to make a difference . . .

That was almost ten years ago now.

Nina opened the door on the left at the far end of the corridor with her security pass and went into the women's cramped changing room, making her way through the maze of blue lockers until she came to her own. She dropped her bag on the floor with a thud. Her arms felt heavy as she shrugged off her jacket, took off the belt containing her holster and handcuffs, the extra ammunition and baton, then took off her bulletproof vest, boots, and uniform trousers. She glanced at the clothes; they were muddy, splattered with vomit and snot from one of the accident victims. It would all need washing. She sighed.

Oh well, she had three days in which to do it.

She opened her bag and looked at her helmet, shin pads, cap, scarf, protective gloves, map, and underwear. No, nothing else needed washing.

She showered and washed her hair, then dried herself until her skin glowed, and put on her civilian clothes, jeans and a gray sweatshirt. She closed her locker and made a brief attempt to brush her hair, then went over to the armory and locked up her Sig Sauer in the correct place. She should really have done that first of all, but she was on her own there.

She stood for a moment, looking at the rows of locked-up weapons.

I don't know, Nina, oh God, I don't know, I'm sure I put my pistol in alongside David's.

She headed for the main entrance with a sense that she was about to be released from captivity, when her mobile rang.

"Nina? It's Holger."

Julia's father.

She stopped abruptly.

"Have you found him?"

"No, but I'd like to talk to you. Nina, is there any chance that you could come down?"

She could hear the rain lashing in the background; he must be standing outside somewhere.

"Of course," she said, trying to get her heart to stop racing. "I've got a few days off now, so I could get the train down first thing tomorrow morning . . ."

"I'd rather you came straight away, Nina. We've found something."

She put her hand out to the brick wall.

"What?" she said. "What have you found?"

Someone said something in the background, she couldn't make out what.

"Holger?" she said. "Where are you? Who else is there? What have you found?"

Julia's father came back on the line.

"There's four of us, and we're standing on the marsh at Sågkärret. Do you know where that is?"

"No," Nina said.

"Three hundred meters southeast from Björkbacken, you turn off toward Nytorp then take the first left. The road leads straight here. We'll be waiting for you here."

"Holger," Nina said, "can't you tell me what you've found?"

There was a whistling sound on the line from the squalls of rain. Julia's father's voice sounded hollow when he replied.

"We'll talk when you get here," he said. "We don't want to make a fuss in case we're wrong. It would be best if you made the decision."

"And it's not the boy?" she asked.

"No."

"But you have to call the police," Nina said.

"That's what I'm doing, isn't it?" Holger said. "We won't go anywhere. Drive carefully."

He ended the call.

She stood still, feeling her pulse race.

Have to get to Södermanland, have to get there now!

I'll take car 1930, that's closest.

She started to run toward the garage; she knew exactly where the keys to the car were kept.

Then she stopped.

I'm crazy. I can't just steal a patrol car.

She stopped dead and stood in the corridor.

Where can I get hold of a car, any car?"

She rushed back into the station, to the duty officer's room.

"Pelle," she panted, "have you got a car?"

Her boss looked at her in astonishment.

"What?"

"That's your blue Merc in the garage, isn't it? Can I borrow it? I'll be back before the end of your shift."

He looked at her for several long seconds.

"I don't suppose there's any point asking what you want it for?" he said, fishing the keys out from his trouser pocket.

Nina gulped.

"I'll tell you later," she said. "At least, I hope I will."

He got up and walked round the desk, holding the car keys out.

"It's almost worth it," he said, "just to see you in civilian clothes and with wet hair."

Then he dropped the keys into her palm.

"My shift ends at 2200," he said. "If you're not here, you can pay for my taxi home."

She closed her fingers round the keys, turned on her heel, and hurried toward the garage.

Annika had just passed Norrtälje and was following the E18 toward Spillersboda when the rain started. She didn't have the nerve to ask Berit to babysit the children again today. So Kalle and Ellen were sitting in the backseat playing with their Game Boys, bribed temporarily with a packet of sweets each. She wasn't sure how sensible it was, taking them to a home for young drug addicts, but at the same time she didn't want to be prejudiced.

The Vårtuna Home was supposed to be on the outskirts of the town. She turned up the speed of the windscreen wipers and peered out, trying to find the right turning. When she reached a more built-up area, she turned off right toward Klemensboda, carrying on past Gravrösen, toward Måsholmen.

Right now she was seriously regretting setting off at all. She had had a terrible night, full of nightmares, and had woken up in tears twice. She felt absolutely exhausted, down to her very marrow. There were houses burning all around, the children were screaming, and Thomas was screaming, and she was completely alone in the world.

She knew what she really needed was to lie on the sofa in Berit's living room and watch a Sunday matinee with the children.

Instead she was on her way through driving rain to meet a born-again drug dealer who was going to sing David Lindholm's praises.

I don't need to do this. I'm going home.

She was considering turning round and driving back, when she realized that the Vårtuna Home was right in front of her.

"Why are we here?" Kalle said as she parked the car between an old Volvo and a misshapen birch tree.

She let out a deep sigh.

"I'm ever so sorry I had to drag you out here," she said. "I'll try to get it finished as quickly as possible."

She had read about the place on the Internet. It was actually an old campsite and youth hostel that had been bought by a Free Church organization and turned into a care home for young drug addicts. There were several buildings scattered across the slope toward the sea. To the left was a large building that Annika assumed was the main house. Ahead of her were several small cabins with little porches that were probably where the clients lived—unless they were called patients?

"I want to go home," Ellen said.

"I know, but we can't go just yet," Annika said, far too sternly and loudly. "I promised I'd come and talk to a man out here, and now we're here. Right, off we go!"

She got out of the car quickly, holding an old copy of the *Evening Post* over her head, yanked open the rear doors and pulled the children out, then ran toward the main building with them round her feet.

The three of them were soaked through by the time they reached the porch. The door had swollen in the damp and they all had to push on it, and when it finally opened they tumbled into an old cafeteria. Annika helped the children to get up and they stamped their feet, instantly making a puddle of water round her trainers.

"We're ever so wet," Ellen said, blinking as the rain from her fringe dripped into her eyes.

There were seven people in the large room. Kalle huddled closer to her and took hold of the sleeve of her jacket.

"Hello," Annika said, raising one hand in a little wave.

Four young men were sitting and playing cards on a table by the window. They were all staring hard at them, and the dealer had frozen in the middle of what he was doing.

Annika looked round uncertainly.

The room was simply furnished, rib-backed chairs and kitchen tables with laminated tops. The floor was yellow linoleum, and the walls had different layers of colored paint.

She pushed the hair from her face.

Immediately ahead of them was a counter with cakes and a hot plate for a pot of coffee. Behind it stood a middle-aged man, and behind him were two more young men.

"Are they junkies?" Kalle whispered.

"Yes," Annika whispered back. "They all are."

"Are they dangerous?"

"No, I don't think so. They're all better now."

The middle-aged man came toward them.

"What terrible weather," he said. "Welcome! I'm Timmo."

His Finnish accent was sharp and pronounced. The man himself seemed gentle; his shoulders were slightly hunched, and he had a bald head with a ring of pale blond hair.

Annika tried to smile.

"It's good of you to see us at such short notice."

"Not at all," he said. "It's nice to have visitors. This is the dining room, where we have our meals and group activities. Shall we go into the office? Make sure you don't cut your fingers off."

This last sentence was addressed to the two lads who were evidently learning how to use a food processor.

"This place was bought by the association almost four years ago now," Timmo Koivisto said, squeezing through a narrow corridor lined with crates of soft drinks and big sacks of jasmine rice. "Reoffending rates among our lads" (he pronounced the word as *latts*) "are very low . . . This way."

He held the door open for Annika, gesturing for them to go through.

The children trod on her heels and they went in.

"Mum," Kalle said, tugging at her arm. "I left my Game Boy in the car. Do you think the junkies will take it?"

"You can never be too sure," Timmo Koivisto said, leaning toward Kalle. "Never leave valuables in the car, because opportunity makes the thief."

The boy was on the point of tears.

"There are no thieves about today," Annika said quickly. "It's raining far too hard. Thieves don't like getting wet."

Timmo Koivisto nodded.

"That's actually true," he said. "Crime figures go down when the weather's bad. In harsh winter there are hardly any opportunistic rapes, because sex offenders don't like getting cold backsides."

Dear God, what have I brought the children to?

She forced herself to smile.

"Maybe we could get down to business? I don't want to take up any more of your time than I have to."

"Oh," Timmo Koivisto said politely, "we've got all afternoon ahead of us."

There was only one spare chair in the room, Annika sat down and lifted one child onto each knee. The manager sat down carefully on the other side of the desk.

"There's one thing I must ask you," he said. "You can't write anything that reveals the identity of any of our clients. They weren't all very happy when I told them someone from the *Evening Post* was coming. But I think it's really great that you want to write about what we do."

Annika could feel her desperation rising as the flow of blood to her legs was slowly cut off.

"I'm sorry," she said, "but I think you might have misunderstood me. I'm sure what you do here is extremely interesting, but I was wondering if you could tell me anything about David Lindholm? I'm writing an article about him . . ."

Timmo Koivisto raised one hand and nodded.

"I know," he said. "I just wanted to explain that the Vårtuna Home is the most important thing in my life. Serving the Lord and helping my fellow unfortunates gives my life meaning, and it was David Lindholm who set me on the right path."

Annika moved the children so that they were standing beside her instead, then took her pen and notebook from her bag and leaned over to write.

"I didn't know David was religious," she said.

"Well," the man said, "I wouldn't know about that. I didn't actually know David Lindholm, but after my encounter with him I came to a new awareness. I had a choice, and I chose Christ."

She wrote "chose Christ" in her notebook, feeling the rainwater running down her spine.

Should I ask the children to wait outside? They shouldn't be hearing this. But can I trust those young men out there?

"So it was after the attack in the Central Station that you decided to . . . change track?"

Timmo Koivisto nodded.

"I was a sinner," he said. "I had let down a lot of people around me, my mother most of all, I think. The mothers of this world never get enough recognition."

He nodded thoughtfully to himself.

"I was only a small-time dealer, selling drugs to other small-time dealers to fund my own habit. It was my fault other young people became drug users, but my income still wasn't enough to keep me going. I started cheating, diluting the smack with icing sugar, but they found out, and they gave me a warning I'll never forget."

He turned his head to show the hearing aid in his left ear.

"And I see double," he said. "My eyes don't refract the light properly. I have special glasses, but they make me dizzy."

Oh, why ever did I bring them? I'm a terrible person! If Thomas finds out about this, he'll take them away from me.

She gulped.

"Why did he do it? Why did David beat you up like that?"

The look in Timmo Koivisto's eyes was calm and clear.

"They wanted to show me that I could never get away. Wherever I went, they would find me. If even the police did their bidding, then there was nowhere to run."

"And who were 'they'?" Annika asked. "The drugs mafia?"

"That's one way of describing them?"

"Mummy," Kalle said. "I need a wee."

Timmo Koivisto reacted at once.

"I can take him."

Annika flew up.

"No!" she said. "There's ... no need. I'll take him ..."

They went out of the office, Ellen too, and went a few meters to the right.

"Can you wait here until I've finished talking to the man?" she whispered once they had entered the small toilet.

"But I want to be with you, Mummy," Ellen said.

"I'll be back soon," she said, closing the door and hurrying back into the office.

"So, you were saying that David Lindholm did errands for some drug syndicate? Why?"

She sank onto the chair.

"I don't know, but I wasn't the only one he went for."

"Tony Berglund," Annika said.

Timmo Koivisto nodded.

"Among others. There were more who never reported it. I've met Tony; things didn't turn out too well for him. The last I heard, he was homeless, selling the *Big Issue* at Medborgarplatsen."

"And why did he attack Tony?"

"The same reason he attacked me."

"Yet you're still grateful to him?" Annika said. "You say he saved your life?"

Timmo Koivisto smiled.

"It's true. I woke up in hospital and found myself in the valley of death. David Lindholm had showed me the only way out, and I took it."

"Why did you retract everything during the trial?"

"Surely you can work out why?"

She could hear Kalle crying out in the corridor.

Annika stood up.

"I'm really sorry," she said, "but I think I'm going to have to go now."

I've got poor judgment, genuinely poor judgment.

The man stood up.

"Mind you, there's one thing I must admit."

"What?" Annika said from the doorway.

"I'm very pleased he's dead."

*   *   *

The storm and rain had turned the road ahead of her into a muddy ditch.
Nina stopped the car and peered into the darkness between the fir trees.

Pelle Sisulu's car was a two-seater soft-top with a ground clearance of
about five centimeters. Whenever there were any stones sticking up from
the mud, she heard them scratching the whole of the chassis.

She paused, wondering how much further it could be. A couple of
hundred meters? A kilometer? It had almost stopped raining, and the
wind had eased. Should she park the car and walk?

She looked up at the sky; steely gray was the right description.

The marsh of Sågkärret was right in front of her. She had taken the
motorway to Åkers styckebruk, then gone across country through Berga
to join Route 55, until she got to the junction at Sköldinge. She then followed the Stöttasten road until she reached the turning to Nytorp.

Then the first turning on the left, and here she was.

She put the car in first gear and accelerated cautiously. The wheels
slid a little in the wet, then found their grip, and the car moved off.

She had never driven such a responsive car; it held the road like a
limpet.

It has to be here somewhere!

She had hardly finished the thought before the wall of trees opened
up to reveal a large clearing in the forest. A mirror of water was visible
between the reeds and moss, and some stunted birches struggled against
the wind on a small island further out.

She put the car in neutral, pulled on the handbrake, and leaned forward to peer into the growing darkness.

Is this it?

There, to the left of the island with the birches, not far away at all
really, stood a small group of men. One of them waved to her, and she
could tell by his hat that it was Holger.

She switched the engine off, opened the car door, and got out. Her
foot sank into the boggy ground straightaway, and she gasped as the
water soaked through her trainer and reached her skin. The wind was
buffeting her from behind, almost making her fall.

Holger was holding his hat on with his right hand and slowly making his way toward her with long strides. Nina clung on to the car door as she waited for him to reach her.

His eyes looked red when he finally stopped beside her; it was hard to work out if that was the result of the weather or something else.

"Thanks for coming," he said, and in spite of the chasm in his voice she recognized her Holger, with all his strength and stability.

She took a step toward him and gave him a hug, holding him tight for a whole minute.

"I'm so sorry," she whispered.

Holger nodded.

"So are we," he said. "You haven't got any better shoes than those?"

Nina looked down at her Nikes and shook her head.

"Hold onto me," he said, stretching out his arm.

Together they set off across the marsh. Sometimes the ground held their weight fine, but occasionally Nina sank into the mud to her ankles; Holger managed better in his heavy hunting boots. The wind was pushing them from behind, making them take long steps. The rain picked up and started lashing them again, and soon Nina could feel the damp soaking through her denim jacket and gathering at the small of her back. The birch trees out on the island were twisting in the wind.

They soon reached the other men, Kaj from the neighboring farm and two more that she didn't recognize. She held out her hand in greeting, and noted that her hands were frozen while theirs were dry and warm. Their eyes were wide and mute, and none of them said anything.

She realized that they were now standing on firmer ground, a small island similar to the one farther out, the one with the birch trees. They had rock and hard-packed earth underfoot, and the rain was running off the sides.

"Here," Holger said, pointing to a rod sticking out of the water close to them. "When Kaj pulled the pole this floated up."

He pointed to a bundle next to the pole, just at the edge of the solid ground.

Nina took a few steps over to the little bundle, then leaned down to look at it.

Cloth. Muddy, but not torn.

She felt the ground with her hand until she found a stick. She carefully prodded the bundle to see how stable it was.

It doesn't split, so it hasn't been in the water long. But what is it?

She didn't want to touch the cloth, even though it could hardly hold any vital evidence. Instead she grabbed another stick and poked the fabric to see if she could see what shape it was.

It fell into two pieces. She stretched out the smaller of them.

It was a little shirt.

A child's shirt.

She bent down close to the cloth and scraped the edge with a nail.

No, not a shirt, the fabric was too thick, it was . . .

"Flannel," Holger said.

Pajamas!

She smoothed out the other piece.

A small pair of trousers.

A pair of flannel pajama trousers.

She pulled one sleeve of the shirt over her wrist, not caring about possible evidence, and wiped the mud away to see the original pattern and color of the fabric.

Pale, with blue and green balloons.

"Blue and green?" Holger wondered.

Nina nodded.

"Do you recognize it?" he asked.

"Not off the top of my head," she said.

"What about that, then?" Holger said, pointing to a tree root close to the pole.

Nina stood up and stepped closer to the root.

It was about twenty centimeters long, muddy and twisted, with odd pieces sticking out of it. She poked it with her stick and was surprised at how soft it was.

"We thought it was just a piece of wood as well," Kaj said.

Nina let go of the stick and picked the object up with both hands, wiping the end of it on her arm.

A pale-blue eye looked up at her.

She wiped the other side.

Another eye.

She scraped the mud off and a pair of ears and a nose appeared.

"Is it him?" Holger asked.

Nina nodded.

"Yes, it's his teddy," she said.

"You're sure?" Holger wondered.

She turned the bear over and inspected one of its paws. The seam along the leg had been repaired with dark blue cotton, although now that it was wet it looked black.

"Yes," she said. "I'm the one who did this sewing."

"Viola bought Alexander a pair of flannel pajamas last Christmas," Holger said. "I don't know if these are the ones. But you're sure about the teddy bear?"

Nina gulped, could feel water running down her face.

It's only rain, it's only rain.

"Yes," she said. "It's Alexander's. He never went anywhere without Bamse."

The four men around her bowed their heads to the ground.

The office was on the thirteenth floor, and had a view of the Skanstull bridge and the whole of what was once the industrial part of Hammarby. The furniture was gray, the walls white, the floors polished. The chairs in the corridor were black leather, designed to be uncomfortable.

Annika felt constricted and sweaty in her knitted cardigan, and her jeans had got muddy crossing Berit's lawn. She pulled her feet under the chair and looked at the time.

Thomas ought to have been here by now.

The damage assessor was talking on the phone behind the closed door in front of her; she could hear his chuckling laughter through the cracks in the door.

For him this is just another day in the office. For me it's Gehenna.

She'd slept badly again. The visit to the care home was still burning inside her. She hoped desperately that the children would never tell Thomas that she had dragged them out there.

The office door opened.

"Mrs. Samuelsson? Please come in."

The insurance advisor held out his hand, smiling broadly and disingenuously.

"Bengtzon," Annika said, standing up and taking his hand. "It's my husband who's called Samuelsson."

The lift pinged behind them, the door slid open and Thomas stepped out. Annika turned toward him and could feel how her chest lurched. *God, how lovely he looks!*

His briefcase was swinging from one large hand, his hair had tumbled down across his forehead, and he must have bought a new suit over the weekend, because she had never taken this one to the dry cleaners before.

"Sorry I'm late," he said, shaking the damage assessor by the hand a little breathlessly.

He glanced quickly at Annika, and she turned away hastily.

"My name's Zachrisson," the man said, and his smile was slightly more genuine now. "If you'd both like to come in . . ."

Annika picked up her bag and went into the office, noting that the whole of the exterior wall was glass. The clouds pressed against the panes and the water was visible far below. She could feel Thomas's presence behind her, his tall, sinewy body in the new suit and ironed shirt, and he smelled *different*, he smelled of *her*, and she was struck by an urge to run straight through the glass and fly, fly, fly away across the Hammarby Canal and off into the sky.

"This of course is an entirely new situation for most people," Zachrisson said, trying to smile in a conciliatory way. "I appreciate that it's a shocking experience, seeing your home burn down, with all the memories and . . ."

Annika was staring into the middle distance, into the grayness above the man's head. She heard him running on, going through the same speech he must have made to hundreds of other clients over the years, about how sympathetic the company was, about how they would offer almost unlimited help. And she could feel Thomas sitting beside her, and she realized that she wouldn't ever be able to live with him on Vinterviks-vägen again, not there, not in that part of town.

"Does the house have to be rebuilt?" she asked abruptly.

The assessor lost his train of thought and his smile fell.

"Er, no," he said. "Your insurance covers reconstruction and contents, but if you choose not to restore the house to its original condition, there are other alternatives . . ."

"Hang on a minute," Thomas said, leaning forward toward the official. "Can we take it from the start? What would be the usual course of events in a case like ours?"

He cast an annoyed glance at Annika.

Zachrisson fingered some documents on his desk and adjusted his glasses.

"What usually happens is that the house is rebuilt as it was. Plans are drawn up, planning permission sought, and the reconstruction of the house is organized. Usually this is done as soon as possible, and in most cases begins at once."

"And if that's not what we want?" Annika said, refusing to look at Thomas.

The official thought for a moment.

"In that case we would evaluate the house as it was, and get a valuation of the property such as it is now: burned down, in other words. Because it can still be sold, of course, in spite of that. The plot itself has a value. The clients would get the difference paid into their account. They would also be recompensed for the loss of contents, furniture, clothes, television, DVDs, and so on."

"I think that sounds like a reasonable option," Annika said.

"I don't know if I agree with that," Thomas said, beginning to look absolutely furious. "Even if we don't want to live there, there's probably much more to be gained from selling a newly built property than a smoking pile of ruins . . ."

Zachrisson raised both hands as if to stop them, and looked rather upset.

"There is a problem in this case," he said, "which we must take into account before we can begin discussing any form of payment. No insurance company would pay out damages to anyone under suspicion of arson on their own home."

The silence that fell in the room ran right through Annika's body. Suddenly she could hear the hum of the air-conditioning and the noise of the traffic below on Götgatan. She glanced quickly at Thomas and could see that he had frozen, leaning forward with his mouth half open. The damage assessor was also sitting with his mouth open, as if he were surprised that the words had actually emerged from his mouth.

"What?" Thomas said. "What are you saying?"

Zachrisson loosened his tie, and it looked like sweat had broken out on his brow.

"As we understand it," he said, "there's an ongoing police investigation into your case. There are suspicions of arson."

"It was definitely arson," Annika said, "but neither of us started it."

The assessor leaned back, as if he were worried about coming into contact with something infectious.

"We can't make any payment until the police investigation into the circumstances of the fire is complete," he said. "Even if the preliminary inquiries don't lead to a full investigation, we still wouldn't make a payment. We carry out our own investigations as well . . ."

Annika looked at the bespectacled man on the other side of the smart desk, and felt the same feeling she had had when facing the cashier in the bank a few days before.

"But that's ridiculous!" she said, and could hear that her voice was all wrong, too loud and too shrill and too emotional. "Someone tried to kill us, and now you're insinuating that we started the fire ourselves. *Ourselves! Would we really have tried to kill our own children?*"

"We have to take everything into account," Zachrisson said. "We can't pay out any money to arsonists."

Annika stood up so quickly that the leather chair almost toppled over behind her.

"Take everything into account?" she said. "For whose benefit? Your shareholders? What about us, the people paying for your fucking view all these years, you don't feel like taking account of us? And now you're accusing us of *arson*?"

Thomas stood up as well and grabbed her hard by the arm.

"I must apologize for the behavior of my . . . wife," he said in a restrained voice, and dragged her out of the room.

"Ow," Annika said, following him like a helpless doll in his huge fist, her bag slapping against her legs.

They got into the corridor and then the lift. Thomas pressed to go down to the lobby and didn't let go of her arm before the metal door had closed. Annika was breathing fast and could feel her heart racing in her chest.

"Sorry," she said. "I didn't mean to blow up."

Thomas was leaning forward against the wall of the lift; his hair had fallen forward, and he was staring down at the floor.

She wanted to reach out her hand and brush his hair aside, stroke his cheek, kiss him, and tell him that she loved him.

"Sorry," she whispered again.

The lift stopped with a little shudder and the doors slid open. Thomas took a better grip of his briefcase and walked quickly toward the main entrance. Annika followed him, running to keep up with him, her eyes on the back of his head.

"Wait," she said. "Wait a minute, we have to talk . . ."

They emerged into the gray haze, the noise of the traffic hitting them at the same time as the exhaust fumes.

"Thomas," she said, "don't you want to see the children? What are we going to do about the children . . . ?"

He stopped and turned round and stared at her with his new eyes, swollen and predatory.

"What the hell are you playing at?" he managed to say.

She held out her hand to stroke his cheek but he pulled back, and it looked like he felt like spitting on her.

"Thomas," she said, and the world around her dissolved and all sound vanished. The hand that had tried to caress him landed on her own chest.

"You're completely out of control," he said, taking another step back.

She went and stood right next to him and felt like touching his hair.

"I'll do anything," she said, suddenly aware that she was crying.

"Where are the children now?"

Her hands started to shake uncontrollably and she recognized the signs of an imminent panic attack. *Nice and calm, there's nothing to be afraid of, there's nothing to be afraid of . . .*

"They're with Thord, he offered to look after them while I . . ."

"*Thord?* Who the hell's Thord? I'm going to get them right away."

She let his fury wash over her. What was he saying? What was it he wanted?

He's angry and upset and he wants to cause trouble.

The world came back, with its driving rain and traffic noise.

"No, you're not," she said, noticing that her pulse had actually slowed down.

He turned away and took several steps toward Götgatan, then turned back and stopped in front of her with his eyes on fire.

"My children aren't going to be looked after by someone like you," he said. "I'm going to apply for sole custody of them."

She looked into his eyes and saw nothing she recognized.

"You won't manage to look after Kalle and Ellen," she said. "You never have."

"Well, at least they won't have to live with some fucking *arsonist!*"

He screamed the last word.

So this was what they had come to.

She suddenly became completely calm.

Okay, if it was like that.

She looked away and felt grief spreading through her whole body.

"I'll see a lawyer today," Thomas said. "I want to get divorced as soon as possible, and the kids are mine."

She looked at him through her tears.

I've been here before. This has happened before, with Sven.

She gasped, her whole body tensed and made ready for flight. Thomas's face was hovering above her, his jaw clenched so tight that his cheekbones turned white.

This isn't the same thing at all, he's not going to try to kill me.

"I think we should have them alternate weeks for the time being," she managed to say. "You can pick them up on Friday."

He took a firmer grip of his briefcase, looked away from her, and turned to go, marching determinedly toward Götgatan, leaning forward, his shoulders hunched against the wind.

I'm not dying, I'm not dying. It just feels like it.

Nina came into the station with a nagging anxiety in her stomach. She had called during the night and explained that she wouldn't be back with the car before the duty officer finished, but Pelle Sisulu had already reached the end of his shift by then and gone home.

She headed toward the duty officer's room but stopped a meter or so from the door.

Christer Bure was in there, talking to the station commander about a case involving a dead body. There was some question about the death certificate and the seizure of prescription medications from the scene.

Nina hesitated. Should she go away and come back later?

"Don't worry about passing on news of the death," she heard Pelle Sisulu say. "I'll take care of that."

Christer Bure walked out of the duty officer's room and glanced quickly at her, and his eyes narrowed.

Nina adjusted her hair and walked up to the door. Her boss was standing with his back to the door, putting a file back on top of a bookcase. His back almost blocked the window.

She knocked on the doorframe, and he looked over his shoulder.

"Ah," he said, turning back to his desk, "so it's you."

"I really can't thank you enough for the loan," Nina said, feeling oddly embarrassed. "I know you had to get a taxi home, of course I'm going to pay for it . . ."

"That was a joke," the duty officer said, tucking in his shirt again. "Was everything okay with the car?"

"Absolutely," she said, "but it's very muddy, and I didn't dare take it through a car wash because I didn't know if a soft-top would be okay in there, what with the roof and everything, but I'm happy to take it to the garage and wash it by hand if you like . . ."

"Thanks," he said, sitting down. "That would be great."

She nodded.

The duty officer looked at her for a few seconds, nodding at her uniform.

"Aren't you supposed to have today off?"

"Yes," Nina said, "but I have to go to the remand hearing."

"Is Julia being officially remanded today?" he asked.

Like he didn't know.

"Three o'clock," Nina said.

He stood up and came and stood in front of her.

"There's something I've been wondering about," he said quietly. "I understand that you were on the scene when the Katrineholm police picked up the evidence of the Lindholm boy. How did that come about?"

She looked out of the window and refrained from answering.

The man sighed.

"I'm not trying to catch you out," he said. "Just let me say that I'm impressed by your contacts. Because I don't suppose you happened to be at Sågträsket by accident?"

Nina sat down on a chair by the wall.

"Sågkärret," she said. "Julia's dad called. He and the other men in the village had been searching the marshland around Björkbacken all day. It was the neighboring farmer who found the things. Holger wanted to make sure that they could really have been Alexander's before he made a fuss."

"And how come he thought you would be able to judge that better than him?"

"Holger's color-blind," she said. "He thought he recognized Alexander's pajamas, but he wasn't sure about the teddy bear. Its name is Bamse Lindholm, you know. Holger didn't want to frighten his wife if they weren't actually Alexander's things, and by phoning me he was actually phoning the police as well, so . . ."

She fell silent, worried that she was babbling.

Pelle Sisulu looked at her for several seconds.

"And what did his wife say? She was the one who made the formal identification?"

Nina nodded again.

"She bought the pajamas from H&M last Christmas, slightly too big but she thought he'd grow into them . . ."

"You've got no theories about how they might have ended up in the lake?"

Nina thought for a moment, seeing the scene in front of her.

"It's not a lake, it's more of a marsh. Before all this rain it was probably possible to walk there without getting your feet wet."

"How far from a public road?"

"There's a forest track that goes all the way to the marsh."

"So someone could have driven a vehicle to the edge, dumped the body, and then left the scene. Any tire tracks?"

Nina looked at her boss.

"No body was found," she said. "Just a pair of pajamas and a teddy bear."

"Did you happen to see if there were any journalists there?"

Nina frowned.

"Yes," she said, "the local reporter from Flen was there. Oscarsson, he lives in Granhed and heard about the discovery on police radio. If I've done something wrong, if I've broken any rules, I'd like you to tell me."

"I think you did exactly the right thing," he said. "You made the initial decision that the find was interesting and encouraged the finder to contact the local police authorities."

He paused.

"And I appreciate that this wasn't just an ordinary police matter for you."

She folded her arms and leaned back.

"How do you mean?" she asked.

The station commander smiled slightly and turned toward the window so that Nina could only see his face in profile.

"I can still remember the day you and Julia turned up here for the first time. People always keep an eye out for girls on practical experience, and I can hardly claim to remember them all, but I remember you two."

Nina was still sitting with her arms folded, unsure if she should feel flattered or insulted.

He glanced quickly in her direction.

"So keen," he said, "big eyes, long hair . . ."

He looked down at his hands, then stood up.

Nina followed his example.

"So you won't be reporting me for doing anything stupid?" she wondered stiffly.

The duty officer shook his head.

"Why would I do that?" he said, then added in English: "*Go and sin no more.*"

She looked at him in surprise.

"You speak American? I thought you were 100 percent Swedish."

The big black man burst out laughing.

"*Oh man,*" he said, "now that's good! I've been called coon and nigger and monkey, but never 100 percent Swedish!"

She could feel the blood rushing to her head, turning her cheeks bright red.

"Sorry," she said, looking down at the floor.

"My dad's from South Africa and my mum's from the US. And I grew up in the Stockholm suburb of Fruängen. Leave the car in the garage when you've finished washing it."

He was still laughing as he sat down behind his desk, and Nina headed out of the door toward the main entrance.

Anders Schyman was staring at the front page of the *Evening Post*.

It was dominated by a grainy picture of a marsh with the photograph of the Lindholm boy in the top right-hand corner.

ALEXANDER'S GRAVE was the uncompromising headline.

No question mark, no doubt.

Is this all right? Isn't this just unpleasant speculation?

From the teaser on the front page it was clear that the boy's pajamas and teddy bear had been found pushed down into marshy ground close to the main suspect's summer cottage.

"Now it's just a matter of time before we find the boy," a source said.

The last line reported that Alexander's mother was due to be remanded in custody that afternoon.

The editor in chief ran his fingers through his hair.

No, this isn't all right. We're going to get hell for this.

He let out a deep sigh.

Through the glass wall he could see the members of the Journalists' Association heading over toward the long table shared by the day-shift reporters for their annual general meeting. Judging by their body language, it didn't look like anything of any great importance was on the agenda.

The other evening paper had missed the story about the findings in the marsh—they hadn't mentioned it at all in their first edition and had only had text but no picture in their late Stockholm edition—so on those grounds he could be pleased . . .

The intercom buzzed.

"Anders, there's a call for you."

The receptionist's nasal voice sounded even more adenoidal than usual.

"Well, put it through then!"

"It's the press spokesman from Stockholm Police."

Oh no . . .

Anders Schyman closed his eyes for a couple of seconds before picking up the receiver.

"Yes," he said abruptly.

"I'm not trying to find out your sources," the press spokesman said in his characteristically weary voice. "And I have no ethical opinion on your wild speculations about crime and guilt. But I would like to let you know that you're publishing confidential material from the preliminary investigation in today's paper."

"I can't agree with you on that," Schyman said. "We've done nothing but go about our usual journalistic business, just as we always do."

"That's bullshit and you know it," the press spokesman said. "But I don't want to argue with you, I just want to clarify some of the circumstances surrounding our mutual interests."

"Really?"

"Both I personally and the police authorities in general have long been very keen on having an open and honest relationship with the media, a sort of mutual loyalty and respect for each other's specific working conditions."

Schyman groaned inwardly.

He doesn't half make a meal of things.

"Of course."

"When you consciously break our agreement, I have to react; you must understand that. You're printing details of evidence we've found about the boy in today's paper, making it completely worthless in any future trial. It's entirely possible that we'll never solve this crime, thanks to you."

Anders Schyman let out a deep, audible sigh.

"Well," he said, "that has to be something of an exaggeration. Aren't you supposed to be remanding someone this very afternoon for this particular crime?"

"That's not the point. The fact that she's in custody is no thanks to the media. As a result, I've decided to follow your lead and reevaluate our shared activities, which will naturally have consequences not only for us, but for you as well."

"And . . . ?"

"The series of articles that Patrik Nilsson is planning about the south of Spain, with the working title 'Costa Cocaine,' is, as you are no doubt aware, the result of close collaboration between the Stockholm Police, the Justice Department, and the *Evening Post*. I'm afraid that we're going to have to disregard any agreements reached on this matter and look for another newspaper . . ."

Anders Schyman sat up in his chair.

"No hold on a minute," he said. "That's our series of articles, it's grown out of our angle and our research . . ."

"I'm terribly sorry, but I'm not the one who decided to break our agreement."

"No, but . . ." Schyman said.

"And I'm going to have a few conversations with some of the officers that I know usually supply you with the more informal details concerning our investigations. That's all over now. We've got other papers we can talk to. Good afternoon to you, then, sir . . ."

God, what a pretentious bastard!

Schyman put the receiver down and leaned back in his chair again, holding the paper up in front of him.

It wasn't that bad, was it?

He looked through the articles again, with a more critical eye.

Patrik Nilsson had written the articles about the find in the marsh the previous evening.

HEROES was the headline across pages six and seven. The picture desk had bought the rights to a photograph from the *Katrineholm Courier*, in which the missing boy's grandfather and some other men were standing gloomily at the scene of the find. The subtitle picked up the speculation of the front page: *Have They Found Alexander's Grave?*

At least they had managed to squeeze in a small question mark at the end.

The article said that the old men had braved the terrible weather and carried on the search when everyone else had given up. They had recognized Alexander's clothes and favorite teddy bear immediately. Now the search was focusing on that particular piece of marshland; the whole of the Södermanland police force was involved, and the army was going to be called in.

The description of the marsh was rather gothic and dramatic, all about unyielding stagnant water and swarms of buzzing mosquitoes.

Surely that wasn't worth getting too excited about?

He lowered the paper to his lap where it crumpled untidily.

Why draw a connection between a series of future articles and a possible case of overstepping the mark? That was a little far-fetched, wasn't it? Did the press spokesman have a hidden agenda?

He glanced through the glass wall out into the newsroom. A few latecomers were on their way to the union meeting.

Once upon a time he himself had been active in the union. Seriously militant, if he remembered rightly. Hadn't he actually been union representative on one of the local radio stations up north somewhere, Radio Norrbotten, maybe? Or was it Radio Gävleborg?

In those days, before the commercial stations, journalists would spend years out in the bush. In the eighties, employment regulation had been incredibly strict: eleven months probation, then you were out on your ear. People used to end up stuck in the middle of nowhere, with no chance of ever getting to Stockholm and the national television channels. No permanent positions had come up since TV2 launched in 1968, providing work for an entire generation of agitators.

Those were the days. All appointments lasted a whole lifetime, and everyone knew who the chancellor of justice was. And no reporter was ever in the lap of the police.

Well, that last one may have been a bit dubious even then, he thought, as he watched Berit Hamrin making her way to the meeting.

If Berit was going, then maybe they were going to be discussing something important. What could it be?

Of course, they were going to be choosing a new union representative, he'd almost forgotten.

He got up, grabbing the crumpled newspaper, and went and sat down opposite Spike.

"You're not going to the union meeting?" the editor in chief asked, putting his feet up on the desk.

"I've been expelled," the head of news said. "I forgot to pay my sub."

"That's a bit mean of them," Schyman said.

"Sixteen years in a row," Spike said. "So I have to say I don't blame them."

"What have we got on the boy for tomorrow?" the editor in chief asked, pointing at that day's front cover.

"We're trying to find a new picture of the kid, ideally wearing the pajamas and hugging the teddy."

"So how's the search going?"

"No luck so far. His relatives just snap at us and put the phone down."

Schyman opened the paper again, looking at the picture of the marsh. Voices from the union meeting bounced between the desks toward him, they had got as far as approving the agenda.

He slumped deeper into his chair and tried to close his ears.

"How exactly did we find out what they found in the marsh?" he asked.

"How do you mean?"

"Who leaked?"

"Hell, no one leaked anything. The old boys talked to the *Katrine-holm Courier* last night. That's where we got it. *KC* were running it on their website just after midnight."

"So we can thank the local press, new technology, and the uselessness of the competition in that order," Schyman said. "When things like this come up I want to be involved in the discussion. I've just had a conversation with the police press spokesman, and he wasn't particularly happy."

Spike looked up at the ceiling.

"He's a long-winded bastard."

Schyman turned the page. The union meeting was accepting the accounts.

"He's tearing up our agreement on Patrik's series about the Costa Cocaine. Either he really was as cross as he sounded, or else he just needed a reason to get us off the story."

"I always thought that was fucking weird," Spike said. "I mean, why should we send people all over Europe just to write how fucking great the Swedish police are?"

Over at the day shift's table, the committee was being granted the authority to act on behalf of the members. The election committee had two proposals for a new chair. Seeing as they couldn't decide, both names were being put to the membership. The first nomination was the political reporter, Sjölander, and the second was the newsroom secretary, Eva-Britt Qvist.

Really? Schyman thought, pricking his ears. I wonder why Sjölander is suddenly taking an interest in the union?

The reporter, who was a former head of crime reporting, former American correspondent, and currently a political commentator, had none of the characteristics usually associated with union representatives. Sjölander was smart, ambitious, and highly regarded. Unlike most union reps after a short while. The ones who made the union into a career were usually whiny, untalented, and work shy.

Eva-Britt Qvist, on the other hand, more than met the criteria usually associated with local union reps. He'd managed to get her out of his hair by making her responsible for the office budget and attendance rates, and the fact was that she was at the top of the list of people he wanted to get rid of.

It's hardly surprising that she's put herself forward, he thought. As union representative, she'd finally have a bit of power and influence.

"Lindholm's wife is being remanded this afternoon," Spike said. "If we're lucky, we can get something from that."

"I doubt it," Schyman said. "The prosecutor will batten down the hatches, and refer to the confidentiality needed for the preliminary investigation."

"Yes, and the killer's evidently completely mad," the head of news said.

Tore from reception was talking.

"There are plenty of us here who'd like to see a new sort of union rep. Someone who listens to us. This year it's time for the whole orchestra, not just a soloist. It's time we got a bit more influence."

There was a murmur of agreement. A show of hands was asked for.

Why is Tore in the Journalist's Association? Schyman wondered. Didn't he used to work in graphics?

"I make that twenty-seven votes for Sjölander," Tore said. "And twenty-eight for Eva-Britt Qvist. We have a new chair!"

Scattered applause.

Anders Schyman sighed.

Now he would have to sit and discuss cutbacks with the person who used to open his post.

"Did Patrik go down to Södermanland last night?" he asked, nodding toward the article containing the evocative description of the marsh.

"Bloody hell, no," Spike said. "Why ever would you think that?"

"Unyielding stagnant water and buzzing mosquitoes," Schyman said.

"Everyone knows what a marsh is like. Have you seen this?"

Spike pointed at the screen.

"The Foreign Ministry are hinting that Viktor Gabrielsson is about to be released."

Viktor Gabrielsson? Who the hell was he, again?

"Really?" Schyman said. "How come?"

"They're getting close to a 'diplomatic solution.' This is from the main news agency: 'After spending fifteen years in a New York prison as an accessory to the murder of a police officer in Long Island, the Foreign Ministry in Stockholm has indicated that Viktor Gabrielsson could soon be extradited to Sweden . . . '"

Ah, that one, the old police murder.

"I'll believe that when I see it," Schyman said.

Spike clicked on and read the next message.

"The girl who won *Big Brother* is going to have an operation to remove her silicon tits," he announced. "She's going to bury them symbolically in a Plexiglas coffin and then auction them on the Internet. The money's going to kids in war-torn Rwanda."

Anders Schyman stood up.

"Check with the staff at Alexander's nursery if we can go and look at the pictures on the walls," he said. "Nowadays they always have loads of pictures of the kids that they pin up on notice boards."

The head of news looked up, eyebrows raised.

"So where the fuck do you think we got the pictures of the kid in today's paper?" he said.

Ander Schyman went back to his office, closed the door carefully behind him, and sighed deeply. He was about to sit down when there was a knock on the door.

Annika Bengtzon was standing outside. She pulled the door open before he had time to wave her in. Her hair was all over the place and she had that terrier-like expression on her face that never boded well.

"What?" he said wearily.

"I've found some really interesting stuff on David Lindholm. He was charged with beating people up, twice, because he was doing favors for the drugs mafia and beat up small-time gangsters who tried to con them out of money."

Schyman made an effort to keep his facial expression neutral.

"He was charged? When?"

"Eighteen years ago. And twenty years ago."

"You say 'charged.' Was he found guilty?"

"No, and that's really dodgy as well. He was let off both times."

"And you want to write about this?"

"I think it paints a completely different picture of David Lindholm."

"And the information comes from . . . ?"

"The preliminary investigations, and I've also met one of the men who was beaten up. He says he's pleased David's dead."

He had to cover his eyes with his hands to summon up a bit of strength.

"So you want me to publish a story saying that a murdered hero was actually a thug working for the drugs mafia, and we're basing this on the fact that he was found *not* guilty of charges of using excessive force? Twenty years ago?"

She bit her lip.

"You're twisting everything . . ."

"Slandering the dead," he said. "That's a serious offense. Editors in chief have gone to prison for that."

"Yes, but . . ."

"I've already been hauled over the coals for our editorial decisions once today. I don't want to hear any more about this. Go and find yourself somewhere to live."

"Yeah, yeah," Annika Bengtzon said as she walked out.

He sat down in his chair and leaned his head in his hands.

It can't just be my imagination.

This job has got a hell of a lot messier over the past few years.

The remand proceedings were announced in one of the high-security courtrooms, and Nina stood up quickly, before everyone else. She felt uncomfortable in her uniform, something she really should have got over by now, but this situation was particularly exposed and unusual.

There were a lot of journalists in the hall outside the courtroom, reporters from press and radio, and at least two television crews. She could see them studying her, wondering what she was doing there.

Hyenas! Here to get their mouthful of flesh.

She shook the thought aside and headed toward the courtroom.

Detective Inspector Q slid up alongside her and held the door open.

"Go and sit right at the front," he said quietly.

She looked at him in bemusement.

"We're going to be on our own on the public benches," he said.

She did as she had been told and sat down on the front bench. The judge's seat was right in front, the prosecutor to the left, and the defense to the right.

Nina had been in this room many times before; she had been a witness in a lot of remand proceedings.

But nothing like this one.

She glanced over at the door behind the defense bench. It led to a waiting room which was linked directly to Kronoberg Prison via the Walk of Sighs. That way they could bring people held in custody straight into the high-security courtroom without having to steer them through the crowds outside.

You're sitting behind there now. Do you realize what's happening?

The room quickly filled up, reporters with recording equipment, court artists with large pads. They rustled and jostled and chatted, their muttering sounding like an expectant and irrepressible waterfall.

Nina leaned toward Detective Inspector Q.

"Which public defense counsel has been assigned to her?" she asked in a whisper.

"Mats Lennström," Q said quietly.

Who?

"Who's he? What's he done before this?"

Before Q had time to answer the door behind the judge's platform opened and the chief judge and chief clerk took their places. A second later a dark-haired man in a suit came in from the waiting room, followed by a prison guard who led Julia to her seat.

Nina leaned forward instinctively. *God, what did she look like!* Her hair was messy and unwashed, her prison outfit all creased as if she'd slept in it.

She felt her throat constrict and gulped audibly.

"Why didn't she get a different lawyer?" she said. "Can he really handle a case like this?"

Q gestured to her to keep quiet.

Prosecutor Angela Nilsson came in as well, sat down, and adjusted her skirt beneath her thighs. She had changed her clothes; this outfit was blue verging on gray.

The presiding judge banged his gavel on the desk and complete silence fell.

Nina stared at Julia. She was looking at her face from slightly off to one side, and her eyes seemed shiny and empty. There was something innocent about her messy hair and the outsized collar of the prison shirt.

How thin you look. You're probably not eating the food; I bet you think it's disgusting.

The judge cleared his throat and started to explain the formalities, remand proceedings, the parties summoned, and Nina watched Julia's reactions.

"This isn't working," she whispered to Q.

"If you can't be quiet you'll have to leave," he hissed back, and she closed her mouth.

Angela Nilsson began.

"Mr. Chairman, I propose that the court remand Julia Lindholm in custody on suspicion of having committed murder in Bondegatan in Stockholm on June 3," she said in a monotone. "As justification for this action, I note that the penalty for this crime is longer than two years imprisonment. I also refer to the two motivations for holding the suspect on remand, as documented in my proposal: the danger of collusion, and the danger of the suspect reoffending. I also propose that the court impose certain restrictions upon Julia Lindholm."

Nina held her breath and studied Julia's reaction.

Nothing at all.

The presiding judge turned to the lawyer, Mats Lennström.

"Mr. Lennström, please go ahead and present the position of the accused."

"Thank you. We object to the prosecutor's proposal of remand. There are no reasonable reasons to suspect . . ."

He lost his train of thought and leafed through his papers.

Nina groaned inwardly.

"What is the position of the accused toward the matter of guilt?" the judge asked.

The lawyer hesitated.

"Mr. Chairman, I would prefer that this matter be dealt with in a closed session," he said, glancing toward the public benches.

The presiding judge turned toward the prosecutor. Angela Nilsson shuffled slightly in her seat and glared at the defense lawyer.

"Considering the confidential nature of the preliminary investigation, the prosecution would also prefer a closed session."

The judge turned to the public benches.

"Then I must ask members of the public and representatives of the media to leave the courtroom," he said, and banged his gavel on the desk.

The next moment the room was full of hubbub and noise, and Nina kept her eyes firmly on Julia.

She didn't seem to notice that people were moving about in the room.

When the doors closed the silence in the room was almost tangible.

"So, about the question of guilt?" the judge said.

The lawyer put his expensive ballpoint pen down on his documents and looked right at the judge.

"The fact is that my client is too ill to offer any opinion on the question of guilt. It is simply not possible to conduct a conversation with her."

"What do you mean?"

"I was appointed to this case on Saturday. Since then I have tried to communicate with my client, but I don't think she understands who I am. I have reason to believe that my client is in need of acute psychiatric care."

The judge leafed through his papers.

"I thought she had already received treatment?" he said. "At Södermalm Hospital, just after she was apprehended?"

"My client has a long history of psychiatric problems," the lawyer said. "She has been on sick leave from her position with the police for almost two years on grounds of stress. She spent some time in a psychiatric ward for depression. I have serious reason to believe that this treatment must be recommenced immediately."

The judge looked up.

"What has led you to that conclusion?"

Mats Lennström clicked his pen.

"My client refers repeatedly to another woman who was present in the apartment on the night in question," he said. "She calls this other woman 'the evil one' or 'the wicked one,' but she can't name her."

The presiding judge stared at Julia.

"So you believe that she . . . might have more than one . . . ?"

"It is incompatible with the criminal justice system's responsibility to provide care, to allow an unwell individual to be remanded in custody, even in a medical facility."

The judge shook himself and turned to Angela Nilsson.

"Does the prosecution share the opinion of the defense?"

The woman sighed theatrically.

"This notion of hearing voices is starting to become far too popular."

"What do you mean?" the judge said, raising his eyebrows.

"Julia Lindholm has chosen not to cooperate with the investigation. I wouldn't like to speculate upon her reasons."

"I see," the judge said. "On what grounds does the prosecution base its request that the accused be remanded in custody?"

Angela Nilsson sorted through her papers and composed herself for a few seconds before she started to speak.

"David Lindholm was found dead in his home at 0339 on Thursday, June 3. The preliminary postmortem report indicates that he was shot in the head, which was the direct cause of death. After that the body was shot once more, in the torso."

"Could any other woman have been present when the fatal shot was fired?" the judge asked.

Angela Nilsson turned a page and the silence echoed.

"The suspect was apprehended at the scene of the crime. A gun, type Sig Sauer 225, was found at the scene, and a preliminary forensic investigation has been able to prove that this gun bears the fingerprints of the accused. The pistol is registered as being the accused's service revolver. Whether or not this weapon is also de facto the murder weapon is currently being investigated by the National Forensics Laboratory, but the caliber matches the bullets found during the postmortem and there are two bullets missing from the clip . . ."

The was dead silence in the courtroom. The clerk was taking notes. A fan was whirring somewhere.

"Then we have the situation regarding the suspect's son," Angela Nilsson went on after a short pause. "The boy, Alexander Lindholm, who is four years old, hasn't been seen since his father was murdered, and is currently still missing."

Nina leaned forward on her bench. Julia had raised her head when the prosecutor mentioned Alexander's name, and now she was looking round the sealed room. She looked at the lawyer sitting next to her as if she didn't recognize him, and stood up.

Nina saw the lawyer put one hand on her shoulder and persuade her to sit down again.

"As things stand, I don't want to specify any particular suspicions surrounding the boy's disappearance," Prosecutor Nilsson continued.

"There is still a chance that there is a straightforward explanation for his disappearance, but if Alexander Lindholm is not found alive and well in the very near future, I will apply to have the preliminary investigation expanded to cover the murder or kidnapping of Alexander Lindholm ..."

Every time the boy's name was mentioned Julia reacted and looked round. Eventually she twisted on her chair in such a way that she caught sight of Nina sitting in the public benches.

No, Julia, not now!

The thought didn't get through. Julia stood up and took a hesitant step toward Nina. Her eyes were wide open and innocent, like the time she hadn't dared to jump from a haystack, and she was standing with her feet slightly turned in, the way she did when she was scared or needed a pee badly.

Pull yourself together, Julia, I can't help you now.

"Will the accused please sit down during the proceedings," the judge said.

Julia took an unsteady step toward the public benches.

"Alexander?" she said. "Where's Alexander? *No!*"

She hit the lawyer's arm when he tried to get her to sit down again.

Nina looked down at the floor and clenched her hands helplessly. Julia was only making things worse for herself if she didn't cooperate. All she had to do was tell the court what her life had been like. No one had anything to gain from her protecting David, least of all she herself.

Nina looked up again. Two prison guards who had been standing by the door leading to the Walk of Sighs each took hold of one of Julia's arms and bent her forward.

Julia struggled. She was making small whimpering sounds as she tried to get free. The guards sat her back down on her chair again, and she slumped visibly to one side.

You should have reported him. You should have listened to me. I would have stood by you. They would have had to believe you.

"If only he'd hit me. A couple of serious bruises, at least, ideally a few broken ribs as well."

What he's doing to you is worse. It comes under a different category. He can't lock you in like this. Unlawful imprisonment, coercion ...

Suddenly Julia toppled off her chair.

She fell to the floor with a dull thud and lay there on her side with her legs pulled up. Nina was on her feet at once.

One of the guards grabbed Julia's arm to pull her up but she didn't respond. His colleague came over and took hold of her other arm.

Sit up, Julia, get up!

There was complete silence in the courtroom, everyone had frozen where they were. The only things moving were Julia's legs and feet, which had started twitching spasmodically and uncontrollably, and suddenly the guards let go of her arms and stood up, backing away from her.

Julia lay on the floor with her head back and her body jerking violently. Nina gasped. *Oh God, what are they doing to you?*

"Medics to the courtroom," the judge said into a microphone that was evidently some sort of intercom system.

He sounded unsettled.

Nina took an involuntary step toward the woman on the floor, but Q grabbed her by the wrist.

"Sit down," he hissed.

The judge raised his voice.

"Can we have a doctor or a medic to the courtroom . . ."

Nina sat where she was, completely paralyzed, and watched as a medic ran in clutching a bag. He bent down over Julia's jerking body and spoke into a crackling radio.

"We've got a tonic-clonic attack," he said, holding the radio to his mouth with one hand as he examined Julia with the other. "I repeat, we have a primary, generalized tonic-clonic attack. I need backup and an ambulance immediately, I repeat, *immediately!*"

"Take her out through the side door," the judge said. He was now standing up behind his desk and was staring at the scene in front of him in horror. "Hurry up!"

Another two medics appeared, carrying an improvised stretcher between them. They picked Julia up, and Nina could see that she was stiff as a board, her body completely rigid, stuck in an unnatural pose with one arm and one leg sticking straight out.

Then, as she was being lifted onto the stretcher, it seemed as if the cramps eased and her body relaxed, but Nina wasn't sure if she had got that right, because the medics rushed out with the stretcher, disappearing through the side door.

There was complete silence in the courtroom once the doors had slammed shut. The guards stood there staring helplessly at the door where Julia had been carried out. Prosecutor Angela Nilsson was sitting on the edge of her chair, staring suspiciously at the place where Julia had been lying. The defense lawyer, Mats Lennström, had got to his feet and moved back, and was standing with his back to the wall.

The presiding judge sat down and struck his gavel.

"Well," he said, rather shakily, "if we could bring the proceedings to a conclusion . . . Angela?"

The prosecutor simply shook her head.

"Defense?"

Mats Lennström hurried to sit down again.

"Well," he said, adjusting his hair. "In conclusion I would like to point out that my client has in no way acknowledged liability for the accusations made by the prosecution. But if the prosecution's proposal were to be accepted, I petition the court to order an immediate paragraph seven investigation of my client. As well as immediate treatment, her mental state at the time of the crime needs to be examined at once."

"The court will adjourn," the judge said, hitting his gavel on the desk and standing up. He disappeared quickly into his office to calm down and have a cup of coffee before announcing his decision.

"I'm going," Q said. "I've got an interview to carry out."

He stood up and headed for the exit.

Nina sat where she was, unable to move. She could feel her heartbeat racing and realized that she was sweating all over.

She didn't know that Julia had epilepsy.

She didn't know that Julia had resigned.

I didn't know that Julia was so ill.

The realization came with an audible gasp.

I don't know the first thing about her! I don't know her!

Maybe her Julia didn't exist, the Julia who never put up a fight, who always expected someone else to sort out anything unpleasant, maybe she was gone, or else she had never existed. Her Julia could never have shot David, her Julia couldn't have done the boy any harm, *but what if this was a different Julia, a destructive one?*

Nina forced herself to take some deep breaths.

She looked around the courtroom.

I believe in the system, I know that there is such a thing as justice. This is its very heart!

From that moment she knew exactly what was going to happen.

Once the judge had composed himself and had a second cup of coffee, the doors of the courtroom would be opened again, the media would be allowed in, Julia would be remanded in custody on suspicion of murder, and the case would have to go to court by June 21 at the latest.

There was no question that the preliminary investigation would be completed within a fortnight, which meant that Julia would be remanded in custody again, and again, and again, until the prosecutor had such a watertight case that Julia would never be let out again.

A different Julia, not hers anymore.

Suddenly she felt she couldn't stay in the courtroom another minute, not a single second longer. She stood up and hurried for the exit.

Annika was sitting on a sagging sofa, waiting outside Inspector Q's office on the third floor of Police Headquarters. She leaned her head back and closed her eyes.

For a day that had started so terribly, things hadn't turned out too bad after all.

The children would be able to start back at their old nursery later that week. The manager seemed genuinely pleased that they were coming back, presumably mainly because they would boost the nursery's income.

She had signed Kalle up to go to the Eira School, a bit further away on Kungsholmen, that autumn. Thomas could shoot her if he didn't agree with that.

She had also found a flat. As long as you had money, there were flats to rent even in the center of the city, albeit on business contracts and for absurd sums of money. She had got hold of a three-room apartment on Västerlånggatan, in the heart of Gamla stan itself, for 20,000 kronor per month, on an unlimited contract. A ridiculous amount of money, of course, but she still had three million left from the Dragon's money. Once everything was settled with the insurance company, she'd buy the sort of flat that she really wanted . . .

That *she* really wanted.

She took a deep breath and listened to how it felt.

Alone, without him.

She clenched her jaw to hold back the tears.

My children. Not going to be looked after by someone like you. I'm going to apply for sole custody of them. Not one second longer. I'm going to get them.

She tried to breathe calmly.

She had taken as much maternity leave as she could.

She always stayed at home when they were ill.

She had never neglected them, had always delivered them to the nursery clean and in one piece.

He can't take the children. He's got no case. He'd have to prove that I'm highly unsuitable, otherwise I win.

The detective came walking down the corridor with a mug of coffee in his hand.

"Do you want some?"

Annika shook her head.

"I have to get home to the kids," she said. "So I want to get this over with quickly."

Q unlocked his room and sat down behind the desk. Annika followed him in and sat down on the familiar visitor's chair.

"So, she's been remanded in custody now," Annika said. "I suppose she'll be convicted quick as anything. Unlike David. The cases against him were dropped, after all."

The policeman fumbled with a tape recorder to the left of the computer and said "One two, one two" into a microphone before rewinding to make sure it sounded okay.

"I met the man that David almost beat to death, but there's no need for you to worry. His halo is still firmly in place. No one wants to know what David was really like."

Q leaned toward her.

"This is about the fire in the house on Vinterviksvägen," he said. "Just answer my questions, okay?"

Annika nodded and leaned back in the chair.

He switched the machine on and ran through the usual stuff about the interviewee's name, the time, and location, and then he asked the first question.

"Can you tell me what happened on the night of Thursday, June 3, this year?"

Annika bit her lip.

"Can you switch that off for a moment?" she said.

Q sighed, lowered his head demonstratively for several seconds, then pressed the pause button.

"What?" he said.

"Is it actually suitable that you're conducting this interview with me?"

"Why wouldn't it be?" Q said.

"Won't it be invalid? Because of our special relationship?"

He leaned back slightly and raised his eyebrows.

"Speak for yourself," he said. "I've had special relationships with other reporters, but not with you. Tell me what happened that night."

He turned the machine on again.

She closed her eyes for several seconds, trying to locate the memories she had already had time to file away.

"I was on the upstairs landing," she said. "It was dark. I'd brushed my teeth, even though there was no toothpaste. I was on my way into the bedroom ..."

"Was your husband at home?"

She shook her head.

"No. We'd had a big row earlier that evening. He'd left. Both the children wanted to sleep with me, and I agreed."

"So the children ... ?"

"Were in the double bed in our room."

"What time was it?"

She sighed and thought for a moment.

"I emailed you a draft of an article," she said. "It must have been half an hour after that, forty-five minutes maybe."

The detective rolled over to his computer and opened his email folder.

"It arrived at 0243," he said. "So you were standing on the upstairs landing of your house at quarter past, half past three in the morning, and then what happened?"

She licked her lips.

"There was a crash from downstairs," she said. "Like a window being broken. I went down the stairs, four or five steps, before I realized what had happened."

"And what had happened?"

"Someone had smashed the window. The big picture window right next to the front door. There was glass everywhere. I ran down the stairs, but I couldn't see anyone outside."

"How did you react?"

"At first I was just surprised. Then angry. I wasn't scared until there was another crash from Ellen's room."

"Were you barefoot?"

Annika looked up at Q in surprise.

"Yes," she said, "or rather, I think I was wearing socks."

"Did you cut yourself on the glass?"

She realized what he was getting at and felt the blood rush to her face.

"No," she said, "but I'm not lying."

"Then what happened?"

"The window in Ellen's room smashed as well. I ran back upstairs. The door was open, and I could see the glass was broken. Something came flying through the window—it was dark and rectangular and had a burning tail."

Q was chewing a Biro.

"What do you think it was?"

Annika gulped.

"I realized when it hit the floor and smashed. I just managed to get the door closed before the room burst into flames."

"So the window was already smashed? It didn't get broken by the fire-bomb?"

She looked at him in surprise.

"I hadn't thought of that," she said, "but yes, that's what happened. The glass was already smashed."

"And this is the room at the northeast corner of the house?"

Annika thought for a moment.

"Yes," she said, "that's right. Closest to the junction."

"And then?"

She screwed her eyes shut.

"Kalle's room," she said. "A brick came through the window, breaking the glass, and it landed on the bed. The bottle came a few seconds later, it hit the wall above the bed and shattered instantly."

"What happened when the bottle broke?"

Annika could see the flames in front of her, the way the fire followed the petrol fumes, then the curtains and bookshelf catching light.

"Everything was alight," she said. "There was a smell of petrol and everything was alight."

"And Kalle's room, that's the one facing southeast?"

"That's right."

"Then what did you do?"

She shook her head and scratched her hair.

"I backed away," she said, "because the heat was so intense. I thought of the children and went into the bedroom."

"Did you close the door to Kalle's room?"

Annika stared at Q, wide eyed.

"I don't think I did, actually," she said.

"But you closed Ellen's bedroom door?"

She scratched her head again.

"I think so," she said.

"Why not Kalle's?"

"I don't know. It was so hot. I wanted to get to the children."

"And what did you do when you got to the children?"

"I woke them up and lowered them down onto the terrace using the bottom sheet."

"Both at the same time?"

"No, Kalle first. Then Ellen."

"And what about you?"

"I jumped."

"You jumped."

"And landed on the terrace table. That's when I saw him."

"Who?" Q said.

"Wilhelm Hopkins, our neighbor. He was standing there, hiding in the bushes. I'm absolutely convinced he was the one who started the fire."

Q looked at her, so intently that Annika started to feel her skin itching.

"Are we done, then?" she said.

"What were you doing up so late at night?"

"I've already told you. I'd been up working, then I sent my article to you and the newsroom."

"Yes, at 0243. What were you doing between then and half past three?"

She looked at the detective and felt her throat tighten.

"Mostly sitting and crying," she said in a quiet voice. "We'd had an argument, me and my husband, and I . . . well, I wished we hadn't. I was feeling sorry for myself."

"Because your husband had left you?"

Annika smiled weakly.

"Yes, more or less."

"Any thoughts of revenge?"

"What for?"

"For the fact that he'd left you. Because you were left on your own."

She shook her head.

"No," she said, "not at all."

The detective sighed and picked up some sheets of paper from his desk.

"Do you know what this is?"

She shook her head again.

"A judgment from the district court in Eskilstuna," he said. "Nine years ago you were found guilty of manslaughter and given a probationary sentence."

She was sitting absolutely still, her brain racing. *Where's this going? What next?*

"There's one very interesting witness statement in this report," Q said. "The police officer who was first on the scene after your boyfriend died—do you know what he says you said? Your motive for hitting him so hard that he fell into the blast furnace?"

All of a sudden she was back there again, in the summer heat, in the abandoned foundry in Hälleforsnäs, the dust whirling through the air and Whiskas's dead body in her arms.

"'He shouldn't have attacked my cat. He really shouldn't have done anything to Whiskas. Do you understand?'" Q read out loud.

"Could I have some water?" Annika said.

"You acknowledged revenge as your motive on that occasion when you killed someone," he said. "Now you claim that you had no thoughts of revenge this time?"

"There's quite a different between having your cat killed and being left by your husband, isn't there?" Annika said.

Q looked at her for several long seconds.

"Considerably more people commit murder for the second reason," he said.

Annika felt the room lurch. *What's he saying? What's he doing?*

"It was Hopkins," Annika said. "Hopkins set fire to the house."

"Hopkins was the one who called the fire brigade," Q said.

"He must have been feeling guilty."

Silence descended.

"What?" Annika said eventually. "What is it?"

"Because we have no witnesses and no forensic evidence, there are no obvious grounds for suspicion and therefore no reason to hold you. You're free to go."

Annika sat there staring at Q.

"Free to go?" she said. "Why wouldn't I be free to go? What would have happened to my children if I wasn't free to go?"

Q leaned forward toward her and looked genuinely troubled.

"There is an ongoing preliminary investigation into arson and possibly also attempted murder, but the prosecutor hasn't yet made a decision about that. These are crimes that can carry a lifetime sentence in prison. Someone started that fire, and you were there. Do you understand what I'm saying?"

Annika almost burst out laughing.

"Are you mad? Am I a suspect? Am I the only suspect? Are you telling me that I'm officially suspected of committing these crimes? *Is that what you're saying?*"

Q sighed.

"Not officially, not at the moment. But the fire was started by someone who had a reason to start it. You're at the top of the list of informal suspects."

Annika looked out of the window; it had started to rain again.

I'm going to apply for sole custody. I'm going to get them. My children. Not going to be looked after by someone like you. Not one second longer.

"Nothing will happen until the investigating officers have received all the forensic results," Q went on. "That could take a while, I'm afraid. Then, when we know more, there'll be three alternatives: Either you will be charged, or cleared of all charges, or else the case will be dropped through lack of evidence. In this third instance there would still be concerns about you, but not enough to send you for trial."

"I didn't do it," Annika said. "It wasn't me."

"Do you know," Q said, getting up, "almost everyone says that."

PART 2

November

JULIA LINDHOLM CHARGED WITH DOUBLE MURDER
PROSECUTOR SEEKS LIFE SENTENCE

Updated Nov. 15, 0954.

The case of the murder of Police Superintendent David Lindholm is approaching its conclusion.

Yesterday Lindholm's wife Julia was charged with two counts of murder and aggravated kidnapping at Stockholm City Court.

According to Prosecutor Angela Nilsson, Julia Lindholm shot and killed her husband on the morning of June 3 this year. During the days immediately before that, she also kidnapped, murdered, and hid the body of their son, Alexander, 4.

The findings of the criminal psychiatrist are partially confidential, but the published sections indicate that Julia Lindholm suffers from a psychiatric disorder. This is not severe enough, however, to suggest that she should be sentenced to a secure hospital.

"Considering the brutality of the crime and the vulnerability of the victims, the only suitable sentence is lifetime imprisonment," Angela Nilsson has told eveningpost.se.

The investigation has been protracted as a result of the psychiatric examination, as well as the amount of work required from the National Forensics Laboratory.

One source indicated that the investigating officers have been waiting for Julia Lindholm to confess where she hid Alexander's remains.

"These days it is possible to try someone for murder even if no body has been found," says Professor of Criminology Hampus Lagerbäck to eveningpost.se. "The Thomas Quick case proved that."

Julia Lindholm's counsel, lawyer Mats Lennström, questioned the decision to go to trial.

"As far as the murder of Alexander is concerned, there are no witnesses, no explanation as to what happened, no forensic evidence. I will be asking for that part of the charges to be dropped."

The court case is due to start next Monday, November 22, at 1000 in the high-security courtroom of Stockholm City Courthouse.

The rain had turned into sharp and biting snow, the first of the winter. The flakes dissolved the moment they hit the tarmac, gathering in gray-brown pools of depression.

Nina pulled her zip all the way up to her chin and stuffed her hands into the pockets of her jacket.

There'll be a lot of road accidents today if this keeps up.

She looked at her watch without taking her hand out of her pocket. Her shift wasn't due to start until 1600.

Plenty of time.

She realized her teeth were chattering. *It's only the cold, nothing else.*

Bergsgatan ran uphill all the way from Scheelegatan to Kronoberg Park. The entrance to Police Headquarters at number 52 lay about halfway up the hill. She shouldn't be out of breath after such a short amount of physical exertion.

The wind's against me, and I'm probably a bit tense as well.

She hadn't spoken to Julia since the awful meeting up in her cell some six months before. After she was officially remanded in custody the restrictions had been watertight, but through Holger she had learned that Julia had spent almost the whole time either in psychiatric care or in the hospital wing of the prison. Not one single visit had been authorized, neither for her parents nor for anyone else.

"Are they trying to make an example of her?" Holger had asked.

"I don't know," she had replied. "Maybe."

But now the restrictions had been lifted because the charges had been laid, the court case was imminent, and the preliminary investigation had been made public. Only the presentence psychiatric evaluation was still confidential, but she had seen that thanks to Holger.

"I'm here to see Julia Lindholm," she said in reception to the same guard as before. He pursed his lips and disappeared into the back office, leaving her to sweat.

A female guard, a different one this time, led her through the remote-controled lifts and shiny corridors to an ordinary visiting room on the sixth floor, right next to the women's section. There were no windows, just a table, two chairs, and a tinfoil ashtray.

"If you wait here, we'll be back shortly with the prisoner," the guard said, closing the door.

Nina sat down on one of the chairs.

The room was cool, and it felt damp and smelled of smoke.

Only cigarette smoke, nothing else.

Gray-white walls loomed toward her. A low-energy lamp spread a weak and slightly flickering light from the ceiling. She knitted her fingers in her lap.

Julia has been here for five and a half months. Surely I can handle four minutes, seeing as I'm mentally well.

The paragraph seven investigation into Julia's mental health had proved that she was in a very bad state after the murder. It took an extensive criminal psychiatric investigation to come up with a diagnosis. The examination had been conducted during August by the National Board of Forensic Medicine in Stockholm.

I wonder how Holger got hold of it. Probably through the lawyer...

The door opened, and the light from a window further down the corridor turned the figure in the doorway into a faceless shadow.

Nina stood up.

Julia came into the visiting room, her eyes moist and her hair in a ponytail. She looked older, yet simultaneously younger. No makeup, angular shoulders.

"Nina," she said in surprise. "What are you doing here?"

Nina looked over at the warder who had stopped in the doorway.

"Thanks very much. I'll ring when we're finished."

The woman closed and locked the door.

"Julia," Nina said, going over and hugging her friend. "It's good to see you."

Julia kept her arms down by her sides.

"Why are you here?"

"The preliminary investigation," Nina said, taking a step back. "It's been made public, so now I can finally come and visit you. How are you?"

Julia turned round, went over to the wall by the table and felt the rough surface with her fingertips.

"This is solid concrete," she said. "Every room in the prison is a separate concrete module, making each one its own fireproof cell."

She went on to the next wall, letting her finger trace a crack in the surface.

"This building's been here since 1975, but there's been a prison in Stockholm since 1252. It must have been founded by Birger Jarl, I suppose."

She glanced quickly at Nina, then concentrated on the wall again.

"The whole of the Kronoberg block covers 161,000 square meters of space; the latest extension was finished in 2005."

She turned toward Nina.

"When this is all over, I'm thinking of applying to the College of Architecture. I'm unlikely to go back to being a police officer, after all."

She smiled, a short, fleeting smile.

Nina caught her gaze.

Yes, she's in there. The lights are on and she's at home.

She smiled back, relieved.

"Maybe that's just as well," Nina said. "Doing something different."

"But you're still there?"

Julia sat down beside the table, picking up the tinfoil ashtray and inspecting its underside.

"Yes," Nina said. "My shift starts this afternoon, handover at four. There'll be a lot of single-vehicle RTAs if the weather doesn't change."

"Pettersson in charge?"

"Pelle Sisulu," Nina said. "How are you feeling?"

Julia shrugged and looked down into the ashtray.

"It'll be so good to get out. The flat's still there, Dad's been taking care of the rent . . ."

Nina felt a sense of unease creeping up her back once more.

"So you think you're going to be found not guilty?"

Julia looked up and let go of the ashtray.

"Of course I do," she said. "If there's one thing we learned at Police Academy, it's that the criminal justice system works. I understand that they've had to keep me locked up while the investigation was being carried out, and to be honest I think it's probably just as well seeing as she hasn't been caught. Otherwise she'll just come back and shoot me too."

Nina felt her heart sink.

"So you think they'll let you go home after the trial?"

Julia blinked with her big, blue eyes.

"Where else would I go?"

Nina pulled her chair closer to the table, leaned forward and took one of Julia's hands in hers.

"Julia," she said, "has your lawyer been to see you? Has he been through the preliminary investigation with you?"

Julia shook her head, eyes wide open.

What a useless defense counsel! It's a dereliction of duty for him not to have informed her about the charges.

"The investigation showed that you were suffering from a dissociative identity disorder," Nina said. "Do you know what that is?"

Julia was staring at her uncomprehendingly.

"It's also called multiple personality disorder. It's a psychiatric condition where a person has two or more separate personalities."

"Schizophrenia?" Julia said skeptically.

"A split personality," Nina said. "It's a form of psychotic condition, where there are several different personalities that can act independently of each other. It can occur when the mind is trying to deal with a trauma. If necessary, a different personality takes over."

"That's not what happened," Julia said. "It wasn't me. It was the other woman, the evil one."

Nina nodded and squeezed Julia's hand.

"It's okay," she said. "I understand."

"No!" she said, pulling her hand away. "You don't understand at all. She was there, and she took Alexander away with her."

"Where do you think she took Alexander?"

"How could I possibly know that? If I knew that, I would have gone and got him!"

Nina forced herself to sound calm and collected.

"The blood on the hall floor," she said. "DNA tests have proved that it was Alexander's."

Julia stood up and stared at Nina.

"You don't believe me?" she said. "You think I hurt Alexander? That *I* was the one who fired those shots?"

Nina stood up as well.

"I don't think you should count on being released," she said. "The evidence is pretty solid. You were there, you were mentally unstable, your service pistol was used as the murder weapon, with your fingerprints on it . . ."

Julia turned away and rang the bell to be let out of the visiting room.

"If I'm so mentally unstable," she said, "then they'll sentence me to psychiatric care and I'll be out in a year."

"I don't think you can count on that either," Nina said. "The criminal psychiatric investigation suggests that you committed the crime under a temporary episode of mental confusion, but that you can still be sentenced to prison."

Julia stared at her, her eyes so blue and radiant in the flickering lamplight that Nina felt ashamed.

"I'll come and see you again," she said. "I'm not going to distance myself from you, no matter what you've done."

The door opened and Julia turned away and walked off down the corridor without looking back.

The preliminary investigation was a disappointment, actually something of an anticlimax.

Annika, Berit Hamrin, and Patrik Nilsson were sitting at the crime desk, each reading a copy of the report, getting more and more frustrated. The newsroom was quiet at this time of the afternoon; people had finally learned that there were live broadcasts going on the whole time and had stopped shouting across the room at each other the way they used to. All the television sets had their sound turned down and you could only listen to the radio through headphones.

"How are we going to divide this up, then?" Berit asked.

"I can take Q," Patrik said quickly.

Annika hadn't spoken to the detective since July. In the back of her head there was always a fear that he would call, or that there'd be a knock at the door and someone would say: "You are under formal suspicion . . ." She had no idea how the investigation into the fire was going, and she didn't want to know either, until it was either dropped or she was cleared.

"Go ahead and call. I've got no problem with that," Annika said, trying to maintain a neutral expression.

"Why would you have a problem with me talking to Q?" Patrik wondered.

"It's a good idea for you to talk to the police," Berit said. "I can snout about the National Board of Forensic Medicine and see if I can find out anything about the psychiatric examination."

"I can talk to the defense lawyer and try to get an interview," Annika said.

Patrik snorted.

"Good luck with that," he said, and Annika could feel herself getting angry.

"Then we've got the victim," Berit said. "Admittedly, we wrote a lot about David Lindholm back in the summer, but it's probably time to update things . . ."

"I can do that," Patrik said.

Annika put her pen down.

"Can I interrupt for a moment?"

All three of them looked up. Eva-Britt Qvist was looking at them expectantly.

"Our savior from the newspaper dragon," Patrik said. "What can we do for you today?"

"There's a general meeting tomorrow at two o'clock, at the day reporters' desk. Everyone has to be there. *It's about all our futures.*"

She swept on through the newsroom.

"What are we going to do with the trial?" Berit said, taking off her glasses and looking at her colleagues.

"I've got the children," Annika said quickly.

She had recently endured a week of the Nobel murders in the high-security courtroom. The verdict had only been delivered the previous week: life for the perpetrator. She had no desire to sit through another three days of judicial formalities that wouldn't give them anything new.

"I can take the expert analysis," Patrik said.

"I'm sure you can," Berit said, "but wasn't Sjölander going to organize that? What do you say about news updates for the website?"

Patrik grunted something to the effect that political editors ought to stick to politics.

"If you take the summary of the news for the print edition, I can do the background and fact boxes," Annika said to Berit.

"Are you lot having a coffee morning, or what?" Spike said, dropping a printout on Berit's desk.

"What's that?" Patrik said, snatching the paper instantly.

"The cop killer's free," Spike said. "Viktor Gabrielsson's on a plane on his way back to Arlanda. The Foreign Ministry finally managed to get him out. I never thought they would."

"Bloody hell," Patrik said, standing up, his cheeks ablaze. "Do we know when he's due to land?"

The small-time Swedish gangster Viktor Gabrielsson had been an intermittently recurring story in the media for the past ten years, sentenced on dubious evidence for being an accessory to the murder of a police officer outside New York. He had served eighteen years of his fifty-year sentence, but had always fought for the right to serve his sentence in Sweden.

"Goodness, what a lot of cop killers we're going to have in tomorrow's paper," Annika said. "How on earth are we going to stop them getting mixed up?"

"There's a hell of a difference," Patrik said. "One case was in the US, the other in Sweden."

"The plane took off from Logan in Boston five hours ago," Spike said.

"Okay, we'll get going at once," Patrik said, peering over to the picture desk.

"What about the coverage of David Lindholm, then?" Annika asked innocently.

"You can deal with that, can't you?" Patrik said generously, pulling on his coat as he made hand gestures toward the picture desk across the newsroom.

Everything was quiet around them once Patrik had rushed out. Berit and Annika looked at each other during an uncomfortable silence.

"Don't be too hard on him," Berit eventually said. "He's just young and enthusiastic."

"Really?" Annika said. "He's a year older than me."

Berit laughed.

"Well, maybe he just seems more childish," she said. "Do you want to take over the stuff on David?"

Annika smiled wryly.

"To be honest, I think David's more interesting than Viktor Gabrielsson, but I've already tried to get his murky past into the paper and hit a brick wall. Do you think Julia Lindholm might be innocent?"

Berit looked up at her over her glasses with a look of surprise.

"Not a chance," she said. "Not even the tiniest chance."

Annika dropped her feet to the floor, picked up her bag, and headed off to the day shift's desk. She unpacked her secondhand laptop and logged in to the network. She sat there for a moment looking out across the newsroom.

Eva-Britt Qvist had installed herself in Anders Schyman's glass-walled office, and was talking and gesticulating. She did that most of the time these days. Schyman was leaning back in his chair, looking tired and harassed. He did that most of the time these days as well, actually.

After the summer holidays the management of the paper had announced that there would have to be serious cutbacks across the business, but mainly on the editorial side. The message had detonated like a bomb and caused several days of panic among the journalists. The editor in chief, oddly enough, had done nothing to calm people's nerves. He had allowed the union and the gossips to run on until the whole newsroom was in chaos. Eva-Britt Qvist had burst into tears in one union meeting that she was actually chairing, not because she was under threat, of course—as union representative she was the only one whose position was utterly safe—but because she was *thinking about the collective.*

Eventually Spike had had enough and roared that if people didn't get a grip and come up with a few headlines, they might as well shut down the whole fucking paper straightaway instead of doing it the slow way with a series of cutbacks. Then the reporters, editors, photographers, and web managers had reluctantly, but almost with a sense of relief, made their way back to their desks and got to work on their computers again.

"A fuck of a lot of fuss just because some of us get to take things easy in the future," Spike had said, putting his feet up on his desk as he took a bite of a supersized capricciosa pizza.

"You've given up the diet?" Annika had asked, only to receive a greasy middle finger in reply.

Once the atmosphere in the newsroom had stabilized, it was simultaneously more nervous and more focused. People were more alert, which was something that Annika had nothing against.

Less chat and more work.

She was utterly immune to communal social events like boules tournaments and organized after-work drinks and joint celebrations whenever someone reached a significant birthday, and any other sort of supposedly jolly activity with her colleagues.

Now all that sort of nonsense seemed to have ground to a halt.

Excellent! Just let me get on with my job.

For the first time in several years, she had also had the chance to work full time throughout the autumn, at least during the weeks when Thomas had the children. She had filled the feeling of emptiness in her chest with a series of articles about the gradual dismantling of social services provided by local councils, as well as an overview of discrimination cases in the Swedish Labor Court.

"You should be fucking grateful for the chaos here in the newsroom," Spike had said on the day she turned up with her article about the nine cases in which the Labor Court had decreed that it was okay for women to be paid less than men in the same job, because they had a lower value on the employment market.

"Believe me," Annika said, "I am."

Without the paralysis that the others were displaying, she would never have got a piece like that in the paper, but when the alternative was empty pages even articles with a feminist angle could get in.

No, Annika had nothing against things being stirred up a bit.

If they sacked her, then they sacked her, but Annika didn't think that was very likely. She had been employed on the paper for almost ten years and ought to survive if they decided to rationalize in accordance with employment legislation. This law about employment protection, so cherished by the unions, was based upon the premise of last-in first-out.

If Schyman was allowed to choose personally who he got rid of, she'd be okay too. If that wasn't the case, she would have been history long ago.

But on the other hand, a group of young hotshots, with Patrik Nilsson in the vanguard, had suddenly realized that they were in the danger zone and had therefore shifted into *indispensable* mode. Their ruthless ambition wasn't making them indispensable, it was making them unbearable.

The only drawback of the cuts.

She sighed and logged into the phonebook. She was looking for Julia's legal representative, the lawyer Mats Lennström, from the Kvarnstenen legal practice. The number was engaged eight times in a row (every reporter in the country must have come to the same brilliant idea of interviewing him as she had), then she got through to a secretary who told her that the lawyer was in court and wasn't expected back in the office until the following morning.

So much for that story.

She spun on her chair, irritated that Patrik would be proved right.

Instead she went into the newspaper's archive and pulled out the articles that had been written about David Lindholm around the time of his death.

There, once again, were all the heroic deeds, the eulogies from Christer Bure and Hampus Lagerbäck at the Police Academy. She tried calling them both, at Stockholm Police and the Academy respectively, and left messages saying she was trying to get in touch.

Then she looked through the amazing contributions the policeman had made to society. The hostage crisis in Malmö, solving the raid on the security van . . .

But that was it.

That can't be all? Where are all the heroic deeds?

She repeated the search, broadening the terms of inquiry:

david lindholm achievement* criminal* *search.*

Loads of hits, but no new heroic deeds. But she did find an old article about police officers working undercover. David Lindholm was mentioned at the end of the piece. He was named as an example of an officer who had extensive contacts in the underworld, who had acted as a handler to people wanting to change sides, and had acted as a link between different worlds.

She pushed the computer away from her, deep in thought.

Timmo Koivisto had claimed that David Lindholm worked for the drugs mafia.

Could that really be true? Was there any other explanation as to why he had been attacked?

How well did David Lindholm manage to maintain the balance between right and wrong? And what did the criminal world think of his double-dealing?

She checked the archive again to see what had happened to the hostage taker in Malmö.

After several false starts she found a piece in *Sydsvenska Dagbladet* about what had happened to him, saying that the Appeal Court had upheld the verdict of the City Court.

The man had been sentenced to life imprisonment for attempted murder, aggravated kidnapping, aggravated extortion, and threatening behavior.

Life? Wow! I wonder if he was such good friends with David Lindholm after that?

She called Malmö City Court and asked them to send her a copy of the verdict.

Then she searched for information about the American who had spilled the beans about the raid in Botkyrka, but found nothing.

She rested her chin on her hand and stared at the screen.

How come the information about the American had ever got out? If someone in the criminal underworld talked, then didn't you usually plaster it all over every possible media?

This is bloody weird.

Why did David Lindholm reveal that he had received information about the raid on the security van from that particular prisoner? Was it even true? And if it was, was it really David who had made it public?

And what happened to the American afterward?

She didn't even know what his name was.

She went into the website of the National Correctional Organization and found the phone number of Tidaholm Prison. She got through to a receptionist, and asked to speak to the press spokesman at Tidaholm, and was put through to the main office.

"Our press spokesman has finished for the day," the warder said.

"Oh, that's a shame," Annika said. "That'll probably mean we get it wrong in tomorrow's paper again."

"Er, what?" the warder said.

"That American bloke who was serving a life sentence with you, the one who was friendly with David Lindholm, you know the one. We're running an article about him tomorrow and I just felt that I ought to check with you that our facts are correct, because they seem pretty weird to me . . ."

"But he's not here now," the warder said.

"The press spokesman?"

"No, the American."

Annika waited a couple of seconds, letting the information sink in.

"There, you see! I knew it. The journalist who wrote the article got it wrong. He wrote that the bloke was still in Tidaholm with you."

"No chance. He got transferred right after the accident."

Accident?

"Of course!" Annika said. "And naturally he never came back?"

"I'm not so sure about 'friendly' either," the warder said. "David Lindholm was his trustee. There's quite a difference."

"Trustee," Annika said, noting that down. "Right."

"What's this article about?" the warder said, beginning to sound suspicious.

"It's part of a series about life sentences," Annika said, "but I think I'm going to have to put it on hold; the facts need to be checked properly. Where's the American now?"

She closed her eyes and held her breath.

"You'll have to call our press spokesman tomorrow," the warder said, and hung up.

Oh well, better than nothing!

Something happened to the American, and he was transferred.

I wonder how happy he feels about it all now?

David Lindholm needed to be investigated, as closely as possible. Every little stone he left behind him would have to be turned over.

She looked at the time, she had to get something to eat first.

She pulled on her jacket and went out.

Thomas was sitting at his desk on the fourth floor of the government building at Rosenbad, looking down onto Fredsgatan. It was snowing, and the flakes were being blown onto the window, where they slid jerkily down toward the sill. He could see people hurrying along the pavement, all hunched up with upturned collars, squinting through the snow.

The view really wasn't anything special.

He sighed and looked at the time, then checked again that the memo and outline were in the folder where they should be.

The task of evaluating the cost implications of abolishing lifetime sentencing had been more complicated than he had imagined at first. Not that the calculations themselves were particularly difficult, but because of the political aspects of the inquiry . . .

The intercom buzzed, making him jump.

"Thomas, where the hell are you? I'm sitting here waiting like some old maid."

What do you think I'm doing, then?

He straightened up and pressed the button to reply to his boss.

"I thought you were going to let me know when you were free."

"Free, I'm never free. Come over now."

Thomas stood up, pulled the hem of his jacket down, made sure the top button of his shirt was done up. With the folder in his hand, he headed out into the corridor and off toward Per Cramne's room.

"So tell me what's bothering you most, then," the assistant undersecretary said, gesturing toward a chair as he rolled up the sleeves of his white shirt.

"It's turned out to be slightly problematic," Thomas said, scraping the chair on the floor as he pulled it out. "I don't know that it's possible to abolish life sentences under the remit we've been given."

"Of course it is," Cramne said, walking round the room and stretching his arms. "Nothing lasts a lifetime anymore. Why should prison sentences?"

Thomas sat up and put the folder on the desk in front of him.

This isn't going to be easy.

"I'm thinking specifically about the frame of the inquiry," he said, crossing one leg over the other.

Cramne stopped with his back to the room, looking out over the water of Riddarfjärden.

"I mean, we can forget marriage," he said. "If that lasts a lifetime, then I've lived three lives—so far, I should add . . ."

He doesn't want to listen.

"Are you thinking of getting married again?" Thomas asked, moving the folder slightly.

Cramne sighed, turned round, and sat down in his chair.

"Employment is another one we can take off the lifetime list. No one has the same job from cradle to grave anymore. Nowadays people don't just switch employer, they switch career several times during their working lives."

Thomas nodded and felt in his pocket for a pen.

"We also swap our friends along the way," the assistant undersecretary said. "We can choose not to have anything to do with our siblings . . ."

"Children," Thomas interrupted, looking up, pen at the ready.

"What?" Cramne said.

"They're for life," Thomas said. "You can't escape being a parent."

Cramne snatched at the memorandum.

"Shall we stop wasting taxpayers' money and do some work?"

Thomas coughed.

"The directives," he said, picking up the document as well. "They clearly specify that the cost of the criminal justice system mustn't increase if life sentences are abolished. But my calculations indicate that the costs will rocket if this is pushed through."

"Be more specific," the head of section said, leaning back in his chair.

"You know the background, of course. The longest fixed term we currently have is ten years. Prisoners sentenced to life get an average of twenty years and six months, in terms of the actual sentence. Because they get out after serving two-thirds of the sentence, that means they're out in fourteen years, more or less. If we abolish life sentences, the new maximum term for murder would be something between twenty-one and twenty-five years, probably closer to the latter, meaning that there'd be a difference of up to fifteen years between the highest and next-highest penalty. That doesn't make sense, which opens the way for all sentences to be adjusted upward as a result. And the current option of imposing tougher sentences would also be exploited more often . . ."

"This is just speculation on your part," Cramne said.

Thomas took a deep breath.

"Not at all," he said. "I've discussed this with three professors of criminal justice, five researchers at the Council for Crime Prevention, and with the political group, of course . . ."

"And what do they say?"

"Within three years every level of sentencing would have increased so that we had a plethora of penalties attracting sentences of twelve, thirteen years . . . Experience in other countries shows that sentences rise across the board when lifetime sentences are abolished in favor of lengthy statutory penalties. The next time we come to sentence a multiple rapist, he'd get eighteen years."

"And?" the section head said. "You're a civil servant. What you're doing now is making political judgments, and you're not supposed to do that."

The man's voice was as silky as ever, but his words had an edge that wasn't usually there.

"These aren't political judgments," Thomas said, "they're realistic. My task was to evaluate the cost implications of a specific legislative change, and that's exactly what I've done. If we abolish life sentences, all other sentences will increase, and it will happen within three years, and that would mean a 30 percent increase in the cost of the prison system according to the most cautious estimates . . ."

Cramne stood up, walked round his desk and went over to the closed door. Thomas looked at him in surprise, noting that his face seemed slightly swollen, his eyes a little red.

Is he drinking too much?

"It's like this," Cramne said, sitting on his desk close to Thomas. "Criminals have been shown a hell of a lot of consideration throughout the time this minister has been in office. The sentencing guidelines need to be adjusted upward, the whole criminal justice system demands it, but the politicians are putting the brakes on. The minister even wants to abolish certain crimes."

"Such as?"

Per Cramne stood up again, held his hand out, and went back to his chair.

"Treason," he said, catching the blank look on Thomas's face. "Throwing pies at the king, although perhaps that's a bad example."

He sat down with a sigh.

"Sentencing guidelines are the only thing this government has left to deal with. They've thrashed their way through all the other big issues, including the whole wretched question of bugging, but they've always shied away from this. How much more bloody obvious do I have to be?"

He leaned over the desk and laid his hairy hands on Thomas's folder.

"The directive about this not costing any more money is a restriction imposed by them. You have to find a way of getting round that. We have to make sure that this gets through. We have to be able to lock criminals up, and there has to be an end to all this kid-gloves treatment."

Thomas stared at his boss.

He wants me to falsify the calculations in a parliamentary inquiry so that he can push through a policy that has no democratic basis.

With his eyes firmly fixed on the other man's, he nodded slowly.

"Okay," he said. "I understand what you mean. Thank you for making it so clear."

Per Cramne's face cracked into a broad smile.

"Excellent," he said. "I look forward to seeing your new cost evaluations. What the hell, consider them cost proposals!"

Thomas gathered his papers, stood up, opened the door, and floated out into the corridor without quite touching the ground.

Two other reporters were sitting there tapping away on their laptops when Annika returned to the day shift's desk. One of them had put a mug of coffee on her folded laptop.

"Excuse me," Annika said, pointing at the half-empty mug, "but I need to do some work."

The reporter, a young temp called Ronja, of all the ridiculous fashionable names, looked up and moved her mug demonstratively so that it was no longer on top of Annika's computer, but half a centimeter away from it.

The other reporter, Emil Oscasson, was one of the blokes who had found an extra gear in order to cling onto his job. He looked up for a moment, then stared back at his screen again.

Annika leaned over, knocking the mug so that the contents spilled onto Ronja's notes.

"Whoops," Annika said, sitting down and switching her laptop on.

"What the hell are you doing?" the temp said, jumping up as the coffee dripped onto her trousers.

Annika logged into the national database and pretended not to hear her.

"You, what did you spill my coffee for?"

Annika looked up at Ronja in surprise.

"Well, go and dry yourself off, for heaven's sake," she said.

She could see that the girl was on the verge of tears.

Bloody crybaby. If you fuck with me, I'll fuck you right back.

"You're crazy," the crybaby said as she headed off toward the bathroom.

Emil was hammering away at his computer, pretending he hadn't noticed.

Are all their generation named after characters in Astrid Lindgren books?
Oh well, she was called Annika, so she could hardly talk.

She went into the national ID database and typed in David Lindholm, male, the postcode for Bondegatan, and there he was.

Personal information, "THE PERSON IN QUESTION IS DECEASED."

But the Swedish state didn't let go of its citizens just because they had died. Here were all of David Lindholm's personal details, his ID number, full name (Lindholm, David Zeev Samuel), his registered address on Bondegatan, the date he was registered, county, local council, parish, and then the information: *Deceased*, June 3 that year.

He must have been Jewish. Zeev isn't a common Swedish name. Named after Zeev Jabotinsky, the Jewish activist?

She clicked to get his personal report. When the image appeared on the screen, David's ID number was already included in the menu.

This isn't a game anymore.

She clicked *Select all* and, two seconds later, was rewarded with all the information available about David, financial records including repayment defaults, debts, tax information, details of any bankruptcies, official roles in registered companies, self-employment records, the registration number of his own company, any restrictions, and what vehicles he owned.

"You really ought to pay to get my jeans dry-cleaned," Ronja said, gathering her things in a lovely little briefcase.

The cutbacks start to be implemented in December. She'll be history in a few weeks' time.

Annika smiled at the temp.

"I usually put mine in the washing machine. But perhaps you haven't got one of those?"

"Well, at least I haven't set fire to it," the girl said, and marched out of the newsroom.

Annika glanced quickly at Emil. His face hadn't moved a muscle.

She stared at the screen in front of her and had to hold onto the table to stop herself falling through the floor.

At least I haven't set fire to it.

That was no coincidence, and Ronja was hardly Einstein. If she knew, then everyone on the paper was aware of the police's hypothesis.

Is that what they all think? Is that what they're whispering? That I set fire to my own house? Tried to kill my own children?

She stared at the computer screen for another long minute before she pulled herself together and scrolled down to read further.

She leaned forward and suppressed the falling sensation.

There!

David Lindholm had had ambitions as a private businessman.

He had been on the boards of four different companies, two of which had been delisted, and a third was about to be declared bankrupt.

She printed out the information and pondered what to do next.

It would probably make sense to get to the bottom of all the information from the start, dealing with things as they came up.

She fetched a cup of coffee from the machine, walked back via the printer and picked up the list, then went back to her laptop again.

The first business on the list was a trading company that had been deregistered fifteen years ago, Fly High Equipment HB, and David was listed as a board member.

She didn't know they kept a record of such old information.

Okay, time to get going!

She went into the database of registered companies and clicked through to the page identifying the nature of the business. Trading in parachute equipment and accessories and conducting associated activities, it said.

So flying high was a literal description of what they did. David Lindholm must have been an active parachutist in his youth, because why else would he own a company selling the equipment?

She clicked to see who the board members were, and who had been its registered signatories. The computer thought for a moment, and from the corner of her eye she saw Emil packing up his laptop and getting ready to leave.

"See you tomorrow," he said, and she nodded to him.

David had been a registered signatory of Fly High Equipment together with two other men, Algot Heinrich Heimer and Christer Erik Bure.

Bure, again. They must have been really good friends.

She went back to the national database and ran a couple of complementary searches.

Christer Bure lived on Södermalm, on Åsögatan.

She checked his details as well.

No debts, no bankruptcies, no links to any companies except Flying High Equipment.

She looked up the second man.

Aha!

Algot Heinrich Heimer was dead.

She checked the date.

February 9, the previous year.

Young, only forty-five, registered in Norrköping.

She bit her lip.

Forty-five-year-old men don't die just like that. Maybe he had a bit of help?

She opened another window, went into the archive of articles, and looked up Algot Heimer.

No results.

She tried "dead *or* murder *or* murdered," February 9 and 10, the previous year.

Site found, *wait ...*

Bingo!

A forty-five-year-old man was shot dead in a car park outside a shopping center in Norrköping during the evening of February 9.

Could that have been Algot Heinrich Heimer? How high could the odds be?

She quickly opened the homepage of the Office of National Statistics, and saw from the population statistics that approximately 91,000 people had died last year. Something like 250 per day, and how many of them would have been forty-five-year-old men living in Norrköping?

Not many.

"Is anyone sitting here?"

One of the evening reporters, a young girl, had stopped by the chair where Emil had been sitting. What was her name? Pippi, maybe?

Annika shook her head and the girl sighed.

"Why can't people tidy up after them?" she said, sweeping Emil's empty crisp packet, empty plastic cup, and crumpled notes into the wastepaper bin. "How do they expect anyone to work if you have to . . ."

"Sorry," Annika said, "but I'm trying to work."

The girl fell silent abruptly and sullenly.

Annika called the Norrköping Police and asked to speak to the press officer responsible for the crime unit. She was put through to a mobile phone and ended up talking to a woman who was picking her child up from nursery.

"Algot Heinrich Heimer?" she said. "No, we never arrested anyone for that murder; it's still an open case for us."

So it really was him!

"What happened?" Annika asked, as she heard a small child crying in the background.

"He was shot in the back of the head as he was walking across the car park carrying a crate of beer. He was alone in a fairly poorly lit car park, the murder weapon probably had a silencer, no one heard anything, and no one saw anything."

"No tire tracks?" Annika wondered.

The child in the background sounded like it was out of control.

"Yes," the woman said, sounding exhausted. "About one and a half thousand. It's a big car park."

Annika thanked her and hung up.

She printed out Heimer's personal details and the article about the death in the car park. She leaned back in her chair, finished her coffee, and looked at the time.

Five to five.

Thomas would be picking up Kalle from his after-school club now, then going to get Ellen from the nursery on Scheelegatan.

She felt a burning sensation in her chest, the searing pain of inadequacy and envy.

I'll never get away from him, as long as I live.

The girl unpacked her laptop from a big rucksack, then unfolded a napkin and put an apple and a banana on it, then took out a china mug, a thermos flask, and poured out what smelled like stewed herbal tea.

Annika went back to the national database and looked up the next company in David Lindholm's records, a limited company that had gone bankrupt.

Pettersson Catering & Arrangement AB, listed as providing restaurant and catering services; the sale, import, and export of foodstuffs; hiring restaurant and serving staff; trading in horses and confidential documents and associated activities.

Trading in horses?

Yes, that's what it said.

The details of board members and registered signatories contained a long list of names, ten in total. David Zeev Samuel Lindholm was a deputy member, two from the bottom.

Annika checked through them one by one. Apart from David, they were all still alive, and they all lived somewhere in the Mälar Valley, not far from Stockholm. The chairman of the board and managing director of the bankrupt company had been a Bertil Oskar Holmberg, registered as living in Nacka, just outside Stockholm.

She did a search for his personal details.

Bloody hell!

The man was linked to fifteen different businesses, some delisted, some bankrupt, and some still active. Among the latter were a solarium, a consultancy firm, a travel agency, and a property company. He had eight notices for bad payment, and owed the enforcement office a total of 509,439 kronor.

Is someone like that actually allowed to run a company?

Apparently so, seeing as there were no restrictions listed.

The young reporter was now typing very slowly and deliberately on her computer on the other side of the desk. Annika concentrated on ignoring her. She printed out all the information about Bertil Oskar Holmberg and looked through the names of the board members in the other companies. There was no one who rang any bells.

Why so many? And why this business in particular? Why was David a deputy board member there? There had to be a reason: that he stood to profit by it, or was doing someone else a favor by being there . . .

Her mobile rang and she let go of the laptop and dived into her bag. She just managed to answer before voicemail took the call.

It was Thomas

"Where are Ellen's winter clothes? How the hell am I supposed to look after the children if you don't let me have their things?"

Annika clenched her teeth to stop herself screaming.

Mondays was when they swapped the children. They looked after Kalle and Ellen for the rest of the week, dropping them off and picking them up from nursery and after-school club, and then had the weekend to wind down with the children. Then they would leave them at nursery and school on Monday morning, and the other one would pick them up in the afternoon. That way they didn't have to see each other.

"I didn't send any winter clothes," Annika said, "because Ellen doesn't have any. They went up in the fire. You'll have to go and get her some new ones, and a pair of decent winter shoes.

"*I'll* have to? You're the one who gets the child support!"

Annika shut her eyes and leaned her head on her hand.

Dear God, give me strength!

"You're the one who says he wants sole custody of the children, so you can show a bit of bloody initiative for once, just this once . . ."

She ended the call with her heartbeat hammering in her ears.

God, how I hate him!

Thomas was pursuing a case for sole custody of Kalle and Ellen through the courts. He opposed any form of adequate visitation rights between her and the children, but had agreed to supervised visits every other weekend.

That's only so he can have a free babysitter so he can go to the pub with his wretched fuckbunny.

Thomas was claiming that Annika's violent and criminal past made her entirely unsuitable to have custody, and that the suspicion that she had set fire to the home they shared meant that she was a direct threat to the children.

The initial custody hearing had taken place in July, on one of the hottest days of the year, and it had been a truly unpleasant experience. Thomas had been aggressive and arrogant and had boasted about his lovely job in the Justice Ministry to the point where even his legal counsel had looked embarrassed. Annika's lawyer, a woman called Sandra Norén, had laid her hand on her arm for a brief moment and flashed her a quick smile.

This is nothing but good for us!

Sandra Norén had explained that Annika had acted in self-defense on the occasion many years ago when her former boyfriend had died. As far as the allegation of arson was concerned, it was verging on slander. The fact was that Annika had rescued the children from the flames, seeing as Thomas Samuelsson had already left the family to spend the night with his lover instead.

Annika was the one who had taken all her maternity leave, apart from two weeks during the soccer World Cup three years ago, and nine times out of ten was the one who stayed at home and looked after the children when they weren't well.

The judge had taken the interim decision that they should share custody, and Annika and Thomas had avoided each other since then, even over the phone.

She put her mobile phone back in her bag and was settling back down to work on her laptop when her eyes met those of the late-shift reporter opposite. She was openly curious.

The girl had evidently heard the short and aggressive conversation.

"If there's anything you feel like talking about, just say," she said, her eyes sparkling.

"Thanks, but no thanks," Annika said, staring at her screen.

The next company that David Lindholm had been involved in was called Advice Investment Management AB.

So many empty phrases all in a row. Advice *and* investment *and* management, *all together.*

"The company will provide financial advice and business development and associated activities, but nothing that could legally be deemed to be banking or credit related," she read.

David had been a deputy board member in this business as well.

There were two full members living on the outskirts of Stockholm, Lena Yvonne Nordin from Huddinge, and Niklas Ernesto Zarco Martinez from Skärholmen.

She checked out Lena Yvonne Nordin and found that she was linked to two other companies, both deregistered: a cleaning company in Skärholmen and another investment business. She had run the cleaning company together with Niklas Ernesto Zarco Martinez, and the investment business with Arne Filip Göran Andersson.

She sighed and looked at the time. Niklas Ernesto Zarco Martinez didn't appear to be linked to any other companies . . .

Frustrated, she pushed the computer away.

Maybe she should have something else to eat today? Life always seemed a bit easier then.

She pulled out her wallet and checked to see if she had any meal tokens left. There they were!

"Do you fancy hanging in the canteen together?" the young reporter asked.

Hanging?

Annika put the tokens back.

"I think I'll just get something quick from the machine," she said, heading over toward the prepacked sandwiches.

Without knowing quite why, she found herself thinking of Stefan Demert's old song about the railways, and she was back in Grandma's kitchen in Lyckebo listening to the transistor radio on the windowsill, with flies buzzing around and the smell of cinnamon buns.

Treat yourself to a coffee break
Shrink-wrapped sandwiches by the crate
They've been traveling many a day
And they're still going on that way . . .

She chose one with cheese, ham, and a very tired slice of tomato.

The last company on David Lindholm's list was called B Holmberg Property in Nacka AB.

The business was still active; it managed property and conducted legal transactions and other associated activities.

Oh well.

This is pretty boring. Viktor Gabrielsson would probably have been much more fun.

She swallowed a sigh and went through the details of this last company. Again, David Lindholm was listed as a deputy board member, that was evidently his thing. The managing director and registered signatory was a Bertil Oskar Holmberg from Nacka.

Hang on, I recognize that name . . .

Yep, it was the same bloke who had run the bankrupt catering firm that did all those other odd things.

She printed out the details, went over to the printer and waited impatiently as they were spat out, then gathered them into a neat bundle.

So what am I going to do with all this now, then?

Check out the dead man in the car park, look into the bloke with all the different companies, maybe write something about David's complex personality . . .

She looked at the time again—almost time for the early-evening television news.

It'll just be a load of stuff about Gabrielsson.

She thought about getting a mug of coffee but decided against it—she'd never get to sleep. When her mobile suddenly started to ring, she jumped.

Number withheld.

She put the earpiece in.

"The receptionist told me you were trying to reach me. What's this about?"

A man, she didn't recognize his voice.

"Who am I talking to?" Annika asked.

"You don't know who you tried to call? My name's Christer Bure, I'm a detective inspector on Södermalm."

Arrogant, she wrote on her notepad.

"Thanks for calling back. Well, I'm a reporter on the *Evening Post*, and I . . ."

"Yes, I know what number I called."

She fell silent and decided to ignore his rudeness.

". . . I'm writing an article about David Lindholm, and I understand that you were a good friend of his?"

"That's correct."

"I understand that you were in business together a long time ago. Could you tell me something about that?"

The man at the other end cleared his throat authoritatively.

"There's not much to say. We were into skydiving, and bought and sold equipment involved in that, rigs, parachutes, helmets, jumpsuits and so on, weight belts, cutters, straps, and other reserve parts. Altimeters and height alarms, of course . . ."

The man fell silent.

Skydiving?

"You must have been fairly committed parachutists," Annika said politely.

"It was David who got me interested. He was obsessed, jumping whenever he had any time off. If it hadn't been for that one bad landing in Skellefteå, he'd never have stopped."

"Bad landing?"

"The Swedish Cup, he was jumping freestyle and landed all wrong. Fractured his seventh vertebra, he was lucky not to end up in a wheelchair. That was the end of his jumping career."

"How did he take it?"

"How he did he *take* it? How the hell do you think?"

Bitter because of a parachute accident? Annika wrote.

"David was very interested in a lot of other things too, or course," she said. "He was a probation worker, and a trustee . . ."

"Yes," Christer Bure said, "David wanted to make a contribution besides just catching crooks. There aren't many blokes who can maintain that balance."

This might be a way in.

"So this was something that was important for him?" she asked lightly.

"Of course, otherwise he wouldn't have done it."

"And he carried on with this probationary work right up to the end?"

She held her breath.

"Of course," Bure said firmly. "The last time he met Filip Andersson was just a few days before he died."

Filip Andersson? Who's that? Should I know?

"Right, Filip Andersson," Annika said, searching her memory frantically. *Filip Andersson, Filip Andersson . . . ?*

"David volunteered as a trustee as soon as the legislation was passed. He was probably the only person who believed that Andersson was innocent. That was so typical of him, going in and supporting someone who was so despised . . ."

Ah, that was it, Filip Andersson, the financier who was found guilty of the ax murders on Sankt Paulsgatan. *So David was his trustee?*

"Did he have any other cases toward the end, do you know?"

"Why do you ask?"

"Well, he was the trustee for that American in Tidaholm, the one who had that accident . . ."

"That bastard," Bure said. "David gave up on him as soon as he ended up in Kumla, there was no reasoning with him after that."

Annika was making notes.

So the American's in Kumla, thank you very much!

"There's one other thing I've been wondering," she said. "You and David ran your business together with a man called Algot Heinrich Heimer . . ."

"Yes . . . ?" Christer Bure said, sounding thoughtful now.

"Do you know anything about the circumstances surrounding his death?"

There was silence on the line for a few seconds.

"He's dead?" Bure said. "I didn't know that. That's a shame. Was it recent?"

He's lying.

"In that case, I'm very sorry," Annika said. "I didn't mean to break the news like that. He was shot, on February 9 last year, in a car park in Norrköping . . ."

"I don't know anything about that."

His tone was very abrupt, and Annika realized that she had very little time left before Christer Bure lost patience with her.

"I've read the reports into the allegations of excessive force that were made against David," she said quickly. "You know, that business with the two young men twenty years ago. I think you were there, weren't you?"

There was another silence on the line, Annika could hear it crackling. "Hello . . . ?"

"What the hell is this? Where did you dig up that old crap?"

Annika gulped and squeezed the phone wire.

"What's your opinion of it?"

"They were just mudslinging, nothing but slander from the gutter. David was cleared on all charges, after all, the cases were dropped."

He knows exactly what happened.

"Did you see any signs of anything like that ever again?"

"What? People talking shit? Every day."

"Of David being violent, I mean?"

"Okay, this conversation is going in a direction that I don't much care for. What exactly do you want?"

"I just think there are some odd circumstances . . ."

"Listen, if you're planning to write shit about David, I'm not interested in helping. Thank you, and goodbye."

He hung up on Annika.

She decided that she did need that cup of coffee after all.

Then she sat down to write an article about David's background. She could mention that he'd had various positions in different companies, that he'd injured himself in a parachuting accident, and the fact that he'd been Filip Andersson's trustee and had met him just days before the murder was fairly interesting. She could even mention that he'd been accused of excessive force and cleared, as long as she didn't go into any details.

It ended up more like a feature than a news article. She thought it felt hypocritical and rather ingratiating.

She'd added some of the information that Nina Hoffman had given her when they met back in the summer, about David spending long periods working abroad. She had promised to let Nina know if she was ever going to use the information.

She sighed and called Nina Hoffman's mobile.

The police officer answered immediately.

"Just so you know," Annika said, "I'm writing about David for tomorrow's paper. I'm mentioning the fact that he and Julia spent some time living abroad, in Estepona, for instance."

"As long as you don't mention anything about his criminal contacts," Nina said.

Annika was taken aback.

"What do you mean by that?" she said.

"You didn't hear that from me," Nina said.

Annika put her hand to her forehead and thought so hard she could hear the cogs whirring. What did this mean?

"I'm planning to write about it for tomorrow," she said. "About Algot Heinrich Heimer and Filip Andersson and . . ."

There was silence on the line.

"Hello?" she said. "Nina?"

"My colleague has just got back in the car. My shift ends at midnight. I can meet you tomorrow morning. I'll call you."

The police officer ended the call.

There's something here, there's definitely something here.

She packed up her things, closed the laptop, and stuffed all her printouts into a plastic folder.

"Are you leaving?" the late-shift reporter said. "Lucky you, I've got to be here all night. It's stopped snowing now, which is always nice, with a bit of luck we'll get a few decent days before it settles in properly . . ."

Annika smiled toward the young girl.

"See you tomorrow," she said.

The flat was dark and silent.

Annika closed the front door behind her and went into the hall without switching the light on. She pulled off her boots and hung up her thick coat.

She stopped in the doorway to the main room, taking in the silence.

In their flat on Kungsholmen, all the sounds of Stockholm had seeped through the badly fitting windows and loose vents, the vibrations passing through the stone walls and ventilation pipes, the buses' squealing brakes and the sirens of the emergency vehicles. But here it was quiet, the sounds of the modern city didn't reach far into the heart of the medieval city.

She sighed and heard the sound bounce between the walls.

Without turning the lights on she went on into Ellen's room.

The same day she had got the keys to the flat she had taken the children out to the Kungens kurva branch of Ikea and let them choose their own furniture, whatever they wanted, with whatever cushions and duvet covers they liked.

Everything in Ellen's room was pink. Even the gray-black winter light was making the duvet cover and velvet cushions glow pale pink.

She stroked her hand over the head of the bed.

Emptiness, emptiness . . .

With a gaping hole in her chest she went into her son's room. In the daylight everything was blue, but at night it just looked pitch black.

She sank onto Kalle's bed. He had forgotten to take Chicken with him this morning, and she picked the stuffed toy up and hugged it, his new favorite, just the same as the one that burned up; this Chicken just smelled a bit different. She breathed in its smell, the new, clean, antiseptic smell that hadn't yet been erased by the bedclothes and night sweats.

I ought to do the washing-up, but I can't be bothered.

She looked through the doorway out into the main room, feeling the heat from the radiators, listening to the whispers in the corners.

Alone, alone . . .

With silence ringing in her ears and her desire to feel a sense of belonging like a sting in her chest, she crept up onto the boy's bed, clutching the stuffed chicken. There was still a hint of happiness somewhere, a freedom waiting for her in these dark rooms without demanding anything of her.

She felt sleep drift in like heavy veils and let herself be carried off.

The sound of her mobile came from far away, shredding the peace and quiet and making her sit bolt upright. Chicken slid onto the floor. Where had she left her phone?

She staggered through the main room and out into the hall.

Number withheld, damn it. It must be the paper.

She answered, and was met by a solid mass of noise, shouting, music, and voices.

"Annika? Is that you?"

Speechless, she slid to the floor.

"Listen, hello, it's me, Thomas."

He was in the pub, somewhere really noisy.

"Hello," she said into the darkness.

"Listen," he said, "I've reserved two sets of winter overalls. For Ellen. At Åhléns. One dark blue, the other pink. Which one do you think we should get?"

He was slurring, quite badly.

"Where are the children?" she asked.

"They're asleep. I'm having a beer with Arnold . . ."

"Who's with the children?"

"Sophia's at home, so you . . ."

"If you want to go out, I can look after the children," she said.

He fell silent. Disco music pounded in the background. A woman was laughing loudly.

"I don't want to fight with you," he said.

She had to breathe through her mouth to get any air.

You're calling me from the pub when you're drunk. Are you tired of her already?

"Me neither," she said.

"What shall we do about the overalls?"

Why are you really calling? What do you really want?

"What do you think?"

"You always say we have to think about this whole girly thing. And boys. Maybe pink isn't great? I thought . . ."

"Which does Ellen want?"

"The pink ones."

"Get those, then."

"You think?"

She gulped hard to fight the tears.

Don't call me like this. Never again. I can see all the way to the bottom of my loneliness, and it's making me dizzy.

"Let her decide. The color isn't that important."

"Okay. Bye, then."

"Bye."

Neither of them hung up. The music throbbed. The woman had stopped laughing.

"Annika?"

"Yes?"

"Do you mean it? Could you look after the kids if I go out in the evening?"

She gulped.

Hang up! Leave me in peace! You're tearing me apart.

"Sure."

"Bye."

"Bye."

This time she clicked to end the call and put the phone in her bag, then pulled her knees up under her chin, and somewhere deep inside her chest she felt strangely ecstatic and validated.

Nina Hoffman's flat was on Södermannagatan, not far from Folkungaga-tan on Södermalm. The traffic noise from the main road echoed loudly along the walls of the side street; Annika had to stifle the urge to hold her ears.

The building dated back to the 1920s, pale brown with a characteris-tically blank façade, with narrow, barred windows. The flats were usually cramped and dark.

She stepped into the entrance hall. When the door closed behind her, the sound of traffic miraculously disappeared. She studied the list of names: Nina lived on the second floor.

Annika went up the stairs, found the door that said *N Hoffman*, and rang the bell.

The police officer had cut her hair. She was wearing the same gray hooded jacket that she had on the last time they met, that rainy Saturday in June when she had been so upset at the way Julia was being treated.

"Would you like some coffee?" she asked, and Annika nodded.

It really was a rather dark flat, a single room with a small kitchen alcove, facing the inner courtyard. But the room was fairly large, with a polished wooden floor and comfortable furniture.

She took off her shoes and outdoor clothes in the hall.

Nina must have had the coffee ready, because she came into the living room with a thermos flask and two mugs, which she put on the dining table. Annika handed her a copy of that day's *Evening Post*.

"The piece about David is on page eleven," she said.

Nina took the paper and sat down on a chair while Annika poured coffee into both mugs. She sat and drank the hot liquid. Nina was reading in silence. Then she folded the paper and looked up at Annika.

"That wasn't very smart," she said.

Annika took a deep breath and shrugged.

"Okay," she said. "What's wrong with it?"

"I think you should keep away from that side of David's past. The reason he used to spend time abroad was because people were after him. They don't care to be reminded of the fact."

"And who do you mean by 'they'? Different criminal gangs?"

Nina stared down at her mug of coffee without touching it.

"People that David helped put away?" Annika went on. "Crooks that he beat up, or their families and business associates?"

"I don't understand what this has got to do with anything," Nina said, pushing the mug away. "David's dead, and Julia's going to be found guilty of killing him."

She leaned forward.

"I'm telling you this as a favor. It's not all the way it looks. People have hidden agendas. You look at David Lindholm and see a corrupt police officer with a solid façade, but you know nothing about his background. His mum arrived in Sweden on the white buses after the Nazis surrendered, the only survivor in her family. She was sixteen years old when she arrived, and she was already sick then. She's been in a care home since David was a teenager. Don't be so quick to judge."

Annika straightened up.

"I'm not judging. On the contrary, I believe there's a chance that Julia's innocent. There seem to be plenty of people out there who had a motive to kill David, and they haven't even been investigated . . ."

"What would you know about that?"

The answer was abrupt and short.

Annika drank some coffee, staring down at the table and feeling foolish.

"You haven't got a clue about what the police have looked at, have you?" Nina said. "You don't even know what conclusions the clinical psychiatric report reached, do you?"

"No," Annika said. "But she can't have been that ill if she can be sentenced to serve time in an ordinary prison . . ."

Nina stood up.

"It's called dissociative identity disorder, or multiple personalities."

Annika felt the hairs on the back of her neck stand up.

"Like the woman who was described in that book *Sybil*," Annika said. "They think she's got a split personality."

"The diagnosis explains her suppression of events as a temporary mental disturbance in which she assumed the role of a different person, the other woman."

Nina looked out at the courtyard.

"I became a police officer because I wanted to help people," she said. "Sometimes I think Julia followed me because she didn't have anything better to do. She'd probably really have preferred to do something else, become a social worker or a teacher, maybe an artist . . ."

She fell silent and Annika waited.

"I keep wondering if there was anything I could have done differently," Nina went on. "What did I miss, why I wasn't good enough . . ."

"Could there have been another woman in the flat?"

Nina shook her head.

"Everything points to Julia. What I don't understand is why she's still not talking. Now she could explain what really happened between her and David. Not that it would change anything in the trial, but people would be a bit more understanding . . ."

Annika looked down at her hands.

"My house burned down in the summer," she said. "I know the police are investigating whether I was responsible. They think I'm guilty, but they've got no evidence, because if they had I'd have been arrested, even though of course I know I didn't do it."

She looked up at Nina, who had turned round to look at her carefully.

"What if Julia really is innocent?" she said. "What if there really was another woman there? Can you imagine anything that could possibly be worse than that?"

"It's been investigated," Nina said. "There was no one else there."

"Maybe," Annika said, "but *what if* . . ."

Nina walked over to the table, put both hands down on it and leaned forward.

"Don't confuse what happened to you with anyone else," she said quietly and emphatically. "You might be innocent, but that doesn't mean Julia is. Julia's been ill, but she's better now and will be sentenced to prison for a very long time. That's all there is to it."

"But why did she do it?" Annika asked.

Nina sat down.

"Something happened toward the end," she eventually said. "Julia never said what it was, but she was extremely frightened and worried. She hung up whenever I rang, didn't want to meet. I was seriously concerned about her mental state, but I never imagined she'd . . . that she could . . ."

The words ebbed away. Nina Hoffman took a sip of tepid coffee and pulled a face.

"Okay," Annika said slowly. "If I've got this right, this is what happened: David had enemies in criminal circles. He kept in touch with some of them by acting as a probation worker and trustee, and he was on the board of various companies . . ."

Nina looked up.

"You didn't know that?" Annika said. "He was involved in at least four businesses. Is it common for police officers to do that?"

Nina looked at the time.

"I have to go," she said. "I was thinking of going to the gym."

"I've got a union meeting," Annika said, looking at her own watch. "Just one more thing: Did David ever talk about the ax murders on Sankt Paulsgatan?"

Nina was carrying the mugs over to the kitchen alcove.

"Why do you ask?"

Annika scratched her head.

"He was a trustee for Filip Andersson, the financier who was found guilty of the murders. According to Christer Bure, he believed Andersson was innocent. Why would he think that?"

Nina came over to Annika and stopped very close to her.

"David really did love Julia and Alexander," Nina said. "He was a troubled man with a sick pattern of behavior, but Julia and Alexander were the only people he really cared about."

"Did David know anything about the ax murders that nobody else knew?" Annika asked.

Nina pulled on a duffel coat, hoisted a gym bag onto her shoulder, and headed toward the door.

The union meeting started in fifteen minutes. Annika was definitely going to be late.

She walked along Folkungagatan, feeling that she really didn't want to hurry; she was walking through quicksand and it didn't matter.

The whole world was the color of lead. She couldn't shake the vague sense of unreality that was enveloping her more and more often. People drifted past her, floating around like unfathomable shadows, with such rigid expressions on their faces, such empty mouths, that she wondered if they were really alive or just pretending.

She'd woken up that morning and not known where she was. The light had been falling on her bed in the main room, gray and heavy, making it difficult to breathe.

She had lived there for five months, spending the whole summer on Västerlånggatan in Gamla stan, with tourists dropping their ice creams in the doorway and the busker's out-of-tune version of "Streets of London" outside the window so often that she felt like throwing up.

She knew she should be used to it, but she understood what the problem was.

It was time that was the problem, time suddenly spreading out around her, as much time as she liked, day and evening and night alike.

The gap left by the children, she thought, aeons that could be used for something urgent, so much responsibility that just vanished to be replaced by a flood of unscented, colorless *time*.

She had no idea what to do with it.

The weeks without the children had been a period of free fall, without any frame of reference, minutes and hours full of shrieking emptiness.

Berit had gone off on holiday with Thord to visit her children, so she hadn't been able to spend time with her.

Her mother had got in touch after her little sister's thirtieth birthday to ask why she hadn't been there to celebrate, and Annika had said she had been working and hadn't been able to get away. It was a complete lie, which her mother took for granted and started reproaching her for.

Anne Snapphane had sent a few emails with confused and aggressive accusations that went around in circles, mainly repeating the things she had said the night the house had burned down: that Anne had given up her own life simply to support Annika, that she hadn't given herself space to grow, that she had let Annika's shaky marriage ruin her own relationship with Mehmet, that she had realized that she always backed down and therefore had to *grab what she could now and live the best life she could* . . .

Annika hadn't bothered to reply, presuming that she would only be fueling the flames.

The solution was work.

Every day *without the children*, in this new, scentless reality, she had spent at work, from when she got up until she collapsed in bed.

It hadn't resulted in many articles. The torrent of time took a lot of effort to overcome.

And now Thomas was calling her in the middle of the night from pubs and tearing down all her frames of reference.

She looked at the time.

Eva-Britt Qvist's big union meeting had started, the meeting about "their shared future."

She stopped on the pavement, shutting her eyes against the grayness. People carried on streaming past her, from in front and behind, bumping into her and muttering apologies for treading on her toes.

One point of stillness, something to cling onto, a shape and a color in all the emptiness.

There was a great mass of people around the day-shift desk. Annika could see Eva-Britt Qvist's spiked hair sticking up in the center of the crowd, and presumed that the union representative must have got up on the table in a effort to conjure up some of the spirit of '68.

"This is about solidarity," she said in a voice that sounded on the brink of cracking.

Annika stopped beside the news desk and put her bag on Spike's desk.

"Have they been going on for long?" she asked quietly.

"A fucking eternity," the head of news said without looking up from his morning paper. The *Norrbotten Courier*, she noted.

"We have to stand up for each other!" Eva-Britt Qvist cried. "This isn't the time for soloists, but for the whole orchestra!"

Scattered applause.

"Don't they use that metaphor every time?" Annika said, opening a can of Ramlösa mineral water that happened to be sitting on the desk.

Spike groaned and turned a page of the paper.

"If we accept management's demands to abandon the list dictated by employment regulations, our employers will be able to fire people completely as they choose. We can't let management have their way, we have to stick together here..."

"What exactly does the paper want?" Annika asked, taking a swig from the can.

"For people to shut up and do some work," Spike said, pushing the *Norrbotten Courier* into the recycling bin.

"After all the hard work we've put into this paper! After all the times we've shown how dedicated we are, time after time after time! Through reorganizations and online launches and cutbacks, we've put up with all of that and struggled on, recognizing our responsibility to our readers..."

An appreciative murmur ran through the crowd.

"We have to show that we stand united in our struggle against management and their blinkered focus on profits. We have to come up with powerful counterproposals. Therefore, we in the union are today proposing a united, collective, and aggressive strategy to show the bosses that we're serious. We're going to sign ourselves off sick!"

Annika choked on a mouthful of mineral water.

Sign ourselves off sick?

She stared at Eva-Britt Qvist, who had raised her arms toward the ceiling as if she were expecting thunderous applause.

"Sign ourselves off sick?" Annika said. "Is she mad?"

She put the water down on Spike's desk.

"We'll show them what happens when none of us comes to work. We'll make them realize the consequences of failing to listen to their colleagues..."

"For heaven's sake," Annika said, "she's off with the fairies now."

Ronja turned around and shushed her irritatedly.

"What?" Annika said. "Do you think it's okay for everyone to go off sick at the same time?"

Ronja turned her back on her and folded her arms.

"No, seriously, tell me," Annika said. "Do you think it's okay to exploit the social welfare system to take revenge on our employers?"

There was now complete silence around them, as Annika's last words filtered through the union members.

Eva-Britt Qvist had lost her thread up on the table; she was looking round the crowd until her eyes came to Annika, and she raised one hand and pointed a trembling finger at her.

"Do you have something to say?" she said indignantly.

Everyone turned toward Annika, who felt her heartbeat quicken, and just shrugged.

"Signing yourself off sick isn't an aggressive strategy," she said. "Exploiting the social welfare system like that is actually against the law. False certification."

Two red marks had blossomed on Eva-Britt's cheeks.

"Solidarity," she cried. "Do you know what that is?"

Annika shuffled uncomfortably, feeling her colleagues' stares burn into her.

"Well," she said, "what about our solidarity with anyone who's really sick if we use their money just to cause trouble for Anders Schyman?"

"Solidarity is when you unite in a collective," Eva-Britt Qvist cried. "It's when you look toward something bigger than yourself, but that's something you've never done!"

Suddenly Annika was utterly incensed. That stupid bitch was standing here in a union meeting and pointing her out to the whole newsroom. She took a couple of steps in among her fellow workers and felt her throat tighten.

Don't be pathetic, for fuck's sake don't start crying.

"Okay," Emil the temp said beside her, "surely we can debate the subject? This is a meeting, after all."

"Everyone has to work together," Eva-Britt Qvist shrieked. "We've agreed on that!"

Annika looked in surprise at the little reporter beside her. Bloody hell! A temp with a bit of go in him!

"Who's agreed what?" Annika said, turning to face the union rep. "You and who else? What about us, your fellow members?"

"Annika's got a point," she heard someone say behind her.

"This is a collective action!" the union representative cried. "We have to stick together to get our demands through."

"What, firing people according to the 'last-in first-out' list?" Annika said. "So how come that's so fair?"

"Exactly!" Patrik Nilsson called out.

People were shuffling about now, considerably more animated than before.

"We have to stick together!" Eva-Britt Qvist shrieked, and by now her voice had cracked completely.

"So that you keep your job," someone on the far side shouted. "What about us, then?"

"Yes, exactly, what about us?"

Annika took a few steps back, walked around Ronja, and picked up her bag from the news desk. There was now so much noise that she couldn't actually hear the union rep croaking.

It would take a while before she could sit and work at the day reporters' desk again.

Anders Schyman watched Annika Bengtzon fish a lunch coupon from her wallet and disappear in the direction of the canteen.

He was sitting in an empty radio studio watching the union meeting through the open door.

Eva-Britt Qvist was an even bigger disaster as union representative than he had been able to imagine, and that was saying something.

She's not worth fighting for.

He remembered the huge fuss when one of the papers in Småland had tried to get rid of an intransigent union boss a few years back. The man had made himself utterly impossible in his workplace. He opposed everything, refused to work repeatedly on the grounds that the tasks he was being given were beneath him, claimed he was busy with investigative reporting when he was actually surfing the net for porn, and when he realized that he was on the point of being sacked, he got himself elected union boss at the paper. The paper's management still tried to get rid of him, with the result that the whole of the Swedish trade-union movement lined up behind this one incompetent reporter. It ended with him being appointed as an ombudsman at the headquarters of the Journalists' Association on Vasagatan in the center of Stockholm. The whole of Media Sweden celebrated: What a victory!

The fact that the man left three months later when his probation was over was something that nobody saw fit to report, apart from the Newspaper Publishers' Association. Today he was driving a taxi out in Sundbyberg.

Playing to the gallery. That's how it works. Let them have their headlines.

Now they had had their big meeting. Now the masses were riled. Now it was time for him to come with concessions.

He stretched his legs.

The meeting had been interesting. It had revealed a couple of rebels he hadn't noticed before. He had taken it for granted that Annika Bengtzon would oppose Eva-Britt Qvist's imbecilic ideas. Partly because she couldn't stand the former editorial secretary, and partly because she reacted instinctively against rule-breaking (unless the rules were being broken by her or someone close to her, in which case it was fine).

One advantage with Eva-Britt Qvist, from his point of view, was of course that she was a woman. She'd never have the same authority as a man. Her lack of success would be seen as her own personal failure, and the rest of the union committee wouldn't be tainted as a result.

She'll be easy to rationalize away when this is all over. No one's going to fight for her.

After a long series of local negotiations, he and Eva-Britt Qvist had agreed on a framework for the cutbacks. According to the agreement, undersigned by the union representative, members of the paper's editorial management were excluded from consideration under most aspects of employment legislation, and would not be included in any lists relating to the cutbacks. Schyman had claimed than anything else would be unreasonable, and she had soon backed down.

Maybe she was counting on becoming part of that group herself.

No exceptions had been specified, and there was no attempt to define precisely what "editorial management" meant—very little explanation at all, in fact.

That new lad, Emil, and Patrik, of course. The young lads on the online edition, and the girls in entertainment.

All of them would have to go, according to the union's list.

He sat and looked at the group of newsroom staff gradually breaking up into smaller groups before dissolving and disappearing, each person going back to his or her own work.

The editor in chief got up and headed back to his office.

This is going to be the newspaper with the largest editorial management team in the world.

The day shift's desk was littered with coffee cups, Coke cans, and orange peelings. Annika swept the rubbish from one place into a large recycling bin and made an effort to block the rest of the mess from sight. She unpacked her laptop and logged in. She took out her notes from the previous evening, the jottings of phone calls she had made, the sheets of information she had dug out.

The only question was: Could any of this ever be used?

There were all the people in the various companies, the forty-five-year-old who had been shot in the car park in Norrköping, the American serving a life sentence who disappeared from Tidaholm after an accident . . .

She paused when she got to her notes from the call to the warder in Tidaholm Prison. The warder had said David Lindholm had been the American lifer's *trustee.*

Trustees were contact people for prisoners serving life sentences, a sort of aristocracy within the probation system.

Which other prisoners did David Lindholm have official links with? How do you find that sort of thing out? Would that be in the public domain?

She couldn't recall ever having thought about it before.

She went into the website of the National Correctional Organization, checked their contact details, picked up the phone, and dialed the number in Norrköping. She was put through to a lawyer who dealt with freedom-of-information requests.

"This is covered by legislation guaranteeing confidentiality to those within the criminal justice system," the lawyer said. "It's a matter of individual concern, which means that such dealings aren't in the public domain."

"Is it possible to apply to see them?" Annika wondered.

The lawyer hesitated.

"Yes, it's possible. If we were to receive a request, we'd deal with it in the usual way."

"Where?"

"Here, at our national head office. We have access to all the information here."

"So you think it might be possible to find out if someone has been a trustee, and if so, who for?"

The lawyer was thinking out loud.

"Well, we can't give out any information that could harm an individual. But revealing whether or not someone is acting as a trustee could hardly be regarded as harmful. But it might be more sensitive if the person in question had served a prison sentence themselves and was now acting as a trustee. We'd have to judge each application on its own merits."

"Great," Annika said. "I'd like to make an application, then. How long will it take to get the answer, and who will I get it from?"

"Decisions like that are usually dealt with by our clerical staff, so it shouldn't take long. You'll have an answer within a few days."

I want an answer NOW!

Annika asked for the woman's email address, thanked her, and hung up.

Then she quickly composed a request to find out who David Lindholm had been a trustee or probation contact for, going back as far as it was possible to check.

She sighed and pushed the computer away.

Oh dear. I'm treading water badly.

Behind her she could hear Patrik Nilsson discussing something with Spike in an extremely agitated tone, presumably something about the homeward-bound cop killer.

"It's a fucking scandal," the reporter roared.

Spike muttered something.

"My source is rock solid. The government gave the Yanks something in return for Gabrielsson. We have to find out what it was. Raids on people making sour milk? Landing rights for the CIA at Bromma?"

Annika stood up. She didn't want to hear any more.

Please, dear proprietors, put us out of our misery and get rid of the people you're going to get rid of, and let us get on with our work in peace.

She went over to the coffee machine and selected black coffee, +strength, –sugar, and—milk. She stood there fingering the plastic mug by one of the tables, thinking about Julia Lindholm's diagnosis.

Multiple personalities. Sounds like a bad film.

Practically every murderer these days claimed to suffer from some sort of psychological disorder. If they didn't hear voices, they were on anabolic steroids or blamed poor potty training and broken toys when they were little. Everyone should feel sorry for the unemployed because they didn't have jobs, sorry for people who had jobs because they suffered from stress, sorry for the young who'd never been given a chance, and sorry for the old who had never made the most of the chances they had been given.

Wife killers obviously always felt *really bad* because they hadn't been able to control their wives, not been allowed to fuck them whenever they felt like it, and not been able to decide who they talked to. All too often the courts actually showed a degree of understanding to these poor wife beaters, producing page after page justifying why they should be treated as leniently as possible. Often they managed to get the names of the victims wrong as well, Annika had uncovered several instances of that. The murdered women were called Lundberg and Lundgren and Berglund more or less at random, while the poor murderer, who of course beat his wife to death in a nice, humane way, was sentenced to the shortest term permissible by law because he was so sad that she had ended their relationship. Ten years in some low-security institution with a herd of cows and nice lawns, and then they were out after six and a half.

And now Julia was supposed to have a split personality, like the woman in that old American bestseller.

How sorry should we feel for her?

Anyway, didn't they turn Sybil's story into a film?

She tipped the rest of the coffee away and went back to her desk. Patrik Nilsson had left the news desk and was sitting at his place hammering away at his computer in the crime section, and she breathed a sigh of relief.

She did a Google search and discovered that *Sybil* was both a novel and a television drama based on the true story of a young woman who was treated so badly in her childhood that she developed sixteen different personalities. "Sybil," whose real name was Shirley Ardell Mason, suffered nervous breakdowns and prolonged blackouts as a young woman.

When she started having therapy, involving hypnosis and antipsychotic medication, with a psychiatrist, Cornelia B. Wilbur, it turned out that her periods of memory loss were the result of one of her other personalities taking over her body and doing loads of things that she never remembered.

Was that what happened to Julia? The "other woman" took over her body without she "herself" being conscious of it?

She found a site about dissociative personality disorders and read that two different personalities could deny each other's existence or reject each other, while they each identified the same body as their own.

God, how weird! The things the human mind is capable of!

"The sufferer switches between different personalities depending on circumstances and neither can remember what the other has done. In some cases the gap between them isn't as pronounced, and the sufferer can be aware of their different personalities but has a more complicated relationship to them."

So Julia could be aware of this other woman? That could actually be possible?

She clicked to read more.

Truly split personalities were extremely rare, she read. In total, there were something like a thousand known cases worldwide.

Multiple personality disorders shouldn't be confused with schizophrenia, as often happened.

"One reason for the misunderstanding is that the word *schizophrenia* literally means 'split mind.' This, however, reflects changes in associations and logical reasoning. A schizophrenic person has only *one* personality, but his or her thoughts and actions can often appear extremely disorganized . . ."

She picked up a pen and began chewing on the end of it.

She ought to be able to write about this. All she needed was one other source who could confirm what Nina Hoffman had told her about the psychiatric report. Who would be able to spill the beans?

The lawyer! He didn't seem to be particularly blessed with intelligence.

She looked up his name and number again. Mats Lennström at the Kvarnstenen law firm.

"Mr. Lennström is in court until late this afternoon," the secretary chirruped.

She hung up and called the prosecutors' office, but Angela Nilsson wasn't available. She called the National Board of Forensic Medicine, only to be told that they never commented on their reports.

Which left Q, and she didn't want to talk to him.

Damn! Why couldn't Lennström be in?

She leaned over the computer, thinking.

Who else could give her some gossip?

About Julia, and about David?

Was there anyone who had no interest in protecting David Lindholm?

The people he betrayed. The ones he shopped. The ones who got life because they trusted him.

Names, she thought. Got to find their names and work out where they're serving their time.

She wrote a list on a piece of paper.

The American who had something happen to him at Tidaholm: moved to Kumla, in the central province of Närke.

The father who had taken hostages at a nursery in Malmö: now in Kumla.

The ax murderer from Södermalm, the financier Filip Andersson: also in Kumla.

Maybe it would be worth taking a trip to Närke to visit a few criminals? But what the hell was the American's name?

She had the name of the man from Malmö, Ahmed Muhammed Svensson. Yes, that really was his name. The name was there in black and white in the court report she had been sent.

How the hell am I going to find the American?

She picked up her pen and started jotting things down. What did she actually know?

He was an American and he was serving a life sentence.

That ought to reduce the options enough to make him easy to identify. There were currently 164 people serving a life sentence, 159 of them men. And it was hardly likely that many of those were American citizens. Because he had been tried within the Swedish judicial system, he would be in the public records.

I need to identify the trial. What could he have been found guilty of?

It had to be either murder, kidnapping, arson, posing a serious danger to the public, aggravated sabotage of some kind, or aggravated dissemination of poison or an infectious substance . . .

She stopped at the third item on the list.

Arson.

She heard Q's cold voice echo in her chest.

The fire was started by someone who had a reason to start it. You're at the top of the list of informal suspects.

She took a short walk round the newsroom to get some air.

The other crimes that were punishable by life imprisonment would hardly apply to an American, not in Sweden during peacetime.

She put her pen down and checked them out on the Internet just to be certain: incitement to mutiny; insurrection; high treason; treachery in dealing with a foreign power; arbitrary conduct in dealings with a foreign power; aggravated espionage; aggravated insubordination; undermining morale; disregarding preparations for war; unauthorized surrender; dereliction of duty; betraying the country; unauthorized possession of chemical weapons, mines, and nuclear material.

Unauthorized possession of mines? Good grief.

She sighed.

So, which court? There were dozens of them in Stockholm alone. Probably a hundred or so throughout the country. Where to start?

She looked up Stockholm City Court and its various subdivisions.

She stopped, her fingers hovering above the keyboard.

If you're given a life sentence, you appeal.

So his case ought to have been heard in one of the Courts of Appeal.

There were only six of those: one each for the regions of Götaland and Svealand, Upper and Lower Norrland, Western Sweden, and finally one for the southern provinces of Skåne and Blekinge.

She looked at the time; they usually took calls until four.

She started from the far south and worked her way up.

She was looking for a verdict in which an American was sentenced for life, probably for murder.

On her sixth and final attempt, the Court of Appeal for Upper Norrland in Umeå, she was put through to a helpful young man in the archive.

"That sounds like Stevens," he said.

A minute or so later he sent her the case report against Michael Harold Stevens.

Annika leafed through to the summary of the verdict and let out a whistle. *An impressive catalog of crimes.*

The American had been found guilty of murder, grievous bodily harm, kidnapping, attempted extortion, posing a serious danger to the public, obstructing the course of justice, and breaches of firearms legislation.

Sounds like a hired thug who messed up badly.

She flicked through the document, all thirty-eight pages of it.

In summary:

Michael Harold Stevens admitted that he had blown up a car in a quarry outside Skellefteå, which accounted for the charge of posing a serious danger to the public. Inside the car was a thirty-three-year-old man who died in the explosion; hence the murder charge. He had forced a thirty-two-year-old man inside another car (kidnap), driven him to a hunting cabin outside Kåge, put a pistol in his mouth (breach of fire-arms legislation), and made two demands: that he withdraw a witness statement (obstructing the course of justice) and pay off a drugs debt (extortion).

The two victims, the thirty-three-year-old and the thirty-two-year-old, both had criminal records. They were in the same criminal gang.

He had also admitted taking part in the planning of the armed raid on the security van in Botkyrka the previous year.

She sighed in annoyance, and let the document fall to her lap.

This has to be the right American, but where does David Lindholm fit into the picture? What has he got to do with any of this? Who can I call and ask?

She looked back at the first page of the report to see who had been appointed to defend Stevens: a lawyer named Mats Lennström from the Kvarnstenen law practice.

Mats Lennström? But he's Julia Lindholm's lawyer!

She picked up the phone and dialed the number for the Kvarnstenen law practice.

"You're in luck," the secretary trilled. "Mr. Lennström has just walked through the door. We weren't sure if he'd make it back here today."

Annika shifted restlessly on her chair as the talkative woman transferred her call.

"Lennström," he answered, and Annika got the impression that he wasn't even sure of that.

"I'm calling about three things," she said, once she'd introduced herself. "Firstly, I'd like to interview Julia Lindholm; we've met before so she knows who I am . . ."

"A lot of people would like to interview my client," he said heavily.

"Yes, of course," Annika said, "but I know that all restrictions have been lifted now and she can see whoever she wants, so perhaps you could pass on my request?"

He sighed.

"Then there's this business of dissociative identity disorder," Annika said nonchalantly. "What do you think about the fact that the National Board of Forensic Medicine has decided that Julia can serve time in prison, even though she's evidently been acting as someone else, this other woman . . . ?"

"Er," the lawyer said, "well, that's their expert opinion, so I don't really have any comment on that . . ."

Hurray! Confirmation! Now it was publishable!

"And I was also wondering what really happened to Michael Harold Stevens," Annika said.

There was a moment's silence on the line, then the lawyer cleared his throat.

"Why are you wondering about that?"

"David Lindholm was his trustee, of course, but Stevens had some sort of accident at Tidaholm and was transferred to Kumla, and after that David was no longer his trustee. I was just wondering what happened."

"Have you read the report from the trial?"

"Yes, I have."

"Then you know that Mike confessed."

"Yes."

The lawyer paused, and from the noises on the phone it sounded like he was taking his jacket off.

"Well, it must fall outside the statute of limitations now," he said. "The policeman's dead, and Mike's never going to pursue the case . . ."

Annika waited in silence.

"David Lindholm was in charge of questioning Mike," Mats Lennström said. "He confessed to everything he was charged with, and quite a bit more besides. The armed raid in Botkyrka, for instance."

Mats Lennström fell silent.

"But?" Annika said.

"When the sentence was upheld by the Court of Appeal, Mike was taken to Kumla for evaluation; everyone sentenced to more than four years goes there first. Then he was sent to Tidaholm, and presumably that's when Mike realized that he'd been completely fooled."

"Fooled?"

"Yes, I should have checked it all a bit more thoroughly. Mike and David Lindholm had come to an agreement under the terms of which he would have served a shorter sentence at the facility in Ljustadalen, in Sundsbruk just outside Sundsvall; his wife worked at the horse-riding center nearby. But none of what David promised him was legally binding. I ought to have realized . . ."

Annika sat up straight in her chair.

"Do you mean to say," she said, "that you didn't know if it was legally binding or not? And that you didn't check, if you weren't sure?"

"You trust the police, don't you?" he said. "Especially such a renowned figure as David Lindholm."

Bloody hell, what an imbecile! It's hardly surprising that they picked him to defend Julia, if they wanted to get her put away.

"What sort of accident did he have?"

"Mike slipped in the shower and fell on something sharp."

Annika had to suppress an audible snort of derision.

"Puncture wounds," she said. "Mike talked, and five men were locked up for the Botkyrka raid, and they weren't exactly happy about it. They had friends in Tidaholm. They sharpened their toothbrushes or cutlery and attacked him in the shower."

"That's all speculation on your part."

"Tell me one thing," Annika said. "What did Stevens do in return? Did he get back at the Botkyrka gang, or David, maybe? Or his wife? Or his son?"

"If you'll excuse me, I've got a lot to do," he said, and hung up.

Annika sat there staring into thin air for a whole minute.

There was nothing remotely heroic about the way David Lindholm had solved the raid on the security van in Botkyrka. Quite the reverse. He used his public reputation to gain a man's trust, then betrayed him.

What an arsehole!

She moved on to the second man on the list, Ahmed Muhammed Svensson. She pulled out the report of the trial in Malmö City Court: attempted murder, aggravated kidnap, aggravated extortion, and threatening behavior.

Ahmed Muhammed Svensson had married a Swedish woman and taken her surname to make it easier to fit into Swedish society. It hadn't worked out very well. Ahmed Muhammed couldn't find a job and became depressed, his marriage started to look a bit rocky, and he began to hit both his wife and their four-year-old daughter. In the end Mrs. Svensson asked for a divorce.

Then Ahmed Muhammed got hold of his neighbor's hunting rifle and went off to their daughter's nursery. He arrived just in time for the afternoon break, when all the children were sitting eating rose-hip soup and almond biscuits. He announced loudly and in tears that he was going to shoot the children, one by one, until his wife stopped the divorce proceedings and the Swedish government gave him a million kronor. And a new color television.

God, how tragic.

The hostage drama got out of hand at once.

One young man, a student at a nearby sixth-form college, was doing work experience at the nursery and managed to get out through the balcony door to the car park at the back of the building. Ahmed Muhammed Svensson fired three shots at the boy and hit a parked car and a lamppost; hence the charge of attempted murder.

The lad naturally sounded the alarm and ten minutes later the whole nursery was surrounded by police and emergency vehicles. At the trial, the staff described how Ahmed Muhammed Svensson was terrified by all the commotion and sat there hugging the rifle as if it were his only salvation.

The local police had obviously tried to talk some sense into Mr. Svensson, but he hadn't been willing to enter into any form of dialogue.

It just so happened that the experienced negotiator, David Lindholm, was in Malmö for a seminar that day. Someone high up in the police was aware of this, and Lindholm was called to the scene as an expert.

David Lindholm had, entirely of his own volition, gone inside the building and talked to Ahmed Muhammed Svensson for about two hours. First the children came out in groups of five, each group accompanied by a member of the staff. Svensson's daughter had been in the last group.

Finally, the hostage taker himself emerged, arm in arm with Detective Superintendent Lindholm.

In court David Lindholm had testified that Svensson had threatened to shoot the children, the staff, and himself, and that he had believed that Svensson was likely to carry out his threat at any time.

Ahmed Muhammed himself hadn't said much, just that he regretted what he had done and would never have been capable of harming children.

And he was given a life sentence. Poor bastard!

Because David Lindholm had betrayed someone, again.

I wonder what he did to the third one, Filip Andersson?

She shivered slightly: those terrible ax murders. The paper had printed acres of coverage, she typed "facts filip andersson" into the computer and waited.

And waited and waited.

What's this? Why's it going so slowly?

Then the screen flickered and a short list of articles appeared.

"Notes and facts filip andersson" she read on the first one. *This looks very odd . . .*

She leaned forward and studied the screen, and realized that she'd typed the terms of the search into the wrong box. She hadn't searched the Internet or the newspaper's archive, but the hard drive of the laptop itself.

So what's this?

She clicked on the file and up popped an ordinary Word document.

"Is he innocent?" she read.

"Facts pointing to FA: 1. He had evidently been at the scene of the murders. His fingerprints were on the door handle, on the female victim's handbag, and in four different places inside the flat. 2. He must have been present when the murders were committed. He left his trousers to be dry-cleaned the following day; the police found the ticket in his wallet and managed to pick the trousers up just before they were cleaned. On one trouser leg were traces of blood whose DNA matched the female victim. 3. He had a motive. The three people in the flat had deceived him somehow, although in what way is unknown."

Yes, so far this all makes sense.

"Facts against FA being the killer: 1. Why weren't there any traces of blood from the other victims on his trousers or other clothes? Chopping up the victims like that means you have to be in close contact with them. You can't just swing at them: You have to stand on the arm or leg to hold it down on something solid, in these cases usually the floor, but in one instance a table, and for that to work the victims have to be either drugged or otherwise rendered compliant, in this case with blows to the head. It seems extremely unlikely that the murderer could have avoided getting any blood on his body and clothes, considering the quantity of blood involved. 2. Where's the murder weapon? Is it really just an ordinary ax? Wouldn't some sort of broadax or mattock or chopping tool like a meatcleaver have been more effective? 3. Why didn't he throw his trousers away? The traces of blood that were found were microscopic. Might he not have know they were there? Why not? NB check tomorrow. 4. There were a lot of fingerprints in the flat, many of them unidentified. 5. Most importantly: There were traces of blood and DNA from another person at the scene of the murder, and these have never been identified either. An accomplice who was injured in the struggle?"

She was staring openmouthed at the laptop.

This wasn't a published article. It wasn't even publishable. It was a list of notes someone had made to help them keep track of the case, possibly because they were covering the trial or . . .

Sjölander! This was his old computer, after all!

She clicked *archive*, then *properties*, and sure enough, Sjölander was listed as the author of the document. It had been written almost four years ago to the day, just before Filip Andersson's trial.

So Sjölander had doubts about his guilt.

So had David, according to Bure. More than just doubts.

He was probably the only person who believed that Andersson was innocent . . .

Why? How could David be so sure of Filip Andersson's innocence? What did that mean? And why was Filip Andersson so quiet? If he was that innocent, why didn't he cooperate with the police?

She opened up the website of the National Correctional Organization again, and checked visiting times at the huge prison in Kumla: Monday–Friday, 9–15, weekends 10–14.

Brilliant! Open every day! That's what I call service!

Then she dialed the number of the main prison office and introduced herself.

"Well," she said, "I'd like to visit one of your inmates, a Filip Andersson." The warder transferred her to the acting prison governor and Annika repeated her request.

"That won't be possible," the governor said.

"Really?" Annika said. "Why not? I thought you were open for visits every day."

"We're open 365 days a year, except leap years," the governor said. "Then we're open 366 days."

"So why can't I come?"

"You'd be very welcome," the governor said, sounding simultaneously amused and weary. "But the same rules apply to the mass media as to everyone else. Inmates can apply for permission to receive a visit or phone call from a particular individual, with their full name, postal address, and ID number. They must also specify their relationship to the visitor. Then we would evaluate the visitor, performing a criminal background check, and then the inmate is informed either that a visit permit has been granted or denied, or if a visit can only take place under supervision. Inmates are then permitted to contact their visitor, who must then book a time with us."

"Wow," she said. "There are three men I'd like to visit. Can you ask them to apply for permits for me?"

The governor was a master of patience.

"I'm afraid not," he said. "We don't act as go-betweens anymore. You'll have to contact the inmates yourself by letter or fax."

"I assume I can't email?" Annika said.

"You assume correctly," the governor replied.

"But they're allowed to reply by fax or letter?"

"Not by fax, but they're allowed to write letters. But I should warn you that they often don't reply. Most of them don't want any contact at all with the media."

"What a nuisance," Annika said.

"What's the purpose of your visits?" the governor asked amiably.

Annika hesitated. What did she have to lose by being honest?

"I'm writing an article about David Lindholm, the police officer who was murdered. Three of your inmates had some sort of relationship with him. How long does it take to get a visitor's permit, assuming that they do want to talk to me?"

"It usually takes about a week, ten days. But I have to tell you that you can only visit one of our inmates, unless you're a close relative."

Annika closed her eyes and ran a hand through her hair.

"What?"

"If you have three brothers, you can visit them all, but you can't have permits to visit three different prisoners without there being an exceptionally good reason. You'll have to pick one of them."

"You don't seem terribly keen on having the media visit your prisoners, do you?"

"Not terribly, no," the governor said. "But we don't prohibit it. And if you do come, I must warn you that photography is forbidden."

Annika straightened up.

"What? Why? That's . . ."

"Chapter one, paragraph nineteen of the Criminal Custody Act 2006:26. 'Audio recording and photography are not permitted within the premises of the facility . . . '"

She slumped back in her chair.

"Okay," she said. "Should I use the fax number on your website?"

"That would be splendid," the governor said.

She pushed the computer away from her, glanced at the time, and looked out across the newsroom, with its flickering screens and bowed necks and coffee-stained desks.

He'll have picked up the children by now.

They'll be on their way home.

The lift doors were the lovely, old-fashioned sort, two folding gates that had to be pushed aside to reveal the polished brass interior to the better class of people who inhabited the property in Upper Östermalm.

Thomas could still remember how well thought out the period detail had seemed the first time he took the lift up, with his own keys, to his own flat, in his own building . . .

"Daddy, she's pushing me!"

He moved his briefcase from one hand to the other and couldn't help sighing.

"Listen, both of you," he said, grabbing his son by the collar to stop him hitting his sister. "Will you please stop fighting, we're almost home now . . ."

Yes, this is my building. Well, it's hers, but . . .

He tugged the outer gate open.

A howl of pain echoed through the stairwell. He looked down in surprise to see Ellen's contorted face lifted toward him. Her fingers were utterly trapped in the folded gate, her eyes overflowed and her cheeks were bright red.

He quickly shut the gate in order to free the little girl's fingers, and she curled into a little ball at his feet, holding the other hand around the squashed fingers.

"Oh, little one, what on earth were you doing? You mustn't put your fingers there when Daddy's opening the door . . ."

Blood was dripping onto the marble floor, making the girl's scream rise to a falsetto.

"It's blooding, Daddy, it's blooding . . ."

Thomas could feel himself going pale. He wasn't good with bodily fluids.

"There, there, let Daddy see, do you want me to blow on it?"

He crouched down beside the girl and reached out for her hand, but she turned her back on him and clutched her hand to her new winter overalls.

Damn, now those were going to get covered in blood.

"Listen, darling, let Daddy see . . ."

"You hurt me!"

"I know, darling, I'm sorry, I didn't mean to but I didn't see, I couldn't see that you had your hand there, I'm so sorry . . ."

He picked the girl up, taking care not to get blood on his coat. That backfired immediately when she burrowed her head against his neck and wiped her tears and snot against the collar of his jacket.

"It huuurts . . ."

"There, there," Thomas said, feeling himself breaking into a sweat all over his body.

"She's always so clumsy," Kalle said, staring wide eyed at the blood that was already turning dark on the floor.

"Okay," he said, "into the lift now."

He guided his son in with one arm, holding his daughter with the other, then grabbed for his briefcase and put it inside the lift, closed the gates (first one, then the other), and let Kalle press the button for the sixth floor.

The loft apartment.

The penthouse, as Sophie described it on her website.

"It huuurts, Daddy . . ."

"There, there," Thomas said, watching impatiently as the floors slid past, the chandelier on the third floor disappearing past his feet, the paneled walls of four with its patrician portraits and double doors sliding past.

"What are we having for tea?"

Kalle was always hungry these days.

"You know, I'm not sure. Sophia was going to make something."

The lift stopped at the top of the building with a little shudder.

"Now, keep your fingers out of the way," he said unnecessarily loudly before he opened the gates.

He couldn't be bothered to hunt through his briefcase for the keys to the flat, so rang the bell with his free hand as he hoisted Ellen up better with the other. She was sobbing and crying and nursing her fingers.

"Shush, shush," he said, rocking her rather helplessly.

Nothing happened. Ellen's screaming started to subside slightly. He couldn't hear any sounds inside the flat. The little girl was starting to feel very heavy on his arm. Was Sophia not at home?

He rang the bell again.

The door flew open before the ringing stopped.

Sophia was wearing an apron and had her sleeves rolled up. There was a tiny wrinkle between her eyebrows.

"Did you forget your keys?" she asked before noticing that Ellen was crying.

Thomas pushed past her and knelt to put his daughter down on the hall floor.

"Okay, now you have to show Daddy where your fingers got hurt," he said, taking the girl's hand.

"Has there been an accident?"

He closed his eyes for a second and swallowed, letting go of the girl's hand, then stood up and smiled.

"Darling," he said, kissing her on the cheek. "Ellen got her fingers caught in the lift, she's bleeding quite badly, I need to get her cleaned up."

"You were the one who caught her in the lift," Kalle said sullenly, glaring at Sophia.

"Take your clothes off and hang them up, then go and wash your hands," Thomas said, shrugging off his own coat.

It would have to be dry-cleaned before he could wear it again. He glanced down at his jacket. Same thing there.

He looked at Sophia. She didn't notice his silent plea and turned and went back out into the kitchen again.

Annika always took care of the dry-cleaning.

The thought hit him from out of nowhere and made him blink.

Yes, that was how it had been, ever since the time when he managed to lose the ticket for the old angora cardigan her grandmother had given her.

He pressed his coat and jacket into a pile on the hall bench.

"Right, then," he said, picking up the little girl. "Let's go and put a plaster on it."

She had almost stopped crying now.

He carried her into the bathroom and discovered that there was a cut right under the cuticle on her right ring finger. She'd probably lose the nail.

"It's blue," Ellen said, staring in fascination at the end of her finger.

"Like blueberry pie," Thomas said, and she giggled.

He sat down on the lid of the toilet and put his daughter on his lap, rocking her gently.

"Sorry," he whispered. "I didn't mean to squash your fingers."

"Do you get sweets if you've squashed your fingers?"

The child looked at him hopefully as she wiped her nose on her sleeve.

"Maybe," he said. "If we've got any."

"You can get them in the shop. Foam cars are good."

They went out into the flat, hand in hand. The girl's body was still trembling slightly with the aftershocks from her tears.

She's so fragile, I have to take more care of her.

Kalle hadn't hung his outdoor clothes up, leaving them in a heap on the hall floor. Thomas swallowed an annoyed comment and bent down and hung them up.

When he stood up he saw Sophia watching him from the door to the kitchen.

"If you keep tidying up after him like that, he'll never learn," she said.

He shrugged lightly, smiled, then held out his arms.

"You're right," he said, tilting his head to one side.

She smiled back.

"You can sit down at the table, dinner's ready."

She disappeared into the kitchen again. Thomas went through to the dining table in the studio and ducked instinctively in the large, open space of the room. The normal ceiling height in the hall and bathroom exaggerated the difference. The studio space dominated the flat, and only the sloping wall separated it from the sky. It had to be seven or eight meters tall at its highest point. The oblong skylights and muddle of beams made you think of Tribeca or some other hip New York neighborhood (not that he had ever been in an apartment in Tribeca, but Sophia had, and she had explained the similarity to him).

"Kalle," he called over his shoulder. "Dinner's ready."

He could hear the bleep of a PlayStation game from the boy's little room, which wasn't really much more than a cupboard, and sighed. Then he picked Ellen up and sat her on top of a cushion so she could reach her plate. Sophia had thought buying a high chair unnecessary—"She'll soon be taller"—which was true enough.

She came in with a bowl of mashed potato and a frying pan full of slices of fat sausage.

"Kalle!" Thomas called again, sitting down. "Dinner's on the table!"

"I just need to die first," the boy called back dully.

"No! Come out here, *now!*"

Sophia was looking down at the table, she didn't like it when he shouted.

There was a demonstrative sigh, then the noise of the game stopped and the boy came out into the studio.

"I was about to beat my high score, *actually.*"

Thomas ruffled his hair.

"Well, you can have some sausage instead."

"Yum!" the boy said, scrambling up onto the tall, leather-covered chrome chair. "Are those onions? Yuk. Can I scrape them off?"

"Just try one," Thomas said.

"Here we eat what we're served," Sophia said. "Some wine?"

She was smiling at him. He smiled back.

"Thanks, I'd love some."

All food tastes so much better with wine. Meatballs and pasta taste better. Sausage tastes better. Even instant mashed potato becomes edible. I've drunk far too little wine up to now.

They touched glasses.

"How was your day?" she asked, tasting her rioja.

He took a sip and closed his eyes. *Divine.*

"Oh," he said, putting his glass down. "Cramne's ignoring me since I pointed out how impossible it was to follow the directives. He just thinks it's a good idea to raise the sentencing guidelines, and I don't really think I have much of an opinion on that, but the costs are bound to increase, which conflicts entirely with the directives we were given for the inquiry..."

He took another sip, and Sophia nodded understandingly.

"It's very good that you've pointed that out," she said. "Now this socialist government will have to think again, and that will be thanks to you."

He put his glass back and looked down at his plate. He'd voted for this socialist government and actually thought that they were doing a reasonable job. He knew Sophia didn't share that opinion, but she probably imagined that he shared hers.

Annika always voted left of center.

He pushed the thought away.

"What about you?" he said. "How has your day been?"

Just as Sophia opened her mouth to speak, Ellen started crying.

"It hurts again, Daddy," she said, holding up her plastered finger toward him. He could see that the plaster was tight, the top of her finger had swollen up.

"Oh dear," he said, blowing on her hand. "We might have to give you a little pill so you can get to sleep with that silly hand."

"Or sweets," the girl said, wiping her tears.

"Maybe you're allowed to have sweets even if you haven't squashed your finger," Kalle said.

"You have to eat up first," Thomas said, "then you can have a look in my briefcase."

"Hurray!" Kalle said, waving his knife and fork and splashing some fat from the sausage onto the wallpaper.

"Oh no," Thomas said, "look at what you just did!"

Sophia got up to fetch a clean dishcloth and wiped the wall. There was already a stain.

"Now sit nicely at the table," Thomas said, and Kalle shrank away from his gaze.

They ate in silence.

"Can I get down?" Kalle said, putting his knife and fork together.

"Wait for your sister," Thomas said and the boy groaned.

"But she's so slow."

"I've finished now," the little girl said, pushing her half-cleaned plate away.

"Okay," Thomas said, and breathed out quietly, relieved, as the children had got down and rushed out into the hall.

He looked at Sophia and smiled. She smiled back at him. They touched glasses again.

"This is the life," she said, looking into his eyes as they drank.

He didn't answer, just looked at her glossy blond hair and bright eyes.

Sausage and powdered mash. This was the life?

"It's not hard to make the world sparkle for a party," she went on. "But an ordinary Tuesday, like this, this is what we need to make the most of. Adding a bit of sparkle to everyday life, that's the important thing."

He looked down at the table, obviously she was right.

So why does it make me feel so embarrassed? Why am I just thinking "Bollocks!"?

"Are you thinking about work?" she asked, putting a hand on his arm.

He looked up at her.

"I'm afraid so," he said. "The verdict in the first appeal for clemency is due in Örebro District Court tomorrow."

She looked at him quizzically.

"Clemency?"

He opened his mouth to go on, then realized that she didn't know, that she didn't understand the workings of the judicial system.

Of course not, why should she?

"Up to now, people serving life sentences have only been able to get their sentences limited by the government, by asking for clemency, but that system was never entirely legally sound. The government never gave any explanation for its decisions, and they couldn't be appealed against. But for a while now lifers have been able to turn to Örebro District Court as well, to get their appeal for clemency adjudicated. They get represented by a legal ombudsman and are given a judicial motivation for the decision. The first verdict's due tomorrow."

He took a sip of wine.

"It wouldn't be a bad thing if the case was rejected," he said. "Obviously it wouldn't be good if the first signal was that it was much easier to pursue cases in Örebro than with the government."

"But," she said, "why Örebro?"

He smiled at her.

"Where are the largest prisons?"

"Which prisons?"

"Kumla and Hinseberg. The largest male and female prisons, respectively. And where are they?"

She opened her eyes wide.

"In Örebro County?"

"Bingo!"

She laughed.

"Imagine," she said, "I never knew that. What a lot I'm learning now I'm with you!"

He looked over toward the children, who were sitting by the door to the hall sharing out the sweets between them.

He had had the same discussion with Annika long before, when the location of the new clemency procedure was still under discussion. She had also questioned Örebro as a suitable site, and he had said the same thing then: "Where are the largest prisons?"

"Bullshit!" had been Annika's response. "By the time they come to apply for clemency they're no longer in Kumla or Hinseberg. They're out in some open prison in the middle of nowhere waiting to be rehabilitated. The only reason this is being linked to Örebro is that the minister has his constituency there."

He remembered how taken aback he had been: That thought hadn't actually occurred to him.

"You're making that up," he had replied, and she had shrugged.

Now he looked at Sophia again.

"What about you, then?" he asked. "How are you?"

"Such a funny thing happened today," she said, but at that moment Kalle came racing toward him.

"Daddy, tell her off! She took the last sweet because she said she was the one who got hurt."

He emptied his glass and stood up.

"If you fight about the sweets, I'll have to take them away," he said, then turned back toward Sophia. "You stay there, I'll do the dishes later. I need to get her overalls in the wash, there's blood all over them."

He headed off toward the hall, and from the corner of his eye he saw Sophia refilling her glass.

p. 13

EVENING POST—STOCKHOLM EDITION
THURSDAY, NOVEMBER 25

"IT HAS TO BE LIFE"
EXPERTS UNANIMOUS AFTER POLICE TRIAL

By Berit Hamrin
Evening Post (Stockholm). Life imprisonment. Anything else would be unthinkable.

Prosecutor Angela Nilsson was absolutely certain when the trial of Julia Lindholm concluded at Stockholm City Court yesterday.

"I've seldom been involved with such a calculated and brutal crime."

Prosecutor Nilsson didn't spare the accused during her final statement in the high-security courtroom yesterday afternoon. She called Julia Lindholm "emotionally cold" and "cunning," and demanded nothing less than life imprisonment.

"Killing your child, refusing to say where you hid the body and then pretending that you're a different person . . . There aren't actually any words to describe what I think of that," the prosecutor said, among other things.

The three-day trial in Stockholm City Court has seen a lot of emotion and a great deal of grief. The presiding judge has had to call for calm on several occasions. David Lindholm's colleagues have been seen sobbing openly in the public benches. Julia Lindholm's parents have attended all three days, and her mother broke down several times.

Julia Lindholm herself was extremely concise in her testimony. She answered in monosyllables and showed no emotion. She claims that there was another woman in the flat on the night of June 3 this year, and that it was this other woman who shot her husband and then took her son with her when she left.

According to the forensic examination of the crime scene, there is nothing to suggest that anyone else was in the home, which is one reason why a psychological evaluation determined that Julia Lindholm was suffering from a mental disorder at the time of the crime.

Julia Lindholm's lawyer, Mats Lennström, maintains that there are clear gaps in the prosecution's case.

"Most troubling is of course the fact that Alexander Lindholm's body has never been found. But there are also other assertions that I believe must be questioned. Julia has already said that she had mislaid her service revolver. And there were no traces of gunpowder on her when she was arrested."

The prosecutor dismissed the defense lawyer's objections in her final statement.

"You can't get away with murder simply because you have managed to make the body disappear. The fact that the defense claims that she had mislaid her service revolver and had time to wash her hands before the police arrived on the scene does not count as extenuating circumstances, but rather the opposite."

The verdict will be announced on December 2. Until then, Julia Lindholm will remain in custody.

Hampus Lagerbäck, professor of criminology, who was close friends with the victim, is in no doubt about what this means: "Clearly, she's going to be found guilty.

"No one I've spoken to expects anything but a life sentence."

PART 3

December

It was snowing. Hard white ice crystals were lashing at Annika's face as she made her way along Vasagatan. The streetlamps were blurred and yellow in the darkness, and when she peered across at the Central Station she couldn't see anything but swirling snow. She felt giddy and groggy, wasn't used to being up this early. She was having trouble judging distances and kept putting her foot down wrong.

Taking the train instead of driving had been a stroke of genius, not just because she was so tired. The traffic was solid, car wheels were spinning at the red lights, and no one was getting anywhere. She checked the time: fifteen minutes to go.

Almost two weeks had passed since she faxed off her letter to Filip Andersson in the prison in Kumla.

The acting prison governor had been right. Neither Stevens, the American, nor the Arab, Svensson, had replied to her faxes, despite the fact that she had written three times.

But Filip Andersson, the ax murderer, on the other hand, had written back by return. He would be very happy to see a member of the media, and if she could send him her personal details at once, he would arrange a visitor's permit for her. He also took the opportunity to send her a lot of information about his case, and there was a heavy stench of miscarriage of justice from the envelope. He had news for her, he said, and it was important that she was well acquainted with the facts of his case.

With a degree of reluctance, she sent him her personal details. Of course there was nothing confidential in what she was sending, her address and ID number were matters of public record, but it had still felt uncomfortable faxing them off.

What could he possibly do, though? Hide under her bed clutching an ax?

And that was hardly likely, seeing as she slept on a mattress on the floor.

In fact, out of the three of them, Filip Andersson had been the one she was least keen to meet. She persuaded herself that this was because he was least likely to dish the dirt on David Lindholm.

A stairwell, gray stone landings. Blood on the yellow walls, blood dripping down the steps. The smell, thick and heavy. "Police! There are guns aimed at you! Julia, get the door. Annika, get out of here!"

She shook the image away.

On the other hand, Filip Andersson was probably the most likely of the three to be able to express himself articulately. According to the report of the trial, Svensson had spoken through an interpreter, which suggested that his Swedish wasn't good. Maybe he hadn't been able to read her fax, but she hadn't been given any other way of contacting him, so she had to give up the attempt.

There had been nothing about interpreters in the report of the Stevens trial, so she presumed that his Swedish must be reasonable, but her limited experience of hired thugs suggested that he was hardly likely to be particularly talkative.

Which left the ax murderer from Sankt Paulsgatan. She had booked a time at the visitors' section of Kumla prison for 1100 today, December 1.

She had to admit that she had slept badly.

Not just because she was going to be locked in a confined visiting room together with a violent mass murderer, or because the children were back with Thomas and his wretched ice maiden, but because something was gnawing away at her, something she had missed. No matter how much she twisted and turned under the covers, she hadn't managed to work out what it was.

I'll have to try and wheedle it out of him, whatever it is.

She had been through the verdict in Filip Andersson's case carefully, and had checked Sjölander's old computer for any more files relating to the case, but had found nothing else.

There were certainly weaknesses in the case, but she hadn't found any glaring errors. Filip Andersson had been at the scene of the murders; he had both the opportunity and motive. According to one witness, the three victims had tricked Andersson out of a large sum of money, which was presumed to be the motive. Revenge. It wasn't mentioned in the report of the trial, but Annika knew that theft rarely went unpunished in Filip Andersson's world. Not to respond could be seen as an invitation to further attempts, which was evidently why Andersson had decided to make an example of them.

A gossip blog for journalists had provided more details about the nature of the victims' deception, but Annika had no way of knowing how accurate that was.

The blog claimed that the three of them had been involved in an elaborate money-laundering scheme largely based on the Spanish coast. Through a number of different property deals, mostly conducted through Gibraltar, they had managed to process the considerable profits of trafficking cocaine from Columbia via Morocco.

Annika had some difficulty envisioning the staid Swedish financier as the business partner of a South American drug lord, but what did she know?

The three murder victims, who were all fairly low down in the criminal food chain, had put the money in their own pockets instead and believed that Andersson wouldn't notice. Which is why he chopped their hands off, to show that they should have kept their greedy fingers to themselves.

But there were undoubtedly some details of the case that struck Annika as very odd.

Most significantly, if Filip Andersson was so high up the food chain, why would he want to get his smart trousers splattered with blood by doing the dirty work himself? Were all the hired thugs on holiday at the same time? Or was he simply a sadist?"

If he had the ability and ruthlessness to build up an advanced drug-smuggling syndicate, would he really have left his fingerprints on the handbag of one of the victims?

And why wasn't there more blood on his trousers?

And why on earth use an ax?

The entrance to the Central Station emerged through the swirling snow in front of her, and she went inside, stamping her feet.

She had booked first-class tickets, so she could sit in peace and do some work on the journey. The train was due to leave at 0715, and after a change at Hallsberg she would get to Kumla at 0932. She had booked a return ticket for 1328, and was already looking forward to it.

The Central Station was literally black with people, even though it was still extremely early in Annika's world.

Why doesn't anyone ever wear bright red in winter? Or orange? Do nature, the climate, and the Swedish need to drain all the color out of us?

She hadn't had time for breakfast, so she bought a yogurt drink and an apple from a kiosk.

The train was due to leave from platform ten.

It rattled into the station just as she emerged onto the platform. She found her carriage, then her place, took off her coat, settled into the seat, and fell asleep immediately.

She woke with a start when the speakers announced "Next stop Hallsberg, Hallsberg next stop." Groggy with sleep, she struggled into her coat and tumbled out onto the platform seconds before the doors closed and the train headed off further south.

She was on the point of getting into a taxi when she realized that she wasn't in Kumla yet; she had a six-minute trip on a local train still to go.

I have to pull myself together, I have to be focused when I meet the ax murderer.

She shook herself to clear her head. She had to run to catch the local train to Örebro. The flat countryside with its brown fields and gray farmhouses spread out around her as the train set off, and her eyes found nothing to focus on until they saw a strip of pine forest over on the horizon, blurred by mist.

She was the only passenger to get off in Kumla.

It had stopped snowing. Dampness hung heavy and cold over the town. The train rumbled off, leaving an echoing silence behind it. She stood there listening to it for several seconds, looking round. A big ICA supermarket, a Pentecostal church, the Hotel Kumla. Hesitantly she set off toward the exit, her heels loud on the concrete platform.

She descended into a gray tunnel and emerged into a gray square, beside a Sibylla fast-food kiosk. Her stomach was rumbling. She had left the apple and yogurt drink on the first train. She went over to the hatch and ordered a thin-bread roll with two sausages, prawn cocktail sauce, and a can of Ramlösa. She couldn't hear if the lad inside said twenty-three or seventy-three, so she offered him a hundred to be on the safe side, and got back change from seventy-three.

For a thin-bread roll!

And the "Ramlösa" was ordinary tap water in a Coke cup.

Hardly surprising that people turn to crime here.

She gulped down the food in three minutes flat, threw the napkin and half the roll in the bin and headed across the cobbles toward the taxi rank in the distance, feeling decidedly unwell.

"Viagatan, number 4," she said as she got into a large Volvo.

"That sounds like a very big prison," the taxi driver said.

"Yes," Annika said. "I've had enough. Farewell, cruel world."

The taxi driver shook his head.

"Wrong place," he said. "There's no place for you there. Hinseberg's in Frövi, on the other side of Örebro."

"Damn," Annika said.

The car swung to the right, and there it was. The walls and barbed wire began almost in the center of town itself. The taxi drove alongside an endless electrified fence that eventually made way for a large metal gate.

"Okay," he said, "I can't get any closer than this."

The drive cost sixty kronor, less than the thin-bread roll.

She paid, and the taxi disappeared, leaving her alone in front of the huge entrance. A double layer of fencing stretched out on either side, first a chain-link fence with several layers of barbed wire at the top, then an electric fence that must have been at least five meters tall. The wind was whistling through the metal wires.

She hoisted her bag onto her shoulder and went over to the entry phone.

"My name's Annika Bengtzon, I'm here to see Filip Andersson."

Her voice sounded small and thin.

This is how they must feel, anyone visiting their husbands in prison. Only even worse, of course, because for them it's real.

There was a whirring sound from the gate and she pulled at it cautiously and went in. She found herself on a tarmac drive leading to the next gate. The fencing continued on either side of her; she was walking through a caged enclosure with the wind pulling at her hair and around her legs, one hundred or so long meters of bare no-man's-land before she reached a building with two doors.

VISITS TO INMATES it said on the left one, so that was hers.

She pressed another entry phone.

The door was extremely heavy; she had to use both hands to open it.

She stepped inside a long entrance hall, with a stroller parked just inside the door. A young woman with a ponytail was standing there tapping at her mobile phone with her back to Annika, ignoring her.

Three of the walls were covered with white metal lockers. The fourth wall had windows with closed blue curtains. Beneath the windows was a row of chairs. It looked like a dentist's waiting room.

She pressed a third entry phone.

"Someone will be with you shortly," a voice said curtly.

The girl with the ponytail put her mobile in her bag and left the building without looking at Annika.

So this is what it's like. There's no sense of solidarity, even among prison wives.

She stood in the middle of the floor for a while. She leaned over and peeked behind the curtains. Thick metal bars, of course, white.

She let the curtain fall.

She went over to a notice board next to the phone and read about opening hours and information about the renovation of the overnight rooms.

"Take off your outdoor clothes and leave them in a locker."

She straightened up and stared around her.

The voice had come from a loudspeaker. She looked up at the surveillance camera in the top-left corner of the room and felt the blood rush to her face. Of course, they were bound to be watching her.

She quickly took off her coat and scarf and stuffed them into locker number ten, as far from the camera as possible.

"You can come in now," the voice said.

The lock clicked and she opened the door to the visitors' section and found herself at a security check. A metal detector to the left, and an X-ray machine and conveyor belt for bags on the right.

Two uniformed guards, one male, one female, were watching her through a glass screen.

"You can put your bag on the belt and go through the detector."

She did as she was told with her pulse beating in irritation. Of course she managed to set the alarm off as she walked through the machine.

"Take off your shoes and put them on the belt."

She obeyed. The noise stopped.

Then she was allowed to step behind the glass screen and go up to the desk.

"ID, please," the man said, and she handed him her press pass.

"Would you mind opening your bag, please," the woman said.

Once again, Annika did as she was told.

"There's a knife in your bag," the female guard said, pulling out a penknife with the slogan *The Evening Post—sharp and to the point.* "You can't take that in. Not that pen either."

"But what am I supposed to write with?" Annika said, hearing that she sounded almost desperate.

"You can borrow one from us," the guard said, handing her a yellow Bic.

"You'll have to leave your mobile as well," the male guard said.

"You know what," Annika said. "I'll leave my bag in the locker and just take my notepad and pen in with me. Your pen."

The guards nodded. She took back the penknife and phone and went back out into the waiting room again, opened her locker and put her bag inside, then went back through the door to the visitors' section and skirted around the metal detector without going through it. She smiled uncertainly and felt oddly eager to be pleasant.

"Do the prisoners get many visitors?" she asked.

"We have five thousand visitors a year, but they're fairly evenly spread out. Forty percent of inmates never get visitors."

"Goodness. Am I the first visitor to see Filip Andersson?"

"No, not at all," the female guard said. "His sister comes at least once a month."

"And David Lindholm? As I understand it, he was here a few days before he died."

"We see trustees and probation contacts here quite a lot," the woman said.

The male warder had stuck her press pass onto a notice board with a big metal clip. He put a document on the counter in front of him and pointed at a series of directives without taking his eyes off her.

"You could be asked to take off your clothes and be searched by two female warders," he said, "and you have the right to refuse. But if you do, you won't be allowed in. You could also be checked for drugs by a dog from the drugs squad. Again, you have the right to refuse. Same thing there, you won't be allowed in. You can't take any food in, and smoking isn't allowed anywhere. You have to sign to say that you agree to being locked inside the visiting room with the inmate."

Annika nodded and swallowed. It was suddenly very quiet. She signed with the yellow Bic to acknowledge that she accepted the conditions.

"We provide fruit and coffee, and if visitors have children they can have juice. Would you like anything?" the female guard said as she led the way down a corridor with numbered doors. She gestured toward a table of refreshments.

The thought of anyone bringing children into these surroundings sent a cold shiver down Annika's spine. She declined the offer with a shake of the head.

"Here's room number five. I'll just check it's okay. You'll have to tidy up after yourselves."

The guard opened the door and went into the small room ahead of Annika.

"There's a toilet and shower here," she said, pointing. "This is the intercom, if you want the central warders' office. And next to it is the alarm. Oh, someone's left some toys out . . ."

She bent down and picked up a pink stuffed animal and a plastic spinning top from the floor.

"One of the inmates had his little son to see him yesterday," she said apologetically.

"That must be difficult," Annika said lamely.

The guard smiled.

"We try to make the best of the situation. The children get balloons when they leave. Jimmy blows them up for them."

"Jimmy?"

"The other guard."

She gestured toward a low cupboard.

"There are sheets and blankets in there. I'll put a call through for the inmate now."

She went over to the door, leaving Annika standing paralyzed next to the item of furniture that took up almost the entire floor area of the room: a narrow bed with a foam-rubber mattress.

The door closed with a muffled clang, and the lock turned.

Holy fucking Christ, what have I let myself in for?

She started at the walls. They were creeping toward her, making it hard to breathe.

How am I going to handle this? I need a strategy, now!

There was one chair in the room, and she made up her mind to take it under occupation. There was absolutely no chance that she was going to end up on the bed next to the ax murderer.

She put her notepad and pen on top of the cupboard, deciding to use it as a desk. She glanced around the walls. There was one picture, a black-and-white image of some dockworkers laboring on a quayside, in a brownish-red frame. It was a poster for an exhibition of Torsten Billman's work at the National Museum, June 17–August 10, 1986.

Behind her were two windows, and she peered behind the curtains. The same white metal bars as on the windows of the waiting room with all the lockers.

I wonder how long I'll have to wait? The inmates may have to come a fair distance.

The minutes crept past. She looked at her watch four times in three minutes, then pulled her sleeve down over it to stop herself from looking. She looked up at the metal box that was evidently an intercom, and her gaze settled on the alarm next to it.

She could feel that she was sweating, even though the room was fairly cold.

There was a rattle from the lock, a clunk, and then the door swung open.

"Just let us know when you're done," the guard said, then stepped aside to let the prisoner in.

She stood up to introduce herself and stared at the man who walked into the room.

Who the hell is this?

Pictures of the trial had shown a long-haired man, pretty muscular, with suntanned skin and a curl to his lip. This was an old man with cropped, graying hair and a serious beer gut, in washed-out prison clothing and with plastic slippers on his feet.

Four years—was such a transformation possible in just four years?

He held out his hand.

"I hope they weren't too hard on you with all the security checks?" he said.

Annika had to stifle an impulse to curtsy.

This place does weird things to people.

"No worse than flying to Gothenburg," she said.

"Us inmates come from the other direction, and go through the same thing," he said, without letting go of her hand. "I agree, it's not that bad, although we have to change our shoes. Apparently there's a risk that we might hollow out the soles of our trainers and fill them with drugs."

Annika pulled her hand away.

"Mind you, it's worse when we leave here and go back to our sections. We have to strip off. Then go naked through the metal detector. They have to check that we haven't hidden any weapons up our backsides, of course."

She quickly sat down in the chair, leaving the bed for him. He sat down, and their knees almost collided. She pulled back and picked up her pen and notepad.

"They check the metal detector every day," Filip Andersson said. "That might seem a bit extreme, but the fact is that it works. Kumla's a damn good prison, in the eyes of society. Hardly any drugs here. Very few escapes. None since the break-out that summer, and we don't kill each other very often either . . ."

Annika gulped.

He's trying to shock me. Nothing to worry about.

"A life sentence," she said. "How does anyone deal with that?"

That wasn't the question she had planned to start with, not at all. It just popped out.

He looked at her in silence for a few seconds. There was something watery about his gaze.

Is he on happy pills?

"I've got some information for you," he said. "New information about the case. I've applied for a retrial in the Supreme Court."

He said it as if he had just detonated the news story of the century. Annika looked at him and tried not to blink. What did he mean? How was she supposed to react? *Really? Goodness, how exciting!* Or what? Every small-time criminal tried to get a retrial in the Supreme Court.

She fumbled in the silence of the room, trying to think of something polite to say to move things on.

"What sort of new information?" she asked, and he nodded for her to pick up her pen and notepad, which she did.

"Have you read the documents I sent you?"

She nodded, she had actually glanced through them. At least, the ones at the top.

Filip Andersson rested his elbows on his thighs and leaned forward. Annika moved back slightly.

"I was convicted even though I'm innocent," he said, emphasizing every word. "The application for a retrial proves that."

Had the application for a retrial been among the papers he had sent her? She didn't think so.

"In what way?" she said, drawing a small question mark on her note-pad.

"The mobile phone," he said, nodding emphatically.

She looked at him, at his bulging stomach and pale arms. The earlier impression of him being muscular had probably been wrong, the result of very well tailored suits. Maybe he used to dye his hair. She knew he was forty-seven years old, but he looked considerably older than that.

"What?" Annika said.

"The police never checked the call log! I wasn't in Sankt Paulsgatan when the murders were committed."

"So where were you?" Annika said.

He opened his eyes wide, then they narrowed to thin slits.

"What the hell has that got to do with you?" he said and Annika felt her pulse race once more, and had to make an effort not to draw away from him.

"Nothing," she said, "it's got nothing to do with me."

Her voice sounded far too high.

Filip Andersson lifted a finger and pointed right at her face.

"You don't know shit!" he said, with a ferocity he couldn't quite live up to.

Suddenly Annika's heartbeat slowed down. She looked into his damp eyes and found desperation and hopelessness, someone clutching at straws.

He's like a cornered dog barking, but he can't bite in here. There's no danger, there's no danger.

The man stood up quickly and went over to the door, two short steps, then turned and came back. He put his hands on the arms of the chair and leaned over her. He had bad breath.

"You're here to write about my application for a retrial," he said. "Not to ask a load of fucking questions!"

"No, you're wrong there," she said, not bothered by the fact that she was talking right into his face. "I'm the one who asked to visit you, so this is on my terms."

He let go of the chair and stood up.

"If you calm down and listen, you'll find out what I want," Annika said. "If you carry on making demands, I'll leave."

"Why should I listen to you?"

"I know a lot more than you think," Annika said. "I was there."

"What?"

"I was there."

He sat down on the bed with a little thud, his mouth half open.

"Where?"

"I was in the patrol car that was first to arrive on the scene in Sankt Paulsgatan that night. I didn't see much, but I noticed the smell."

"You were there? What did you see?"

She didn't take her eyes off him.

"The blood. It was splattered all over the walls, and it was dripping down the stairs, slowly. It was thick, but bright. Bright red. The walls were yellow."

"You didn't see anything else?"

She glanced up at the dockworkers, struggling under the weight of heavy sacks in Torsten Billman's picture.

"Her hair. It was dark. She was lying on the landing, moving her head. Julia Lindholm was first up the stairs, then Nina Hoffman, and then me, I was last, Julia first, but Nina took charge of the situation, she was the one who drew her gun."

She looked back at him.

Filip Andersson was staring back at her.

"Did she say anything?"

"She shouted 'Police,' and then 'There are guns aimed at you. Julia, get the door. Annika, get out of here.' That's what she shouted. Then I turned and ran out."

He was shaking his head.

"Not the police. Olga."

"Who?"

"The dark-haired woman."

He means the victim.

Annika couldn't help gulping again.

"I don't know," she said. "I don't think she said anything. She died before the ambulance arrived."

The silence in the room had changed now, it was no longer uncertain, but heavy and suffocating.

"What do you know about Algot Heinrich Heimer?" she asked, and Filip Andersson started, just a little twitch around his mouth, but Annika saw it.

"Who?"

"He's dead, but that's hardly your fault. How did he know David?"

Annika already knew this, at least in part. They had both been involved in the parachute equipment business.

The financier looked at her with empty eyes.

"If you haven't got anything more to say to me, then I'll go now," Annika said.

"They were childhood friends," the man said quietly. "David was like a big brother to Henke."

Henke?

"But things went badly for Henke?" Annika said.

"David really did try to help him, but it was no good."

"Why was he shot?"

Filip Andersson shrugged.

"Maybe he did something stupid."

"Or else he was just a way for someone to get back at David. Mike Stevens is in here, do you know him?"

Another shrug.

"What about Bertil Oskar Holmberg, then? Who's he?"

"I don't know."

"You're sure?"

"I didn't do it. I wasn't even there. I wasn't in Sankt Paulsgatan."

Annika studied the man before her, trying to see his eyes.

The pupils are an opening into the brain. I should be able to see his thoughts.

"If you're telling the truth, that means someone else did it."

He stared at her.

"If you're telling the truth," Annika said, slightly louder now, "that means you know who the real killer is, but you'd rather sit in here serving life than say what you know. And do you know why?"

His mouth was hanging open again.

"Because at least you're alive in here. If you say what you know, you're dead. Aren't you? And why did you ask about Olga? Are you worried she had time to talk?"

He didn't answer. She stood up, and he followed her with his eyes.

"I can just about accept," she said, facing the door, "that you'd rather keep quiet about who really beat those people to death in order to save your own skin, but there's something else that I just don't understand."

She turned round and looked at him.

"Why was David Lindholm the only person who thought you were innocent? Well? How come one of the most famous policemen in Sweden was the only one who believed you? Was it because he was so much better than all the other cops? Did he see something else in the investigation that the prosecutor, the defense, and the court missed? No, that's not it, is it?"

She sat down on the low cupboard with the sheets and blankets.

"The only reason why David believed you was because he knew something that nobody else did. He believed you because he knew who really did it, or else he thought that he knew. Is that right?"

Filip Andersson didn't move.

"I can understand you keeping your mouth shut," Annika said. "After all, you are where you are. But there's one thing I just can't understand. Why did David keep his mouth shut?"

She stood up again.

"No one believes you," she said, "but David had every chance in the world to say what he knew. He would have been hero of the hour yet again. There's only one reasonable explanation for the way he acted."

The man was looking straight ahead at the curtains. He didn't answer.

"I've thought a lot about this over the past few weeks. David must have been terrified as well," Annika declared. "Not of being killed: He doesn't seem to have been scared of death. No, he was scared of something else."

She went over to the chair and sat down again, leaning to one side to catch Filip Andersson's eye.

"What was important to David?" she asked. "What meant so much to him that he would keep quiet about a mass murderer? Was it money? Reputation? His career? Or girls? Sex? Drugs? Was he an addict?"

Filip Andersson looked down for a moment, and his hands fumbled with a handkerchief.

"What exactly were you and he involved in? What's the connection? He knew you before the murders, you were in touch long before then, weren't you? I have no idea whether or not you're guilty of carrying out these executions, but you're pretty damn crooked. How were you involved with a famous policeman? And why on earth did he risk his career by associating with you?"

Filip Andersson sighed deeply and looked up.

"You really haven't understood a single thing," he said. "Do you know that?"

"So, tell me then!" Annika said. "I'm all ears."

He looked at her with a sadness so great that it seemed to go on forever.

"Are you really sure you want to know?" he said. "Are you willing to pay the price of knowing?"

"Absolutely," Annika said.

He shook his head and stood up slowly. He didn't look at her as he put one hand on her shoulder and called for the guards.

"Believe me," he said. "It isn't worth it. We're done now."

This last sentence was directed at the intercom.

"Don't go," Annika said. "You haven't answered anything at all."

The look on his face was almost tender.

"You're welcome to write about my application for a retrial," he said. "I think there's a real chance that they'll consider it. I was in Bromma when the murders took place."

Annika picked up her notepad and pen.

"Your mobile phone was there. What's to say that you were the one using it?"

He stared at her but didn't have time to reply, because the door opened and he left the room, his plastic slippers slapping on the floor.

What is it I'm not getting here? There's something else, something I should have asked him about. Shit!

She drifted toward the exit, through the hundred-meter-long metal enclosure. The wind was blowing a gale, but otherwise it was completely quiet.

She stopped when she reached the outside gate. The fence stretched off into the distance on either side of her, and she turned her head from one side to the other, suddenly feeling so giddy that she had to grab hold of the gate. She pressed the intercom, time after time in quick succession, like a child.

"Can I get out, please!" she cried, and the lock clicked, and the gate swung open, and she was out, standing outside the metal fence, and the air was instantly colder and clearer. "Thanks," she said to the mute surveillance camera above her.

She let the steel door click shut behind her. She walked and walked along the edge of the enclosed site until finally she was back in town again. She turned left into a road called Stenevägen, which went on and on, with different schools on either side, then wooden houses and brick houses and even a few prefabs. Eventually she could see the railway line ahead of her. She stopped and shook her sleeve to uncover her watch.

An hour and twenty minutes before her train.

She looked toward the station, over on the left. She had had quite enough of Sibylla's fast-food kiosk.

To her right lay something called Svea's Café. She took a deep breath and went in. She settled down at a window table with coffee, biscuits, and the local newspaper.

A woman on a bike had been knocked down and slightly injured at the junction of Fredsgatan and Skolgatan in Örebro just before 1300 the previous day.

Another woman was demanding seven thousand kronor in damages because someone had spat on her in a pub.

A Social Democratic youth group in Pålsboda had been awarded a council grant of ten thousand kronor to build a music room.

She closed her eyes and could see the stairwell on Sankt Paulsgatan before her.

She pushed the biscuits away from her and went to get a glass of water instead. She sat down at the table again and looked out at the fast-food kiosk.

Are you really sure you want to know? Are you willing to pay the price of knowing? Believe me. It isn't worth it.

She rested her forehead on the palms of her hands.

He had actually confirmed what she had said. It wouldn't hold up in a court of law, but he had more or less confirmed the scenario she had outlined.

David Lindholm was involved in some sort of shady dealings with Filip Andersson, although exactly what remained unclear. But they had know each other for a long time and were somehow mixed up in the ax murders on Sankt Paulsgatan, both of them.

Now David had been murdered as well. And Filip Andersson had chosen to spend the rest of his life in prison rather than be killed too.

It couldn't just be coincidence. It had to fit together somehow.

The three victims on Södermalm were beaten to death with an ax.

David was shot.

No similarities there.

Apart from the excessive cruelty. The symbolic castration.

She gasped.

Thou shalt not steal. Off with their hands. Thou shalt not commit adultery. Off with his cock.

If Filip Andersson is innocent, then the real killer is still out there somewhere.

Bloody hell! It could be the same person!

The next conclusion crashed into her head.

Which means that Julia didn't do it! So maybe Alexander's still alive!

She pulled out her mobile and called Kronoberg Prison in Stockholm. There was no point trying to go through her useless lawyer. The restrictions placed on Julia Lindholm had been lifted, so there was no legal reason why she couldn't visit her.

"My name is Annika Bengtzon, I'm a reporter from the *Evening Post*," she told the warder. "I spent a night in a patrol car with Julia Lindholm four and a half years ago; we were both pregnant at the time. I believe she's innocent and I'd like to interview her. Could you pass on my request, please?"

She left her mobile and home phone numbers.

Then she got up and ran over to the station, even though the train wasn't due for half an hour.

*   *   *

She changed trains in Hallsberg, the same as on the journey down. She forced herself to think calmly, trying to structure her thoughts and evaluate them objectively.

Am I really onto something, or I am just chasing shadows?

According to her first-class ticket, she was in carriage one, seat ten.

Only when she had made her way through all the carriages did she realize that there was no first-class compartment anywhere in the entire train. All the seats looked exactly the same, squashed together like sardines, without so much as a folding table on the seat in front.

Typical of the Swedish railways. Taking your money but not coming up with the goods.

The only seat that happened to be occupied in carriage one was number ten. A large man had settled down and spread his briefcase and thick coat over her seat.

She sat down in an empty seat. The train started to move with a jolt. Just thirty seconds later they had left the town behind them. She stared out at the landscape rushing past, naked woodland with blackened branches, barns, an abandoned car, a yard full of firewood, red cottages, plowed fields. The Swedish Drawing Pin factory, stone-walled farms, and endless forests of fir trees.

She took out her mobile, thinking carefully as she formulated the text message. Didn't want to promise too much.

Have met Filip Andersson. Food for thought. Think Julia may be innocent. Can we meet?

She leaned back in her seat with a sigh.

She caught a glimpse of some brownish-gray water in Kilsmo, and three deer ran across a patch of felled woodland. She stared after them, trying to see them through the undergrowth and scrub, but they were already gone, the moment had passed, and she was overwhelmed by the familiar landscape, the Södermanland she had grown up in, with its stubbornness and watchful isolation.

Grandma!

The intensity of the thought made her gasp, as the memories burned in her chest. She shut her eyes and was back in the kitchen in Lyckebo, in the drafty cottage in the middle of the woods, with the lake, Hultsjön, down below and the tops of the fir trees swaying halfway to the sky. There was a smell of damp moss and dripping branches, rustling in the bushes and the babble of a half-frozen stream. There was the transistor radio on the windowsill with the Top 20 on Saturday afternoons and Eldorado late at night, "nighttime pleasures and the music of the stars." And Grandma, pottering about doing her chores and knitting and reading. She remembered the silence and her own breathing, the way the chanterelles turned brittle in the frost and how the cold nipped at your fingers when you picked them.

The train slowed down as it went through Vingåker and she opened her eyes: a soccer field, a car park, a block of flats with brown and white paneling. She blinked, and then they were gone, a bird of prey in a tree, more water, could that be Kolsnaren?

Where will my children have their firm foundations? Where will they find security? In which smells? In which rooms? In what space, in which music?

A scrapyard, a residential suburb: They were approaching Katrineholm.

Time is all that anyone has. Like youth, and life, it seems obvious as long as you have it, then it's just gone.

It was getting dark and she could see her own reflection in the window, she looked tired and thin. Not beautifully emaciated like Hollywood stars, but bony and hard.

The train stopped, in among the Savings Bank and McDonald's and all the buildings round the square, so painfully familiar and out of reach. She had belonged there, but she had chosen to leave. Those would never again be her streets, and they would never be her children's.

She turned her head away to shut out all the people flooding into the carriage.

Think Julia may be innocent.

Nina read the text again before deciding what to reply.

Think may be.

Think may be.

Irritated, she clicked to get rid of the message.

She had taken two weeks holiday, and was going back on the night shift at 2000 that evening. First she had spent three days supporting Holger and Viola through the trial, then she had spent a week with them at their farm outside Valla. She had walked the fields with Julia's father and watched television serials on the sofa with Julia's mother, and all the while the space in the rooms and stables had been dominated by a total and overwhelming emptiness.

They've only got me now.

She sank back on her bed, looking around her cramped one-room flat.

Holger and Viola had decided to stay in Södermanland and not drive up to Stockholm to watch the sentence being pronounced. She had said they could stay at hers if they liked, just as they had done during the trial, but they had declined the offer. They thought they'd just be in the way, even though she had assured them that wasn't the case, but they didn't really want to leave the farm, although they no longer had any livestock to look after.

People were talking behind their backs. Nina had seen that with her own eyes. The way people turned away demonstratively in the local supermarket. They had both got older and more frail over the past six months. Viola's hair was completely white now, and Holger had developed a limp.

The sentence was due to be pronounced at 1330 tomorrow.

The trial had been stiff and conventional, the same as usual. For Holger and Viola, the formalities had been a drawn-out nightmare. In the wait for the sentence they were like cats around hot porridge. Surreptitious questions from both of them when they thought the other couldn't hear.

What does it mean, Nina, what the prosecutor said, you know about this sort of thing? Is it bad for Julia? Will she go to prison? How long for? Oh . . . Where will she be, then? Örebro? Well, that's not too far, we'll be able to visit. She'll be let out for Christmas, won't she? No? Maybe later on, in a few years time?

And now that journalist had popped up again, with her *think may be.*

She pressed the keys hard as she replied.

Don't agree. Julia guilty. She's done her parents a lot of harm. What do you want?

It sounded unpleasant, but she didn't care.

She sent it quickly before she had time to change her mind.

She went and got a drink of water in the kitchen, and the reply reached her mobile with a bleep before she had time to put the glass down again.

Have been to Kumla & met Filip Andersson. Interesting. Cd be worth discussing. I'll be at Sthlm C in 5 mins.

Discussing?

Filip Andersson. Think may be.

That could mean anything at all, it didn't impose any obligation on her.

She quickly grabbed the phone.

At home. Come over.

She gathered together some bills from the dining table and put them on the bookcase, straightened the bedclothes, and put some coffee on. Then she sat down on one of the dining chairs waiting for the water to stop gurgling through the machine.

She had just set out mugs, milk, and sugar when the doorbell rang.

The journalist looked like an unmade bed, more or less as usual. She marched into the flat with her great big bag and thick coat and the words poured out of her.

"There's a pattern I didn't see before, and I probably wouldn't have believed it if Filip Andersson hadn't reacted the way he did. He claims he's innocent, and there are certainly a number of questions surrounding the evidence that convicted him. Either he's a very good actor, or he really is scared and browbeaten . . ."

"Please, take a seat," Nina said, pulling out a chair for her, using the voice she usually reserved for difficult drunks and cocky boys on mopeds. "How do you take your coffee?"

"Black," the journalist said, perching on the edge of the chair as she fished a little notepad out of her bag. "I've written down a few things that I can't make any sense of."

Nina poured the coffee, glancing at the reporter from the corner of her eye.

There was something slightly manic about her, something a bit too intense. She was like a fighting dog whose jaws had locked shut, unable to let go.

She could never have been a police officer. She's not diplomatic enough.

"The sentence is due tomorrow," Nina said, sitting down opposite Annika Bengtzon. "It's a bit late to be presenting evidence that could change things."

"This isn't evidence, exactly," the journalist said. "It's more circumstantial assumptions."

Nina sighed to herself. *Circumstantial assumptions.*

"I see," she said. "And what do they tell us?"

The reporter hesitated.

"It's a bit of a long shot," she said. "The fact is that it's so awful I don't quite believe it myself. It's too cruel, too calculated, but if you were violent and ruthless enough, it's just about possible."

Nina couldn't think of anything to say, so waited in silence.

Annika Bengtzon bit her thumbnail as she read her notes.

"There's a link between the murders on Sankt Paulsgatan and David's murder," she said. "Has that ever occurred to you?"

Nina waited silently for her to go on.

"All the victims were hit in the head first, the ones in Sankt Paulsgatan with an ax, David with a bullet through the forehead. Then the bodies were mutilated. Thou shalt not steal, off with your hands. Thou shalt not commit adultery, off with your cock. Both cases show very strong symbolic gestures . . ."

Nina could feel her eyes widen in disbelief.

"Do you know what?" she said. "There are more than four years between these crimes, and apart from the fact that they both took place on Södermalm, there's no connection between them at all."

"There are several connections," Annika said. "You and Julia were present at both crime scenes, for instance."

"Pure coincidence," Nina said.

"Maybe," Annika said. "But the most important connection is David himself. He knew Filip Andersson, they'd had dealings in the past. According to the gossip in the blogosphere, Filip Andersson had some sort of business on the coast of Spain, and didn't you say that David and Julia lived down there for a while? Six months, in a row house outside Malaga?"

Nina shifted irritably on her chair.

"That was to get away from some gang in Stockholm, it was nothing to do with Filip Andersson."

The journalist leaned over the table.

"Are you sure? There couldn't have been another reason? Was he infiltrating Andersson's gang? Or working for him?"

Nina didn't answer.

"How long is it since David and Julia were in Spain? You said Julia looked like a ghost."

"She'd just got pregnant and was throwing up all the time," Nina said.

"So it was just before the murders on Sankt Paulsgatan," Annika noted. "Julia was in her fourth month that night we spent together."

Nina shook her head.

"There's nothing to suggest that David ever had any dealings with Filip Andersson. Nothing at all."

"David became his trustee when he was given his life sentence, and according to Christer Bure, David was the only person who thought Andersson was innocent. They must have known each other before that, and David knew something about the murders that no one else knew."

Nina couldn't hide a deep sigh.

"Sorry to be so blunt," she said, "but you sound like an overenthusiastic private detective."

"There are other common factors," the journalist went on. "There are the murders, the symbolism, and the desire to catch the wrong killer."

Nina stood up.

"Now, hang on a minute," she said.

"Sit down," Annika Bengtzon said, and the look in her eyes was suddenly pitch black, and Nina did as she was told. "If you manage to carry off the challenge of first killing several people and then getting someone else convicted of the crime, you'd have to be astonishingly cunning and calculating. There's only one thing that I can't get to fit."

"What?" Nina said.

"Julia's service revolver. David was shot with her gun."

Nina could feel herself going pale. A new sort of silence had settled around her and she could feel her hands getting clammy.

"What do you mean?" she said, and her voice sounded odd.

"That's the missing link. I can get everything else to fit, but I can't find an explanation for the murder weapon."

"Julia's gun went missing a year ago," Nina said. "It was when she was at her worst point, it was all very embarrassing. She couldn't remember what she'd done with it. That's nothing new, it came out during the trial."

Now it was the journalist's turn to go pale.

"What are you saying?"

Nina rubbed her hands together in an attempt to warm them up again.

"We always have to lock our weapons in at the station when we finish a shift, but Julia sometimes kept hers at home. David had permission, and they had a special gun cabinet in the bedroom."

"So she used to keep it in more than one place?"

"That's right. And if a police officer is going to be off duty for more than thirty days, they have to hand their service weapon in to the weapons store. When it became clear that Julia was going to be off sick for a long time, she was asked to hand in her pistol, and that was when she realized it was missing."

"Missing?"

"It wasn't in the gun cabinet at home in Bondegatan. She went to the station and checked if she had left it at work, but she hadn't. She was beside herself, of course, couldn't work out where it had gone."

"So what happened?"

"She reported the gun missing. She didn't want to say it had been stolen, she just couldn't work out where it had gone. An internal inquiry was set up to find out if Julia was guilty of breaking the law, or of dereliction of duty, or possibly just misconduct, seeing as she had evidently managed to lose her Sig Sauer . . ."

"Why haven't I heard any of this before?"

"You can't have been paying attention. The defense mentioned it during the trial, but nothing much was made of it. I can only assume that it
wasn't in Julia's interests to reinforce the image of her as a confused and
irresponsible person."

"So what happened in the inquiry into the disappearance of the
weapon?"

"It hadn't reached any conclusions before the murder, but everything
pointed to misconduct, which wouldn't have had any consequences. The
lenient findings were mostly for David's sake, of course. When the gun
reappeared the inquiry was dropped, seeing as she had evidently found
the weapon or had it in her possession all along . . ."

"But she hadn't," Annika Bengtzon said. "Someone started planning
this murder a very long time ago, and Julia was being lined up to take the
blame right from the start."

"That can't be true," Nina said. "It sounds like a conspiracy theory in
the same class as the Roswell landing."

But the journalist was no longer listening to her. Her gaze had turned
inwards and she seemed to be talking out loud to herself rather than to
Nina.

"If Julia is actually innocent, then Alexander really was kidnapped.
Which suggests that the real perpetrator is capable of almost anything.
Chopping the hands off people who are still alive with an ax, for in-
stance."

She looked at Nina again.

"Could David have been gay or bisexual?"

"I doubt it," Nina said. "What's that got to do with anything?"

"The murderer must have had a personal relationship with David,
otherwise he or she would never have blown his cock off."

Annika Bengtzon nodded to herself.

"There really was another woman in the flat. Someone who had access to the keys, or could make copies of them, to the front door and
the gun cabinet. It must have been one of his lovers, and she must have
been desperate to get revenge for something. She must have known
about Björkbacken, seeing as she hid Alexander's things in the marsh

there. Talk about the ultimate revenge: shooting the man, getting his wife locked up for the murder, and stealing their child."

Nina was sitting like she'd been turned to stone, unable to think anymore.

"The sentence is due tomorrow," she said.

"It can be appealed," Annika Bengtzon said. "Can you help me get in touch with Julia somehow, or at least arrange for me to talk to her? Or maybe write a letter? I've called the lawyer a hundred times and left messages at the prison, can't you help me?"

Nina stood up.

"I'm working tonight, and I've got a lot to do."

There was a cold, bitter wind as Annika stepped out of the front door. She thought about taking the underground, but decided to walk. She needed to burn off the disappointment of her failure.

I begged her, like a little child. She must think I'm completely mad.

If Nina isn't willing to see the connections, no one will.

She pulled on her gloves and started walking toward Slussen, forcing herself to leave the conspiracy theories on the pavement of Södermannagatan.

But everything could have fitted together, especially as Julia's service pistol had been missing for some time.

Annika shook herself, she had to pull herself together and get a bit of perspective.

It wasn't up to her to free Julia Lindholm. Julia wasn't necessarily innocent just because she was herself.

Am I going mad? Have the angels fallen silent only to turn into obsessive behavior instead?

She struggled up Östgötagatan, forcing her legs to move faster in the cold. Her eyes were watering, mainly because of the wind.

Does anyone know when they're on the brink of going mad?

What if she started finding secrets codes in the morning papers, like the Nobel Prize winner in the film *A Beautiful Mind*? The one who wrote masses of incomprehensible gobbledygook on scraps of paper and thought he was the cleverest man in the world.

She quickened her pace as she reached Mosebacke Square, skirting round the Sodra Teatern and stopping to look at the view of Stockholm harbor.

This was one of her favorite places on the entire planet.

If she could live anywhere she liked, she'd buy a flat on Fjällgatan or somewhere up near Ersta Hospital. The view was incredible, all the water and light, with the medieval buildings along Skeppsbron to the left, Skeppsholmen with all its museums straight ahead, Djurgården and the amusement park to the right, and Waldemarsudde jutting out into the water in the distance. One of the Vaxholm boats was heading toward the quayside, its lights twinkling in the water. People had been living here for a thousand years, even before Birger Jarl decided to build the capital of Sweden on these islands at the opening of Lake Mälaren.

If I can only get hold of the insurance payout. If I'm cleared of all suspicions of arson. Then I shall live here.

She looked away from the view and hurried home, so that she could look up the main online estate agent to see if there were any flats for sale with a view of the harbor. With every step she got further away from the sense of failure that was left on the pavement of Södermannagatan.

She had just crossed the big junction at Slussen and turned into Västerlånggatan when she first got the feeling that she was being watched. The cobblestones of the medieval streets were wet and slippery, and she slid slightly as she looked back over her shoulder. She stopped and listened, slightly out of breath.

The street curved to the right ahead of her, empty and deserted. The wind had torn an old poster down, whirling it around her feet. The shops were all shut, but the bars were open; she could see people eating and drinking and laughing through steamed-up windows. The light from the candles on the tables flickered over the façades of the buildings.

Nothing. No steps, no voices.

Am I getting paranoid as well?

She hoisted her bag up on her shoulder and started walking again.

There it was again, the sound of footsteps. She stopped again and spun round.

No one there.

She was breathing fast.

Pull yourself together, for God's sake!

She had gone past the 7-Eleven and was just passing the arched opening of Yxsmedsgränd when someone stepped out of the shadows and grabbed her arm. She looked up in surprise. He was wearing a balaclava. His eyes were bright. She took a deep breath to scream. A second person, someone else, came up behind her and put a gloved hand over her nose and mouth. The scream ended up as a rather surprised and stifled whimper. She opened her mouth and felt a finger slip between her teeth, and she bit down as hard as she could. There was a muffled curse in her ear, then he hit her hard over the head. As she was falling she was dragged into the alley. It was completely dark in there. She was pulled into a doorway. The wind was howling but her whole body felt strangely hot. The two men—they had to be men—pushed her up against the wall. She caught a glimpse of a knife flashing in the gloom.

"Don't poke your nose into things that don't concern you," one of them said.

It was a whisper, not a real voice.

"What things?" she said quietly, staring at the knife. It was pointed at her left eye.

"Leave David in peace. It's over. No more poking about."

She was panting now, feeling panic closing in. She couldn't reply.

"Got it?"

Give me some air! I can't breathe!

"Do you think she's got it?"

One voice whispering to the other.

"No, I think we're going to have to make it a bit clearer."

She felt them grab her left hand and pull her glove off. The knife vanished from in front of her eye. At last she got some air.

"If anyone asks how you cut yourself, you did it cooking," the voice whispered, then the glove covered her mouth again, and she felt a fierce pain through her hand and up her arm into her chest. Her head was thudding with the shock, and her knees gave way.

"Stop asking questions about David. And not a word about us. Next time we'll cut your children instead."

They let go of her, and she sank onto the cobbles as warm blood pumped out her wounded index finger.

At A&E she said she'd cut herself in the kitchen.

A stressed doctor sewed her together with eight stitches, and told her to be more careful in future

"What were you making?"

She looked up at him. How could doctors be so young these days? Younger than the temps at the paper.

"Making?"

"Was it chicken? Some other meat? The wound might be infected."

She closed her eyes.

"Onions," she said.

"If you're unlucky, you could have lasting damage. Some of the ligaments were cut."

He sounded unhappy, as if she were wasting his time with her carelessness.

"Sorry," she said.

"Make an appointment to see the district nurse in your health center, and change the dressing every day. She'll make sure you haven't got an infection and will take the stitches out in a week or so."

"Thank you," Annika said.

She didn't mention the bump throbbing on the back of her head, and took a taxi that was waiting outside the entrance. She told him to drive to number 30, Västerlånggatan, then leaned her head back in the seat.

"Is it okay if I drop you off at Kåkbrinken?" the taxi driver asked.

Then I'll have to walk past Yxsmedsgränd.

"No," she said. "I want you to drop me off at my door."

"I can't, there's no traffic allowed up there."

"I don't care."

He dropped her off at the top off Kåkbrinken, and she slammed the door so hard the window shook.

She was left standing on Västerlånggatan with her heart hammering in her chest like church bells, staring at the archway that covered the entrance to Yxsmedsgränd. Her left hand was throbbing and stinging, and she could smell the man's glove, taste the leather.

They're not here now. Whoever they were, they're not still here. Pull yourself together!

She put one foot in front of the other and slowly walked down the street, staring hard at the opening of the alley.

The shadows in the alley were deeper than any other sort of darkness, sucking up all the oxygen and making her gasp for breath. She hugged the plate-glass window of Flodins on the other side of the street and made her way past, beyond the alley and down toward her building, without once letting Yxsmedsgränd out of her sight.

"Annika," someone said, putting a hand on her shoulder.

She screamed out loud and spun round, her right arm raised ready to strike.

"Goodness, whatever's the matter?"

Annika stared at the person who had stepped out from the doorway of number 30, Västerlånggatan. Tall, blonde, not exactly thin, with a shocked and reproachful expression on her face.

"Anne!" Annika gasped. "What the hell are you doing here?"

Anne Snapphane smiled nervously.

"I'd like to talk to you. It's important to me."

Annika closed her eyes and felt anger and impotence flooding through her, everything she had kept dammed up from previous snubs and insults.

"You know what?" she said. "I don't give a damn about what's important to you. Frankly I couldn't care less about you."

"I understand that, Annika," Anne said, "and that's what I'd like to talk to you about."

"Go away," Annika said, feeling in her jacket pocket for her keys.

"If you just give me a chance to explain . . ."

Something snapped inside Annika's head, and she spun round and pushed Anne away with her uninjured hand.

"Go to hell," she shouted. "I hope you die, you egocentric little parasite."

Somehow she managed to get the door open and pulled it shut behind her, then ran up the stairs without turning the lights on. She stopped outside her front door and listened for any sounds from below, but everything was silence and dusty shadows.

She unlocked the flat and went into the living room without turning the lights on, as had become her habit. She stood still on the wooden floor and waited as the cares of the day gradually subsided and died.

There was something comforting about the darkness and silence, in finding herself in something soft and dark. The darkness itself didn't scare her, it never had. On the contrary, it hid her and gave her the space to explore new paths.

The telephone rang, shredding the silence.

She went over to her mattress, which she had left unmade that morning, and hesitated over whether or not to answer, then picked up the receiver.

It was Thomas.

"Sorry to call so late, but things are a bit of a mess."

Sober this time, calling from home.

She sat down by the window and looked up at the dark sky between the buildings.

"In what way?"

"Ellen's not well, so I'll have to work at home tomorrow, which isn't really a problem. But we're supposed to be going out tomorrow evening. It's Sophia's mother's birthday, and we've got tickets to the opera. I can't leave the children alone, and the babysitter has just called to say that she isn't well either, and you did say . . . well, I was wondering if you could maybe look after the children tomorrow night . . ."

He said all this without taking a breath.

He means well. He sounds desperate.

"How is Ellen?"

"She's been sick, and she's got a temperature, but she's always like that when she gets ill, isn't she?"

"Is it serious? Have you spoken to a doctor?"

"It's nothing serious, but I don't really want to move her. So I was wondering if you could maybe come here?"

Come . . . where?

"Here, to Grev Turegatan. That way she won't have to leave her room."

Her room? Her room is here. With a pink duvet!

"I thought that maybe they could come here," Annika said.

"Well, this is my week, and she's got a temperature . . ."

Sophia Fucking Bitch *Grenborg is starting to get tired. She wants me to take more responsibility to let Thomas off the hook.*

"Okay," she said quietly. "I'll come. What time?"

He told her the address and she hung up with a giddy feeling of failure in her chest.

I want you to be drunk with longing when you call. Drunk! From the pub!

She suddenly felt that she was going to be sick. She was just about to get up and go into the bathroom and stick her fingers down her throat when the phone started to ring again.

"Shut up, for God's sake!" Annika shouted at it, throwing it across the floor. The receiver flew off and bounced across the floor as far as the wire would reach. She covered her eyes, fighting to stop herself panicking.

"Hello? Hello?"

A voice from the phone, it sounded like a woman.

If it's Anne, I'm going to go over to Artillerigatan and strangle her.

She shuffled over to the phone, holding her hand to her chest, and picked up the receiver.

"Hello?" she said quietly.

"Hello?" a high female voice said. "Is that Annika Bengtzon?"

"Yes," Annika whispered, "that's me."

"This is Julia Lindholm. They told me you called, that you wanted to visit."

Annika stood up, trying to breathe properly.

"Hello," she managed to say, "yes, that's right."

"I had a boy," Julia said. "What about you?"

Annika closed her eyes.

"A girl. Her name's Ellen."

"Does she live with you?"

She stared into the shadows dominating the flat.

"Sometimes," she said. "We're . . . getting divorced."

"That's a shame."

"Yes, well . . ."

She cleared her throat and tried to pull herself together.

"I still work for the *Evening Post*. I know your sentence is being pronounced tomorrow," Annika said, "but no matter what happens, I don't believe you did it. I'd like to talk to you about that."

Silence on the line.

"What makes you think I'm innocent?"

"Long story. I'd be happy to tell you, if you'd like to hear it."

"You can come early tomorrow morning if you like. I'm allowed visitors from eight o'clock."

"I'll be there," Annika said.

Anne Snapphane walked down Västerlånggatan and stopped outside number 30. She looked up at the building and saw lights on in some of the windows on the second floor. Maybe Annika was in those illuminated rooms, because she lived somewhere inside this building.

She's bound to be up, she's always been a morning person.

She had walked past here all autumn, every day since she started renting space in the office shared by freelance journalists in Tyska brinken. She had looked up at the building and stopped at its entrance almost every day, wondering if she should go up and knock on her door. She really did miss Annika. Every time she ground to a halt with an article or couldn't get hold of someone she wanted to interview, she had to stop herself from phoning. Annika could always find anybody in a flash; Anne had never been able to work out how she did it. And whenever life got messy and men let her down, she missed Annika particularly, Annika always had coffee and dark chocolate in the house, and usually a pair of new boots to help cheer her up.

Her career as a lecturer had stagnated during the autumn; she hadn't had any new bookings, and the agency stopped getting in touch. Which was just as well. She needed time to herself, to think things through. Her eagerness to be seen in the media and become a famous face was just superficial; she had made up her mind to try to find some inner values, the things that made her a good person. She wanted to live the very best life she could, and to do that she had to come to grips with the people who sapped her energy, the people who had become small stones in her shoes, sitting there and chafing.

Annika was the person she really needed to talk to. She had actually tried to arrange a conversation since the summer, emailing and phoning, but never got any answer.

She shivered, not just because of the raw early morning.

Their encounter here the previous evening had left her feeling wretched. She had been working late and was on her way home to Artillerigatan, and as usual she had stopped at number 30 and looked up at the building, thinking about important things. She had stood there for a minute or so, two minutes maybe, when she saw Annika coming toward her, all the while looking back over her shoulder.

It hadn't been a good meeting, Annika had been incredibly cruel, and Anne didn't want to have to put up with that sort of thing anymore.

She took a deep breath, pulled out her mobile phone, and dialed Annika's familiar number.

The call went through, one ring, two, three, four, and then she was there.

"Hello, it's Anne. I'd like to talk to you."

"What for?"

She sounded very tired, but not newly woken.

"Yesterday was all wrong . . . Listen, I'm standing outside your door, can I come up?"

"What are you doing here?"

"I'm not stalking you, I share an office with a few other people in Tyska brinken, you know, in that building I used to live in . . ."

"Really."

She sounded curt and extremely dismissive.

"Can you spare me a few minutes?"

"I'm just on my way out."

"At half past seven in the morning?"

She didn't reply.

"I'll wait down here. You can choose to go past me if you like."

Anne ended the call.

It really was dreadful weather. The damp paved the way for the cold, getting right into your marrow. She stamped her feet and rubbed her hands together. Darkness was still clinging heavily to the rooftops. The sound of the traffic on the Munkbro highway skirting Gamla stan stood no chance of finding its way through the cold and the stone buildings. The medieval streets were left eerily silent and deserted.

God, I couldn't live here. I can't imagine how Annika puts up with it.

The lights in the stairwell came on, and thirty seconds later the door opened.

Annika stepped onto the pavement with her mobile in her hand.

She looked pale, and her hair was a mess.

"What do you want?" she said without looking at Anne.

"I want to say I'm sorry," Anne said. "I've been behaving like an idiot, and I hope you can forgive me."

Annika looked at her with her enormous eyes, so open and vulnerable and trusting.

She doesn't even know she's got them. She doesn't know how revealing they are.

Anne wanted to reach out a hand and touch her, but resisted. Annika wasn't good at physical contact. It took a lot for her to exchange any form of touch.

"You've helped me every way a person could," Anne said, noting that she felt tense and nervous. "You've helped me with work and contacts, you've given me money and childcare and friendship. You were always there and I took you for granted . . ."

She stopped and took a deep breath and decided to stay calm.

"You were always there, and I got myself muddled up with you. I thought I should have everything that you had. And when I didn't get everything that you had, I thought it wasn't fair."

Annika was standing completely still, not saying anything, just looking down at the ground. Anne noticed that she had got a few gray hairs.

"I realize that was wrong, at least I do now, anyway. But I didn't realize before."

Annika looked along Västerlånggatan.

"I'm on my way to a meeting," she said.

"I miss you," Anne said. "You're one of the people I like most of all. I'm very sorry if I've hurt you."

Annika looked up, a quick glance with those naked eyes.

"I have to go now," she said.

Anne nodded.

Annika walked away, her mobile phone in her hand, in her thick padded jacket, her skinny legs inside a pair of black cowboy boots.

Communication really wasn't Annika's strong point.

*Oh well, I'll just have to be the communicator. She can't be best at ev-
erything, after all.*

Annika walked quickly in the direction of Kronoberg Prison.

Over the past six months, since the terrible night of the fire when
Anne hadn't let her in when she was standing in the stairwell with the
children, she had blocked Anne Snapphane from her mind. She had
turned her into a nonperson, the sort of person you didn't say hello to.
The fact was, she had started to forget Anne.

And the fact that she had suddenly turned up to say sorry had shaken
things up.

*I made myself into her curling assistant, someone who ran ahead
sweeping the course to make things easier for Anne to glide along.*

She stopped at a crossing and swallowed the feeling of injustice.

With her eyes wide open and self-criticism resounding through her
body, she admitted to herself that she had only swept the course as she
wanted to, and had directed Anne to go in the direction she wanted.

And their friendship had capsized. Anne took it for granted that Annika would sort everything out for her, from money and clothes and a
flat to lectures and new jobs. Annika in turn had assumed that Anne was
an inferior loser who was incapable of doing anything for herself.

*As if I wanted her to become dependent on me, so that I could feel im-
portant.*

The lights went green, and she hurried over the road.

*Anne refused to be there for me when my life was falling apart. She
sent me out onto the street with the children when Thomas left me and the
house had burned down.*

Her anger was still sharp and white-hot.

She arrived at Kronoberg Prison at 0759, went into reception and
showed her ID, put her things in a locker, and took the lift up with just
her notepad and pen.

No metal detector, no X-ray machine.

She was shut inside a windowless room containing a table and four chairs.

Annika stopped and stared at the walls.

Imagine, we're still locking people up like this for breaking rules imposed by someone else. It's utterly barbaric.

The door opened. The warder stood to one side and a petite blond woman came into the visiting room. She was wearing jeans and slippers and a gray top, and her hair was tied up in a ponytail. A few locks had escaped and were dancing round her face. She stopped inside the door and pulled at the sleeves of her top.

"Hello," she said.

"Hello," Annika said.

"You look just the way I remember you."

"So do you."

That isn't true. She's shrunk. Older and smaller. Unless the uniform just made her seem bigger last time.

They shook hands and sat down on opposite sides of the table. Annika put her pen and notepad down. The weak low-energy lamp in the ceiling was casting deep shadows under Julia's eyes. Her top sat limply on her shoulders.

"So you had a girl," she said. "Is she sleeping okay?"

Annika nodded.

"Always has done. My first, Kalle, used to scream every evening until he was six months old. I got so tired I thought I was going to go mad."

Julia relaxed.

"I know just what you mean. Alexander didn't go through the night until he was two. Do you think it's easier with girls?"

Annika studied the woman's eyes behind the shadows. They were wide open and empty in a way that sent a shiver down her spine.

This isn't at all healthy.

"I think it's easier with a second child," Annika said. "You've had time to practice. And you know it's all going to pass, the colic and sleepless nights and all the bad stuff . . ."

Julia shook her head.

"I don't know if I'd ever dare have any more children," she said. "I felt so terrible after Alexander."

"Maybe that wasn't just because of the birth or him," Annika said, "but the result of other things as well."

Julia's eyes stopped at a point on the wall. She sat in silence for a long time.

"They think I killed him," she eventually said.

"I know that's what they're saying," Annika said, "but I don't believe that."

The shadows under Julia's eyes deepened as she pulled back against the wall.

"Nina says I'm going to go to prison. Do you think that too?"

Annika felt her throat go dry, as doubt crept into her eyes.

"The experts seem to think so," she said, "and if they're right, then I believe a great injustice will have been done. I don't believe you did it. I think there was another woman in the flat, and I think she took Alexander."

Julia was sitting completely still.

"Why do you think that?"

"I think there's a connection between David's murder and that terrible triple murder we stumbled upon that night I was with you in the patrol car. Do you remember Filip Andersson?"

Julia Lindholm leaned her head back and looked up at the ceiling.

"No one believes me," she said. "Not even Nina. They just keep asking what I did, not what the other woman did."

She turned her eyes toward Annika.

"You know Nina, don't you? I feel rather sorry for her, she's so alone. She lived with her mum in a little cottage outside Valla. She had brothers and sisters, but they were much older. Her mum was a real hippie, she lived in some commune on the Canary Islands when Nina was little. She was nine years old when she started at Valla School, and she couldn't read or write. She used to stay with us on the farm most nights. Has she ever mentioned that?"

She leaned forward over the table.

"There's one guy at the station, a really great inspector called Pelle

Sisulu. He's been in love with Nina for years, but she refuses to take it seriously. She doesn't think she's worth loving. I wish I could help her . . ."

She leaned back in the uncomfortable chair again and looked closely at Annika.

"I feel so sorry for people," she said. "David grew up without his dad, he only had a stepfather who kept coming and going. When David was nineteen, he disappeared and never got in touch again. I think that's why David went into the police."

She tilted her head to one side.

"Should I feel sorry for you, Annika?"

Annika took a deep breath.

"No, I don't think so."

"So you've got someone who loves you?"

Yes, the children.

"Should I feel sorry for myself?" Julia asked.

Annika nodded.

"Is that why you believe me?"

"No," Annika said. "There are several connections between the murders, and I don't think the police have investigated them properly."

"So you believe there was another woman?"

She nodded again.

"That's what I've been telling them all along!"

"I know. The question is: Who is she, and where could she have taken Alexander? Do you have any ideas?"

Julia shook her head slowly.

"Do you remember Filip Andersson? The ax murderer?"

Julia shivered. Her gaze slid along the wall.

"I went to visit Filip Andersson in Kumla Prison a few days ago," Annika said. "I think he might be innocent too. Someone else might have committed those murders, and if that person got away then he, or she, could have murdered David as well . . ."

They sat in the visiting room without speaking for a long while. The ventilation hummed somewhere up in the ceiling. Julia was sitting completely still, staring into the wall.

"I know there was someone there when I woke up."

Annika sat in silence, the hairs on the back of her neck standing up. Julia was fiddling with some of the strands of hair that had come loose, tucking them behind her ear.

"There was a bang," she said in a shaky voice. "I think it was the bang that woke me up. I didn't know what it was. I thought I might have been dreaming or something."

She looked up at the ceiling.

"There was a funny smell. Something horrible, not the way our bedroom usually smells. A bit burnt, maybe . . . Someone was moving about in the room, I think I said something."

The sound of the ventilation seemed to get louder in the silence. Annika stared at the woman, unable to take her eyes from her mouth.

"Then there was another bang, and my ears popped, a sort of ringing, howling sound . . ."

The shot to the groin. Thou shalt not commit adultery.

Julia took a deep breath. It sounded rough and shaky.

"I've got a bit of a cold," she said apologetically. "I'm a bit bunged up. How on earth that's managed to happen, seeing as I've been shut away for the past six months . . . I suppose I got it from the guards, or warders, as we're supposed to call them . . ."

Annika was breathing with her mouth open so as not to clear her throat or swallow.

Julia nodded to herself and wiped her nose on the sleeve of her top.

"My heart was pounding right through my head, my body, I don't know how I can describe . . ."

She brushed the hair from her face.

"Did you see someone?" Annika asked in a rather hushed tone. "Did you see who fired the shot?"

"It was completely dark. David can't sleep if it isn't pitch black. I don't know, I didn't see anyone."

"Do you remember what you were thinking?"

Julia shook her head. They sat in silence for a while. Julia pulled a paper handkerchief from her jeans pocket and blew her nose, then crumpled it into a little ball.

"Then what happened?" Annika asked.

"Alexander was crying. I could hear him crying, even though my ears had gone deaf. So I got up to go and see if he was all right."

"Where was Alexander?"

Julia looked up at her in surprise.

"In his room, of course. He was asleep. I mean, it was the middle of the night."

"And then what happened?"

Julia seemed to shrink and her shoulders hunched, it looked like she was trying to make herself smaller. Locks of hair tumbled in front of her face.

"Alexander was standing in the hall. He was hugging Bamse. She was standing behind him, holding the knife. He said 'Mummy.' She looked at me. I could feel her looking at me."

"The other woman? The one who was in the flat? What did she look like?"

Julia's eyes flickered across the wall.

Annika had read her description of "the other woman" in Berit's report of the trial. Medium-length hair, possibly short. Not fair, not dark. Medium height, normal size.

Julia looked down at the table. The psychiatrists had concluded that she was describing herself when she told them about the murderer. The lawyer must have explained that to her.

"It wasn't me," she said, scratching her wrists. Annika noticed that she had scabs on her arms from where she'd scratched herself before.

"What did she do with the knife?"

The scratching got more frenetic.

"She cut . . ."

"It's all right to tell me," Annika said.

Julia's hands stopped, she looked at the wall without really focusing.

"She . . . she cut him on the cheek and put her hand over his mouth . . . and she was wearing gloves . . ."

"She cut Alexander on the face?"

Tears were welling up in her eyes.

"And I did nothing," Julia said. "She said, 'I'll suffocate him. I'll smother him if you scream. It's so easy to kill little children.' That's what she said . . . Oh God . . . what have I done . . . ?"

And Julia Lindholm started to cry, calmly and gently.

Annika sat still on the other side of the table and watched.

Then she reached for her bag to give Julia a tissue, but remembered that she'd had to leave it in the locker down in reception.

Julia let out a deep, sobbing sigh and wiped her face on her sleeves.

"I didn't help him. 'If you follow me, I'll cut his throat,' she said. He was crying. He said 'Mummy.' That's when she cut his cheek, she cut his face, and I know I tried to scream, but nothing came out, and after that I don't know what happened . . ."

She shuddered and started crying again.

"I couldn't help him. She cut his face with the knife and I didn't know what to do, I was so frightened he was going to die . . ."

The blood on the floor. Alexander's DNA.

"I think the woman knew David," Annika said. "Can you help me track her down?"

Julia shook her head, felt for the used tissue and dried her eyes.

"She's lethal," she said. "David was terrified of her. 'She's mad,' he said. 'Don't go anywhere near her.'"

Annika got goose bumps. *Is she talking about herself now?*

"Who is she? Do you know her name?"

Julia shook her head again.

"She had an abortion," she said. "While I was expecting Alexander. David never admitted it, but I knew that was what had happened. I found a picture of the ultrasound; it would have been a girl. I should have left him then, I should have realized. He was never going to stop seeing other women."

"Was she the one who used to call?" Annika asked. "The one who used to phone when Alexander was little, telling you to let go of him?"

Julia shrugged.

"Don't know. Maybe. He had more than one."

"When did David say that about the woman being so dangerous?"

Julia looked up at her in surprise.

"What woman?"

"You said David talked about her, the dangerous woman. When did he do that? Was it when Alexander was small?"

"Oh," Julia said, "no, not at all, it wasn't that long ago."

"Just before he died?"

Julia put a hand over her mouth, her eyes filled with tears.

"It was my fault," she said. "I did absolutely nothing, because I was so scared she was going to hurt him even more. She was evil! The blood was running down his cheek—you should have seen how terrified he looked—and she put her hand over his nose and mouth so he couldn't scream, or even breathe—she had gloves on—and I was so scared . . ."

"But when did he say it?"

"When he was drunk. Alexander and I had been out to the cottage, cooking sausages outdoors, and we went to watch the May Day Eve bonfire in Hälleforsnäs, and when we got home he was so drunk. He wasn't angry, mostly just scared."

"Earlier this year? Four weeks before he died, then?"

She nodded.

"You say David was scared? Did he say why?"

She shook her head.

"How could you tell that he was scared?"

"He asked me to forgive him. Said he'd hurt me. That he hadn't meant to. That I should take care when I answered the phone, and not to answer the door if anyone knocked."

Annika recalled Nina describing how distraught Julia had been during the last few weeks before the murder, how she'd shut herself away and not answered the phone.

"But he never said what her name was? Nothing about who she was?"

Another shake of the head.

Annika shifted on her chair.

"This has to be a seriously disturbed individual," she said. "She's probably got criminal connections. If she did have an abortion and sent David a picture of the ultrasound, he must have been the father. Which means that she must have had some sort of contact with David over a long period, at least four and half years. Right back to the time you spent living in Spain, at least. Had you ever seen her before?"

Julia merely shook her head again.

"Would you recognize her if you saw her again?"

Julia hesitated, then nodded.

"If I got hold of pictures of women David had dealings with for different reasons, would you take a look at them and see if you recognize any of them?"

Julia nodded again.

"One more thing," Annika said. "I'm a reporter on the *Evening Post*, after all. Can I interview you and write about you for the paper?"

Julia looked at her, bewildered.

"But what would I say?"

"Well, you could start by telling me what it's been like for you here in prison."

Anders Schyman welcomed the chairman of the newspaper's board into his little office with a flamboyant gesture.

"Can I offer you anything?" he said, taking Herman Wennergren's coat and laying it ceremoniously across his desk. "A glass of water? Some coffee from the machine?"

"You don't have to make a fool of yourself," the chairman snapped, adjusting his cuff links.

Schyman had been invited to lunch with Herman Wennergren on the veranda of the Grand Hotel, but had declined out of consideration to the poor finances of the paper's proprietors. That hadn't gone down well, evidently. There was now an item on the agenda of the next committee meeting proposing that his own entertainment budget be cut—not that he gave a damn about that really. It was the petty act of revenge that annoyed him.

"I have to say that I think this sounds deeply troubling," the chairman said, sitting down on the rather flimsy visitor's chair. "An editorial management team consisting of eighty-two people: That's completely unreasonable. How on earth can we afford that?"

Anders Schyman walked round the desk, sat down, and pulled his chair closer to the desk. He pulled a sheaf of calculations out from under the chairman's coat and handed them to his visitor.

"It's the simplest, cheapest, and quickest way to make the necessary cuts," he said. "In accordance with locally negotiated wage agreements— you've got those in appendix four—there are no premiums paid to members of the editorial management team. Any such premium is included in their basic salary or recompensed in other ways. We chose to introduce a 'responsibility bonus' instead, and those payments are only made to people in active leadership roles."

"Ahem," Herman Wennergren coughed, leafing through the documents. "And this will solve the problem of the cutbacks?"

"We have to take into account the union's demand that we follow the 'last-in first-out' principle. Sixty-two posts are going, most of them on the editorial side. As you can see from the proposals, we're clearing out top management as well. The committee would remove the managing director of his position and transfer his responsibilities to me instead. I'm going to negotiate with the local union representative straight after this meeting. Which is why I wanted to run my alternative proposal past you before I set to work."

"I see," Herman Wennergren said. "Well, we can certainly manage without our current MD. So, what's this alternative proposal of yours?"

"If the union kicks up a fuss, I'll dismiss the entire editorial staff. They would all have to reapply for their jobs, and I'll reinstate those I want."

The chairman frowned disapprovingly.

"We've tried that before. There's always some catch."

Anders Schyman threw his arms out.

"You're the ones who want to impose the cuts; I'm just a simple facilitator. Will the Family support my proposal, even if it means a certain amount of turbulence?"

Herman Wennergren stood up and looked at his watch, a Rolex Oyster (which Anders Schyman regarded as a completely ridiculous watch).

"We would appreciate it if any turbulence could be kept to a minimum," he said. "Can I have my coat, please?"

Anders Schyman smiled, aware that by having this meeting here and not on the veranda of the Grand Hotel, he had saved the Family at least two thousand kronor, and himself at least three hours of his life.

"I'll do my best," he said.

As soon as the chairman of the board had disappeared toward the lifts to go back down to his waiting chauffeur-driven Volvo, he asked the receptionist to call Eva-Britt Qvist.

She must have been standing by the starting blocks in her running shoes, because she appeared outside his room ten seconds later.

"What did Herman Wennergren want?" she asked, pulling the glass door shut behind her.

Yet another good reason for meeting him here.

The editor in chief adopted a deep frown.

"I wanted to make sure that the board and our owners in the Family were absolutely sure about the cutbacks, one final time, and make sure that they understand how serious this is. But they won't be moved, they really do want this to be carried out. They're not even sparing their own ranks: Our new MD is one of the people who will lose his job. The whole committee is behind our preliminary proposal, but is also prepared to support our alternative plan."

Eva-Britt Qvist nodded thoughtfully and sat down.

"We think it's excellent that the paper has accepted its responsibilities and is following our preferred list when it comes to redundancies."

He handed over a document containing a list of names.

"Based upon our locally negotiated agreements, the list of posts to be lost looks like this," he said.

Eva-Britt Qvist began reading.

I wonder how long it will take before she realizes.

He checked an urge to look at his watch and time her.

At least two minutes passed.

"But," Eva-Britt Qvist said, "this doesn't follow the last-in first-out principle. Where's Emil Oscarsson, for instance? He was the last person to be taken on, surely he only arrived this summer?"

"Ah," Schyman said, handing her another list. "This is the new list of editorial management."

Eva-Britt Qvist turned pale. She read for a long time in silence, going through the whole list several times. Then she lowered the document.

"So this is how you think you can get away with it," she said. "But let me tell you, we won't agree to this."

She stood up.

"Sit down," Schyman said.

"No," she said, in a loud, clear voice. "I'm going now."

"In that case we have an even greater problem, you and me."

He stood up as well, a head taller than her.

She stopped, her hand on the door handle.

"I have just been authorized by the chairman of the board to dismiss the entire editorial staff," the editor in chief said. "Then I will reinstate those I actually want, rather than those I am obliged to keep. Even if it means the closure of the paper, we're going to get this through. Because we don't actually have any alternative. Carrying on as we have done up to now merely means that we will simply reach the same disaster more slowly."

"And if we protest?"

He looked at her hard.

Bet everything on one card.

"There'll be a lot of important work for you at this paper, Eva-Britt. Don't let something like this ruin your whole career."

She gasped.

"That's a threat."

"Not at all," Schyman said, looking affronted. "I'm just keen to keep you, even after the cuts. We need experienced administrators, and we have to bear one thing in mind. Not even my position is secure."

He opened the door.

"Nothing lasts a lifetime."

Annika Bengtzon was just walking past.

"So you've heard?" she said. "Mind you, it was entirely predictable, with that idiot defending her."

"What?" Schyman said.

"She's the sixth woman ever to be given a life sentence in Sweden."

"We won't accept this," the union representative whispered, looking close to tears.

"We can probably come to an agreement," he said in a quiet voice, and smiled amiably.

As she headed to her place at the day shift's desk, it occurred to Annika that Eva-Britt Qvist had looked terrible. She took out her laptop and all her notes and documents relating to David Lindholm. First she wrote up her interview with Julia, under the heading "Accused Wife of Police Officer Speaks Out." It didn't reveal much of what Julia had said. Annika left out everything about the other woman and what she had done. The article was more a description of the prison and Julia's time there, nothing remarkable, with no contentious allegations.

She wasn't feeling well, and went over to the coffee machine to get herself a mug of tar. She took some headache pills and persuaded herself that the fact that she was feeling unwell had nothing to do with the evening ahead, when she had agreed to look after the children in Sophia *Fucking Bitch* Grenborg's flat. She was doing it for their sake, Ellen and Kalle's, because they needed her and were missing her.

Once she had sent the article to the shared filestore, she sat down to structure her real work.

Women who had had personal dealings with David. Who had he been together with? Where do people meet their bits on the side? At work? In bars? In their free time? Among mutual friends, with shared ambitions and business interests?

And how was she going to get hold of pictures, even if she managed to put together a list of names?

The passport register was no longer open to the public, nor the register of driving licenses. A lot of people were in pictures on the Internet, or in different image archives, but she needed definite identification of everyone. Otherwise, it would all be a complete waste of time.

Well, she'd deal with that later.

The criteria were fairly clear. There shouldn't be too many alternatives.

Someone who knew David well. Who had a sexual relationship with him. Who had access to his home. Who was sufficiently criminal and ruthless to murder David, frame Julia, and kidnap Alexander.

This is an attack on a whole family. She must have been planning it ever since the gun disappeared.

She shrugged off an image of Thomas, Sophia, and the children.

The woman must have got hold of the keys to the flat in Bondegatan and stolen Julia's Sig Sauer from the gun cabinet in David and Julia's bedroom without ever touching it with her fingers and without smearing Julia's fingerprints.

It wasn't actually any more complicated than that.

She quickly laid out the printouts she already had and pulled her notepad and pen from her bag, and decided to try to structure the search.

1. Women who had been on the same committees as David.

Easy, but there would probably be a lot of names. And it wasn't a particularly likely list either, so she decided to wait with that one.

2. Women related to the men who were in prison thanks to David: wives, mothers, daughters, sisters, and ideally lovers as well.

Harder to dig out the information, but not impossible, and more likely to produce something interesting. She'd make this one her first priority.

3. All the women David had worked with.

There must be hundreds. The best way of checking them would be to find group photographs.

4. Women he'd acted as a probation contact for.

Were there any?

She realized that she hadn't heard anything from the National Correctional Organization after her freedom-of-information request to see the list of David's trustee activities, so she looked through her notepad and rang the lawyer's direct number. She picked up after four rings. She disappeared to look up Annika's request and returned a minute or so later, and there was a rustle of paper on the line.

"I can confirm that David Lindholm was active as both a probation contact and as a trustee over a period of many years," the lawyer said. "Sometimes he was a probation contact for, let's see, up to three people simultaneously, but while he was a trustee he had no other responsibilities."

"Is it more demanding being a trustee?"

"Yes, you could probably say that. Providing support to someone serving a life sentence is a tough responsibility."

"Can you tell me anything about who the inmates were?" Annika said, then held her breath.

"No, I can't identify them. We're bound by confidentiality legislation within the prison service and have to protect individual privacy. We've come to the conclusion that this isn't public information and therefore can't be handed out."

"Okay," Annika said. "Could you answer just one question: Was any of them a woman?"

The lawyer leafed through the documents.

"Well, I don't know . . ."

"Could you check? I don't know how this works. Could a man be a probation contact for a woman?"

"I don't think there's anything prohibiting that, or the reverse, of course."

"You don't have to tell me who she is, just if there was anyone . . ."

More paper shuffling.

"No," the lawyer said. "No women, only men."

"Thanks," Annika said, and hung up.

Okay. She could get rid of point four.

She got going with the second group on the list.

She went into the national ID database and typed in "Stevens, Michael Harold." It was a nuisance not being able to use her left index-finger when she typed.

Stevens was registered at an address in Sundsvall. Annika kept the address and surname but changed the gender of her search, and bingo! There were two women at the same address with the same surname, Linda Helena and Sarah Linda Hillary. The former was thirty-three years old, the latter eight.

Wife and daughter. The wife will do nicely!

She printed out the details, then looked up Ahmed Svensson from Malmö in the database. She found an old record and tracked back until she had found both his daughter Fatima and his ex-wife, Doris Magdalena.

I'll have her as well!

Filip Andersson, full name Arne Filip Göran, wasn't married, and never had been. It didn't look like he had any children either. Because he had such a common surname, it was impossible to track down his mother through the database.

She stretched her neck. Her headache was starting to ease. The pills must be kicking in.

I'll try googling him instead.

He was listed in Wikipedia under the category "Swedish criminals," but there was nothing about a wife or fiancée. The search terms *filip andersson wife* brought up loads of results, but nothing to suggest that the ax murderer was married.

She sighed. Thin pickings so far.

She tried the national police website instead to see if she could find any group photographs of the staff at different police stations, but all she found were a few portraits of gray-haired gentlemen with titles like national head of police and general director, as well as a few blond-haired women, senior directors, and the head of national crime.

Shit. This isn't going well at all.

She pulled out the printouts of David Lindholm's business activities and decided to list the names and ID numbers of any women who had been involved in any of his old companies.

The first file she looked at was the one about Fly High Equipment, the old parachuting company David had run with two other men, Christer Bure and the prematurely deceased Algot Heinrich Heimer, also known as Henke.

She decided to check out any women in Henke's life, and now things started to move.

Algot Heinrich Heimer had left a wife, Clara Susanna, and three daughters who were now twenty-three, twenty-one, and nineteen years old. Their names were Malin Elisabeth, Lisa Katarina, and Claudia Linn.

It was likely that David had known these women. He could well have had sex with them, or at least one of them. Annika made a note to try to find pictures of all four.

The next company she checked was Pettersson Catering & Arrangements AB, the one with such a large number of board members, which dealt with catering as well as horses. She made a note of the four women on the board. She also looked up Bertil Oskar Holmberg's wife, Victoria Charlotta, eighteen years younger than her husband.

This could be something!

She glanced at the remaining printouts, Advice Investment Management Behzad Karami and B Holmberg Property in Nacka AB. She looked at the time. She wanted time to get home and do some washing before heading to Grev Turegatan.

Oh, what difference does it make what clothes I'm wearing? Thomas has seen me without plenty of times. Anyway, they won't have time to dry properly...

She shook herself and concentrated on the people behind Advice Investment Management AB, Lena Yvonne Nordin in Huddinge and Niklas Ernesto Zarco Martinez in Skärholmen.

She added Lena Yvonne to the list and checked her other professional dealings, the cleaning firm in Skärholmen that she ran with Niklas Ernesto Zarco Martinez, and the investment company with Arne Filip Göran Andersson...

The room around her went totally silent. The light from the windows turned corrosive white, and she opened her mouth to say something, but nothing came out.

Arne Filip Göran Andersson.

The ax murderer from Sankt Paulsgatan.

She gasped for breath.

It couldn't be anyone else.

I knew it! I knew I'd seen his full name somewhere before, it was in these printouts, this is what I've been looking for...

With her hands trembling, she hunted through the printouts she had just got from the national database. Yes, bloody hell, the financier Filip Andersson was also named Arne and Göran.

Annika glanced back at the woman that connected them.

Lena Yvonne Nordin.

She sorted the documents in front of her, trying to see the links.

Lena Yvonne had run two investment companies, one with Niklas Ernesto Zarco Martinez, and the second with Filip Andersson.

This is the link! Here's the evidence that David and Filip Andersson had dealings with each other! A woman called Lena Yvonne Nordin.

Annika made a note of her name and ID number; then, with her hands still trembling, she took out her mobile phone and called Nina Hoffman.

"I've found something!" she said, standing up, unable to conceal the excitement in her voice. "Damn it, I think I'm onto something. You know I said there was something I couldn't quite work out? I know what it was now! You know the ax murderer, Filip Andersson . . . Nina . . . ?"

She stopped and listened to the silence on the phone.

"Nina? What is it? Has something happened? Are you crying?"

"Life," Nina said, taking a deep breath. "I knew she'd get a custodial sentence, but *life*! And for killing Alexander as well, this is just awful . . ."

Annika swallowed and sank back down onto her chair again, and her finger started to throb and ache.

"I know," she said lamely. "It's really . . ."

"Her lawyer, the useless little idiot, says he's considering an appeal, seeing as Alexander's body hasn't been found. As if that makes any difference!"

She was crying out loud now, angrily and violently.

"What does Julia say?"

"Don't know, Holger's been told they've taken her back to the medical wing again. She must have collapsed."

Annika tried to think of something sympathetic to say, but failed.

"This is typical," Nina went on. "They gave her an inexperienced little know-all to represent her, knowing full well that he'd fail. I've never seen such a show trial in my life, or such a sloppy murder investigation! Of course she was going to get life! Anything else was out of the question! Just because David Lindholm's dead, and someone had to pay, and they made up their minds it was going to be her, it was going to be Julia, and then they decided to sacrifice her child as well while they were at it . . ."

"Nina," Annika said. "There's something you could do to help me. I've been looking through various archives and I've found something I'd like to look into."

"What?" Nina said.

"I've found a connection. There's a woman who links David Lindholm with Filip Andersson."

"What sort of connection?"

"Two investment companies. They were both owned by a Lena Yvonne Nordin; she ran one together with David Lindholm and the other with Filip Andersson. Does that name mean anything to you? Lena Yvonne Nordin?"

Nina Hoffman fell silent, breathing shallowly down the phone a few times, then she blew her nose.

"Not a thing."

"There are others as well, other women . . . I've got a list of names and ID numbers. Would you be able to find photos of them from the National Police Registry?"

"What for?"

"I think the woman in the flat might be one of them. I can't get into passport records anymore, so . . ."

She could hear Nina Hoffman breathing on the other end of the line.

"Why do you want pictures of them?"

"Julia thinks she'd recognize the woman who took Alexander."

The police officer groaned.

"So you're thinking of showing them to Julia?"

"Of course."

"I can't do it," she said. "I can't help you."

"Of course you can!" Annika said. "It's just a matter of putting in a request for them!"

"I don't want to get involved . . ."

"Oh, don't try that one!" Annika said, more harshly than she intended. "I'll send the list to the station straight away."

"No!" Nina said. "Absolutely not. My colleagues mustn't know."

"A letter, then? Do you want me to send it to your home address, or the station?"

"Well, I'm working tonight, if you want to post it . . ."

"I'll get it couriered over at once."

Annika hung up and looked at her watch.

It was high time she went home.

She packed up her laptop and put the list in an envelope, then called reception to arrange for a courier.

The flat was a mess; Annika hadn't bothered making the bed since the children went to Thomas's. She dropped her bag on the hall floor and stood in the doorway, looking at the state of the living room.

Seeing as she was living in an unrenovated office space, there were no wardrobes anywhere, which meant that she had her clothes, bed linen, and towels piled in dusty heaps along one wall.

I have to sort my life out, and I have to start with my home.

She sighed, hung up her coat, then rolled up her sleeves.

Twelve names, there were no more than that for Nina to dig out pictures of.

Stevens's wife, Svensson's wife, and Henke's wife and daughters. The four women on the board of the catering company, Bertil Oskar Holmgren's wife, and the woman from the investment companies.

Twelve in total.

She started picking up clothes frenetically from the living room floor and stuffing them into a laundry basket, and was halfway through when the phone rang.

"Hello?" she said crossly into the phone, dropping the dirty laundry on the floor.

"Yes, I'm trying to reach Thomas Samuelsson," said a deep male voice with a pronounced Stockholm accent.

"Are you, now?" Annika said, putting her healthy hand on her hip. "He's not on this number anymore."

"Do you know how I can get hold of him?"

"Do what everyone else does, call him on his mobile."

"I've tried, but it's switched off. Have you got his new home number?"

Annika took a deep breath and let rip.

"He's moved in with his mistress," she said. "You can try calling him there."

"Oh shit," the man said, and to Annika's annoyance he sounded almost amused. "So the mistress has a phone?"

"Who can I tell him called?" Annika said, hearing how unfriendly she sounded.

"My name's Jimmy Halenius, I'm calling from the department. Is that Annika?"

Annika straightened her back.

Jimmy Halenius, the undersecretary of state. Thomas's boss, and the minister's right-hand man.

"Yes," she said, "it is."

"Thanks for dinner, I should say, although it was a while ago now."

They had met once, at the fateful dinner she and Thomas had held in the villa out in Djursholm a few days before it burned down.

"Thanks," she said curtly.

Was that right? Is that what you said when someone thanked you for your hospitality? She'd have to buy one of Magdalena Ribbing's books on etiquette.

"I've read Thomas's memo in my email, and I need to get hold of him at once. Can you give him the message?"

"Why?" she said. "What's so urgent?"

The man fell silent. His bantering tone had led her to expect something oily and sexist—*Nothing for you to worry your pretty little head about*, or something in that style—but he didn't say anything of the sort.

"I've left a message on his voicemail, but he hasn't called back," he said, sounding rather at a loss.

Annika took a deep breath.

"He's working from home today. Ellen isn't well. I'll be seeing him this evening. I'm looking after the children so that he and Sophia can go to the opera . . ."

She fell silent and chewed the inside of her cheek. Why was she telling Jimmy Halenius all this?

"Just ask him to call me," he said.

"Because otherwise I'll read about it in tomorrow morning's papers?" she blurted out, and could have bit her tongue off. *What the hell did I say that for?*

But the undersecretary of state just let out a little laugh.

"Something like that," he said, and hung up.

She was left standing there with the phone in her hand for a few seconds.

Thomas had evidently not said anything about their divorce at work. Mind you, why would he?

She put the phone down and gathered up the rest of the dirty washing. The last thing on the pile was the blue top Thomas had given her last Christmas, the only thing that survived of her former life. She had been wearing it the night the house burned down. That's why she was thinking of wearing it again tonight, because it brought time together, the person she was then and the person she had become. Besides, she knew Thomas liked the way she looked in it. It was a feminine cut, slightly sculpted at the front with a deep neckline, not her style at all really, but she like the cornflower-blue color.

She squashed it into the basket, fighting back the tears. *Why do I care what he thinks?*

The color of honey, heavy with stucco detailing, bay windows with leaded glass. This was one of the Grenborg family's rock-solid investments.

Annika was standing in the darkness on the other side of the street, looking up at the attic flat, at the sharp light coming from the windows in the roof.

In there, they're in there. In that white light.

She had been here before. A year ago, last November, the day after she realized Thomas had been having an affair, she had stood in this exact spot and looked up at the building. She felt a lurching sensation in her head and had to grab hold of the wall behind her to stop herself from falling. She struggled against dizziness and the urge to be sick for a few seconds before she was able to cross the street to the main door, dark brown and ornate.

She pressed the entry phone; she hadn't been given the code.

She answered. Sophia *Fucking Bitch* Grenborg.

"Come in, come in, you're very welcome. Sixth floor, at the top, the penthouse . . ."

The penthouse . . . ? Christ!

The entrance hall was all yellow and black marble, the lower portion of the walls clad in dark wood paneling, smoke-colored brass lamps. The carpet was dark blue, soft as eiderdown.

She took the stairs, slowly and unsteadily.

The attic floor was much less interesting than the rest of the building, a white security door in the middle of a whitewashed brick wall. She remembered the nameplate, brushed steel, and there was a handwritten note beside it.

T. Samuelsson.

She rang the bell.

Thank goodness, it was Thomas who opened the door.

She hadn't seen him since July.

He'd cut his hair. His fringe was sticking straight up and looked a bit odd. It made him look much older. His features looked sharper than she remembered them. He was wearing a black suit and polished shoes.

I was always the one who polished his shoes. I wonder if he's started doing it for himself now?

"Aren't you allowed to have a first name?" she asked, pointing at the note.

"You're a bit late," he said. "We have to go straightaway."

He was visibly nervous, turning away and reaching for a coat hanging from an ornate wrought-iron coatrack.

Sophia *FB* Grenborg skipped out behind Thomas with her hand outstretched and an ingratiating smile glued to her face.

She was wearing a bright yellow top, which, together with her yellow hair, made her look like an Easter chick. It took a moment before Annika realized that the top was exactly the same design as her cornflower-blue one. *What a fucking relief I didn't have time to wash it.*

"Mummy!"

The sound came from the living room, and was accompanied by the sound of quick footsteps. Kalle shoved Sophia *FB* Grenborg out of the way and threw his arms round Annika's legs. Ellen came skipping along behind him, clutching her new Poppy in her arms, also forcing her way past *FB*. Annika dropped her bag and coat on the floor and crouched down, taking both children in her arms, laughing and rocking them from side to side. It felt like she hadn't seen them for months, even though it had only been Monday when she dropped them off at school and nursery. She kissed their hair and cheeks and hugged them and tickled them, and kissed Poppy as well just to be on the safe side.

Thomas cleared his throat.

"Well," he said, "we ought to get going . . ."

"How are you?" Annika asked, stroking her daughter's hair from her face and looking at her carefully. "Have you been sick any more today?"

The girl shook her head.

Annika looked up at Thomas.

"So she hasn't got a temperature?"

"Since about lunchtime," he said. "She can go to nursery tomorrow, so she ought to be in bed by eight. What have you done to your hand?"

Annika stood up with her daughter in her arms.

"Cut myself cooking. I need to do some work once the children are asleep. Is there a computer I can borrow?"

"Of course," Thomas said, gesturing with one hand toward a large studio space that seemed to take up most of the flat.

Annika went past Sophia *FB* Grenborg without taking any notice of her.

"This is my office," Thomas said, opening the door to a cramped little space beyond the kitchen. "You can work in here. We won't be late, will we, Soph?"

Soph? Bloody hell!

"Well," Soph *FB* Grenborg said, pulling on her coat and a pair of nap-leather gloves, "I think Mother wanted to have dinner afterward, I think she may even have booked a table at Operakällaren . . ."

Mind you, he used to call me Anki . . .

"I'm not planning to go anywhere," Annika said curtly without look-ing at the other woman, then took Kalle's hand and headed off toward the sound of the children's favorite television program. Thomas came after them and watched as they settled down on the black leather sofa in front of the plasma television. He stopped in the doorway; Annika could sense him looking and felt her pulse rate increase.

He's so lovely, he still looks lovely even with short hair.

"Thanks for doing this," he said quietly.

She swallowed and kept her eyes on the television screen.

"Thomas, are you coming?"

How can he put up with that voice?

He disappeared from the doorway, and she heard the sound of keys and mobiles being dropped in pockets and bags, then the door closed and silence spread through Soph *Fucking Bitch* Grenborg's horrible pent-house suite.

The children went to bed at the same time and with the same amount of fuss as at hers; there wasn't much difference. They washed and brushed their teeth and sorted out their clothes and put the dirty ones in the laundry basket and chose a bedtime story and then huddled down ever so tightly under the covers and got comfy. Ellen was a bit difficult; she'd had a sleep during the day and had trouble settling down. Annika lay down in her narrow little bed and sang to her quietly until she fell asleep. She stroked her hand over her round head and soft shoulders, closing her eyes and inhaling the smell of her hair, feeling it tickle her nose.

You're a little miracle.

She carefully disentangled herself from the girl's warm body, then stood in the doorway looking at her. She was getting more and more like Thomas, with her blond hair and blue eyes. She felt a tightness in her chest and turned her head away, then went out into the chill of the flat. She shivered and wished she'd brought a cardigan.

It wasn't just that the temperature was low in the flat, there was a draft coming from somewhere and the pared-back furnishing only strength-ened the sense of cold. Everything was white apart from the leather seating, which was black, and the tables, which shimmered with glass and chrome.

The children had small rooms next to each other in the furthest corner of the large studio room. There was just enough space for their beds and a small shelf with a few toys, the walls were bare, and there were no rugs on the floor, no curtains, and no extra blankets.

I'm just looking for faults. The children aren't suffering here. As long as Thomas cares about them, they'll be fine.

She had never thought she would end up getting divorced. Naïvely, she had assumed that love would be enough: If only she loved him enough, everything would turn out all right, pretty much like a bedtime story.

I forgot to live with him, and now it's too late.

She looked in on Kalle, tucking him in and picking up Chicken, who had fallen onto the floor. Then she walked through the flat, over to the little space behind the kitchen, and sat down in front of Thomas's laptop. He hadn't changed his user ID or password, still using his first name for both. The connection was fast, as good as at the paper.

She went onto the national ID database and typed Lena Yvonne Nordin's details into the search page. She called herself Yvonne, she was forty-two years old, and her address was a post-office box in Skärholmen, on the outskirts of Stockholm. According to the list of old records, she had previously lived in Uppsala, and her marital status had been "widow" for the past ten years. She tried searching for other people called Nordin, male and female, age unspecified, registered at the same postal-box address to see if she had any children.

Nothing. At least none called Nordin, at any rate.

Annika couldn't see a printer in the office. She went out into the hall and fetched her notepad and pen from her bag and jotted down the details by hand. She opened another window in her browser and checked the basics, to see if she had a landline or a mobile. She got forty-nine results for Yvonne Nordin, from Boden in the far north to Simrishamn in the south, but nothing in either Skärholmen or Uppsala. Lena Yvonne Nordin brought up one result, in Uddevalla, but that woman was also named Mari, so it wasn't her.

She went into the register of property and searched for any legal reg-
istrations connected to Lena Yvonne Nordin's ID number.

Nothing.

Annika logged into the database of car registration numbers.

Nothing there either.

She chewed her lip.

Companies, she used to run more than one company . . .

She went into the registry of companies and brought up the details of
the three companies that Lena Yvonne Nordin had been linked to. The
only one that was still active was Advice Management Investment AB,
the company on whose board David had sat. The other two had been
deregistered.

But there was a name there that she had seen before and not yet
checked: Niklas Ernesto Zarco Martinez, also registered as living in
Skärholmen.

She opened another window and looked up his details.

Deceased.

Annika blinked.

Niklas Ernesto Zarco Martinez, thirty-five years old, had died on
Christmas Eve the previous year.

She had a remarkable ability to spread death around her, Lena Yvonne.

Feeling uneasy, she looked up Advice Investment Management AB's
business activities. The company was based at the post-office box address in Skärholmen, like Yvonne herself. Going back to the vehicle-
registration site again, she typed in the company's registered number and
there it was. *Bloody hell!*

The company owned a Toyota Land Cruiser 100, registration number TKG 298. The vehicle was a couple of years old, but was listed as
being taxed, insured, and roadworthy, which meant that it was in use and
on the road somewhere in or not far from Sweden.

Yvonne, I've found your car.

Encouraged by this success, she went into the property register again
and typed in the company number there as well, waiting patiently as the
laptop chewed through several million legal transactions.

I ought to be pleased he cares about the children. It's a terrible thing to

accuse me of having set fire to the house, but can I really blame him? Every-
one thinks I did it, after all. And he does look after the children . . .

The computer bleeped and Annika looked up at the screen.

One result.

Number 2:17, Lybacka, in the parish of Tysslinge, in Örebro council
district.

What?

Yvonne Nordin's company owned property north of Örebro?

Annika's pulse started to race.

The transaction was dated exactly a year before, December 2.

What does this mean?

Number 2:17 Lybacka, that wasn't an ordinary address, but one of
those hopeless property allocations that didn't tell her anything.

Where could she look to find out where 2:17 Lybacka was?

She went into the website of Örebro Council, to see if they had any
maps, and—would you believe it!—you could search for specific properties using their virtual satellite images.

I love the Internet! This is almost too easy!

She entered the property details in the search box, the map on the
right flickered, and then a low-resolution satellite image popped up, apparently showing a patch of forest.

It said 2:17 in the middle of the picture, and she zoomed out to see
where on earth it was.

A couple of clicks later, she could see from the satellite picture that
2:17 Lybacka was a small house with an adjoining barn located in the
middle of the forest. Another couple of clicks took her to an ordinary
map, showing roads and villages. Because she didn't have a printer she
sketched a map by hand, then zoomed out a bit further to discover that
the property lay northwest of Örebro, through Garphyttan and up in the
forest.

So why did you buy that place a year ago, Yvonne? Does it play a part
in your plan?

She went back to the Örebro Council website and looked up the information about Tysslinge parish and the area known as Lybacka, and
discovered that there was a small national park there, and a few aban-

doned earthworks known as the Lybacka Pits. Nearby was a bog called Ängamossen, which was described as being "covered in scattered, low-growing pines. The bog is surrounded by magical, ancient woodland . . ."

She clicked away from the natural description and went into the on-line telephone directory, but couldn't find a number for 2:17 Lybacka. In the end she went and got her mobile from the hall and rang directory inquiries instead, but that didn't work either.

She hesitated for a moment, then called Nina Hoffman and asked if she had got the photographs.

"I haven't had time," the police officer said.

"It's going to be interesting to see if Julia recognizes any of them. I'm sitting here checking . . ."

"Sorry to interrupt, but I'm in the car. Can we meet outside Police Headquarters early tomorrow morning? Eight o'clock?"

Annika could hear the rasping voice of the police radio in the background.

"Sure," she said.

They hung up, and Annika closed all the windows.

Her eye was caught by the Outlook Express icon.

I've read Thomas's memo in my email, and I need to get hold of him at once. Can you give him the message?

Why? What's so urgent?

She started up the email program, clicked on *sent messages*, and looked through the list of recipients. The last one was sent to sophia. grenborg@sdcc.se, Swedish District and County Councils, presumably, and had the heading "miss you darling."

She gulped and carried on looking.

Almost at the bottom of the screen she saw it.

jimmy.halenius@justice.ministry.se, with the heading "memo."

She opened the email and clicked to open the attachment without even blinking.

She shivered as she read it.

Thomas was telling the undersecretary of state that the directives he had been given to work with in the inquiry were impossible to follow. It simply couldn't be done.

If lifetime sentences were abolished, the cost of the criminal justice system would increase so greatly that the long-term state budget would have to be renegotiated.

Bloody hell! This is absolute dynamite!

That was followed by a careful analysis of the effects that time-limited sentences would have on the criminal justice budget. The reasoning seemed to be that a very long fixed-term sentence instead of life would drive up all the other levels in the criminal code, which would result in the cost of the prison system rising by at least 25 percent within three years.

She left the computer on and went out into the big room. She stopped and looked up at the ceiling. It felt a bit like standing in a church.

Penthouse flat! How pretentious could someone actually get?

She glanced at the time; the operagoers ought to be back soon. She walked restlessly round the studio, dogged by her own footsteps, past the dining table and the stylized seating area, and went back into the television room. The late news was due to start in a few minutes. She managed to get the digital box working and find the right channel just as the program began.

Julia Lindholm's life sentence was the lead item. The news presenter, a young woman with a doomsday voice, managed to call Julia both "double murderer" and "police killer" in her short introduction to the piece.

First on was Prosecutor Angela Nilsson, marching quickly, her back ramrod straight, with the cameras wobbling about like the worst Danish Dogma film. She declared that the verdict was both expected and justified. She looked simultaneously pleased and stern.

"The court unanimously shared my opinion," she said. "So I think it was a well-motivated sentence."

Anything else would be rather odd.

The crush inside the court building on Fleminggatan looked like it had been chaotic. Journalists kept bumping into each other, and Prosecutor Nilsson had to raise her hand against the camera lights to see where she was going.

"There are no words to describe the calculated cruelty that Julia Lindholm has shown the families of the victims," she said, sweeping through a security door.

What families? She's the only one left, along with her parents. And Nina, I suppose.

Then her lawyer appeared on screen, the young Mats Lennström, his hair stiff with gel and with beads of sweat on his forehead. He seemed to be leaning so far forward that he actually bumped his nose on the camera, leaving a little smear on the lens.

"Well, it was obvious that the court was going to reach this verdict, seeing as my client was kept in custody while we waited for the sentence," he said, his eyes flickering over the crowd of journalists. "But I don't agree with the sentence imposed by the court. In particular, I find it difficult to understand the court's reasoning with regard to the boy, er, Alexander. The problem is that we still don't know how he was killed."

Annika shifted irritably on the sofa. *How do you know he's dead?*

"Will you be lodging an appeal?" one male reporter shouted.

"Well, I'm considering that, but I haven't had time to talk to my client yet, so I really can't comment . . ."

Mats Lennström stumbled further along the corridor and disappeared through another security door.

A third person appeared on the screen, Professor Lagerbäck, an expert in criminology of the more populist persuasion, and he briskly summarized the verdict against Julia Lindholm in four cliché-ridden sentences:

"It was obvious she was going to get life, nothing else was ever on the cards. She blasted the manhood off an iconic police officer, and then tried the old line about hearing voices. The only thing that I think has been astonishingly shoddy in the investigation of this case is that the police haven't managed to find the little boy's remains. I actually think that's a great scandal."

Annika switched off the television, leaving a deafening silence.

Everyone's so sure. Why can't I let go of the idea that the boy is still alive?

She checked the time: twenty past eleven.

Where on earth are they?

Annoyed, she stood up and went out into the hall to get her mobile. She sent Thomas a fairly neutral text message.

Do you know when you'll be back?

A minute later she got a reply.

In an hour or so.

She sighed. What on earth was she going to do until half past twelve?

She walked over to the rooms where the children were sleeping, then leaned over and kissed their necks. She went out into the kitchen to get something to eat from the fridge but changed her mind, didn't want to touch any of Soph *FB* Grenborg's nasty food.

She ended up standing by the door to the bedroom, their bedroom. She stood there listening to noises from outside, from the stars up above, and out in the stairwell.

At least an hour before they get back. I'll make sure I leave everything as I find it.

Holding her breath, and without making a sound, she pushed the door open. One bedside lamp was on. The bed wasn't made. She walked over to the double bed. The bed linen was black. There were dried white stains on the undersheet. On the floor lay a pair of black panties with stains in the gusset. She looked away toward the wardrobes.

They filled an entire wall. She went over to the first one and cautiously opened the door.

Suits. Thomas had bought new ones. She opened the door wide.

These were more expensive than his old ones, the ones that had gone up in the fire. Carefully she stroked the material, wool, cotton, silk.

He's always had good taste, although he looks best in jeans and a T-shirt.

She closed the door and opened the next.

Soph's dresses. They were yellow and red and white and black and flowery, a few of them covered with sequins.

The pressure in her chest increased. She closed the door and opened the next one.

Her underwear. Panties and suspender belts and bras, all made of lace with hooks and pearls.

I don't have a single bra like this, I never have done. Does this sort of thing turn him on?

They were cream colored and red and deep purple and black, some with shoulder straps, some without, some wired, some not.

She picked up a particularly silky push-up bra, decorated with lace, and held it up in front of her. It was far too small. She made to put it back, then stopped.

She'd never find out I took it. She might wonder where it's gone, but she'd never know for sure.

She closed the wardrobe door with the bra in her hand, looking around the room. She hadn't touched anything else.

She quickly went out, closing the bedroom door behind her, then went into the hall and stuffed the bra into the inside pocket in her bag.

At that moment a text message arrived.

From Thomas.

We're going to be a bit late.

She tossed the mobile away.

I don't want to be here any longer now! Fuck!

Tears welled up in her eyes. The chalk-white walls leaned in on her and she ran into Kalle's room and knelt down by his bed.

"Darling," she said. "I miss you so much . . ."

The boy opened his eyes and looked at her, bewildered.

"What is it, Mummy? Is it time to get up?"

She forced herself to smile.

"No, not yet, I'm just giving you a kiss. Go back to sleep."

She got up and backed out of the room, stumbled through the studio space and stopped at a low cupboard against the far wall. Above it was a row of pictures in elegant frames, the sort they had in American television program. They showed Thomas and FB with their arms round each other on a yacht, Thomas and FB with their arms round each other in front of the Eiffel Tower in Paris, a group shot of Thomas and FB and the children at his parents' place in the country, out in the archipelago . . .

All of a sudden she couldn't breathe. *The bastard!*

She started to cry.

His mum must be so pleased now I'm out of the picture. I bet she thinks Soph Fucking Bitch *Grenborg is a much better mother than me. How could he do this to me?*

Self-pity hit her like a wave, with a force that knocked the breath out of her.

He's going to pay, the bastard!

She hurried back to Thomas's office behind the kitchen, sat down at the computer and wiped her tears with angry fingers. The computer was on standby but woke up at once when she touched the mouse.

She pulled up the email to the undersecretary of state again.

If this memo leaked out, the consequences for the whole inquiry would be immense. If the basic directives couldn't be followed, the entire proposal would collapse. The whole thing would have to be scrapped and they would have to start from scratch again, with the government formulating the terms of reference for a new inquiry with new directives and new members.

Thomas would lose his job.

She stared at the memo, feeling her heart race. She looked at the time. Half past twelve. They would be back soon.

He'll be okay. After all, he's got little Soph.

So how could she make sure no one knew where the email came from?

She couldn't just forward it, because Thomas's email address would be visible. And she couldn't send it from her own account, because everyone would be able to work out how she had got hold of the memo.

She would have to set up a fake address, anonymous and inconspicuous, but still credible enough for her colleagues on the paper to sit up and take notice of it when they saw it in the tip-off inbox.

She checked the time again, and went into hotmail.com.

With her fingers trembling, she created an entirely new email account. deep-throat-rosenbad@hotmail.com.

It took all of three minutes.

Then she forwarded Thomas's email to the new address, waiting nervously until it appeared in the Hotmail inbox. She deleted all the details that identified the writer of the memo and where it had come from, then sent it off again, this time to the email address used by the *Evening Post* for members of the public to give them tip-offs.

It ought to pop into the inbox at the paper more or less straightaway.

The reporter checking the email account would discover a new sender, Deep Throat Rosenbad, named after the confidential source used by Bob

Woodward and Carl Bernstein when they uncovered the Watergate Affair. They'd open the email and read her short message:

> *What I am sending you here is an internal and highly confidential memo from the Ministry of Justice. The contents will have serious consequences for the future program of the government. Undersecretary of State Halenius is aware of its contents.*

No more than that. That was enough. All the key words were there, the ones that got tabloid reporters going: internal, confidential, government, Ministry of Justice, serious consequences, undersecretary of state, aware . . .

Finally she deleted all the Hotmail files from Microsoft Explorer's browsing history, went back into Outlook and deleted the forwarded email from the list of sent mail, and shut down the computer.

In the silence that followed she heard the lift machinery whirring into action out in the stairwell.

She quickly switched off the light in the office and ran quietly through the studio, landing on the black leather sofa just as the front door opened. She got up at once, went out into the hall, and did her best to look tired and uptight.

"How did you get on?" Thomas asked.

"Fine," she said, and without looking at either of them she picked up her bag and coat and disappeared through the door.

Annika went into the 7-Eleven on Klarabergsgatan and bought a breakfast chorizo and both evening papers. Her hands were trembling slightly as she put the money on the counter, slightly uneasy about what the paper would have done with the confidential memo.

What if it leads to a crisis of government?

What if they didn't understand what it meant and just ignored it?

She wasn't sure which would feel worse.

With her eyes wide open, she inspected the cover of the *Evening Post*. It was dominated by a photograph of a smiling Julia with a garland of flowers in her hair and the headline: *Lifetime.* Below stood the words: *Exclusive—Police wife Julia Lindholm speaks out about the murder of her husband David, her son's disappearance, and her future in prison.*

That didn't match what she'd written, but she didn't have the energy to get upset.

There was nothing about the memo on the front page.

She quickly leafed through the paper, then realized that she was standing in the way of other customers and moved to the back of the shop, spreading the paper out on top of the ice-cream freezer. She took a large bite of the sausage, getting mustard on her bandage. *Damn!*

Her interview with Julia Lindholm was on pages six and seven. Eight and nine carried analysis of the lifetime sentence, but there—*Ah, there it is*—on page ten, was the article about the Ministry of Justice's confidential memo.

Emil Oscarsson had written the piece. He had realized the potential of the story and had called and woken the undersecretary of state and the minister's press secretary, as well as the leader of one of the opposition parties. The angle was that the inquiry was heading for disaster and the

Ministry of Justice had been forced into emergency measures to stop the costs of the prison system careering out of control.

Annika swallowed hard.

What am I up to?

She wondered if the main radio news broadcasts had picked it up and were running with it in their morning bulletins, but she had no radio so had no way of knowing.

What are the consequences of this? For Thomas, and for the government?

Her mobile rang and she dropped the sausage on the floor when she grabbed for her bag to dig it out.

It was Nina.

"Julia's still in the medical wing. She's not allowed any visitors."

Fucking hell!

"Give me two minutes."

She pushed the sausage and both papers in the bin and ran off towards Bergsgatan.

Nina Hoffman was in her police uniform. She looked like she hadn't slept a wink all night.

"No, I haven't," she said tersely. "At half past four we found a man's body in a flat near Hornstull. Took a while."

"Do the papers know about it?" Annika asked breathlessly.

"It looked like an overdose, I doubt they'd be interested. But we still have to investigate it, of course. What have you done to your finger?"

They were standing outside the entrance to Police Headquarters on Kungsholmen. Annika pulled her sleeve down over her left hand.

"I cut myself cooking," she said, looking off toward Scheelegatan, feeling Nina's stern gaze on her.

"That's a pretty serious bandage," the police officer said.

Annika looked down at the ground, at the leaves stuck to the pavement, at her own shoes and Nina's heavy boots.

"Do we trust each other or not?" the police officer said, pulling her to one side to let a woman with a pram get past on the pavement.

"There were two of them," Annika said once the woman had gone past. "Two men, they pulled me into an alley when I was on my way home from yours the other evening, close to where I live in Gamla stan. They cut my finger, told me to say that I hurt myself cooking. And if I told anyone about them, they'd cut . . . my children . . . next time . . ."

She was having trouble breathing.

Nina took hold of her hand and looked at the bandage.

"What's this you've spilled on it?"

"Mustard. The strong sort."

"I suppose you had to have stitches."

"Eight. They cut a ligament. I bit one of them, and he hit me over the head to make me let go."

Nina looked at her, her eyes black from lack of sleep.

"You know what I've been saying. You have to be careful. You can't mess with these people."

She looked off down Bergsgatan.

"I think you should drop this," she said. "Think of your children."

"Have you got the pictures?"

Nina hesitated, then nodded.

"Come on," Annika said. "The café over on Hantverkargatan will be open now."

They sat down at a cramped little table by the window.

Annika got some coffee, but Nina didn't want anything. She took off her cap and leaned her head against the wall.

"This is verging on professional misconduct," she said flatly. "I'm not supposed to go anywhere near this case."

She felt in her pockets and pulled out an envelope. Annika took it, feeling her pulse speed up. She opened it carefully and looked through the pictures.

"Which one's Yvonne Nordin?"

"Which one do you think?" Nina said in a dull voice.

Annika spread out the Polaroid pictures from the National Police register on the little table in front of them, picking them up in turn and looking at them carefully.

"No," she said. "I can't guess."

Nina turned one of the pictures over and pointed at the back, where it said the woman's name and ID number.

Yvonne Nordin had mousy blond hair and unremarkable features, and looked to be in early middle age. She had a serious expression on her face, and it looked as if she was slightly overweight.

Annika picked up the picture and inspected it.

"Do you think she's got money?"

Nina snorted.

"That's a completely hypothetical question."

Annika was looking intently at the photograph.

"If she was responsible for the murders on Sankt Paulsgatan, then she must also have been involved in Filip Andersson's shady affairs, which means she's got secret bank accounts hidden away on various tropical islands. I tried to look her up last night. She's registered at a covering address in Skärholmen, but I don't think she lives there."

"Why not?" Nina asked.

"If she really did shoot David and kidnapped Alexander, then there's a reason why. I think she's still got Alexander, and he mustn't be seen by anyone, not for a long while, anyway. Which rules out Skärholmen. Whereas . . ."

She pulled her notepad out of her bag and showed the police officer some uneven lines on one of the pages.

". . . She bought a small house in the middle of the forest exactly a year ago, north west of Örebro. Just outside Garphyttan, here!"

She pointed with her pen at a cross on the page.

Nina was looking extremely tired.

"Julia mentioned that a couple of different women, unless they were the same one, got in touch with David and demanded that he leave Julia. One of them had an abortion. Do you think that could be important?"

"Maybe I will have a cup of coffee after all," Nina muttered, and Annika got up quickly and fetched her one.

"Do you think the abortion is important?" Annika repeated as she put the cup down in front of the police officer.

"It can be a very traumatic experience," she said, blowing on her drink. "Some women never get over it."

"Well," Annika said, sitting back down on the other side of the table, "we shouldn't over dramatize it. It doesn't necessarily have to be that traumatic. I had an abortion when Ellen was six months old, and I'm very happy I did."

Nina took a sip of coffee.

"So you didn't see it as a problem at all?"

Annika stuffed her notepad back in her bag.

"Well, getting them to answer the phone was a nightmare. I spent ages ringing around trying to book an appointment anywhere in Stockholm, but all the clinics that could be bothered to pick up the phone had no vacancies for several weeks. In the end I gave up and had the abortion in Eskilstuna. I can still remember how relieved I felt when I got back to the car park. What is it, you look like you don't believe me?"

"Not everyone reacts like that. It can be a great sorrow, an act of betrayal . . ."

Annika shifted on her chair in irritation.

"That's what everyone's expected to say. It's like it's not acceptable to say that you're pleased you had an abortion, but I really was. I really didn't want to have another child at that time."

She could see Nina's look of disapproval.

"What? You think I'm a bad woman because I'm pleased I had an abortion? Have I forfeited my right to be a mother?"

"No, no," Nina said. "But I really do have to go now."

She got up, and Annika saw the woman behind the counter glance furtively in their direction. The police uniform had a way of making people feel guilty, even if they hadn't done anything.

"I'll hold on to these pictures," Annika said, putting them back in the envelope.

Nina stopped, and it looked like she was hesitating. Then she leaned toward her and lowered her voice.

"Be careful," she said. "The people who cut you mean business."

Then she put her cap back on and disappeared through the door, heading down toward Scheelegatan.

Annika pulled the pictures out again and stared at them, one by one.

They were dark and fair and young and old, some wearing a lot of makeup, others scruffy.

She stopped at Yvonne Nordin, with her rather sad eyes and thin hair.

Are you a crazy mass murderer? How on earth am I going to show your picture to Julia?

She bit on her coffee spoon a couple of times, then took her pen and a sheet of paper out of her bag and wrote a short note to Kronoberg Prison.

"These pictures are to be handed to Julia Lindholm. Best wishes, Annika Bengtzon."

She got up and hurried off toward Bergsgatan, where she handed the envelope in at the reception desk. Then she ran back to the bus stop outside number 32 Hantverkargatan, her old address, her home in Stockholm until the disaster of Vinterviksvägen. She refused even to look at the door and got on the bus.

The weather was uniformly gray and heavy as lead. The sun had probably risen somewhere beyond the iron curtain of damp and grayness, but she wasn't sure if it was ever going to show its face here again.

The bus was full and she had to stand, swaying this way and that as the bus swung around corners. The air was fusty with damp clothes and bad breath.

She got off at Gjörwellsgatan, breathing out deeply.

The newsroom was almost empty. Anders Schyman was sitting in his little glass room with his feet up on the desk and that day's *Evening Post* open in front of him.

"Damn good piece about the cop killer speaking out," the editor in chief said when she walked into the room without knocking. "But have you seen the article on page ten? We've got hold of a confidential memo from the Ministry of Justice that proves that life sentences can't be abolished, it would be too expensive."

"I saw that," she said, sinking onto the visitor's chair. "I'm working on something really big. Julia Lindholm says she's innocent, she's been saying that all along. There might be a way to prove that."

"It came in as a tip-off last night," Schyman said. "From a 'Deep Throat Rosenbad.' What does that say to you?"

"I think she's right, I don't think she did it. Alexander's still alive."

The editor in chief lowered the paper.

"I presume you have some sort of concrete evidence to back that up."

Annika started by going through the triple murder in Sankt Paulsgatan four and a half years before, the way the victims had first been hit in the head with an ax, then each had one hand cut off, and how the financier Filip Andersson had been found guilty by both the City Court and the Court of Appeal, even though he maintained he was innocent.

She outlined the parallels with David's murder, first the shot to the head, then the mutilation of the body, and how Julia claimed she didn't do it.

She explained about David's business interests, and how he had sat on the same board as a woman called Yvonne Nordin who was also involved in a different company with Filip Andersson—"Do you see the connection?"—and that he had told Julia about a crazy woman who was stalking him and threatening to harm him, "But we think she was the one who had an abortion . . ."

There was complete silence when she had finished.

Anders Schyman was looking at her sternly and intently.

"The abortion?" he said.

"Yes, but I don't know how important that is."

"What about Alexander's clothes and teddy bear, how did they end up in the marsh next to Julia's cottage, then?"

"She put them there."

"Who? This Yvonne? And she was the one who had the abortion? The one who's supposed to have Alexander, in other words?"

Annika pulled out her roughly sketched map from her bag and put it on the editor in chief's desk. He picked it up and studied it dubiously.

"There," Annika said, pointing to the cross representing number 2:17 Lybacka in the parish of Tysslinge in Örebro County.

"And Filip Andersson is innocent, and Julia Lindholm is innocent?"

"Filip Andersson is doubtless guilty of an awful lot of things, but not the murders on Sankt Paulsgatan."

"And Alexander isn't dead?"

"It was an attack on the whole family: Kill the man, frame his wife, and kidnap the child. He's alive."

Anders Schyman put the sheet of paper down on his desk and looked at her carefully.

"Did they ever find out who set fire to your house?" he asked.

"What's that got to do with anything?" she asked.

The editor in chief looked genuinely concerned.

"How are you really, Annika?"

She flew into a rage.

"So that's your conclusion!" she said. "That I'm trying to clear my own name by proxy!"

"Don't start harassing innocent people, Annika. Think before you do anything."

She got up, knocking the map to the floor, and Schyman bent down to pick it up.

"Do you know what this reminds me of?" he said, handing it back to her.

She looked at the crooked lines and abbreviated road names.

"*A Beautiful Mind*," she said quietly.

"A what?"

She swallowed hard.

"Do you need help?" he asked.

She shook herself in annoyance.

"I've been a bit off form, that's all," she said, "with the divorce and everything."

"Yes," he said, sitting down on the desk and folding his arms. "How's that going?"

"It's going to court soon, in December," she said. "Then everything's over."

"Everything?"

She brushed the hair from her face.

"No," she said, "not everything, of course, just the rough stuff. After that it'll get better."

"Are you still living in that old office? When are you going to get somewhere proper to live?"

"When the police investigation's over, and I can get hold of the insurance money."

"And your husband?"

"He's living with his mistress."

"If the divorce is almost legal, she's his partner, isn't she?"

She picked up her bag and put the map back in it.

"Is he still at the Ministry of Justice?"

"As far as I know."

"What was it he was doing there? The inquiry into the abolishment of life sentences, wasn't it?"

"Can I have a car for the day? I'll be back this evening."

"What are you thinking of doing?"

"Meeting a source."

Anders Schyman sighed.

"Okay," he said, reaching for a requisition request. "But I don't want you going off and doing anything stupid."

She left without looking back.

The car was an anonymous Volvo, an old model, dark blue and pretty dirty. She drove out of the garage and swung up onto the Essinge motorway.

There were two ways of getting to Örebro, north or south of Lake Mälaren. Without even thinking she headed south, toward Södertälje, then Strängnäs and Eskilstuna. She chose that way instinctively, just because she was used to it.

That's what we're like. We'd rather stick to what we know, even if it's no good, than change to something better but new.

There wasn't much traffic and the road was reasonably dry, so she could have driven faster if she wanted. Once she'd got past Södertälje and turned off onto the E20, she set the cruise control for 135 kilometers an hour, just below the point where she'd lose her license if she got caught. Anne had taught her that, that you could drive "with VAT." On roads with 30 and 50 km/h limits you could drive 20 too fast, and in limits of 70, 90, and 110 the VAT increased to 30. Of course you were breaking the law if you drove with VAT, but it only cost you a fine.

Look upon it as a congestion charge, Anne had said.

She laughed as she thought about it; she'd missed Anne. She passed an articulated lorry from Estonia, and the car flew along the road. The landscape drifted past without her really noticing it; she'd seen it all her life, grew up in it. The flat, brown fields around Mariefred and Åkers styckebruk, the water of Sörfjärden shimmering dully to the right as she passed Härad, then the forests as she approached Eskilstuna.

She glanced at the digital clock on the dashboard: one minute to ten.

Ellen would be back at nursery now, and Kalle would be having his first break at school.

She turned on the radio to hear the news. The newsreader was a man who had a corset as strong as tank casing. The lead item brought her out in a sweat.

"The parliamentary inquiry into prison sentences and the abolition of life sentencing is being shut down because the directives were impossible to follow, the Ministry of Justice has announced in a press release this morning. This means that lifetime sentences will remain part of the judicial system in Sweden for the foreseeable future. This has provoked harsh criticism from the opposition . . ."

No reference to the *Evening Post*, and no mention of what would happen to the people working on the project.

She turned the radio off and the silence that followed was deafening. The rumble of the wheels on the tarmac echoed through the car, forming new words in the voice of the newsreader. She leaned over and turned the radio back on again, turning the dial toward the end of the FM frequency. Mix Megapol had a strong signal around Eskilstuna on 107.3, and she found herself in the middle of a relentless series of adverts that ended with a cheery jingle declaring that the station mixed today's hits with the best of yesterday. She turned up the volume to block out all the voices and thoughts, Anders Schyman and Anne Snapphane and the newsreader and Nina Hoffman and Soph *Fucking Bitch* Grenborg . . .

She turned off toward Kungsör to find a petrol station; it would make sense to fill up. She indicated and turned off into a petrol station on Kungsgatan. She filled the tank with diesel and went in to pay.

Then she went into the bathroom for a pee and discovered there was no toilet paper. With a groan she grabbed her bag to see if she had any paper handkerchiefs, and as she rooted round in the bag her hand touched something soft and silky smooth.

The lacy push-up bra from Sophia Grenborg's wardrobe.

She put the garment in the sink, rinsed and washed her hands, then sat down on the toilet seat again with the silky rag in her hands. The price ticket was still attached. It had been bought in Paris. One hundred sixty-nine euros.

She remembered the photograph of the Eiffel Tower, and the children on the veranda out on the island in the archipelago, Gällnö.

Her chest felt tight and she could feel her anger boiling inside her.

She leaned over and pulled the penknife from her bag, *The Evening Post—sharp and to the point*, then she cut Sophia Grenborg's luxury bra to shreds, thin at first, then coarser and messier, the knife threatened to glance off the metal frame and cut the index finger of her left hand again, she cut and tore until she was completely out of breath, until the little item of clothing was nothing but tattered lace and frayed fragments. She felt like crying but clenched her teeth against the pain, pulled out some paper napkins, wetting them under the tap and wrapping them round the fragments of lace and flushed them away.

There. Gone forever, and good fucking riddance.

She tried to feel pleased, put the penknife back in the mess inside her bag and went back out to the car. She headed off toward Arboga. She had to slow down and switched off the radio, as she ended up behind a tow truck that was trundling along at 60, almost sending her mad.

Finally she overtook it with a sense of relief and turned onto the E18 toward Örebro.

What am I going to do if she's there? What am I going to do if she's standing there with Alexander?

She wouldn't do anything at all, she decided. She'd just take a little look and then leave and call the police if she had to.

Happy with her decision, she cruised through Örebro and eventually found the turning toward Garphyttan. The road became narrow and twisting again, in some places slippery with frost. The thermometer inside the car was hovering around zero, and she slowed down even more.

When she got to Garphyttan she turned right at a co-op supermarket, following the road past detached houses on the right and thick forest on the left. She drove past a recreation ground with a soccer field and a running track, and then she was out in the countryside again.

It started to snow, big, hesitant flakes that swirled round in the air, unable to decide where to land. The forest was getting denser and darker. She turned on the radio to get a bit of company, but the only station she could get was P1, where a serious man was reading something literary about brown envelopes that were dissolving in damp and mold. She switched it off again.

I'll have to put up with silence. I've got to learn how to live with myself.

The landscape opened up and she drove past some farms in a village called Nytorp, then she turned off left and found herself on roads that reminded her of the forest tracks around Hälleforsnäs.

After a kilometer or so she reached a junction where she had the choice of going right or left. She pulled the map from her bag and peered at her directions. She had to go right here and then left almost at once, then follow the road until it stopped.

She tried to shrug off Anders Schyman's reaction when he had handed the piece of paper back to her.

She drove down the winding road for almost twenty minutes, passing a few cleared patches of woodland, without seeing a single person, or a single house.

You like your peace and quiet, don't you, Yvonne?

Finally she reached a turning circle that she had seen on the satellite picture, pulled to a stop, and let out a gasp.

A huge 4x4 was parked next to a barrier at the far end of the circle. She looked at the license plate: TKG 298.

That's her car, her Toyota Land Cruiser. She's here! I knew it!

Annika pulled up beside the SUV and turned the engine off, opened the car door, and got out, her heart pounding. She went quickly over to the Toyota and peered in through the windows. No child seats. No toys in the backseat. No sweet papers on the floor as far as she could see.

In the back of the vehicle a piece of gray fabric had been pulled across to conceal whatever was in there. She'd had something similar in her SUV before it went up in flames.

She looked around, trying to get her bearings. Yvonne Nordin's cottage should be a few hundred meters north of there.

She must have heard the car approaching. There's no point trying to creep up on her.

She zipped up her jacket, hoisted her bag onto her shoulder, and dodged under the barrier.

The forest was thick and dark, pressing in on her from both sides of the path. Annika tried to think of it as unthreatening, noting that it was mainly fir trees with a few birches. The moss was as thick and untouched as the carpet in the entrance hall where Soph Grenborg lived. The treetops stretched up toward the steely gray sky. It had stopped snowing, but she could still smell snow in the air. In the hollows and behind rocks lay the remnants of earlier snowfall.

The frozen mud crunched under her boots, even though she was trying to tread softly.

A stream was burbling somewhere nearby. She peered through the trees but couldn't see any water. Did she dare leave the path? Would she ever find it again? She had a terrible sense of direction; she could never find anything without a map.

She decided to hang her bag on a branch beside the path as a marker. Then she stepped in among the trees.

If Alexander is here, he'd love playing by the stream. He's probably built a dam where he can sail his little boats.

A minute or so later she found the water. It was trickling gently through the rocks and small chunks of ice, a constant, harmonious burble unimpeded by any dams or little boats.

She swallowed and suppressed a feeling of disappointment. She followed the water both up and downstream for a bit, but there were no signs of any human activity at all.

Luckily she managed to find her way back to the gravel track.

A short while later she glimpsed a red façade through the trees and slowed down, finally coming to a halt behind a large fir tree.

It was an old cottage, with windows on either side of the door and a double chimney. Smoke was coming out of one chimney and there were lights on in two of the windows, which had open, white-painted shutters. There was a large satellite dish on the roof. To the left of the house was an outbuilding, what she had taken to be a barn on the satellite image. Now she could see it was more like a storeroom; maybe it had been a henhouse or workshop once upon a time. The little forest track ran past the house and disappeared off to the right. It was completely silent around her, even the wind and the trees were holding their breath.

Then she focused her attention and looked to see if there were any signs of a child being there. A sandpit, a bike, a plastic spade, anything at all. She took a couple of steps out from behind the tree, and at that same moment she saw a woman emerge from the outhouse with a couple of large suitcases in her hands. The woman caught sight of her, stopped, and put the suitcases down.

Annika's first instinct was to run.

She's going to chop me up. She'll hit me over the head and then cut off my hands.

"Hello!" the woman said cheerily. "Are you lost?"

Annika gulped and stepped forward.

"I'm afraid I must be," she said, walking up to the woman and holding out her hand. "My name's Annika."

"Yvonne Nordin," the woman said with a smile. She looked slightly surprised but not remotely worried. "Can I help you at all?"

It was the woman from the passport photograph, no doubt about it. Average height, short ash-blond hair under a crocheted cap, warm and rather sad eyes.

"I'm trying to find the quarry," Annika said. "The Lybacka Pits, they're supposed to be somewhere round here, aren't they? Is this the right way?"

The woman laughed.

"You're not the first person to get that wrong," she said. "That little track is completely impossible to find. I've told the people in charge of the project that they have to improve their signage, but it's like everything else. If you want anything doing, you have to do it yourself."

Annika couldn't help laughing.

"So I've driven too far?"

"About four hundred meters. There's a little red-painted post on the right, and the turning's immediately after that."

"Thanks very much," Annika said, looking around, unwilling to leave just yet. "You've got a nice place here," she said.

Yvonne Nordin took a deep breath and closed her eyes in contentment.

"I think it's fantastic," she said. "I've only had the place for a year, but I really love living here. When you're in my line of work you can work pretty much anywhere these days, it's a great privilege."

Annika saw the opening and grabbed at it.

"How exciting," she said. "What do you do?"

"I'm a consultant," she said. "I run a company that deals with investment and management. I have to spend a lot of time physically at the companies that employ me, like a sort of stand-in MD, but as soon as I get the chance I come out here to recharge my batteries."

"Doesn't it get lonely?"

The question slipped out before she could stop it, and it sounded far too sharp.

Yvonne Nordin looked at her in surprise, then she looked down at the ground and nodded.

"Well," she said, "sometimes."

She looked up at Annika and smiled rather sadly.

"My partner died last year, on Christmas Eve, actually. I haven't got over it yet. The forest gives me some sort of solace. I don't think I could have got through this past year without this place."

Annika felt a sense of shame rising through her chest, and she couldn't think of anything else to say.

"I'd ask you in for coffee," Yvonne said, "but I was just about to set off."

"Duty calls?" Annika managed to say, looking at the suitcases.

The woman laughed.

"Isn't it silly that we always pack so much? All I really need are passports and tickets."

Annika hoisted her bag onto her shoulder and fought to suppress the burning sense of guilt inside her.

"Have a good trip," she said, "and thanks for your help."

"Don't mention it," Yvonne Nordin said. "Look in again sometime . . ."

Annika went back along the gravel track, past the point where she had gone into the forest to find the stream, ducked under the barrier, and got back to the car.

It was incredibly cold now, and snow was falling again. She got in the car, turned the engine on, and turned the heater up full. She screwed her eyes shut and folded her arms over the steering wheel.

God, how embarrassing. Bloody hell, I'm lucky.

She closed her eyes even tighter and felt the sense of guilt rising into her throat, almost making her feel sick.

I'm lucky I didn't make even more of a fool of myself. Imagine, if I'd actually said anything . . .

She could hear Anders Schyman's words echoing in her head.

Don't start harassing innocent people, Annika. Think before you do anything.

She swallowed hard, the sense of shame throbbing inside her.

Sorry for being such a naïve fool. Sorry for stealing and wrecking and sabotaging things.

All of a sudden she started to cry, tears that stung her cheeks.

Stop being so pathetic. You've got no reason to feel sorry for yourself.

She shook herself, wiped her tears on her sleeve, and put the car in gear. She headed back along the winding track, and after a few hundred meters passed the red post that Yvonne Nordin had mentioned.

I've got to get a grip on myself, I can't go on like this.

She drove on through the countryside. There was snow in the air without it ever quite getting going. Her stomach was rumbling, and she realized that she hadn't eaten anything all day, apart from a couple of mouthfuls of chorizo at quarter to eight that morning.

She found a pizza restaurant in Garphyttan and ordered the set lunch. It turned out to be a pizza and soft drink.

Annika got a can of Loka mineral water and sat down at one of the window tables.

There was a large factory opposite, Haldex Garphyttan AB, and she looked out at its car park.

So many cars. So many people who own those cars, washing them and looking after them and getting them serviced, living their lives in Garphyttan without me having the faintest clue about it . . .

She was on the point of bursting into tears again, but pulled herself together.

I should follow Anne's example. I ought to ask for forgiveness.

Without thinking, she pulled out her mobile and saw that she had one missed call. Number withheld, so it was probably the paper.

She gathered her thoughts, then dialed a number she hadn't thought about for six months, a number that she had dialed at least twice a day before then, but had since tried to erase from her memory.

"Hello, this is Anne Snapphane . . ."

"Hello," Annika said. "It's me."

A short silence.

"Hello, Annika. It's good to hear from you. I'm really very pleased."

"Sorry," Annika said. "I've been behaving like an idiot too."

Anne put the phone down and said "Can I call you back?" into another receiver, then came back.

"You don't have to say you're sorry," she said.

"I've got so many people I need to apologize to," Annika said. "I crash on like a steamroller without thinking about anyone but myself. Thomas is right, I shape my view of the world so that it fits me and my own criteria. And I completely ignore everything else."

"You give a damn," Anne said, "and sometimes you go just a bit too far."

Annika laughed, a small, joyless laugh.

"That's probably the understatement of the day. I exploit people, and I steal, and I lie. I refuse to admit when I'm wrong."

"Everyone gets things wrong," Anne said. "Everyone makes mistakes.

You're not the only person on the planet who does that. And that's a good thing to try to remember."

"I know," Annika whispered, looking over at the pizza oven. A flour-dusted cook with a beer belly and bright red hair was sprinkling oregano over her capricciosa.

"Where are you?"

She laughed again.

"In a pizzeria in Garphyttan. My lunch is on its way."

"Where the hell is Garphyttan?"

"You don't want to know, and you don't want to know what it looks like . . ."

"Don't say any more. Textured wallpaper, flouncy, flowery curtains that are all shiny on one side."

Annika laughed out loud.

"Exactly."

"What are you doing there?"

"Making a fool of myself, as usual. Could you bear to hear about it?"

"Of course."

The pizza arrived in front of her, she mimed "thank you" to the red-haired cook who evidently doubled up as waiter as well.

"I behaved like a real cow toward Thomas. I've sabotaged his work, and I went through the wardrobes in his new home, really mean."

"Really mean," Anne agreed. "And really nasty."

"And I've been poking about in the background of a murdered police officer, and I've been absolutely convinced that there's evidence, patterns that no one else has noticed. I've been assuming I was better and smarter than everyone else."

"You do have a tendency to think the rest of the world is full of idiots," Anne said. "That's just part of your character."

Annika sighed and rolled the pizza into a long sausage, then picked up one end and took a bite. Grease ran out of the other end, making a little trickle that spread out across the tablecloth.

"I know," she said with her mouth full of cheese and pizza base. "I've done so many stupid things, I've made a fool of myself in front of my boss, and a police officer called Nina, but I'll just have to live with that."

Not to mention what I've done to Thomas.

"Schyman must have seen most of your bad sides before now," Anne said.

Annika sighed again.

"Now he thinks I'm starting to go mad as well, but that doesn't really matter. I'm just sullen and stubborn, and I always have to be proved right."

"But at least you're starting to get a bit of self-awareness," Anne said. "That should make life a bit easier for you."

Annika swallowed the mouthful of pizza.

"I've been very unfair to you," she said.

"Oh, well," Anne said. "I'll survive. I'm just happy you're prepared to get a grip on yourself and your life. Maybe you should go and talk to someone, what do you think?"

"Maybe," Annika said quietly.

"It's probably not a good idea for you to see the same therapist as me, but I can ask if she could recommend someone."

"Mmh."

There was silence on the line.

"Annika?"

"Yes?"

"Take care on the drive back to Stockholm, and get in touch when you're back. I've got Miranda next week, she's really missed Ellen and would love to see her again."

Tears welled up in Annika's eyes again, this time tears of relief.

"Definitely," she said.

"Well, let's speak soon."

She stayed in the pizzeria for a while, drinking coffee that was surprisingly good and playing a song on the jukebox in the corner, "Losing My Religion" by REM. Breathing started to feel a bit easier. It had been the right decision to swallow her pride.

She paid (the red-haired man worked on the till as well) and went out into the hesitant twilight. The air was clearer and colder, the skies were less cloudy and there was a stiff wind.

She got in the car and had just turned onto the road to Örebro when her mobile rang. It was on the passenger seat beside her and she glanced at the number. Number withheld. Probably the paper again. She sighed and answered it.

"Annika? This is Q. Where are you?"

Suddenly the fear was back, big and black and sucking all the oxygen from the air.

"I'm driving. Has something happened with the investigation into the fire?"

"Julia Lindholm got the envelope with your pictures."

Oh no. Fucking hell.

"The prison staff called me after she'd spent an hour screaming."

Annika slowed the car and pulled in at the verge.

"I'm really sorry, I didn't mean . . ."

"You know, it's really bloody irritating to have you poking about in our investigation."

She closed her eyes hard and felt her cheeks color.

"I'm really sorry if I've made a mess of things."

"It says on the back of the picture that one of the women owns a cottage somewhere near Garphyttan. Is that your information?"

"Er, yes, she lives there. In a cottage not far from the Lybacka Pits. I was talking to her about an hour ago."

"You were *talking* to her? Bloody hell. Where the hell are you?"

Her voice was little more that a squeak when she answered.

"In Garphyttan. And I'm really sorry I left those pictures, it was all a misunderstanding."

"Julia says she recognizes Yvonne Nordin. She says it was Yvonne Nordin who was in their flat that night. That she was the one who took Alexander."

"I'm so sorry I've made a mess of everything," Annika said. "I really am. It's all wrong, there's no child up at the cottage. Yvonne Nordin has nothing to do with this."

"I intend to make my own mind up about that," Q said. "I've just sent a patrol from Örebro Police to bring her in for questioning."

"Oh, no," Annika said. "But it isn't her, everything she said was true."

"What? What was true?"

"When she bought the house, and that her partner died. The company she runs, and the car she drives. She's a decent person."

She could hear Q groan.

"Anyway, she probably isn't there," Annika said. "She was just about to leave. She said she was going away on a job."

"Where? Did she say where?"

"Abroad, I assume, because she mentioned her passport. Has the patrol set off?"

"They'll be leaving any minute. Do me a favor and keep out of the way."

"Sure," Annika said. "Of course. Absolutely."

She was left sitting with the phone in her hand, wishing the ground would swallow her up.

She'd made Julia think there was hope. Yvonne Nordin might end up missing her flight . . . God, she was such a loser.

She put her hand on the ignition key again, then stopped.

Miss her flight? Tickets? Isn't it silly that we always pack so much. All I really need are passports and tickets.

She let go of the key.

Passports and tickets?

Why did Yvonne Nordin use the plural? And why did she need several suitcases if she was going away for work?

Because she wasn't going alone.

Because she was going to be taking a child with her.

She forced herself to get a grip on her thoughts.

I'm getting carried away again.

You couldn't keep a child locked up for six months. It wasn't possible to hide a four-year-old boy in a house in the woods without someone finding out about it.

Or was it?

In that case, he wouldn't have been out in the fresh air for six months. Hadn't been allowed to build dams in streams or dig in the mud with a spade. He hadn't been allowed to eat sweets in the car or pick films from the video store . . .

The satellite dish! He's been watching Cartoon Network!

She looked at the time. Quarter past two. In an hour or so it would be completely dark.

But Julia had actually recognized her.

It would take her a couple of hours to drive back to Stockholm, although the car didn't actually have to be back until the following morning.

She paused with her hand on the key. *What if she gets away before the police arrive? I've got half an hour's head start on them.*

She started the engine, turned the car around, and headed back toward Garphyttan. She drove through the center and past the soccer field, up through the forest and the cleared patches of woodland without meeting a single car.

Could there be any other roads? Of course there must be. Forest tracks, and you don't even need those with a vehicle like that.

The Toyota Land Cruiser 100 was the sort of vehicle that American special forces used when they invaded Iraq; she'd recognized them on the news footage. Thomas had commented on it once when they were watching the evening news, that the US used Japanese cars when it really mattered.

Yvonne Nordin could drive straight through the forest all the way to Norway if she wanted.

She reached the red post showing the way to the Lybacka Pits, the flooded quarries where iron ore had been mined even in prehistoric times. She turned off and parked behind a fir tree, pulled on the handbrake, and switched off the engine. She sat in silence in the car listening to the sound of her own breathing. She looked around the forest. There was quite a gale blowing outside.

I don't have to go all the way, I can just take a look. The police are on their way, they should be here in thirty minutes at most.

She got out of the car and closed the door carefully.

Yvonne's house ought to be about a kilometer away through the forest. She looked at the trees; the wind was coming from the northeast. She hoped that the sound of the car engine hadn't made its way to the cottage.

She pulled out her bag and started to walk, having the sense to put her mobile on silent. Her footsteps crunched on the path, and she frowned and went in among the trees instead. The moss swallowed her steps with a soft sucking sound.

It was getting dark very quickly, particularly down among the bases of the trees. She was forced to tread carefully.

Soon she caught sight of the turning circle ahead of her. The car was gone.

She bit her lip. *Shit!*

Then she noticed that the barrier was open.

Maybe she's driven up to the house to put her things in the car.

Annika jogged through the trees and found the little stream, and decided to follow it through the forest toward the house. She was panting in the wind, partly from exertion but mostly from the tension. She stumbled on a rock and fell head first into the moss, picked herself up, and hurried on.

The car was standing in front of the house, its headlights on and engine running. Yvonne Nordin was just coming out of the house with a suitcase in each hand; it looked like they were heavy.

Annika pressed her light-colored bag into the moss and crouched down behind a narrow fir tree.

Yvonne Nordin went to the side of the car and put the cases in the backseat, then closed the door and went back into the house without shutting the front door.

Annika waited in the darkness and tried to control her breathing.

Then the woman came out again with another two cases. This time she went to the other side of the car and disappeared from view. The light inside the vehicle went on when the rear door on the passenger side opened, and Annika saw her put these bags in the backseat as well. Then she went back inside the house again, and this time she closed the front door.

Annika sat there in the darkness staring at the car, at the house, at the door, at the shadows inside the windows whenever someone moved. It was damp and windy in the forest, making the trees and branches sway.

I've got to stop her from leaving. Can I get any closer than this?

To the left lay the outhouse where Yvonne Nordin had fetched the suitcases, and to the right were wheel tracks disappearing up into the forest.

Halfway toward the house was a well with a bucket and a traditional hand pump, and from there it was just a few meters to the car.

She looked for shadows in the windows, no movement.

She took three deep breaths, grabbed her bag and ran in a crouch over to the well.

How was she going to stop a Toyota Land Cruiser? She didn't know the first thing about cars.

She opened her bag and felt about through the mess inside. Was there anything there she could use?

Her hand landed on the penknife with the slogan *The Evening Post— sharp and to the point*, the one she'd used to shred Soph *Fucking Bitch* Grenborg's bra with.

I've got to stop thinking of her that way. It's beneath my dignity.

She took out the knife, hesitated for half a second, then rushed out and stuck it in the rear left-hand tire. The rubber gave way and started to let out air with an audible hiss. She moved two steps to the right and pierced the other rear tire as well. Then she ran back to the well again in a crouch and had just crept behind it when the front door opened.

Yvonne Nordin stepped onto the porch, and she was holding a little girl by the hand. The child was wearing a pink dress and had blond curls that hung down over her shoulders. Yvonne dragged the girl, making her stumble on the steps, but the child didn't protest and just followed her obediently toward the car.

Why isn't she wearing a coat? It's freezing out here.

Annika curled up into a little ball as they approached the vehicle, and she stopped breathing when they went past the two side doors and stopped at the rear door. She didn't dare poke her head out, but she heard the door open and Yvonne Nordin say: "Get in."

She couldn't help it, and stuck her head out far enough to see the girl crawl into the car and lie down in the boot, then Yvonne Nordin pulled a gray fabric over the compartment and shut the door.

Then the woman paused, stopped, and looked round. Annika ducked down behind the well and screwed her eyes shut.

As long as she doesn't discover the punctures! Don't look down!

Then she heard footsteps going away and peeped out incredibly cautiously.

The woman was on her way back into the house, presumably to turn the lights out and lock up.

Annika took a deep breath and ran over to the car. She opened the rear door, folded back the cloth covering the boot, and stared at the girl lying there.

The child stared back with eyes that seems utterly dead, and Annika realized at once that it wasn't a little girl at all. It was a boy, and he was pale and frightened. He had a vivid red scar along one side of his face. Annika gulped, felt in her jacket pocket, and found a bag of sweets.

"Hello," she said breathlessly. "Would you like some sweets?"

The child looked at her, and his eyes flickered.

"I've got a whole bag," she said. "They're really good. Here!"

She put a bright green sweet in his mouth and the boy chewed and sat up.

"Come with me and you can have some more," she said, holding out her arms to him.

And before she knew it the child was in her arms and she put the gray cloth back in place, closed the rear door, and rushed off toward the well, then abandoned her bag to its fate and rushed off toward the forest.

She crouched down beside the little fir tree again as the lights inside the house went out and the front door opened. She put the boy down in the moss, took off her coat, and wrapped it round him.

"Here," she said, giving him another sweet. "There are different-colored ones. I think the pink ones are best."

The boy took the sweet in his hand and popped it into his mouth, then snuggled up to Annika with the coat wrapped tight around him.

Yvonne Nordin went over to the car, put her handbag on the passenger seat, then went round to the back of the vehicle.

Don't open it! Don't open it! Just go!

Annika tried to send thoughts to the woman through the darkness, but it didn't work. Yvonne Nordin opened the rear door, pulled the cloth aside, and saw that the child was gone.

She moved incredibly fast.

She raced back to the house, opened the front door, turned the light on, and disappeared inside.

Annika picked the boy up and rushed in the other direction, in among the trees and the wind and the shadows. It was now completely dark; she couldn't see a thing and kept stumbling and almost falling. The treetops above her were whistling and singing, and the cold was biting.

Yvonne Nordin would have a gun, and quite possibly night-vision sights.

I have to get away, as far away as possible, preferably somewhere toward the car.

She ran, the boy bouncing in her arms, following the little stream down toward the turning circle. The moss was soft and slippery; she stumbled and fell. *Is this the right direction? Am I going the right way?* She stood up again, clutching the boy to her, one arm round his body, the other round his fair head.

The first shot hit a tree trunk a few meters away to her right.

Don't panic, just don't panic. Run, run!

The second shot was closer, just to the left.

It's a hunting rifle, or some other heavy-duty gun. Hard to aim properly.

The third shot whistled past close to her head.

She won't miss next time. I have to get out of sight.

She ducked down behind a stump, holding the boy close.

"I know you're here," the woman screamed through the darkness, the wind carrying her words. "It's hopeless. Give yourself up, and I'll let the child live."

Where the hell are the police?

"Are there any more sweets?"

The boy was looking up at her with shining eyes.

"Of course," she said, pulling another sweet out of her jacket pocket. Her hands were shaking so much she could hardly keep hold of it.

A fourth shot hit the stump in front of them, throwing shards of wood up into her face; she felt a splinter hit her cheek and had to clench her teeth to stop herself crying out.

The boy started to cry.

"She's horrid," he said. "She's really horrid."

"I know," Annika whispered, and at that moment the forest was lit by the headlights of a car. A police car was heading slowly up the gravel track toward Yvonne Nordin's cottage. Another shot rang out and the windscreen of the police car exploded and Annika heard someone cry out in pain. The car stopped and then reversed, leaving the forest as suddenly as it had arrived.

Come back, don't leave us, she's shooting at us!

She sat completely still with the child beside her, utterly still as a whole minute came and went. There was no movement, no sound. Another minute passed, then another.

Her legs were on the point of going to sleep because of the uncomfortable position she was sitting in. She tried to move her feet to bring back some feeling.

"Come on," she whispered. "I've got a car, we'll go to my car."

The boy nodded and took a firm grasp round her neck.

She stood up carefully and looked toward the house. Then she heard a car engine start up, and far off in the trees she saw the headlights go on.

She can't drive and look through the rifle sights at the same time.

Annika stood up straight and felt her coat slide to the ground, but ignored it and ran like the wind toward the road, with the boy clasping her neck, off toward the turning circle, toward the police.

A headlamp was shining right in her face, blinding her, and she fell.

"There are guns aimed at you," she heard a man say from where she lay on the ground with the boy beside her. "Are you armed?"

"No," she managed to say. "But she's getting away, Yvonne Nordin, she's just got in her car . . ."

"Are you Annika Bengtzon?"

She nodded toward the light.

"Who's the girl?"

The light vanished, leaving her in complete darkness.

"It's no girl. This is Alexander Lindholm."

The wind was singing in the trees. The stars were visible in the gaps between the clouds and the moon was rising. Annika was sitting wrapped in a thick blanket behind the police car without a windscreen. The boy had fallen asleep with his head on her chest. She leaned her head back and looked up at the sky but gave up, closing her eyes and listening to the song of the wind.

She could hear the police radios crackling, and the sound of men muttering.

The ambulance would soon be here to pick up the police officer who had got splinters of glass in his face. The rapid-response unit and dog patrol were also on their way, and the police helicopter was on its way from Stockholm with floodlights and heat-seeking cameras.

"And you're sure she won't get far in the car?" the police officer asked her.

"She might be able to change one tire," Annika said quietly without opening her eyes, "but not two. And you can't drive off road on your wheel rims for long."

A comprehensive approach was being carefully planned, seeing as the suspect was evidently prepared to shoot at the police. Annika let herself be rocked by the sounds around her, as she sat with the child beside her, feeling his warmth and regular breathing.

When the rapid-response unit arrived in their van they helped her up and put her in the back with the boy. They left the engine on to keep the inside of the vehicle warm. Annika tipped the rest of the sweets out on the blanket.

"Do you think the pink ones are best too?" she asked, holding up a sweet. For some reason she knew that each one contained nine calories. Anne Snapphane must have told her.

The boy shook his head.

"I like the green ones."

So they split the sweets by color, green ones for him, pink ones for her, and then shared out the white ones.

The child had just fallen asleep when she heard over the police radio that they had located Yvonne Nordin fourteen hundred meters away from the cottage, trying to change a tire. She had shot at the patrol, which had returned fire.

An ambulance was called to the scene, but there was no rush.

Yvonne Nordin had been hit during the exchange of fire and was believed to have died instantly.

Pp. 6–7

EVENING POST—NATIONAL EDITION
SATURDAY, DECEMBER 4

ALEXANDER'S PRISON
Boy Held Captive For Six Months

By Patrik Nilsson and Emil Oscarsson

Evening Post (Garphyttan). Alexander Lindholm, 4 years old, was forced to spend six months living in a bare cellar two meters belowground.

Sometimes he was allowed up into the living room to watch television, but only if the shutters on the windows were closed.

"Alexander seemed to be relatively well," says *Evening Post* reporter Annika Bengtzon, who met the boy shortly after his release.

The cottage lies deep in the forest, many kilometers from any main roads. A barrier stops any traffic from approaching the house.

This is where four-year-old Alexander Lindholm was found by Örebro Police yesterday evening.

"We think he's been kept hidden in this house since he was kidnapped from his home on Södermalm on June 3," a spokesman for Örebro Police said. "Evidence inside the house supports this theory."

Alexander was forced to live in a potato cellar that could only be reached via a hatch in the kitchen floor.

"We found what must have been his bed down there."

Was there any lighting in the cellar?

"Yes, it had been furnished to look like a room, with rag rugs on the floor and a lamp in the ceiling. There were also some picture books and comics."

There was a television set in the living room of the cottage, and there is evidence to suggest that Alexander was occasionally allowed to watch children's programs.

"We found crisp crumbs and a child's sticky fingerprints on the sofa," the police spokesman said.

The police have not yet released any information about Alexander's kidnapper, the woman who is also believed to have murdered his father.

It is clear, however, that the woman planned the kidnapping carefully. Some of the items in the cellar were bought over a year ago, mainly in Gothenburg and Oslo.

Evening Post reporter Annika Bengtzon was on the scene when Alexander Lindholm was released.

"I don't want to comment on his physical or mental state, but he could certainly walk and talk."

So he seemed to be relatively well?

"Yes."

Alexander's miraculous recovery raises many questions about the reliability of the Swedish judicial system.

"From a legal point of view, this is an extremely interesting dilemma," says Professor of Criminology Hampus Lagerbäck. "Here we have a case in which a person has been sentenced to life imprisonment for the murder of someone who is still alive. It will be interesting to see how the judicial authorities wriggle their way out of this mistake."

SATURDAY, DECEMBER 4

Thomas tossed his dressing gown onto a chair and crept gently back into bed beside Sophia. The sound of the cartoon was effectively shut out by the locked bedroom door. Saturday morning was still young and full of possibilities.

Sophia was asleep. She was lying on her back with one leg pulled up and her back to him. He moved closer to her and put his knee between her thighs. She was moving a little in her sleep. He nibbled the lobe of her ear. Slowly he slid his hand from her stomach toward her breasts. He was still fascinated at how small they were. He carefully squeezed one nipple, and her body stiffened.

She turned to look at him.

"Hello," she said with a smile.

"Hello," he whispered, kissing her neck. He let his fingers trace her spine, down to her buttock, and pulled her to him.

She wriggled loose and sat up.

"I need a pee . . ."

She pulled her dressing gown on, unlocked the bedroom door, and went out to the bathroom.

He lay back in the bed, staring up at the ceiling, feeling his erection subside.

She was taking her time; he could never understand what on earth she did in there.

Rather sullenly, he grabbed the duvet and wrapped it tight around him.

He'd almost nodded off again when she came back in.

"Darling," she said, touching his hair. "Shall we go to the museum today? I haven't seen Rauschenberg's Combines yet."

He looked up at her and smiled, then took a firm grasp of her waist.

"Come and lie down," he said thickly, tipping her over into the bed with a laugh. "Now I've got you!"

She struggled free, annoyed.

"I've just done my hair," she said, sitting up on the bed again at arm's length from him. "And I asked if you wanted to go to the Museum of Modern Art. You could at least answer."

Disappointment turned to frustration and he thumped the pillow, pushing it up against the head of the bed.

"And all I wanted was a bit of intimacy," he said.

"Intimacy," she echoed. "You wanted sex, admit it."

"And what's so wrong with that?"

She looked at him with her pale eyes. They were almost invisible when she wasn't wearing makeup.

"You can actually have intimacy without sex."

"Yes, but I like sex."

"So do I, but . . ."

"Even though you never come."

He said it without thinking. She reacted as if she'd been slapped, jerking and going pale.

"What do you mean by that?"

He felt his mouth go dry.

"It's not a criticism," he said.

"Yes it is," she said, sitting quite still.

"I just thought it might be more fun for you if you could have an orgasm as well. Maybe you could help yourself a bit? Or we could see if I could . . ."

She got up without looking at him.

"It's not important to me. Don't tell me what I should feel. I'll take responsibility for my own sexuality, and you take responsibility for yours."

His clenched his jaw. *Me and my big mouth.*

"I appreciate that it's been really tough on you," she said. "Losing your job that way must feel very unfair, you were only doing your job, after all . . ."

He threw back the duvet and reached for his dressing gown. Saturday morning's possibilities had all drained away.

"I haven't lost my job," he said. "Where did you get that from?"

She looked at him in surprise.

"But you said the inquiry had been suspended."

"Yes," he said, "but my contract runs until October next year. I met Halenius yesterday afternoon. I'm going to be part of an inquiry into cross-border currency transactions."

He studied her face. Was that a tiny hint of disappointment?

She took off her dressing gown and stood to pick some clothes from her wardrobe.

"Do they know who leaked it to the press?" she asked over her shoulder.

He let out a deep sigh.

"It was probably the press secretary. The bosses just seem happy the inquiry has been dropped, they never wanted to increase the sentencing guidelines, which would have been the inevitable conclusion."

"So you're not out of favor, then?"

If he didn't know better, he could have sworn she sounded disappointed.

He looked at her.

"I daresay I'll never work with Per Cramne again," he said, "but that's something I'm more than happy to live with."

She turned back toward the wardrobe again.

"Have you seen my new bra? The French one, with the silk cups?"

He let out another sigh, silent and deep.

Annika stepped into Detective Superintendent Q's office. Her finger ached; she'd got an infection in the wound and the district nurse had given her antibiotics. The splinter of wood in her cheek had been removed but had left a scab covered with a sizable plaster.

She sat down and met his gaze. He was wearing a seriously washed-out shirt today, but it had probably been yellow once.

The policeman nodded toward her hand.

"What have you done to your finger?"

She looked at him coolly.

"Some thugs thought I was digging too hard."

"Have you reported it?"

She shook her head.

"So who do you think did it?" Q asked.

"There are plenty to choose from. Yvonne Nordin's heavies, or Filip Andersson's, or possibly Christer Bure's . . ."

Detective Superintendent Q sighed.

"What the hell were you doing, going back up to Lybacka?"

Annika could feel her eyes narrow.

"Is this a formal interview? Is that why I'm here? In that case I want you to stick to the rules. I want to see it in writing afterward so I can give my consent."

He sighed in irritation, then got up and walked around the desk to shut the door properly. He went and stood by the window with his back to her and his arms folded.

"You can't just go off and pay a visit to a suspected murderer entirely alone, don't you get that?"

She looked at his back.

"I'm almost starting to think you care about me," she said.

"I care about reporters on the evening papers," he said. "Or have done, at least some of them . . ."

He sounded oddly subdued for a moment, then turned round and went back to his desk.

"Has Julia been released yet?" Annika asked.

"The hearing took place at two o'clock this morning," he said, sitting down in his chair. "She's at a care home for families right now with Alexander. They'll be there a while."

"Will there be a new trial?"

"Yes, both the prosecutor and her lawyer have already put in an application to the Court of Appeal, and during those proceedings Julia will be formally declared innocent. Which will mean that the judicial side of things is all finished."

"How is the boy now?"

"He's still got to have a proper medical examination, but evidently he's displaying all the vital functions a four-year-old should, he walks and talks and knows how to use the toilet and so on. You probably know all that better than me . . ."

Annika nodded. She could feel the warmth of his body like cotton wool in her chest. The long wait during the night hadn't left her restless but actually calmer.

A woman from social services in Stockholm had picked him up from Örebro just after midnight, and the boy had cried and wanted to stay with Annika. She'd promised to visit him and bring more of the same sweets.

"I wonder what happens to a small child when they're put through something like this," Annika wondered to herself. "Will he ever be normal?"

"There are a couple of things I want to ask you about," Q said, "but there's no real reason to regard this as a formal interview. Yvonne Nordin obviously won't be charged for David's murder or for kidnapping Alexander, so we can keep this informal. Did she shoot at you?"

Annika swallowed and nodded.

"Four shots. How did she die?"

"One of our marksmen hit her in the chest. There'll have to be an inquiry, but I can't imagine that he'll be reprimanded. The circumstances were difficult: it was dark, the middle of the forest, with all that implies in terms of visibility and complex judgments. And she did actually take aim and fire at the police, which of course she'd already done earlier."

Annika looked out of the window.

"She'd got her bags packed. I wonder where she was going."

"Mexico," Q said. "She had the tickets in the car, from Gardemoen, via Madrid. With a fake passport saying that Alexander was a little girl called Maja."

"So she really was planning to drive through the forest to Norway?"

"That was certainly one option."

Q clicked to open something on his computer. Annika picked at her bandage.

"Do you think we'll ever find out what really happened?" she said. "With David, or the murders on Sankt Paulsgatan?"

"Seeing as Yvonne Nordin is dead, Filip Andersson has decided to talk," Q said. "His lawyer has already been in touch this morning to say that they're applying to have his case heard in the Supreme Court."

"Do you think he's got any chance?"

"There were fingerprints in Sankt Paulsgatan that could never be identified before," Q said. "They were Yvonne's. But we have to find something else tying her to the murders. A murder weapon, for instance, or traces of the victims' DNA in her car, something like that. But the decisive factor will be whether or not Filip Andersson has decided to sing out. He claims it was Yvonne who framed him, that she tipped off the police and left his trousers to be dry-cleaned."

Annika looked at Q and tried to understand what he was saying.

"You don't waste any time," she said. "You've already spoken to Filip Andersson?"

"He knows far more than we ever realized. There are connections between these people that we never had any idea about before."

"They ran a company together," Annika said. "Some investment company."

"Yes," Q said, "but their relationship was considerably closer than that. Filip Andersson and Yvonne Nordin were brother and sister. Well, half brother and half sister, to be more precise."

Annika blinked.

"You're kidding?"

"Why? Most people have brothers and sisters."

"Yes, I mean, I knew Filip Andersson had a sister, but not that it was Yvonne Nordin. She used to visit him in Kumla once a month."

"You've got that wrong," Q said. "Yvonne Nordin, or Andersson as she was before she got married, didn't get on at all with her brother. You don't get someone put away for life unless you're seriously pissed off with them."

"His sister visited him regularly, they told me that when I was there."

"What do you mean, 'there'? Have you been to Kumla as well?"

She squirmed on her chair, and tried to evade the question.

"Why was she so angry with her brother?"

"That's one of the things we're going to have to find out. But she certainly hasn't paid any visits to Kumla, I can assure you of that. I suppose he must have another sister. When were you there?"

"Earlier this week. But what about Yvonne's relationship with David Lindholm, then? Did they have an affair?"

"For several years. They ran the business together and were planning to get married as soon as they'd earned enough money, or at least that's what Yvonne thought."

"And she had an abortion that she never got over?"

"David promised her that they'd have another child as soon as he divorced Julia."

Annika sat in silence for a few moments.

"How does Filip know that? I thought they didn't get on?"

Q didn't answer.

"Well?" Annika said. "How do you know that Yvonne went crazy because she had an abortion?"

Q rocked back and forth on his chair a few times before replying.

"Our colleagues in Örebro found a number of things inside the house that point in that direction."

"Like what? Baby clothes?"

"A room."

"*A room*?"

"There was a sign saying 'Maja's Room' on the door. All done out in pink, furniture, clothes, toys, all with the price tags still on. We haven't had time to go through everything yet, but there are letters and diary entries and little things she'd made for the dead child."

"It wasn't a child," Annika said. "It was a fetus, incapable of life. But perhaps it wasn't the loss of the fetus that sent her mad, but the betrayal of being dumped."

She shook her head at her own thoughts.

"But if you've already chopped three people's hands off, you were probably pretty mad before that."

"If it was actually her who did that," Q said.

They sat in silence again. Annika could see the woman in front of her, her nondescript features, her sad eyes.

"What did she say the first time you spoke to her, when you asked for directions?" the police officer asked.

Annika looked out of the window, it had started snowing again.

"That she'd had the place for a year, that her partner died last Christmas, that she worked for her own company. It all fitted, she seemed so . . . normal. Pleasant, actually."

"Niklas Ernesto Zarco Martinez wasn't her partner. He was a junkie who acted as the stooge in the company, he was the one who was lined up to take the fall when they went bankrupt and emptied the company of its assets. He got a syringe full of dodgy gear for Christmas last year."

She bit her lip.

"So if Martinez was the stooge, what was David doing there?"

Q didn't answer.

"I can understand the fact that he ran the company with Yvonne if they were having an affair, but why was David on the board of those other companies? Do you know?"

Q laced his fingers together and put his hands behind his head.

"The man's dead, and it's not him we're investigating."

"I think David Lindholm was extremely crooked, and those companies whose boards he was on, apart from the parachute business, they were all fronts for money laundering or some other criminal shit. He was probably on the board to keep an eye out, a sort of reminder that no one would ever be able to get away."

"Have you finished?" the detective asked.

Annika looked at the time.

"I ought to go up to the paper. I still haven't handed back the car I borrowed yesterday."

"There's just one more thing," Q said. "We've had a response from England about a forensic sample we took from the fire and sent for analysis months ago, way back in the summer, actually. I think it might interest you."

Annika stiffened, and suddenly it was hard to breathe.

"It was a brick that we found in the ruins of your house. Forensics worked out that it was used to smash the window before the firebombs were thrown in. The Brits have managed to find a fingerprint on it."

Her pulse was racing, and her throat was dry as dust.

"And we've actually been able to identify it," he said. "It belonged to an old acquaintance. I assume you still remember the Kitten?"

Annika swallowed badly and had to cough.

"Her? The hired killer from the Nobel banquet? But . . . why?"

"We're regarding the fire in your house as a closed case, from a police point of view. She was the one who started it."

Annika was sitting there dumbstruck.

"But," she said, "I thought it was the neighbor. Hopkins."

"I know that's what you thought, but you were wrong."

"It must be a mistake. This doesn't fit her pattern. You said so yourself, the fire was a personal attack, a hate crime. Why would she hate me?"

"Just drop it," Q said. "Accept that you were wrong. And you caught her, so how much more personal could it get?"

Annika stood up and walked over to the window, and stopped to watch the falling snow.

"I know I get things wrong," she said. "Fairly often, in fact."

Q sat in silence.

Annika looked away from the snow and turned back to him.

"But you're sure she was in Sweden that night?"

"Off the record," he said.

"What?" Annika said. "What is it?"

He gestured toward the visitor's chair.

"Sit down. We've managed to keep this quiet for six months. The number of people who know is seriously bloody limited."

"It won't last," Annika said. "Everything gets out."

He laughed out loud.

"You are so fucking wrong!" he said. "It's the exact opposite. Almost nothing gets out. So, off the record?"

She looked at her shoes and went and sat down again, then gave a quick nod.

"The Kitten was picked up at Arlanda early on the morning of June 3 this year," Q said. "She was planning to fly to Moscow on a fake Russian passport."

Annika folded her arms.

"So? You arrest criminals every day, don't you?"

Q smiled.

"It's actually rather funny. She was very upset when we brought her in. Not because we'd caught her, but because her suicide pills didn't work."

Annika raised her eyebrows.

"Yes, it's true," Q said. "She'd bought what she thought was cyanide, but it turned out to be Tylenol."

"Tylenol?"

"A common American painkiller, with the same active ingredients as Alvedon and Panodil here in Sweden."

"Ah," Annika said. "My favorites."

"People have got Tylenol and cyanide mixed up before, but the other way round. Seven people died in Chicago in 1982 after taking what they thought were Tylenol pills. Turned out to be cyanide."

"So what's so confidential about the Kitten biting into a painkiller? Why haven't we heard anything about this? She must have been re-manded in custody, so she ought to have been charged by now . . ."

Q sat there silently. Annika's eyes opened wide.

"She hasn't been registered in any Swedish court. Not even her arrest. You've handed her over to the USA! Just like that!"

She stood up again.

"You've sent her back to a country that still has the death penalty! That's a breach of the UN Convention, the same one you broke when you let the CIA pick people up from Bromma Airport . . ."

The detective superintendent raised a hand.

"Wrong again," he said. "Just sit down. The extradition was carried out at state level. She's from Massachusetts, and they don't have the death penalty there."

Annika sat down.

"But the US as a whole does," she said.

"Yes," Q said, "in thirty-eight states. But twelve don't, including Massachusetts. She'll get life imprisonment, that much is certain. And we're really talking about life, none of this eighteen years nonsense."

"So what's so controversial about that, then?"

"Just think about it!"

Annika shook her head.

It wasn't Hopkins! Imagine, that I could be so wrong!

"So he called the fire brigade? He tried to rescue us instead of kill us?"

"We swapped her," Q said.

She stared at him.

"We did a deal with the Americans and swapped her for someone else."

She closed her eyes and remembered an animated conversation in the newsroom, hearing Patrik Nilsson's shrill voice inside her head:

The government gave the Yanks something in return. We have to find out what it was. Raids on people making sour milk? Landing rights for the CIA at Bromma?

Something clicked inside.

"We swapped her for Viktor Gabrielsson!"

"Officially, she was arrested by the FBI. All the documentation shows that. We'll never be able to claim that she was in Sweden that night."

"So you got the cop killer home again. Do you think that was a good deal?"

"It wasn't my decision, but it meant that I had to take charge of the investigation into the fire in your house."

She was trying to understand.

"So you suspected her right from the start?"

"She was one of a very short list."

"What does this mean for me?"

"Like I said, the fire is regarded as a closed case, from our point of view. Unfortunately the files will record it as having been dropped. Sorry."

"What?" Annika said. "So I'll never be properly cleared?"

He shook his head lightly and looked almost genuinely sad.

"But," she said, "what about the insurance money?"

"You can probably whistle for that."

She had to laugh, a bitter little laugh.

"You sold out my home, my children's home, just to get a bit of credit with the CIA and bring home a cop killer."

The detective tilted his head to one side.

"I'm not sure I'd put it quite like that."

"So what do you propose I do?"

"You've got some money left from the Dragon, haven't you?"

She sighed heavily and shut her eyes.

"Thomas and I split what was left over. My half wouldn't even get me a two-room flat on Södermalm."

"You'll just have to get a mortgage, like everyone else. Or get a contract on a rented flat."

She laughed again, a harsh laugh this time.

"A contract on a rented flat? And where would I find one of those these days?"

"The police union has a number of properties throughout the city. I can arrange for you to get a flat in one of them, if you like."

She looked at him and felt her disappointment rising like bile in her throat.

"Christ, this society really is crooked."

"Isn't it?" he said, with a broad smile.

Annika went up to the newsroom and left the car keys in a basket on the reception desk, grateful that there was no one there to shout at her for keeping the car too long.

She felt oddly empty, relieved but sad at the same time.

The divorce would be finalized the following week, after the obligatory six months' breathing space. She would happily have postponed it, would have liked to discuss it calmly with Thomas, but the opportunity had never arisen, she'd never suggested it, and neither had he. The fact was, they hadn't talked to each other properly on a single occasion since the evening when he left her and the house burned down.

I got that wrong as well. I've messed up pretty much everything there is to mess up.

Although she had been right about Julia.

She took a fresh newspaper from the stand and looked at the front page. *ALEXANDER FOUND LAST NIGHT,* it shouted. What followed was an absolute classic: *Grandmother in tears—"It's a miracle!"*

The rest of the page was taken up by one of the pictures of the boy at nursery. (Spike had hit the roof when she refused to take a new picture of him with her phone and send it to him.)

She skimmed the text below the picture. It said that the mystery surrounding the disappearance of four-year-old Alexander Lindholm had finally been solved. The boy's grandmother, Viola Hansen, had given a statement: "There are no words to describe how happy we are."

Readers were referred to five double-page spreads, including the centerfold.

She quickly leafed through the rest of the paper. Patrik Nilsson had written the articles about Yvonne Nordin's death and Alexander's captivity; Annika had provided him with the background information and was cited in several places. She was described as being present on the scene when the events took place, but she wasn't portrayed as an active participant. To her surprise she was actually quite pleased about this, because at the back of her mind was the awareness that she could just as easily have been wrong. Emil Oscarsson had written a summary of David's murder, Julia's trial, and Alexander's abduction in an excellent piece. He was a real find.

She folded the paper and pushed it back in the stand. She felt exhausted. She went into the newsroom to discuss what she was going to write for the next day's paper with Spike and Schyman and was surprised to see so many people there. Saturday morning was usually the quietest time of the whole week, but today the newsroom was close to packed.

"Are they all here because of Alexander?" Annika asked, putting her bag down on Berit's desk.

"Him and the redundancies," Berit said, looking up over her glasses. "The list was made public yesterday afternoon. Schyman's got around the employment regulations by promoting half the staff to management."

"The old fox," Annika said, sitting down on Patrik's chair. "Including you and me?"

"We're not on either list. No need. We've been here so long we wouldn't have gone on the last-in first-out principle. So, I gather you've been off having an adventure."

Annika put her feet up on Berit's desk.

"She was about to take off with the boy," she said. "She very nearly made it."

"But you slashed the tires of her car," Berit said.

Annika stopped short and looked at her colleague intently.

"How do you know that? It wasn't in the paper."

To her astonishment she saw Berit blush, something she'd never done before.

"Someone told me," she said, then began hunting through some documents in one of her desk drawers.

"Who have you been talking to? Someone in the police?"

Berit cleared her throat and pulled out some sheets of paper.

"Yes, I spoke to Q."

Annika raised her eyebrows in surprise.

"With Q? But I've only just come from a meeting with him . . ."

I care about reporters on the evening papers. Or have done, at least some of them . . .

Suddenly the penny dropped with such force that Annika gasped for breath.

"It was Q!" she said. "You had an affair with Q . . ."

"Why don't you say it a bit louder?" Berit said in a clenched voice.

"And there was me thinking he was gay!"

Berit looked at her and took off her glasses.

"Does it matter?"

Annika stared at her colleague, at her gray-flecked hair and wrinkly neck. Tried to imagine her with the detective, the way they met up and flirted and kissed . . .

"Wow," she said. "He's actually quite good-looking."

"And he's also very good in bed," Berit said, putting her glasses back on and going back to her computer.

"Did you see, I've been made a member of management?" Patrik Nilsson said, holding up a copy of the lengthy list.

Annika dropped her feet to the floor and picked up her bag.

"Congratulations," she said.

Patrik's face was beaming with pride as he turned to look at the young temp, Ronja, who was on her way out of the newsroom with a box of her personal possessions in her arms.

"How did you get on, Ronja?"

"I don't care," she said, head held high. "I'm going to go freelance. I'm going to Darfur to cover the conflict there. Something really important."

"Unlike the nonsense we deal with here?" Patrik said.

Ronja stopped and jutted her chin.

"There it really is a matter of life or death."

"Which it never is in Sweden?" Annika said.

Ronja turned on her heel and left them by the desk. Left them sitting on their fat backsides, lulled into the false assurance that their reality was more secure and better than hers.

Suddenly Annika felt ashamed, remembering how insecure and wretched she had felt as a temp.

"Tell me something," Patrik said. "Who tipped you off about Yvonne Nordin? Who told you they were about to arrest her?"

She looked at the young man, who was actually a year older than her, at his inquisitive eyes and smug smile and uninhibited self-confidence, and felt like she was a thousand years old.

"I've got a source," she said. "A really good one."

Then she went over to Spike to find out what he needed from her.

The afternoon had turned into evening before Annika had finished her article. It was a fairly vague account of Yvonne Nordin's background and motivations, without reference to any sources. She was aware that it was fairly thin, but didn't want to expose Nina, Julia, David, or even Filip Andersson, so she stuck to the facts that could be verified: that Yvonne had run a business with David, that she had wanted their relationship to carry on and David to get a divorce, and that she might be guilty of other violent crimes. That the police were investigating if there was any connection to the triple murder on Sankt Paulsgatan, that Filip Andersson was applying to have his case heard in the Supreme Court (she actually did have references for this last fact, with a case number and everything).

She sent the article to the shared filestore, shut down her computer, packed it away, and put it in her bag. As she was walking past Schyman's room she saw him sitting behind his desk, rocking on his chair.

He looked gray and exhausted. This autumn had aged him.

I wonder how much longer he can carry on doing this? He must be close to sixty now.

She knocked, and he started as if he had been immersed in his own thoughts, then gestured to her to come in. She sat down opposite him.

"I daresay an apology is in order," he said.

Annika shook her head.

"Not just now," she said. "I'm overdosing on them. How are you doing?"

The last question just came out, she didn't know where it had come from.

He sighed deeply.

"These cuts almost made me give up," he said.

He sat in silence, looking out over the newsroom, his gaze roaming over the reporters and computers and radio studios and editors and on-line staff. Outside the windows it was dark again, the short day replaced by a long, windy December night.

"I love this paper," he said. "I never thought I'd say that, but it's actually true. I know we get things wrong, and sometimes we go too far, and sometimes we hang people out to dry in a terrible way, but we fulfill a function. Without us democracy would be more fragile. Without us society would be more dangerous, harsher."

She nodded slowly.

"I want to believe that's true," she said, "but I'm not so sure."

"You did a good job yesterday."

"Not really," she said. "I didn't write anything. I refused to take a picture of Alexander."

"I meant more generally."

"It's a messy business," Annika said. "I don't think anyone really knows how it all fits together. Everyone involved had different motives and justifications for acting the way they did. Maybe they're all guilty, just not of what they were accused or found guilty of . . ."

Anders Schyman sighed again.

"I think I'm going to go home now," he said.

"Me too," Annika said.

"Do you want a lift?"

She hesitated.

"Yes, please."

They got up, the editor in chief turned out the lights but didn't bother to lock his room, and they walked through the newsroom and down into the garage to his car.

"Why did you think she was innocent?" he asked as they were driving down Norr Mälarstrand.

She decided to be honest.

"I think I identified with her. If she was innocent, then so was I."

"Have you heard anything from the police? Have they reached any conclusions about the fire?"

She swallowed.

"No," she said curtly, and looked out of the window.

He dropped her off at a bus stop on Munkbron.

"You really need to sort out a proper flat," he said.

"I know," she said, and closed the car door.

EPILOGUE

FRIDAY, DECEMBER 24

Christmas Eve

The train pulled in, brakes shrieking, and stopped at the deserted platform. Snow was swirling around the engine and carriages, creeping in through gaps round the doors and between the joints, enveloping the long contraption in a creaking sheath of ice.

She was the only person who got off.

With a groan the trained rolled off, leaving her standing there alone in the howling wind. She stood for a moment, looking around at the ICA supermarket, the Pentecostal church, and the hotel. Then she headed toward the exit with soft, silent footsteps. She passed through the icy tunnel, carried on past the taxi rank and Svea's Café, into Stenevägen.

The wind was hitting her full in the face and she pulled up her hood and tightened the drawstrings. Her rucksack felt heavy even though it only contained a Christmas present and some sandwiches she had brought for the journey back. She walked slowly past the houses lining the road, holding up her hand against the wind so she could see in past the curtains and Christmas lights. Inside were warmth and friendship, crackling fires and Christmas trees sparkling and smelling of pine.

She hoped the people inside appreciated what they had.

The electric fence appeared in front of her and she turned left into Viagatan. Like so many times before she followed the endless barrier toward the gate and the car park, walking and walking and walking without ever seeming to get any closer.

She had icicles on her eyelashes by the time she eventually reached the entry phone beside the main gate.

"I'm here to see Filip Andersson," she said.

"Come through," the female warder said.

The lock whirred, and she pulled the heavy gate open and walked quickly and determinedly up the tarmac path to the next gate. The snow had settled on the chain-link fence to her left, forming a rough wall of ice.

She reached the third checkpoint and pressed the button again. As usual, she had to use both hands to open the door to the visitors' section. She wiped off the snow and grit inside the door, folded her hood back, and blinked to get rid of the ice around her eyes. Then she walked quickly over to locker number one, where she left her coat and scarf. She opened the rucksack and took out the Christmas present, then locked the rucksack in as well. She pressed the fourth entry phone and was let through to the security check. She put the Christmas present on the belt to go through the X-ray machine and walked through the metal detector. It didn't bleep. It never did. She knew which shoes and belts she should avoid.

"Happy Christmas," the female warder said with a smile as she put her police badge on the reception desk.

"Happy Christmas to you too."

The warder hung the badge on the notice board. Evidently they were going to be in room number five.

"I've already written your details, you just need to sign," the warder said, and she wrote in her neat, legible handwriting: *Nina Hoffman, relative.*

"I heard that the appeal is going well," the warder said.

Nina smiled.

"We're hoping he'll be out before Easter."

"Come on, I'll show you through. Filip's on his way."

Nina picked up the Christmas present and followed the guard into the visitors' corridor, stopping to get an orange and a thermos of coffee from the refreshment table.

"I couldn't help noticing it was a book," the warder said, nodding toward the present.

"*La reina del sur,* by Arturo Pérez-Reverte. A thriller about drug smuggling on the Spanish coast."

The warder looked impressed.

"Filip reads books in Spanish?"

Nina was no longer smiling.

"All three of us used to."

ACKNOWLEDGMENTS

This is a novel. All characters are the work of the author's imagination, and all events depicted are fictional.

Nonetheless, I have taken great care to make sure those institutions and procedures that exist in the real world are correctly described in the novel. As a result, I have, as usual, conducted a great deal of research and taken up various people's time with a lot of often rather peculiar questions to find out how things work.

I wouldn't have been able to write this novel without their help. Their titles below refer to the positions they held at the time of my investigation.

Many thanks for your patience!

Matilda Johansson, a police constable in Stockholm, for research visits, the opportunity to investigate patrol car 1617, help with vocabulary and procedures and other details.

Thomas Bodström, chair of the Parliamentary Standing Committee on Justice, for information about the history and use of lifetime sentences, about directives and the establishment of government inquiries, and for proofreading and more.

Björn Engström, head of information at the Regional Communication Centre, LKC, for details about police service revolvers and the consequences of their loss.

Håkan Franzén, responsible for the regulation of property damage insurance at Folksam in Stockholm, for information about the procedures involved in cases of suspected arson in insurance fraud.

Anna Rönnerfalk, psychiatric nurse, for help with the diagnosis and symptoms of patients suffering severe mental stress.

Peter Rönnerfalk, a director at Stockholm County Council, for details surrounding health service routines, including ambulance transport.

Ulrika Bergling, security adviser at the Kronoberg Prison in Stockholm, for allowing us to visit the exercise yard on the roof and for permission to take the photograph, used on the cover of the Swedish edition of this book, in the section for inmates kept in solitary confinement.

Kenneth Gustafsson, acting governor at Kumla Prison, and also Jimmy Sander and Hilde Lyngen, security officers at Kumla with responsibility for internal sectary, for a tour of the institution's visitors wing and information about telephone and visiting procedures.

Eva Cedergren, legal adviser at the National Correctional Organisation, for help with the application of freedom of information principles for probation officers and trustees within the criminal justice system.

Ulf Göranzon, press officer for the criminal police in Stockholm, and Karin Segerhammar, an administrator within the disciplinary offences committee of the National Police Board, for details about the rules governing freedom of information for cases dealt with by the committee.

Niclas Salomonsson, my agent, and his staff at Salomonsson Agency in Stockholm.

Emily Bestler, my publisher, and all the dedicated staff at Emily Bestler Books and Atria.

And finally, and above all, Tove Alsterdal, who has been the first reader of everything I have written for the past twenty-eight years, for discussion, structural advice, outlines, and character analysis and everything else that features in all my novels.

I have also had a great deal of help from Terése Klein's dissertation at the Legal Faculty of the University of Lund, "Tidsbestämning av livstidsstraff—En jämförelse av nådeinstitutet och lagen om omvandling av fängelse på livstid" ("Determining the Length of a Lifetime Sentence±A comparison of instances of clemency and the law on the commuting of lifetime sentences").

I have availed myself of the author's prerogative and invented buildings, insurance companies, and pizza parlors.

Any mistakes or errors which have crept in are entirely my own.